CROWFALL

Also by Ed McDonald from Gollancz:

The Raven's Mark:
Blackwing
Ravencry
Crowfall

CROWFALL

The Raven's Mark

BOOK THREE

ED McDONALD

GOLLANCZ

LONDON

First published in Great Britain in 2019 by Gollancz
an imprint of the Orion Publishing Group Ltd
Carmelite House, 50 Victoria Embankment
London EC4Y ODZ

An Hachette UK Company

1 3 5 7 9 10 8 6 4 2

A CIP catalogue record for this book
is available from the British Library.

ISBN (Hardcover) 978 1 473 22209 0
ISBN (Export Trade Paperback) 978 1 473 22210 6
ISBN (eBook) 978 1 473 22212 0

Typeset by Deltatype Ltd, Birkenhead, Merseyside

Printed in Great Britain by Clays Ltd, Elcograf S.p.A.

www.edmcdonaldwriting.com
www.gollancz.co.uk

This one is for my mum and dad

Acknowledgements

When you write a book, you tend to get all the credit, but a novel is a team effort. Significant thanks are well deserved by:

My editors, Gillian Redfearn, Jessica Wade, and Craig Leyenaar, for their invaluable contributions in terms of story development, bouncing ideas around, and keeping me focused when impostor syndrome or complete befuddlement threatened.

My agent, Ian Drury, to whom I am immensely grateful for placing his trust in me and sending me tumbling down the rabbit hole.

The hard-working teams behind the scenes, including Miranda Hill, Stevie Finegan, Alexis Nixon, Jen McMenemy, and everyone else who has played a role in helping this series along.

Gaia Banks and Alba Arnau at Sheil Land, for all their amazing work in getting this series into an ever-increasing number of languages.

Everyone at London Longsword Academy who has trained and sparred with me over the last four years, your heads have provided fantastic targets to test out the fight sequences.

Andy Stoter, who named his first talking +3 war hammer 'Spoon' and lived a dozen different lives with me through the worlds of our imaginations.

My grandparents, Mollie and Leslie.

Kit, Ben, Greg, and Henry, who were the first to help reading the pages that ultimately became *Blackwing*.

And finally, my ongoing thanks must go to my mum, who from my earliest memory was instilling me with a desire to create and tell stories, and my dad, who put the first wooden sword into my three-year-old hand. My obsession with goblins and dragons may have puzzled you at times, but I hold you both entirely responsible.

Blackwing & Ravencry:
What Has Gone Before

The Nameless and the Deep Kings have been at war for longer than anyone remembers. The Deep Kings seek to enslave humanity and turn them into drudge-enslaved, deformed creatures that worship them. The Nameless, cruel and caring only for the final victory, stand in their way.

It has been ninety years since Crowfoot unleashed the Heart of the Void against the approaching enemy forces and, in doing so, created the Misery – a toxic, mystic wasteland where ghosts walk and mutated creatures scavenge the sands, and neither distance nor direction are ever quite what they seem. It can only be navigated by specialists taking readings from the three moons.

Ryhalt Galharrow is a Blackwing captain, magically bound to serve Crowfoot, one of the Nameless, and charged with rooting out dissenters, traitors, and spies. With the help of Ezabeth Tanza – a Spinner, able to manipulate light energy into magic, and a woman he'd loved and lost twenty years before – the Nameless were able to destroy one of the Deep Kings, Shavada, and save Valengrad. Ezabeth burned in the process, but her spirit was cast into the light where she lingered on as a spectral figure, seldom seen.

Four years on, an old enemy arose – Saravor, a flesh-shaping sorcerer who had once healed the swordswoman

Nenn. Saravor planned to empower Shavada's Eye atop the Grandspire, and ascend to become one of the Deep Kings. With the help of Ezabeth's spirit and Valiya, his head of intelligence, Galharrow managed to prevent the catastrophe. In the final battle, Nenn was killed, and Shavada was blasted from the Grandspire's roof by a colossal beam of energy.

Though the city was saved, Galharrow's ward, Amaira, took on a raven's mark of her own, and began her servitude to the Nameless. Valiya, seeing that she and Galharrow's affection for one another was bringing only pain, chose to leave, a painful parting for both of them.

The years have turned.

The moons are aligning.

1

I threw myself down in the sand. I hadn't been seen, and I wasn't certain how many they were, but I was going to have to kill a lot of them.

'What's the plan?' Nenn asked. She sat cross-legged on a rock, picking at the threads of blacksap in her teeth.

'Disappear or keep silent,' I said quietly. 'If they see you, this is going to go backwards pretty fast.'

'You taught me not to fight outnumbered,' Nenn said. She found the strand of gristle and tossed it away into the sand, where it disappeared into nothing.

'I taught you to fight smart,' I growled. 'For all the good it did either of us.' Nenn considered that, then snorted derisively.

'At least we had fun.'

'For once would you do as I ask, and shut the fuck up?'

I crawled forwards to get a better view of the desolate, rocky landscape at the foot of the slope. Wavy brown fronds grew from the red sand, but they seemed more like wool than plants. The Misery got confused about what used to be what, but the clumps of false vegetation provided a bit of cover for me to lie in. I took out my scope and twisted it, focused on the troop ahead. Made a quick count. Didn't like what I saw.

A troop of drudge and a train of spare mounts and baggage approached from what was currently the east. Neither the Grand Alliance nor the drudge sent soldiers this deep into the Misery – not until the last couple of months – as the magic rose thick here, soft and malleable. It drew the big things, or maybe they were born here, where the reek of poisoned energy soured the stagnant air with its chemical tang. The first patrol to come this way might have been lost. The second might have been lost too. The third had found me, and three patrols was too many.

A quick count said thirty drudge.

'What you going to do?' Nenn asked. She rubbed at her guts as though she were tempted to slice them open and see what lay beneath the skin. Sometimes she did. Sometimes it didn't make me sick. You can grow used to anything if you live with it long enough. I was living testimony to that.

'I'll do what I always do,' I said, although Nenn wouldn't remember. Ghosts had no capacity to learn.

I eased my matchlock from its canvas bag. There wasn't much about me that wasn't shabby and fraying, but I kept the gun in good working order. She came out to be fired and got wrapped when she wasn't needed. I bit the end from a powder charge, poured, tamped, spat. I only had three matchlock balls left. How long had it been since I'd been back to town to resupply? I couldn't remember. But for what I had in mind, one shot would be enough.

The drudge patrol were of a new breed. Drudge came in a lot of shapes and forms, from the swollen Brides to the waxy-grey-skinned fighting drudge, but these had a bluish tint to their skin and little of their former humanity remained. Through the scope, even at this distance, I could make out the lack of facial features and the smooth planes of glistening flesh. Their eyes were wide black orbs, mouths little more than slits. Noseless. They rode in a tight formation on shaggy, four-legged beasts that no Dortish scholar had named. They were taken from some distant conquered land, heavy bodied and slow. I called them *hurks*, after the noise they made. The drudge had heavy crossbows and lances, good armour, blades and hammers. Well-equipped.

And they were hunting me. There was nothing else out here to find.

I fixed the scope over my matchlock's barrel. There weren't many scopes like mine in the world. Maybe no others at all. Maldon had worked some of his art on it so that it adjusted itself for distance and recoil. I had no idea how that worked, but it had turned me from an average shot to a match for any sharpshooter. I sought out the right target.

The leader was easy to identify. He wore more prayer strips around his muscular arms than the others, dozens of the things hanging down to display his faith in red and black ink. His face was corpse-blue and as blank as the rest of them, but he had a mark stamped on his breastplate in gold leaf. Deep King Acradius' mark, a slaver's brand worn like a medal. I sighted between the captain's eyes, then tracked on. I could kill him, but there'd be a second to take his place, and I'd only get one shot off. I had to make it count.

I found my target in the middle of the plodding column. He was slighter than the warriors around him, warped differently. There was still a remnant of humanity about him; in the nose, lips, hair. He wore antiquated, lavishly decorated bronze armour, a mark of honour from his master. I couldn't be certain that my matchlock had the power to punch through it at this range. He was probably the least dangerous in the whole column, but he was the one that would make a difference. It was the instrument that he carried that singled him out: an astrolabe for measuring lunar positioning. A tangle of brass wheels and lenses, thick and thin. He was the navigator, who used the device to take readings from the moons, the only things constant enough in the Misery to plot a course by.

'You'll only get one shot,' Nenn said. 'They'll hear it.'

'Thanks. That hadn't occurred to me,' I said. 'What do you care anyway?'

She grinned and shrugged.

I hated Nenn's ghost. I knew she wasn't real, but I couldn't help but respond as though it were the woman I'd known. I hated that too.

I got my match-cord glowing, ready to fire the flash-pan. The acrid smell greeted me, an old, familiar friend. I breathed it in. I barely noticed the sourness of the Misery-air anymore. Something else that I'd adjusted to, given enough time. And I'd given it time. I'd given it six years.

'You think they'll come kill you when you shoot?' Nenn asked.

'They'll try.'

I drew the sighting bar over my target. Considered putting my lead ball through the navigator's head, but the drudge had thick skulls and not every hit was a killer. I had a better target. A bead of sweat rolled down my cheek. I breathed out slowly until I was empty, and listened to the beats of my heart.

The trigger clicked, the powder flared, the gun roared, and the brass astrolabe in the navigator's hands exploded into twists of shredded metal and shattered glass. The shot went on, tore through his bronze chest-plate and ripped out the other side. The beasts of burden around him brayed, the ruined tangle of brass dials, hoops, and bars falling in pieces from spasming fingers, and the navigator fell from the saddle.

They were all dead from that moment, sure as if I'd put a ball through every head. The one thing you can't risk in the Misery is your navigator. The endless sands, the twisting of the points of the compass, the way landmarks can grow legs and crawl off someplace else. This deep in the Misery, the drudge had less chance of getting back to Dhojara than I did of winning a beauty contest.

'What if they have another navigator?' Nenn asked.

I sighted on the fallen drudge, but the others had swarmed over him, trying to shield him with their bodies.

'They never do,' I said. 'I don't know what breed the blue ones are, but they won't find their way home without him. Look at that captain. He's just realised how fucked he is.' I glanced right, but Nenn had reappeared on my left. She returned my savage grin.

The drudge were not grinning. They raised their voices in a single, furious funeral-wail and drew steel. Their armour was ornate, engraved with prayers of adulation to their god-Kings, wrapped with streamers carrying their pleas on the wind. I was prepared to bet that none of them had prayed hard enough.

'You sure you thought this through?' Nenn asked.

'You always ask that.'

'How are you going to kill them all?'

'I won't have to,' I said.

The drudge had spotted me now, blank white faces and amber eyes focusing on the rising trail of gun smoke. They knew their chances of sending a crossbow bolt through me were slim at that range, and besides, I was just one man. I stood up so that they could get a better look at me while I began to reload. I tore the end from a second powder charge and loaded another ball.

The drudge kicked at their horned mounts, and the hurks started an uneven amble towards me, hooves thudding against grit and sand as they drove up the incline. They were angry, and surprised, and those two things make both men and monsters stupid.

'Bad odds,' Nenn's ghost said. I shook my head. The drudge charging me were already dead, they just hadn't understood it yet. I gritted my teeth and wiped the sweat from my brow. I was confident, and I had a plan, but nasty plans have the worst habit of backfiring.

'Come on, you bastards,' I snarled. 'Come and get me.' I sighted through the scope, which kindly adjusted itself for the diminishing range as the drudge ploughed up towards me, sand churning beneath driving hooves. The rider at the fore was snarling, his lipless mouth emitting a droning buzz as he heeled his mount towards me, a curved sword held above his head. My gun spat smoke and fire and the back of his skull exploded, spraying brain and bone across the following troops before his body fell from the saddle.

It was a waste of ball and powder. I didn't need to kill him, but being under fire made the drudge whip their beasts harder. They roared with anger, the need to feel anything but hopelessness forcing them on. The drudge are not like us. They measure the passage of time in the great thoughts of their masters rather than by the passage of years, but even they must have understood that with their navigator dead, they'd never hear their god's voice again.

The herd crashed straight through the fronds that lay silent and flat against the sand, translucent as glass and just as sharp. The beasts were halfway across it when the Misery grass leapt to attention, tinkling like tiny festival bells. A rare sound of beauty in the black wasteland, but a beauty that lasted only a moment before the screaming obliterated it. The lumbering beasts crashed to earth as the razor edges slashed through their legs and within moments the glassy fronds were drenched in red. The drudge behind drove into those ahead, the impetus of the charge ploughing them on and into the ground.

The grass had waited until they were all within its clutches. I knelt and put a hand down against the sand. Felt the Misery, the power, the taint on the world. Silently I thanked her.

Shrieking. Screaming. All the right sounds from the drudge. Bellowing and braying from the animals that had carried them, the poor stupid creatures. The Misery grass

6

made short work of drudge and beast alike. I didn't know whether it was sentient or whether it even counted as a plant, but the flexible glass fronds snapped and lashed at the wounded. Legs were severed, and wherever a drudge placed a hand against the ground the blades thrust upwards, spearing palms and severing fingers. Once the fronds pierced flesh, barbs hooked and there was no escape. I sat back, passed my last matchlock ball from hand to hand. I didn't think I'd need it.

At the foot of the slope, the captain stared up at me as his soldiers wailed and died. You can always trust a leader to go in last.

I thrust my fingers into the sand. Something that was part of me, something alien and foreign that had slithered up inside me to live, linked with the corruption below. I barely felt the wrongness of it anymore as it tingled along my hands, my spine. The grass on the slope below was busy feasting, wrapping the last pieces of drudge and drawing them down into the sticky red sand, but it listened. I told it that I needed to pass and the Misery heard me. She warred over it, but only briefly. There was still a part of me that was not hers, still part of me that was foreign, and she wanted it. But I was something else to her now, whatever that was, and in the silent dark where my soul had once lain I felt quiet assurance that the grass would leave me be.

This all sounds pretty grand, as though I were communing with my god and she responded, but the truth is the Misery barely noticed me. I was little to her. A fly on an elephant's arse.

I snuffed the slow match, bagged the gun, and headed down towards the captain. He didn't make any attempt to get away. The grass parted at my approach, only a few barbless juvenile fronds forgetting themselves and spiking at me through my boots. The first time I'd cut through a bank of grass I'd been afraid, but the years will numb you to most things. The drudge was seeing it for the first time, though, and his overlarge, overpupiled fish-eyes were larger and wider than they ever should have been. He got down from his mount and pushed it to go. He was big; not tall but heavy in limb and body. The flat planes of his lips were tattooed with the same sigils the drudge used in their prayer charms, and the great mark on his forehead that declared him King Acradius' creature had a silvery sheen against the matt, rubbery skin. He wore a sword similar to the one that I'd once taken from a drudge guard, out near the crystal forest. I wore that sword now.

I came within a few paces. Killing range. The captain looked me over. He didn't know what to make of me, and I couldn't blame him. I didn't look like a man. Didn't look like drudge either, and he'd just seen me walk through the sea of Misery grass that had devoured his companions without so much as a cut.

'I would have words with you, Servant of Acradius,' I said. A formal way to begin, but the drudge like formality. When they get mind-fucked they tend to lose their sense of humour.

The captain was surprised to hear me clicking and buzzing through its language. He shifted his feet in the dirt, a fighting posture, hand moving to the hilt of his sword. I made no move towards my own. I wasn't threatened by one drudge, no matter how deeply its god had stamped his ownership into its head.

'What are you?' the captain asked.

'I'm a man,' I said. Since he was all nervy with his sword, I put my pack and gun down on the ground, though it wasn't good for the canvas to be in contact with the sand. The Misery has a tendency to decay things, fraying them away a thread at a time until there's nothing left. Cloth, iron, people, it breaks them down just the same.

'You are the Misery's Son?' he asked. His eyes narrowed.

'I'm just a man,' I said.

'No,' the captain said. 'You are something else.' He was right.

'I'm not like them,' I said. 'You understand that I have already killed you, don't you?'

The captain's orblike eyes bulged from his flat face, but they swivelled across to the navigator's bled-out corpse.

'Yes,' he said.

'You were ordered to find me. Why?' It helped to keep the drudge focused if you mentioned their overlords at every chance you got. They were obsessed with them.

'You are an abomination. The gods will not permit your existence,' the drudge said. He bared thick, square teeth. 'I am honoured to die if it means the rightful rulers of this world will at last have their throne. There will be peace at last.'

'You can't kill me,' I said. 'That much should be obvious to you.'

'You cannot defy the will of the Deep Emperor,' he said with utter certainty. Emperor? I kept my face still, but the word rang hard in my chest.

'Acradius styles himself emperor above his brothers now?'

'He is the emperor,' the drudge said, as though I questioned where to find the sky. 'Your death is only a matter of time. Defend yourself.'

We drew swords, and he was strong and skilled, but it was over in a matter of heartbeats. He staggered back a couple of steps as blood welled from his neck. Couldn't believe that I'd hit him that fast. He fell to his knees.

A lot about me had changed down the years. I was fifty years old, but I was stronger and faster than a man of half my years. Maybe too strong. Maybe too fast. I was different, now.

As the captain fell onto his face to bleed into the sand,

I felt a little tug at my consciousness. It was the grass. It wanted the captain's body and couldn't reach it. I was grateful that it had let me pass, so I rolled him up the slope until the glassy blades could began to spear and bite. There'd be nothing left of him before long. The grass wanted the navigator as well, but one trip back up the slope was enough. My leg was still prone to complaining if I exerted myself too much, and besides, I had other plans for the cadaver. I pegged it down using the captain's sword and left it there.

My work was done, but there were still the captain and navigator's mounts to see to, as well as the hurks. They didn't pose any threat, but they'd attract the bigger Misery things. As a general rule the smaller things left me alone, but the really big ones didn't give a shit how much of the Misery I'd soaked up. Lately, I'd seen a heavy black shape in the sky, with scorpion tails, broad wings, and more than one head. It left a trail of black, oily smoke where it passed through the sky – a Shantar. However the Misery had changed me, I'd not last half a minute against one of those. Glancing up now, I could make out a trail in the sky, but distantly, towards what was probably south.

I had a grim feeling that the drudge were not the only things looking for me in the Misery.

The hurks would draw the Shantar, or anything else that came this way. I checked over the baggage for anything that I could use. My knife had suffered over the last months, pitted and growing brittle, and I was glad of a replacement. My boots were worse, but nothing the drudge had would fit me. Dealing with the beasts was simple enough. I got them roped together, then fired a blank into the air. Up close, the noise of it sent the simple beasts into a panic, and they stampeded off the same way that their former owners had gone. That grass owed me a thank-you.

It was time to go home. I knew which way I had come from, but that didn't mean it was the way back. I knelt and put a hand against the Misery's gravel. The magic bled up into my palm like a contagion, a corruption seeking to enter all things and turn them to its darkness. I breathed in, tasted her foulness against my teeth, but I'd spent so long out here in the fume and the ache of it carried a bittersweet tang. I reached down into the earth, breathed out, and let the Misery tell me where north lay today.

I became part of the earth. Not one with it, she was far too grand a thing for me to blend so completely, but we shared.

Through her, I could feel him. Distant. Vast. Somehow both disconnected from the whole and intricately its essence, he was out there, somewhere, beyond. He was in torment, and he was agonised and weak after he and the other Nameless had gone head-to-head with the Deep Kings to stop the rising of The Sleeper, after they broke the world for a second time. Crowfoot. My master.

The sky howled, an aching sob of suffering. Red clouds, threaded with veins of poison black, brewed hard in the east. The poison rain was a new enemy, even out here. It had begun with the Crowfall, bringing lurid visions and madness to those caught in its path. I had to be back under cover before it hit.

I drew my new knife and sliced a shallow cut across my right forearm amongst the lattice of pale scars crossing the old tattoos. A few drops of blood fell onto the Misery-sands, and she welcomed the offering. A part of me, becoming a part of her. It was a bargain of sorts. I took, but I also gave.

I dreamed my way down into the world, and I saw how the land had changed, how reality had shifted over the hours, the months, the moons. I found the Always House, and turned to head in that direction. It had only taken me two hours to intercept the drudge patrol, but it was going to be five hours back, past a lake of black tar that hadn't been there before.

2

The clouds closed in faster than I'd expected. Bad colour covered the world, and I ran.

The tell-tale trail of smoke that rose from the chimney of the Always House appeared ahead of me. It sat atop a rise in the land, a comfortable country cottage, splendid in its isolation.

Little in the Misery survived the Heart of the Void, but the catastrophic discharge of corruption had obeyed no rules. Where it had levelled the cities of Clear and Adrogorsk, it had torn this one cottage out of time and left it there. Unchanging, a blip in the fabric of reality, an island caught in a temporal distortion that meant that every day it was restored to exactly the same state.

I'd cut it close, and I was still a hundred yards from shelter when the sky opened. I pulled my hood up as the hissing drops fell, but the fabric soaked through quickly and the rain stung where it bled through, burning like nettle rash. Nenn's ghost had buggered off, which was a shame since I sometimes thought that, had she lived, she might have enjoyed the stinging rain the way she'd grown to enjoy chillies. I ran harder, seeking a roof before too many of the venomous drops burned my skin, and the visions began to dance before my eyes.

I thumped the door open. It stuck for a moment, as it always did, and then I was out of the rain. I hung my coat by the ever-lit hearth, used an old apron to wipe the sting-ing water from my hands. The sting didn't matter. I had endured worse and more. The visions it brought were the real threat. Terrifying, maddening glimpses of impossible things. A flurry of dark images, little more than impres-sions, and the maddening sense of sand, slipping away through trembling fingers. A face that could not be seen. Distant lives, crumbling into ash one by one. I had thought it had meaning once, but it was overwhelming, senseless, a shivering flurry of warped notions and fluttering pain, echoes of unknowable things. Those that got caught in it were left gibbering for days. The black rain had begun with the Crowfall. Many had died. More collateral damage in Crowfoot's endless war.

No visions today. I wasn't wet enough. I stripped off my sodden things, wedged the door shut, and went to the important business – making sure my matchlock and sword were dry. The little gear I had was too precious to risk rust.

I had discovered the Always House a long time ago, back when I was just gaining confidence in my ability to navi-gate the Misery. Back then, my trips had still been short. A month, maybe two. Over time I had begun to regard the Always House as mine, though given its time-lost nature, ownership was impossible.

Six years. I'd spent the best part of six spirits-damned years out here, alone but for the ghosts. It would be worth it, I told myself. When all was said and done, when it all came to a head and I could cast aside the deceit we had woven, when everyone that needed to die lay broken, it would be worth it. I had to believe that.

The house had been a simple dwelling, a regular farm-house in a regular village somewhere outside the city of Clear. The city had not survived the Heart of the Void, but this one house had. Standing alone, surrounded by a patch of grass that never wilted, never required water. While the elemental devastation had warped and reshaped the world around it, some random stray spiral of magic had taken this house and cast it aside. It still had walls, a thatched roof that was in need of replacing on what was usually the northern exposure, simple panes of yellow glass in the windows. Its owners had been farmers, that much I could tell by the bill hook, the shears, the threshing flail, and other tools left piled in a corner. When the cataclysm had come, someone had been cooking pottage with leeks, onions, and three small bites of mutton. One of those morsels of meat was slightly larger than the others, and a second had a shard of bone in it. I knew them perfectly; every day, shortly after dawn, everything reverted to the state it had been in before. The pottage was always cooking, always contained precisely the same bits of food. The bag of hard old oats was back in the pantry, the mouse droppings lined the wall. The house groaned and trembled just before it happened, creaking as time bent and twisted itself out. I had no desire to know what would happen to me if I ever stayed inside during its reversion. The water barrel had been full when the Heart of the Void struck. That was the discovery that allowed me to become self-reliant for longer periods out in the Misery. At first I'd wished that those long-gone farmers had left me a bottle of brandy or a keg of beer, but after all this time, I found that I didn't miss the drink. It was a quiet, humble existence, but that's what life holds for most folk. There were times when I even found a measure of peace.

I cleaned my weapons thoroughly, treated them with a little oil, then wiped them down with a cloth. It was the last oil I had, my supplies spent. The distortion worked two ways. When the Always House reset what had been there before, it also devoured anything that was left inside. I'd learned that the hard way on my first visit, having left my supplies in what I thought was a safe place, only to find everything gone on my return. I'd tested it with rocks since then. I had no idea what happened to the things that were lost, but if I left the house, I took all of my possessions with me.

Why didn't it devour me? Damned if I knew. Maybe being alive tethered me to the world more firmly, but that was a guess, and in truth it's probably best not to find out. You don't try to understand the Misery, you just try to survive it.

I barred the door. None of the Misery things came near the Always House, not even the big ones. Still, it would have felt remiss to leave them an open invitation.

I dipped myself a cup of water. Cool, clean, fresh. Like farm life turned to liquid. Like life.

Evening darkened the sky, but I had fire and food, water and warmth. All the things a man might need. The rain lasted for hours. The drudge's words had unsettled me, and I brooded, alone with my thoughts. That the Deep Kings knew that I was out here was bad enough. They were hunting me, and would send more of their twisted servants. I only had to slip up once to find myself surrounded and brought down, and I hadn't the supplies to last out here much longer.

I needed to head back to the Range to resupply. Maybe tomorrow. I was out of ammunition, oil, pretty much everything. Station Four-Four were used to me coming and going, though every time they seemed less and less pleased to see me. I couldn't blame them. The Misery had been changing me day by day, year by year. My skin had changed; so had my eyes. They could probably smell the taint upon me. None of it was good.

All three moons had hidden, the only light ebbing from the glowing white-bronze cracks in the sky. When the rain passed I dragged a chair outside onto the decking and leaned back, looked out over what had once been a horror and now – somehow – had become a lonely kind of home. I couldn't have said how long it had been since I'd spoken with anyone

15

who wasn't dead. Hard to chart the progress of days and seasons when there's only the oppressive rising heat of the Misery and the wailing sky. It was a long walk to Valengrad. I seldom left the Misery at all now and it had been six months, perhaps, since my last trek back. The strange looks the civilians gave me hadn't left me champing to return.

Distantly, I saw the dark trail left by the flying thing, crawling so slowly across the sky that it had to be leagues away. Maybe there was more than one, but I didn't think so.

Evenings were long in the Misery. Long and tedious. At first, when I made frequent trips back to the city, I tried bringing books with me. The problem was, if I left them in the Always House they disappeared, if I buried them outside it the Misery might move them, and I couldn't carry stacks of paper around with me. So instead I'd invested in just two small, tightly written little texts that Dantry thought were essential to the plan we'd thrashed out in the days after Marshal Davandein retook Valengrad. Preparations for what had to come. The first was a treatise written on the art of light spinning. The second was a guide to higher-level mathematics. They were dense, impenetrable, and joyless expositions of their respective sciences, but in my ignorance their logic wheels and energy rotations provided puzzles long and deep enough to while away the hours. I had read them over and over, until I could have taught them by rote. It wasn't enough. I still didn't know, not exactly, what I had to do.

I thumbed the overthumbed pages again but couldn't focus and found myself staring off into the cracks in the sky, as though I'd see the final piece I needed in those dim lights.

'Thinking about her again?' Nenn said. She propped her feet up on the decking's rail, as was her wont. Her boots made no sound.

'You seem to think I am, which means either I am, or

16

that I'm thinking about thinking about her,' I said.

'Doesn't help nothing to keep thinking about the dead.'

'That's rich, coming from you.'

Nenn gave me a spectral grin, her teeth translucent green-white where they should have been black as tar.

'It's what it all comes down to, isn't it? Ghosts. You out here. Her, dead but trapped in the light. Even this place. What is the Misery but the ghost of Crowfoot's fury?'

'Such a fucking poet!' Nenn's ghost stood up, stretched her arms, and gave a yawn. Her mouth opened too wide. Any real jaw would have cracked, real skin would have split. I didn't pay it any heed. I'd seen it all before. She rounded it out with a bellowing ghost-fart.

'I liked you much better when you were alive,' I said. The ghost didn't care. She wasn't real anyway.

'You'll get her out of your system one day,' Nenn said.

'It wasn't fair,' I said. 'She didn't deserve to die. Ezabeth saved us all. She deserved better.'

Nenn snorted. 'In all the blades you've swung and bones you've cracked, all the arrows and the cannon fire and the disease and the gangrene, all the Spinners and Engines and Deep Kings, you ever know death to take those that deserve it first?'

She had a point. The drudge I'd goaded to their deaths had been men, once, or at least their ancestors had been. Wasn't their fault they were marked and changed by the Kings. They were just soldiers, same as I was. Same as all those dumb kids I'd got killed in the rout from Adrogorsk, same as the men I'd told to stand on the walls of Valengrad as Shavada tore it out from under them. I shouldn't have hated the drudge for what they were. They were the same as us, but they weren't like us and I did hate them for it. It was a prejudice I could live with. Truth was I'd have killed an empire of them if it would have brought Ezabeth Tanza back from the fire.

What would she have made of me now? Not much. She hadn't liked the old me a whole lot, most of the time. I couldn't claim that the last ten years had done much to improve me.

'Leave me alone,' I told the ghost. Exactly as I'd told her the last time she had come to sit with me. Nenn would come up onto the deck, but her shade never entered the house. Nothing of the Misery would enter the Always House. It was even proof against gillings, although I hadn't seen any of them in a long time. None of the Misery's creatures wanted in. They knew it wasn't theirs.

Night came and went. Dawn brought a fog with it, and I stayed inside until it passed. Fog's never a good thing, but in the Misery it can do strange things. There are creatures that live in the fog and nowhere else, and the spirits only know where they go when the fog dissipates. Best not to tangle with them. There are worse things than being eaten in the Misery. Only when the sun rose alongside the moons, golden Eala and Clada's blue coolness, did I venture out to hunt.

I knelt and put a hand to the grit. The Misery whispered her secrets to me, and I turned what could have been con-sidered north. She told me where to seek, where to hunt. I no longer remembered when we'd started this strange com-munion, but the Misery didn't hate me anymore. She got in my veins, my gums, and when I let myself grow distracted, my thoughts. She didn't like my purpose, didn't like that I wasn't willing to join her completely, but I'd basked in her embrace for long enough that the corruption tolerated me. We were not one, but we coexisted. I held no greater place in her affection than the skweams and dulchers. I was just another thing; a thing that understood. That seemed important. The Misery's Son. That was what the drudge had called me. It was true, after a fashion.

I picked my way back to the site of the previous day's

ambush, though it lay before the dunes rather than beyond them now, and the distance had halved. The Misery's tar lake had become a mere seam of the viscous liquid barring my way. It smoked, bubbled, and stank, sending me on a two-mile detour, but eventually I found the way. The bodies of the drudge and their mounts were gone, devoured by whatever lay beneath that glass-bladed foliage, but it was the navigator's body I'd been interested in. In fact, it wasn't his body I wanted, but the things that had come for him.

They dozed, a pair of bloated, spider-legged maggots amongst the bones they'd picked clean. There were no names for whatever they were. For all I knew, they were the only two of their kind in existence. They'd chewed through the straps of the navigator's bronze armour, pried it open as a fisherman cracks a crab's shell to get at the soft white meat inside. I named them Scuttlers, lying in the afternoon sun, sagging white bellies grotesquely swollen. Senses dulled by satiation, they didn't notice my approach, but they were too bloated to avoid me even if they had. I hacked what I figured to be their heads away, trussed them up like game, and turned for home.

A few miles away, taunting me, a staircase rose up from the sand. Unsupported, it lifted up to a stone arch. I should have seen the sky through it, but instead there was darkness. It led somewhere else. It was not the first time that I'd encountered the dark archway. It had come and gone over the past months, and the Misery's message was clear. It wanted me to enter. Wanted me to climb those stairs, step through into whatever lay beyond.

I kept my distance. The Misery was not my ally. I did not trust her.

I carried the Misery-creatures back to the Always House, then sat outside and went to work. Nenn said nothing as I skinned them. Nothing, as I gutted them, then disappeared entirely as I sat down to my meal.

Nightmares followed. Dreams so vivid I could have painted them in oils if I'd had the talent. I saw the world as it had been before the Deep Kings had come, before Crowfoot had repelled their armies by unleashing the Heart of the Void. The fields patched a luscious country in green, gold, and tan. The wheat grew deep, the olive groves were heavy with fruit. The sun shone hot in summer, the rains came full in spring. The princes and queens who ruled the cities hadn't been saints, and they'd fought hard when the Deep Kings led their armies to trample the wheat, to burn the groves. And when they'd fought with everything that they could, had given everything they had to give, Crowfoot unleashed the Heart of the Void in his desperation. Children looked up from their lessons and work to see the cracks tear through the sky. The energy that came down broke the earth and tore through the stability of reality. Towers crumbled, forests melted. The wheat hissed and spat and sizzled into clouds of poisoned fog, dogs merged with their masters into things that were neither, and they were the lucky ones. I saw the advancing armies of the drudge look up as the moons shivered and their light faltered, and the sky began to howl before they too were twisted, destroyed, and scattered. I lived a thousand hideous, agonised deaths.

As I awoke, my whole body hissed with pain, but I had become accustomed to it. I crawled to the water barrel and tried to wash the foulness away but it lingered and remained, as it always lingered and remained. Sweat slicked my skin, even my fingers glistened. My nails had long ago turned black, my flesh hard and gleaming like polished copper. I lowered my head against my knees, wrapped a blanket around my shoulders, and crawled into the corner. I didn't weep. I didn't ever weep. To mourn took sorrow, and there was no more pity left in my husk. There was only a dry, steady anger. Anger, and the need for revenge.

3

I had to return to the Range. I hadn't the shot, the powder, or the gun-oil to keep going. The rains came eleven days apart, always eleven days. They'd been regular as clockwork for the last three years, ever since the Crowfall.

The earth had shaken. The sky tore afresh, and everything changed.

We were not at the epicentre, whatever it was. Of that I was sure. Nobody knew for certain what caused it, but I had my suspicions. We only caught the peripheral wash, the ground shaking and the black rain falling upon us. It had begun as a day like any other, and then – madness. For a day and a night, nothing made sense. Colours flickered and blended together. Cold water boiled away into nothing, hot water froze into ice. Birds fell from the sky, trees burst into bloom before withering to dry, empty husks. There was no reason behind it. The effects were inconsistent even between one footstep and another. The Doomsayers who'd long since claimed that the world was ending had enjoyed being right for one insane, calamitous day. But the next, they were to be disappointed.

Things did not return to normal but they stabilised. The geese remained different, the crows were gone. New things we'd never seen before crawled out of the dark to pester, to bite, to haunt. It was the deciding factor. What I'd planned with Dantry and Maldon was dangerous. Foolish, even, maybe. But when the world twisted and bucked and every part of reality ground against its own corners, we knew it had to be done. Swore it in blood. One last throw of the dice, before everything was gone.

It would take me six days to make it back to the Range on foot, though it was nearer three weeks' travel. The Misery would accommodate me in this, time and distance swirling like drops of blood in water, provided I was willing to pay her price. I'd learned her moods. Her ways. The passages and flows of change that ran between the fragments of what passed for reality out here. But to work through her meant expending the essence that had bled into me. Everything has a price, and to bend the Misery's pathways to my will took from me the very essence that I'd been soaking myself in all this time. I would spend it only grudgingly, hoarding it as a miser hoards coins beneath his floorboards.

I didn't leave.

I delayed.

I followed my usual routines. Went out across the sands, or the salt flats, or whatever new terrain the Misery's shifting brought to me. When I found things I killed them, and I took what I needed from them. I saw no more drudge, but the hanging archway appeared again, twice, thrust directly into my path. I looked up at the darkness beyond, and not for the first time felt a tugging curiosity to know what lay beyond. It passed as it always did, and I gave it a wide berth.

The one luxury I had found in the Always House was a lonely cigarillo. It was poorly rolled, abandoned halfway. Maybe the owner had tossed it away, running outside to witness his demise as the sky broke asunder and chaos scorched the world. I'd discovered it between two floorboards. It was always a pain in the arse to dig it out, but I dug it out most days. I lit it from the stove and sat out on my porch to listen to the sky. It was red today, red and black and bloody as tar. The wails and howls had always seemed so random before, but there was consistency there, if you knew what to listen for. To say the song was beautiful would have been a stretch, but it was worthy of observation, perhaps.

That was when I saw him. Distant. Just a speck on the horizon. I leaned forwards and squinted against the redness of the sky's glare.

It was a man. Or a man-shape, anyway. The things in the Misery sometimes look like us. The ghosts echo what they were. The gillings parody our beginnings. The limber-men scamper across the dunes on spindle-legs and the behemoths' stony bodies cling vaguely to our shapes. But this was none of those things. It was a man, alone and on horseback. A soldier? A traveller?

No ordinary man could have made it this far into the Misery alone. Not here, into the darkness, where the dread things lay.

I reached slowly for my gun, loaded my last shot and lit the cord, and settled in to get the range. No need for me to go to him – only one place he could be headed. There only *was* one place, around here.

I cocked my weapon, put my eye to the scope. The world leapt forwards into sharp, easy focus, dials rotating as the lenses settled. My eyesight had never been better. The Misery had turned my skin to copper and my veins black, but she'd also sharpened my edges. The rider had not enjoyed such benefits. His mule – not a horse after all – was limping, but without it the man would have been slower. He'd lost a foot, and one sleeve ended raggedly at the elbow. His head hung forwards, and he slumped in the saddle, only his balding crown and dirty brown hair visible. I sighted on him with the targeting bar, lined it up with his chest. It was my last lead ball. A shame to waste it, if he was a lost soldier, a scout, or some other unfortunate detached from his unit.

But he could be something worse. Something that would

erupt from its shell of skin in a flurry of teeth and hate. Something that exploded. Something awful.

My fingers shifted on the firing lever. Put him out of my Misery? Even if he was human, there was no food here that he could take with him, no supplies to get him back home. I could live off the land, but I'd acclimatised slowly. Nobody else could. Better to send him on to whichever of the hells had collected his name and have done.

My hands were steady on the stock. Seemed a cruel thing to see a man survive the Misery's worst only to grack him here. Something nasty had taken his foot and his arm, but he'd got away anyway, and the Always House could keep him alive. For a time, anyway. But it was my sanctuary, and he didn't belong here. I settled my aim nice and steady as he drew closer. With the scope's help, a heart shot was possible at this range.

'Ah, shit,' I said. I lowered my gun, snuffed the match. Instead I fetched out my swords and placed them in easy reach on the table. Better not to waste the shot.

As the mule drew closer, I realised, with the kind of discomfort that rises from blood-clogged drains, that I knew this person. Or whatever he was. 'Person' was a stretch.

I walked out to meet him. The mule was blind and on its last legs. It hadn't the energy to be unnerved by me as I took the small man down from the animal's back and carried him the last ten yards to the house.

'Not inside,' he croaked. 'Don't take me inside.'

His face was thick with dust, scuffed and bloody. The Misery had not been gentle.

'Not refined enough for your kind?' I said.

'Wouldn't go well,' he said. He wasn't smiling. Of all the people that I had expected to see on the back of that mule, Otto Lindrick was well down on the list. Or at least a man – or a thing – that looked like Otto Lindrick.

Nall. One of the Nameless, here in the Misery, alone and

bloodied on the back of a sorry-looking mule. This man – this being – had built the Engine that defended the Range. I had witnessed the vast power that his machinations had wrought, had seen him unpick a god from existence beneath the citadel. He had many bodies; this one had seen better days. I had not expected any guests at the Always House. In no dream had I expected one of the Nameless.

I brought water from the barrel. Immortal wizard or no, the body this part of his consciousness inhabited was feeling the pain of its journey. It must, I realised from its damp clothing, have been caught out in the rain. That couldn't have been easy, even for a wizard.

'Wasn't expecting guests,' I said. I propped Lindrick up in the rocking chair on the deck. 'The place is a mess.'

'"The roads are a mess." That's what the bastard gillings were saying when I woke up,' Nall said, showing me the ragged, chewed-off stump of an arm. 'Nasty little things, aren't they?'

'Not at all pleasant,' I said. My skin was crawling. I brought out a blanket, because Nall's body was ruined and dying, and it seemed fair that a man ought to be given a blanket when he's about to die. Not that Nall really died when one of his bodies failed. His apprentice had once stuck a fruit knife in him, but he'd been back soon enough.

'It took me a long time to find you,' he said. 'Nobody would tell me where you were.'

'They don't know,' I said. I felt a moment of cold. 'Who did you ask?'

'Oh, you know. Your sorts. Drunks and misfits. The Range Marshal. I even tried some of your fellow Blackwing captains.' He cocked an eyebrow at me. 'Not so many of you left, these days, are there?'

He drank, spilling as much water as he took in. The body's eyes were bloodshot. Pained. I reminded myself that it was all bullshit. The whole body was a lie.

'You could have asked Crowfoot,' I said. 'He must know where I am. He always does.'

Nall's eyes glittered through the red streaks. Something of that old wolf's cunning still in there, then. Something alien.

'We both know he doesn't. You've hidden yourself deep in the darkness out here, and the raven is not what he once was. None of us are.'

I'd not heard from my master since before the Crowfall. That was nothing abnormal. He'd gone long periods without bothering me before. But this was different. In those brief, glimpsed flashes in the rain I'd seen things. Terrible things.

'How did you find me?'

'My own captain managed it. Winter found you.'

'Never heard of him.'

'Of course not. My agents don't strut like you Blackwings. Crowfoot never understood the benefits of subtlety.'

Somewhat rich coming from Nall. I didn't think that there was very much subtlety about a towering edifice of iron and concrete spanning the length of the Range, or about a machine capable of wiping lives from the world in their hundreds of thousands.

'You know, Galharrow, you're not looking so good,' Nall said. 'And that's coming from me.'

I got up and leaned against one of the porch's posts. Looked out into the Misery, where the sand was shifting, gliding, and reshaping at the passage of some great presence beneath. The Misery had tried to stop Nall from reaching me. Or maybe that was giving it too much credit. It tried to stop everyone and everything from getting anywhere.

'What do you want?'

'Crowfoot needs you,' Nall said. He coughed into his fist. Sounded like he had wet gravel rolling around in his lungs. 'We're been in disarray since the Fall.'

'The Crowfall?'

26

'If you wish to call it that. But if you think you've seen the Deep Kings make war on us before, what's coming is going to rewrite the definition. It's bad, Galharrow. We're down to our last cards.'

'When you Nameless get desperate you tend to make plays that don't work out so well for the rest of us. What's Crowfoot's angle this time?' I said it without bitterness. Nall accepted it without rancour. It was simply a statement of fact.

Nall hunched over in another coughing fit, came away with red specks on his fist. His body didn't have all that long.

'What does Crowfoot always do when he sees a threat coming? He meets it head-on with all the subtlety of a stampede. He's working on a weapon of some kind. Something new. That much I'm sure of.'

'But you don't know?' I said. 'You're supposed to be the all-powerful Nameless, but you don't feel like sharing with each other?'

'Mortals,' Nall said with disgust. 'Always so caught up being irritable you can't see the truth that's right before you. Look at this body.' I did, and remained unimpressed. 'The Fall shattered me. This avatar was down on the southern coast, selling berths to fishing boats. There were a thousand of me spread across the world. Now? I've less than twenty forms left. I'm not even sure how many of me I still am, or what Crowfoot intends. Or where he is, or how he survived.'

'The day of the Crowfall,' I said. 'That was the day you fought the Deep Kings, to keep The Sleeper buried, wasn't it?'

The Deep Kings had tried to raise The Sleeper from the ocean's depths: some kind of ancient demon even greater and more powerful than they were, in a bid to flood the world. The Nameless had all travelled to a distant place of power, a land of ice and biting wind, to stop them. I had glimpsed their gathering only briefly in a vision my master had sent me, but I remembered the terrible presence that had lived beneath the ice.

'Perhaps,' Nall blinked. 'My memories are full of holes. Torn, frayed, and unravelling. Perhaps another version of me knows what happened. I don't remember much about you, Galharrow. Only that we used you to play the Engine ruse, and it worked. It is a sad state of affairs that I have come to rely upon mortals. But we failed. The Deep Kings are coming.'

'You're confused,' I said slowly. 'If The Sleeper had risen, we'd all be under a hundred feet of water.'

'True,' Nall said. He tried to grin, but the muscles were running out of energy. 'Hah. Hah. You're right. We fought them. But we only contained it. Partly. Deep King Acradius made a deal with The Sleeper. He took on the small part of its power that he could free, and in exchange they became one. Power for freedom. Acradius is something new, now. Vaster and more powerful than any king. Than any Nameless. We don't know how, or why, but the other Deep Kings fought him, and it's taken him three years to win. Philon, Nexor, Iddin, all of them – they're vassals, now. Acradius styles himself emperor now.'

'The Deep Emperor,' I said. I'd been hoping it was arrogance amongst his followers that had given the drudge cause to use that title. A chill crept down my neck, across my shoulders. 'And now he's coming for us?'

'Of course he's coming. We are broken, and with the power of The Sleeper at his call, not even the Engine can deter him.'

We sat in silence for a while. I went inside and dug the cigarillo out from the floorboards, lit it on the stove. Ate the meat from the pottage. Went back outside. I sat down beside Nall's wheezing body.

'You dying, Nall?' I asked.

'This body has seen better days.'

'You know what I mean. The real you. Whatever the fuck you are.'

'We come. We go. Sometimes it's brief, sometimes it's forever.' He coughed, sounding like his ribs were just a tangle of bone in his chest, clattering about in an empty space. Maybe they were.

'Are you scared?'

Nall narrowed his eyes, glared at me. The fury of the cosmos simmered there, burning hard, intense. I was just some petty mortal, and here he was, doing the dying. I doubted that he'd ever been so close to death as this.

'You want me to leave you alone until you're gone?' I asked.

Nall glared at me, then shifted his eyes down, around, away. Embarrassed. Angry. Afraid.

'No.'

I finished the cigarillo and tossed the nub out onto the sand. The smoke curled slowly through the heavy air, reluctant to rise.

'Can anything stop Acradius now?'

'Crowfoot has a plan. Will it work? Not even the spirits know, Galharrow.' He looked up towards the shattered sky, the glowing fault lines spreading in all directions, white-bronze light gleaming. 'But even if it does, I fear for the world. I like this world. I've been here a long time. I'll be gone, soon. But the world deserves to remain.'

'Does it?' I said. The words escaped before I could hold them back.

'It's cold and lonely, out here,' Nall said. 'But you've known love. It's why you've spent six years hiding in the Misery. You can play the bitter old man all you want, but I know what you're planning. Crowfoot doesn't, but I do.'

My muscles went rigid. The knife at my belt suddenly

begged to leap into my hand. I'd sworn I would allow no threats to survive. Allow no one to interfere. Nobody and nothing could get in my way. But this was Nall, and whatever the condition of this body, killing it would achieve jack-shit. I forced my fingers to unclench.

'You don't know anything,' I said.

'I followed Dantry Tanza's enquiries,' Nall said breezily, as though it were nothing. 'The research you've had him doing. The destruction of those mills. I reverse-engineered your plan from there. It's insane, of course. Utterly mad, but that's the brilliance of it. Tanza would be a revered genius, if every prince in Dortmark weren't trying to hang him. It's certainly a bold plan.'

'Will it work?' I asked. Nall laughed wetly.

'No. Of course not. You'd have to be mad even to attempt it.'

But then he smiled.

'You want me to succeed.'

'We all have our roles. Mine is nearly done. It's humanity that matters, now. You can become the anvil all you want, but if you're no longer a man, it won't matter anyway. And I haven't been human for a very, very long time.'

Riddles and half-truths. It was Nall. I shouldn't have expected anything less.

His eyes closed, the wheeze of his chest died away. He lay quite still for a moment, and then his eyes flew wide open. His one hand reached out and snatched my wrist. Or tried to. His fingers were held back, an invisible force keeping us apart. The magic in me and the magic in him did not want to meet, skin to skin.

'Crowfoot's weapon is our last chance at survival. But do not trust your master,' he hissed. His eyes had taken on a fixated intensity. Stared into me like he could see right into my heart.

'Weapons,' I said. I shook my head, turned away from

that gaze. 'We're sitting in the aftermath of his last, flanked by the craters made by yours. Where does it end?' But Nall had no answer for me. His breaths wheezed, rattled in failing lungs. 'What happened to you?'

'The rain remembers, Galharrow,' Nall croaked. 'Ask the rain.'

The body gave up and fell limp, the way the dead do. Empty, a boneless marionette with no operator. An analogy singularly fitting to that particular Nameless. I pulled the blanket up over his head. I'd have to burn the corpse. Wouldn't be wise to leave bits of the Nameless lying around for the Misery things to find. I got up, rolled my shoulders. The raven was calling, and I had to answer.

I'd been gone a long time. It was time to return to civilisation.

4

It is testament to the human spirit that people can not only learn to live with anything, they can usually work out a way to profit from it.

A town that should not have been a town lay between Station Four-Four and Station Four-Five. In the summer it reeked of the Misery as the warm air blew in from the east, and in the winter, everything froze over with ice that bore a greenish tint. Over the years the Misery had crept closer, and if the people that dared to live in that semblance of a town had possessed any sense, they would have turned west and looked for something better. But times were hard, and the people had grown harder. There was something positive to be taken from that, I thought.

I approached along the trade road from the south so that they wouldn't see me coming right at them over the broken sands. The palisade-ringed cluster of two dozen buildings lacked any serious fortification and, officially, Fortunetown didn't exist. There was a fine line between fortune-telling and doomsaying, and neither was permitted in the stations or in Valengrad, and so the tellers had started to settle in the shanty towns that grew up between the Range stations. Soldiers are a superstitious lot, and there was a thriving trade in chicken guts, card turning, and sleep readings.

I walked up the dirt track, noted that the solitary watch tower was unmanned. The palisade gate wasn't manned either, though darkness had already started to descend and there were things in the world that shouldn't have been let in. They must have felt safe here, but since the Crowfall not all of the dark creatures were confined to the Misery.

I was fifty yards from the gate when a coughing fit hit me. I doubled over at the side of the dusty track, feeling the sharp bite in my lungs. Blasting rips of air tore out of me. Felt like someone was jabbing a knife down my throat. I spat out a congealed lump of thick, heavy crap. Something like stewed tar. It had the taste of the Misery behind it, acrid and chemical, bitter and foul. It bubbled and made a feeble pretence at motion on the ground, steaming and staring back at me as I wiped my mouth. Not good.

I did what little I could to hide the oddness of my appearance before I entered Fortunetown, which meant pulling up a hood and showing as little skin as possible. Night would help conceal me, but it was better not to take chances. There would be soldiers here, and it had been a long time since I'd been on good terms with the citadel.

For a small place in the middle of nowhere, the night was lively. Fortune-telling coupled neatly with its sister trades: taverns to drink off a bad reading or celebrate a good one, pleasure houses for one last good time, and even a couple of shrines to the spirits of mercy and solace. Fortunetown drew the soldiers down from the stations and there were people out on the single broad street with cups of beer in one hand and verified certificates of good luck in the other. Neon phos lit the night declaring services to read your life, or ways to make you forget what you'd heard.

'Read your fortune, just ten marks,' an old woman called from a narrow doorway. 'Read your fortune in the sky. University trained, all fortunes sure to pass. Check your luck before you head out.' The lines around her eyes were set deep, her hands wrinkled, but she was dressed in bright silks and jewels sparkled on her fingers. Soothsaying was always profitable around men who risked their lives every time they went out to work. I didn't believe any of it. I'd made my own luck enough times, and I didn't want to believe that my life story was somehow written in the lines on my hands.

For the Misery, though, it was about as cheerful a place as I'd ever come across. It didn't seem like many bad fortunes were being told. Unhappy customers probably weren't repeat customers. Some of the readers probably believed in what they were doing, others were probably charlatans, but I couldn't blame them either way. They made people happy, and for a Misery-fronting town, Fortunetown was about as happy as anywhere got. I could see why Tnota had made it his home.

The wooden buildings bounced laughter and high spirits back into the phos-lit night, but it was a desperate, stretched kind of laughter, and most of it was absorbed back into the sky. I kept my head down and my hands in my pockets all the way to Tnota's house.

It was bigger than the other residential buildings, if a lot smaller than the most prosperous ale-dens. I frowned to see that even in the shadows it was heading towards a state of disrepair. The little garden I'd ploughed out for him hadn't been tended, and sickly weeds overran it. The windowpanes were clouded with dust blown in from the Misery and the whole place had a sad, neglected kind of look to it. Tnota had never been overly concerned with his living arrangements, but I'd thought that Giralt had been a good influence. Times must have changed, and if things had fallen apart on that score, then I'd be a sadder man by the time my visit was over. Tnota had found a good thing here – here, of all places, on the edge of a shattered sky with the hells on the doorstep.

I knocked on the door, three rapid taps. A few moments later, movement within, and it opened.

Age had caught up with Tnota quickly, overrunning him

in a handful of years. I figured that he was halfway between fifty and sixty and though I'd known older men, I'd not known an older navigator. The little hair that remained to him had turned white, and though his Fracan skin was unlined, the years of drink had taken their toll. He opened the door to me half-cut, his shirt hanging open to display an overhanging paunch. He blinked, the earthenware jug in his hand and the glaze of his eyes showing he'd started drinking shortly after dawn and hadn't let up.

'Ryhalt,' he said. He blinked a few times as if he couldn't quite grasp who he was seeing, then stepped out and embraced me with his one arm. He smelled like a three-week-old sock. 'Shit, Ryhalt. It's been an age. Wasn't expecting you. Haven't cleaned the place.'

'Can I get in off the street?'

'Sure. 'Course. Make yourself at home. Grab yourself a jug from the pantry. Whatever you like. What's mine is yours. You know that.'

He was unsteady on his feet, deep under the fug of booze. A pair of long candles cast a bleak light. It was cold, and the smell of disregard hovered in the air like evening mist. Tnota settled into a chair. I'd expected him to be energised to see me, to throw questions my way. Instead he just started to rock slowly in the chair, creaking in time to the ticking of an old grandfather clock, the only other sound in the room. I went to the pantry cupboard. Not a lot that could be called food in there, mostly jars of fish paste. There were a few jars of beer, but it had been a long time, and it didn't call to me the way it had once before. Tnota didn't have anything to drink that wouldn't potentially awaken that old demon. Empty handed, I went back and joined my friend in the dark sitting room. He squinted in the gloom as if focusing was hard.

'It's been a long time,' I said. Tnota looked at me with bleary eyes.

'Wasn't sure you'd come back this time.' He eyed my excessive growth of beard. Nobody to bother shaving for out in the Misery. 'Doesn't suit you.'

'I always come back,' I said.

'Never been gone this long before, though.' Tnota squinted as he performed some mental arithmetic. 'Almost six months.'

'It can't have been that long,' I said, frowning. But it had been late spring when I'd last left town, and winter was blowing in again now. I'd lost track of time. Lost track of myself, maybe. I was impressed that my ammunition had lasted that long.

'Giralt not in?' I said.

'He's away,' Tnota said. They weren't easy words for him to say. I wondered what they implied. Giralt ran one of the general stores that outfitted the miners before they went on their expeditions. A good man, honest and firm. He and Tnota had been of an age, and I'd liked him.

'Gone far?'

'Far enough. We won't see him tonight,' Tnota said. The weight of sadness in his words bore down on me and I chose not to press him. They'd had three years together here on the edge of the world. Maybe that was all that could be asked for. Tnota wasn't an easy man to get along with. He was cowardly, and he drank like a reluctant bridegroom. But he was also loyal, and there was goodness at his core. Giralt had been a good man. I wanted to know what had happened between them, but with your last friend there are some things you don't push.

I stood awkwardly while I plucked up the guts to ask the questions that I needed answered. Tnota sat rocking in his chair, staring into the gloom. You wouldn't have known that his oldest friend had just stepped out of the nightmare and into his home. He should have had questions. He should have cared.

'Have you heard of any sightings of Ezabeth?'

'No,' he said.

'Nothing at all?' I prodded. Tnota turned his yellow-crusted eyes towards me, blinking as if he were dredging memories up from beneath a mountain.

'We don't get news of that kind of thing down here often. It's been years. If she's still in the light, I haven't heard of it. Gone, I think. I know, it ain't what you want to hear.'

He said it as though that weren't crushing, but I just nodded. I'd studied my two impenetrable books. I knew that Ezabeth was fading from the world, even her half-existence destined to come to an end. Nothing lasts forever – except maybe the Nameless.

'And Amaira? Any word of her?'

'Not a whisper. Whatever she's doing for your boss, it took her far away and she hasn't been back. Dantry's still loose, though. They've not caught him yet. He blew up a phos mill, a big one. An accident, I think, although after you've done it three times I'm not sure you can still claim that.'

'Did anyone die?'

'Probably. I don't know. Talents, maybe.'

Melancholy filled the house, so thick that it nearly had flavour. The last time I'd been here, there had been bright-tuned lamps and Giralt had been cooking a shoulder of lamb. There'd been bunches of fragrant herbs strung from the rafters, fresh bread under a chequered napkin. All the life, all the joy had been sapped away. Giralt had never liked me much and I couldn't blame him for that, given I looked stranger each time he met me, and he knew that whatever I was doing, Tnota was mixed up in it and it probably wasn't good. But he was polite, courteous, treated me as a house-guest for Tnota's sake. I'd been happy, knowing that they'd found something worth treasuring.

A knock on the door.

'Expecting visitors?' I rose, my hand moving to my sword hilt. It was paranoia, old caution. Nobody knew I was here.

'It'll just be the boy from the tavern, taking tomorrow's order,' Tnota said wearily. 'Maybe someone looking to get led to the mine. I don't take many jobs these days, but I still have to make a living.'

Tnota pushed himself slowly from the chair, headed out to the hall. I heard a kid's voice, briefly, before the door closed and Tnota returned. He sank himself back down into his chair and stared into the candle flame. Almost as though he'd forgotten that I was there.

My own mood had sunk low as a mouse's belly, seeing my friend in this state. I lived a bad enough way out in the nonsense, but Tnota seemed somehow to be worse. Maybe because he'd had something good before, and now it was gone. Maybe.

I understood how the bleakness can take a man. You feel it in the exhaustion that follows you around, that presses down like a weight just above your eyes, telling you to just sleep through it all. To blot out the world with dreams and closed eyes so that at least you don't have to be aware of it. It tells you to be frantic, to elicit some kind of change to make things better, even as it tells you that there's nothing you can do and no point in trying. It says you had some-thing before, and that will never come back, and that the bottle will at least take it away for a few hours ... though it never does. That bleakness was rooted through Tnota, and not just because he was drunk. One arm had curled around the jug of beer like a child clutched to his breast, and without realising it, he mouthed silent words to the candle flame.

I got up from my chair, crossed to an old trunk. I opened it, poked around inside. Just some old tools, worn and tar-nished from use.

'Any trouble with the geese?'

Tnota shook his head. No interest. He didn't offer anything further. Just stared into the darkness.

I shut the trunk, crossed to a dresser. The first drawer held dishcloths, clean and neatly folded. The sign that someone cared about their life, that they took pride in honest things. Giralt's world, left untouched.

'When was the last time you heard from Dantry and Maldon?' I said. 'No word from them?'

'Not since you were here last,' Tnota said. Said it like it didn't matter. Like what they were doing wasn't vital to everything.

The other drawers contained silverware, an old bottle of cure-all tonic, dishes, licence papers. Tnota watched me rifling through his things without care or comment. I closed the drawers.

'Citadel men came asking for you, couple of months back,' Tnota said.

'Any idea what about?'

Tnota gave a one-sided shrug.

'The usual, probably.'

'Davandein can go boil her arse,' I said. 'You aren't feeling talkative today. Thought you might be glad to see me.'

'I guess,' Tnota said. He put the jug back to his lips. He drank, and liquid spilled into his beard and onto his chest. He was sweating. His health was shot, but I'd seen him drunk, and I'd seen him down, and this was worse than either. Spirits knew, we'd been through the hells and back and we'd seen plenty to bring us low. But this wasn't like him.

I opened the glass door of the grandfather clock. At the bottom, beneath the pendulum, were a couple of old blankets. They shifted a little as I disturbed something beneath them.

'Got you,' I said. I reached down and flipped the blankets. When the Crowfall fucked everything up, it did more than bring the rain. Something had been unleashed on the world, strands of dark and terrible power crafting change where they fell in the aftermath. Hundreds of crows had fallen from the sky, eyes burned out, and so had given the Crowfall its name. In the far south, the colour orange had disappeared for a full year. The people of Pyre had spoken backwards for nearly a month. A new breed of carnivorous geese had appeared, chewing their way through farmyards in a savage display of fanged beaks until the farmers culled them. But of all the odd curses that had appeared to plague the world, the Saplers were the worst.

Beneath the blanket lay a creature. Humanoid in shape, eight inches long. It was milk-white and ill-formed, as if its body were artlessly shaped from clay. It stared up at me with broad eyes, from a face that looked disturbingly close to Tnota's. It had been here a while, then. More than a month. Having been disturbed, the Sapler tried to crawl back beneath the blanket, a shrill screeching erupting from its mimicked lips. I grabbed it around the neck. They had teeth, even if they were small.

'Look what I found,' I said. Tnota stared at the struggling creature with uncaring eyes. Hugged the jug to his chest. 'I'm sorry. This is going to hurt.'

I put the Sapler down on the floor, put my boot over it, and then applied all my weight. There was a crunching sound, a tiny rib cage shattering, a skull breaking. The Sapler gave out a dying squeal. I raised my boot, stamped down hard, one, two. A pan fell from its wall hook.

Tnota stared at me with disinterest for a few moments longer, and then it hit him. The life that the Sapler had been taking from him spilled back to him in a rush. He jerked in his chair. Saplers fed on will, drawing it away and feeding themselves. Over time they took the shape of the victim to whom they had attached themselves. As they drew out the victim's life-spirit, they began to resemble their source of sustenance. Over time they grew bigger. I'd heard of one that had reached full size in a prison, though they were usually found and dealt with long before that. They were a plague on the states. Some kind of aftermath of the magic that had ripped at the world when the Nameless and the Deep Kings went head-to-head.

Tnota gasped as if I'd dragged him out of a lake, sucking in a deep breath of air, then doubling over as if he'd been punched in the gut. I gave him the time he needed to get his shit in order and kept a neutral expression, but there was anger beneath it. I'd put my trust in Tnota, needed him. Why hadn't he realised? He should have known better. I'd taught him better.

'Fuck. Ryhalt. Shitting fuck. There's a problem.'

'There was a problem,' I said. 'It's just a sticky patch on your tiles now.'

'Not that,' Tnota said. He took rapid breaths, like he'd been starved of air for a year and only now remembered how much he needed it. He blinked and tried to get his eyes to focus. 'It's Giralt. They got him, took him away. I don't know where. There was a man. A real bastard. Came south up the Range. Looking for you.'

'For me?'

'Aye … He put that thing in there. Told me he'd send me Giralt's eyes if I didn't leave it alone.' The memory still hurt him. He shook his head to clear it, struck himself on the temple as if he could beat the pain out. 'You gotta move, Ryhalt. That kid at the door comes by every day to check if you're here. He's taking the guy a message.'

I got bright real quick.

'And you're meant to keep me here until they come find me?'

Tnota's eyes said it all. Fear for his man. Self-loathing for having betrayed me. I couldn't blame him for that. The

Sapler had drained the fight from him. I ground the last of the little monster beneath my boot.

'I'm sorry,' he said.

'How long do I have?'

'Depends if you're going to run or fight,' Tnota said. I chewed on it a few moments.

'You got powder? Shot?'

'Same trunk as always.'

I flexed my fingers, joints cracking in the quiet.

'Tell them to bring Giralt. They'll find me at Sav's.'

5

I have always had an affinity for bars. They're familiar, and you know what you'll find. Most bars follow the same kind of layout. They hold the same kind of people. The same ways in and out. I knew One-Door Sav's well. The lights were too bright, the beer was badly brewed, and the resident tellers knocked off at nine. That worked out for me, as there'd be fewer bodies to get in the way. But mostly, I wanted them to find me on familiar ground.

The place was near empty, just a worried-looking man polishing his brassware behind the bar that ran along the left side of the room. I scanned the balcony that ran around the single large room, didn't see any threats. I'd left my dust-guard over my mouth to conceal most of my face, and heavy Talent goggles dimmed the damned amber light that bled from my eyes.

'Cold out there tonight,' I said. My voice was raw, coarse, and dry as sand. 'Whisky.'

The barman swallowed hard.

'Nothing warms you like it,' he said, but there was a tremor in his hand. He was the Sav who gave his name to the joint, and he'd been here from the start. He knew who I was. Any night of the week there should have been at least a dozen desperate Misery-miners gathered around the tables, trading stories about dulchers and limber-men. Evidently the message boy had run his mouth and word had blown down Fortunetown's street like a kicked-up wind; trouble was coming to Sav's. The off-duty soldiers had hit their bunks, the prospectors had gone to lie lower than the silver they craved. No point getting mixed up in something that wasn't their business. That told me that whoever was calling shots in this town had some grit. Dangerous.

Sav poured a measure of whisky, looked back at me, poured two more. I put the smudged glass beneath my dust-mask. Inhaled. It didn't have the same impact it had once had, not since the changes had taken their full hold. I breathed it in without drinking, and left the demon where it belonged.

A red-haired man entered the bar, brushing down his longcoat. He waved a friendly hello to the barman, saw me and didn't like what he saw, hurried away to a table. I was bad for business.

'You haven't been round these parts in a long while. Joining a dig?' Sav said. He hovered near me with the bottle at the ready, but I put the whisky back down without touching it. I wasn't there to drink and Sav was only talking to keep his nerves at bay. Probably wishing that I'd chosen anywhere but his bar.

'Doubt it,' I said. The whisky sat untouched between us.

The barman shivered, took one of the glasses himself, and threw it back. He didn't look me in the eye as he refilled his glass. I couldn't claim to know him, but he'd poured juice for me a bunch of times down the years. I wasn't hard to recognise. I was a sight bigger than most of the emaciated desperadoes here.

'What brought you back here?' he asked. Slightest inflection of nervousness. A glance at the rough, coppery cast of my hands.

'Looking for a man, name of Giralt. Runs a shop across the street.'

'I know Giralt. But he's been gone a while,' the barman

said. Awkward smile. 'Not sure where he went.'

'He'll be along,' I said. 'At least, he better be.'

I reached up and unhooked the mask. Pulled off the goggles. Let the barman see the metallic sheen that coloured me. The black threads of corruption that ran beneath my skin. The amber in my eyes. But it was the look of my face that set him stammering.

'Ah shit,' he said. 'Take the bottle. Get out of here. I don't want trouble in my place. It don't have to be here, man. Choose somewhere else.'

His words were pretty convincing, but his hands were working beneath the counter and they might have got the jump on me if the barman hadn't glanced past me, checking something I wasn't supposed to see.

I felt the change in the air, motion behind me, moved fast and aside as a club swung past. The weapon slammed down against the counter, splintering with a sharp crack. There was a time when I believed in taking men alive, when I wanted to question and pluck the answers from them before I sent them to the hells. That era had passed. My knife was out and shanking, and I barrelled forwards as I pumped the blade in and out of the border-man's guts. He was gracked and done for before he hit the wall, even if he didn't know it, even if he clutched at the redness pouring out of him as though he might grasp a few more hours if only he could hold it in.

'Spirits damn it!' Sav hissed. He went for the pistol he'd been fumbling with below the bar, struggled to yank back the lock. I was already throwing as I spun. The knife hammered into his throat just above the breastbone. He twisted on spasming legs and collapsed behind his own bar.

The proverbial powder keg was about to ignite. I needed cover.

I ran towards the bar, threw myself behind it as a boot smacked door open and a man entered with his matchlock smoking, blinding himself with the coiling trail. I went for the pistols at my belt. He had no shot on me behind the counter, and stark in the doorway he made an easy target. My pistol barked, and the would-be assassin flew back through the doorway, a smoking hole in his chest. I ducked down, reached back, and snagged the whisky bottle. Still had a pistol left, and so long as you have a whisky and a gun, how bad can your luck be?

The front windows shattered as crossbows thumped heavy bolts through them, blasting the mirrors behind the bar into sparkling shards, and a trio of matchlocks barked their loads. Broken glass fell like rain, the phos-lit sign advertising FINEST GRILL sputtered and belched little arcs of lightning. I shut my eyes, shook my head to clear the glass from my hair. Whoever was gunning for me had brought a whole gang. I'd guessed he wouldn't come alone. A couple of cronies, sure, but he'd raised up a whole troop. Old habits, long buried, told me to take a slug of the whisky, but I grimaced and tossed the bottle away, liquid spilling. Never mind. I'd come armed enough to tackle any eventuality short of a battalion.

I spared a glance for Sav. I'd picked his joint because, as its name implied, One-Door Sav's had only one way in, and a gallery that ran all around the top of the room. Under the bar, I saw the switches that operated the lighting, labelled nice and clear with arrows. I flipped three of them, killed the phos tubes everywhere but above the single entrance. Anyone coming in that way wasn't going to enjoy it.

'Galharrow!' someone called from outside. A heavy southern accent, strong voice, neither hurried nor bothered that I'd already taken out two of his men. I didn't reply. I reloaded my spent pistol as quickly as I was able, then took Sav's and put them all in my bandolier. I tested my sword in its scabbard. It slid easily, freshly oiled. I gritted my teeth and waited.

46

'Galharrow. I know you're in there,' the voice came again. 'You're surrounded, neh?'

I yanked the knife out of the barman's unmoving throat and said nothing. Fished in my coat for a cigar. There are times when you realise that there's a good chance that you might not get another.

'You're making this harder than it has to be,' the southern voice called. 'Let's talk.'

You heard all accents up and down the Range. It was a place of strangers and immigrants, the clustering of those brave enough to fight or too unfortunate not to, but that tone was distinctive. From Pyre, the island on which the Lady of Waves made her home, far to the south and always summer.

'Didn't seem like you wanted to talk a minute ago,' I shouted back. I drew on the cigar, flared the nub red. Cheap shit. 'Got a pair of corpses in here as testament to that, and by the sounds the rest of your boys are making out there, there are going to be more soon.'

Time to move. The bar was dark as night, other than the single glow-light over the doorway. I hunkered low, made for the stairs. Stealth isn't easy at three hundred pounds and I had to trust to luck not to make too much noise in the darkness. By now those men had reloaded their weapons, had bolts and balls ready to cut me in half. Someone might take a potshot into the dark.

'Excitable amateurs! Overly enthusiastic,' the spokesman called. 'Jumped the gun, neh? Even gave the first lad a club, didn't I? Hard to hire good help in a place like this.'

'Seems to me if you wanted to talk, there were easier ways of going about it,' I yelled back, but it was just talk, and I was more intent on moving. Along the gallery, until I could see out of an upper-storey window, overlooking the space in the street.

'You're not an easy man to pin down,' the accented man

47

called. He stood at the back of the group, a leader who didn't want to stand in the vanguard. Long black hair, long dark coat. Slender. He had Tnota with him, caught by the scruff of the neck. 'But here's the thing. I got your Fracan out here with me, him and the shopkeep. You don't want to see their tongues coming through the door without the rest of them, you'll come out to talk.'

I caught sight of Giralt, roped up and half-abandoned by a wall. A northern man, looking the worse for his ill treatment. Tnota had been roughed up too, but he was OK. He'd not resisted, though they'd knocked him around anyway. Red scrapes and cuts marred his otherwise uncracked face, and his lower lip was swollen. Men get an idea about who they are, what they need to do. They know that there'll be violence down the line, and they need to prove to themselves that they have it in them, so they get tough on an easy target. I'd seen it a thousand times along the Range. Only this time the man with the long hair had let them test their aggression on one of the few people I actually gave two damns about.

'You're trapped in here,' Nenn said. She lounged against a sideboard, tossing a coin from hand to hand. I blinked and shook my head.

'You shouldn't be here,' I whispered.

'Never did like rules.'

Nenn's ghost missed the coin, shrugged, and gave me a pointed look. She was right, but there was a reason that I'd chosen Sav's. I'd figured that whoever was coming for me wouldn't come alone, and I'd figured that they'd be reluctant to charge the door now they'd realised what a bad idea it was.

The gang were gathered out in the street. Nervous-looking men and women. The matchlock gunners were Range station soldiers in dishevelled uniforms, the crossbowmen looked like Misery-miners or the kind of mercs that walked them out there. Drunks, desperadoes. I doubted that the dark-haired man had needed to pay them well, but they were chancers and they'd already lost men. That would make them twitchy, and nervous enemies are better than calm ones. Nenn didn't offer any further advice – she was gone. She shouldn't have been there to begin with. Ghosts couldn't leave the Misery. They were as much part of it as the rocks and the sand. Maybe the Misery was too deep in me to leave behind entirely, or maybe it was just the pumping blood making things fuzzy. Probably that.

Eleven, not counting the leader. Three matchlocks, four crossbows, the rest were just packing swords, picks, or hammers. No armour. Men he'd had to round up in a hurry. That made him a loner. Twelve in all.

Bad odds.

I once said that I don't fight outnumbered and I don't fight for lost causes. To attack a dozen men would have been suicide. But the Misery had changed me. Twisted me. I had advantages that they couldn't begin to understand.

My first advantage was that whilst I was at Tnota's house, I'd picked up a couple of surprises.

My second was that a bunch of men standing by a single narrow door made for an excellent target.

I puffed twice on the cheap cigar and then applied it to a fuse. The dark-haired man was shouting something about coming out unarmed, but I wasn't listening. I was humming a tune I'd heard Lady Dovaura play on the viola, a lifetime ago now, but the aria had always stayed with me. The sizzling fuses made a static accompaniment. When they were burned down low enough, I kicked the window out. That was Tnota's cue to drop to the ground, and then I tossed the explosives out into the street and covered my ears.

A grenadoe makes one hell of a noise. It makes a lot of shrapnel, a lot of smoke, and a lot of damage too. Two of them make double the mess.

I swung down from the balcony. Everything outside was white powder smoke and the acrid stink of blasting powder. I rushed through the doorway in a low hunch, my drudge-sword whispering from its scabbard. She was no delicate implement, not a weapon intended for dainty pokes and taps, but forged to sever a man's spine.

I moved through the smoke like a wraith.

Most of the posse were sprawled on the ground, some of them in pieces, some of them moaning, some just stunned or clutching at their ears and shrieking. No need to play safe, no need to fence. Broad, savage strokes, slashes and cuts that dismembered and disabled. Nothing that would tangle my sword blade in ribs and innards, but cuts that left people howling as I struck off limbs or silenced their screams altogether. Blinded, deafened, they didn't know who was friend or foe in the roiling, blinding cloud of dense powder smoke, but I had no such fears. I struck through anything that moved or made a sound. A Misery-digger, either brave or panicked, flailed an axe at me but I voided the attack, moved in, and sliced him in half. One of the soldiers swung her broken matchlock like a club but I parried that and my next blow took her head. Not many of them fought. None of them fought well.

Along the town's single, dusty road, shutters banged tight. Lights flickered out. Folk who'd previously been gawking now wanted to get the hell out the way. Dead and dying bodies staggered against walls, to their knees, to the ground. They made sounds, and then, in the aftermath of that flurry, made none.

As the smoke cleared, I stood red and alone.

Looking out over pieces of the men he'd hired, Dark-Hair's face was unreadable behind black-tinted eyeglasses.

'Wasn't expecting something quite so monstrous,' he said, jamming the barrel of a flintlock pistol up against the back of Tnota's skull. His voice was calm, and thick with that southern inflection. The loss of the hired men was only an inconvenience. 'The Misery made you like that?'

Tnota grimaced, but Dark-Hair wasn't going to pull that trigger. If he did, he'd point his weapon at me first. The hostage was a bluff, and I'd called it: if he scattered Tnota's brains then he left himself defenceless.

Blood dripped from my sword blade, across my hand, my wrist, my arm. Hot. Wet. Mine.

Someone had shot me. A crossbow bolt stuck out, high on my chest, and I hadn't even noticed.

I reached up and took hold of the quarrel buried in my left pectoral without breaking eye contact. In the flickering neon phos light, the leaking blood had a bluish hue, crimson as it soaked into the un-white of my shirt. I snapped shaft and fletchings away. Didn't really feel it, part from the battle-rush and part because the Misery's working had made me different. Tougher. Harder. Better able to endure the dust-storms, immunised to the many poisons her creatures dripped with. And damn hard to kill. The bolt-head ground against a rib as I moved.

'The Misery changes all of us,' I said. 'You want to do some talking before I finish this?'

I casually threw the broken, blood-slick stump of the quarrel at him, and his hand flashed out to catch it. He said nothing. Not intimidated. He was thinking about going for it, trying to shoot me dead. The bolt in my chest and the lack of trouble it was giving me making him wonder if I could be killed at all. He could take me down with a head shot – I assumed that I wouldn't survive my brain getting mangled, though I'd not tested that particular assumption. But if he missed even by a hairsbreadth then I'd get to him, and that wasn't going to end well. He was a slim man, well dressed in a knee-length coat, ruffed shirt, eyes hidden behind darkened lenses even though it was night. His hair was oiled, black and curly, past his shoulders. Sun-bronzed skin.

'You came all the way from the coast to find me?' I said. 'From Pyre? You got the look. Got the voice. Makes me wonder what brings you all this way. I don't care much about killing you. Lot of offal lying in the gutter right now. But you didn't come all this way because you don't like the way I look.'

Dark-Hair was weighing up his options. He was a professional. The little I could see of his pistol barrel showed me that it was expensive, a good flintlock. The cut of his coat said money, and the sword at his side said lots of it. But everything was practical. He kept Tnota between us as I circled. Smart move.

'You're a hard man to track down,' he said.

'The discovery must be very disappointing,' I said. I gestured around at the bits that had once been people. Some of them were still making noises, but those would fade in time.

'You look like something that comes from the Misery, neh?' he said. 'How did you get that way?'

He was playing for time. The wound in my chest was bleeding and maybe when the battle-rush faded the pain would hit me. He knew his business, or at least, he was making fair assumptions. Only I'd been hit like this before. A drudge marksman had put a bolt through my liver a while back. After I'd dug it out, it had healed without a scar.

'Time changes all of us,' I said. 'It's not just the outside that's changed. I'm different on the inside. I can read minds.'

'You can, neh?' He turned Tnota in front of me. My friend kept his eyes turned down. Good lad. Didn't want to distract me from what I had to do. He'd taken his pain and fear and held it back. Keeping himself calm, though he had to be shitting himself. It would only take one squeeze of the trigger to end his game. Dark-Hair took a step back, pulling Tnota with him. 'Alright then, mind-reader. Tell me. What am I thinking right now?'

I shifted my feet in the dirt as I got ready to move.

'First, you're hoping this bolt in my chest is going to start slowing me down,' I said. 'It's not. Second, you're wondering whether, when I start ducking and weaving, you can still put your one shot through my head. You're good with a pistol. The best shot you know. How am I doing so far?'

'You're not wrong,' he said. Smiled like a fox. 'I could hit a hawk in full dive.'

I nodded like it was news to me.

'I don't doubt it. But you've seen me cut through the men you hired. You aren't surprised by that, you didn't expect them to bring me down. Maybe to clip me. Maybe to get lucky. But what's nagging at you is how easy it was for me to disassemble them. Look at you. You're sweating just holding that pistol up, but me? You thought you were coming for a Misery-wrecked man of fifty. But I don't even give a shit about a crossbow bolt in my chest. So now, you're thinking, *How's that possible? Why didn't they warn me?*'

Dark-Hair drew Tnota in closer against himself. His lips were set in a hard, bloodless line.

'That sound like what's going on inside your head just now?' I asked.

'We're going to walk away now,' he said. 'You won't follow.'

'No,' I said. 'You're going to stay there and tell me who wants me dead. Then I'm going to cripple you. But if you tell me what I need to know, maybe I'll leave one joint unbroken.'

Dark-Hair reached up and removed his darkened glasses. Beneath them his eyes were the colour of broiling ocean tides. The wave-tossed eyes moved over me. He noted the pebbled, copper-bronze of my skin, the luminance of my eyes, the threads of black running through my skin like veins of gleaming obsidian. He was not afraid of me, but he was weighing up his options. Judging the odds. A cautious man.

I very much wanted to walk up to him, take that one pistol shot head-on, and twist his head from his neck. But Tnota was under the gun, and I wasn't about to risk him more than I already had.

'Perhaps you should ask your own master about that plan. If he ever wakes up again.'

I gritted my teeth. Tightened my fist around the hilt of my sword and flicked blood from the blade.

'D'you know how I know you don't really read minds?' he asked.

'Enlighten me.'

He smiled.

'Because if you could, you'd know I have men on the roof.'

I tried to resist the impulse, but my eyes betrayed me and flitted to the beer-house roof. It was all the opening Dark-Hair needed. He thrust the pistol over Tnota's shoulder and he would have blown my head off if Tnota hadn't thrown himself backwards. Instead the shot sliced across my cheek, split my ear. I looked up properly and saw two men on the roof. Their matchlocks were smoking and I ducked and threw myself in a clumsy roll as the dirt erupted around me with a roar.

Tnota was clear. I drew the barman's pistol in a smooth motion, levelled it at Dark-Hair, and fired. He might have been able to hit a falcon in full dive, but I evidently wasn't half the shot that he was and I only managed to shoot out a window. Dark-Hair leapt for a horse, swung himself over, and spurred away into the darkness. My heart was pounding, blood thumping in my ears, and I could feel the battle-rush coursing through me as I went back into the bar and climbed the stairs, but the men who'd shot at me had already thought the better of whatever pay they'd taken and escaped into the night. Tnota was fine. He'd freed Giralt and they clung to each other, clung so tight that the world could never pull them apart again. I couldn't share in what they had. Worse, I'd done this to them. For most of six years I'd dwelt alone in the Misery, and even so, my friends had suffered for it. I couldn't allow them to bleed for me. I couldn't let them suffer. More importantly, they were getting in the way.

The only way I could pull this off was alone.

6

I felt like a child listening to my parents arguing. I'd shut myself away in a back room that was mostly being used to store Tnota's collection of dog-faced statuettes. They peered at me accusingly from their high shelves as I cleaned my gear and got everything in fighting order. My sword had a new edge, my pistols were loaded and ready to spit. I worked my dirk against a whetstone, the grating squeaks doing little to drown out the row taking place farther along the hall.

'If it wasn't for him, none of this would have happened,' Giralt said angrily. 'And now you want us to follow him to the spirits know where?'

'Ain't so easy as just wanting,' Tnota said. He might have been free of the Sapler's influence but he wasn't entirely recovered. Or maybe I'd just never heard him fight with a partner before.

'I know this isn't much of a place. Much of a life. But damn it, it's *mine*. Do you know how hard I've had to work just to scrape this out? My father abandoned my mother—'

'—and she had to work cleaning grease out of industrial drums,' Tnota finished for him. 'I know. You told me. A lot.'

'What's that supposed to mean?' Giralt snapped back.

I tried to focus on my knife. Keeping a good edge was important. I took pride in making sure that if anything went wrong when the crunch came, it was because I'd made a bad decision in the heat of the moment, not a bad or idle decision days or weeks before. You tended to win more often in life when you stacked the odds in your favour.

The bandage around my chest was coarse, itchy, and annoying me. Giralt had dug the crossbow bolt out. He'd had to use a knife, and he'd had to cut into me to get at it. I don't know what work Giralt had done before he set up trading to the Misery-diggers, but he knew how to work with flesh. It had not been an easy removal. The bolt-head had blunted itself against my ribs, bent back on itself. It had hurt, but not nearly as much as it should have, and Giralt's knife had lost its edge. The smell that rose from the wound was worse than the pain; worse than turpentine and sewers. Giralt had done his best and I knew that I shouldn't, but I couldn't resist looking. I pulled back the bandage and looked at it. Nearly gone already. A few more hours and the scar would have disappeared entirely. The damage done by the pistol shot that had grazed me was already mended. The Misery's gift was doing its work.

I doubled over, a coughing fit taking me as vile black-green sludge fought its way inch by inch up my throat. It was hot in my mouth, and even more vile-smelling than the wound had been. I wiped it on the head of a statue that was giving me a particularly judging look. Perhaps vandalising Tnota's religious curios was a shitty thing to do to a friend, but he was going to have to leave them all behind anyway.

'For the last time, you don't owe him anything!' Giralt yelled, for what I suspected wasn't the first and wouldn't be the last time.

'We all owe him, Gir,' Tnota said. He tried to be quiet enough that I couldn't hear him, but without success. 'More than you'll ever know. But that ain't the point. The point is, if we stay here then we're dead men.'

'You go,' Giralt snapped. 'Do whatever you have to.'

'You know I won't leave without you,' Tnota said. 'And staying isn't an option.'

I wiped the dagger down with a little oil and stuck it in my belt sheath. I looked over some other bits of kit, but I was only killing time. I didn't think that my intervention in a lovers' quarrel was going to be appreciated, but time was up. They'd argued through the night and dawn was rising. I'd no doubt that someone who'd lost a loved one – or perhaps more likely, someone who'd been owed money by one of the casualties – would have gone running to the commander at one of the two nearby Range stations. And while the citadel turned a blind eye to the Misery-diggers and Fortunetown, probably because some of those few valuable nuggets that came back from the wastes made their way into princely pockets, the commanders wouldn't take kindly to a massacre taking place so near their fortresses, or to there being soldiers amongst the dead. Not good soldiers, but soldiers nonetheless, and pointing out that it was only a small massacre was a poor defence. Degrees of scale don't seem to matter much where a massacre is concerned.

I put on my swords, slung on my guns, gathered up the odds and ends that go with them. The gunk that I'd smeared on the Big Dog's image had burned through the wood and he was now missing the upper part of his face. Not nice to think that I carried that stuff inside me, even if I was healing faster than any man had a right to.

I stepped into the room where Giralt was glowering at Tnota, and Tnota looked embarrassed. The air was humid with anger and regret, and they fell silent as I stepped into the midst of their conflict. It was a small thing, compared to the bloodshed of the night before, but important in its own way.

'I get that you don't want to leave,' I said to Giralt. Tnota saw the sense. I looked around at the dresser, the armchairs, the little depressions made by two old men sitting together in front of the fire together each night. 'This is your world, and you don't want to give it up. But you don't have a choice.'

'Don't tell me what I do and don't have. This is all your fault!' Giralt snapped at me. His face was flush beneath his beard. He was proud, wasn't military, wasn't Blackwing, and I wasn't anything to him. I could see his point of view.

I walked to the dresser and picked up a dusty decanter of something amber hued. There were cups. I poured for the two of them and passed them out. They drank amidst the glowers and the bad feeling.

'I want you to go,' Giralt said. His face was flushed. 'Go, and don't come back. I told him you're no good for him. You're no good for him, and you're no good for me either. You don't even look human anymore.' He thrust a finger at me, but he spoke to Tnota. 'Is this what you want? Is it?'

Tnota looked helplessly to me, caught between a stampede and the river it was driving him towards.

'You're not safe here,' I said.

'Soldiers will be on their way,' Giralt said. 'I know the commander, down at Four-Three. He'll see we're taken care of. He'll have men hunt the bastard that did this to me, and if he comes back here, he won't get away so easily next time.' He indicated mottled black-and-purple bruising across his cheek bones. Tnota's eyes were pleading. He couldn't afford to lose this argument. 'How could you understand?' Giralt said bitterly. 'You're barely even human anymore.'

'You're right,' I said. I leaned back against the dresser. 'But I was, once, and even then I wasn't like everyone else. Most people just want to live safe and quiet, do their work, drink a beer in the evening. Build something to stick with. They take their satisfaction from living their lives undisturbed. I don't fit into that world.'

'You're right there,' Giralt snapped. He looked me over, jaw set. His barbs didn't hurt. I'd accepted what I'd done to myself a long time ago. 'Your world isn't ours.'

'True. But that man who hurt you? The man who imprisoned you, who hired men to kill me, who put a Sapler in your clock to break the man you love? He fits into my world. And he'll be back.'

I paused, and let that settle in as the grandfather clock ticked us slowly into the dawn.

'Maybe it will be him again. Or maybe next time his employer will send someone else. It won't matter. They'll be the same kind of man. And when they come, they'll ask around the town. They'll find out that you were involved with me. And they'll know I've moved on. I won't be back. But there's a chance – not a good one, but a chance – that you might know where I went. So they'll come here, and they'll ask.'

'I don't need to know where you're going,' Giralt said. '*We* don't. So we'll have nothing to tell them.' He crossed over to Tnota, put an arm around his shoulders, making it clear that it wasn't Tnota he was angry with. They were a unit, a team. I was the problem. Tnota looked uncomfortable.

'The problem is, for all that he did to you, you don't understand these kinds of men,' I said. 'They'll ask, and you won't have an answer. And then they'll ask again, and maybe they'll use their fists, and you still won't know. And they'll ask again, and they'll ask harder still. They'll ask with knives. They'll ask with pliers. Maybe they'll make you watch while they ask Tnota.'

'You can't know that,' Giralt said, but my words had bitten through whatever thick skin he thought he wore.

'I do know,' I said. 'It's what I would do.'

'He's right, Gir,' Tnota said. 'I know these kinds of men. They won't care about soldiers who might come for them, and they ain't going to care what you know or don't. Please.'

There was dread in his tone. Fear in his eyes. Poor guy had it bad. Tnota wasn't even thinking about his swollen lip, or the cuts and grazes speckling across his face. All his thoughts were for Giralt. Keeping him safe. Giralt's fight withered as he accepted the truth of what he was being told. There was despair, frustration, overwhelming sadness at having to abandon the life he'd worked so hard to carve out for himself. Here, on the edge of the Misery, at the doorway to the hells, he'd made something of himself. What had he been before? A misfit, maybe. A criminal? A servant? Whatever he'd been, he'd since tied himself to this place and now it was roped with lead and sinking fast.

I left him with Tnota to talk through what had to be done and went out into the cold, quiet dawn. The streets were empty. No need to rise with the sun, here. These were hard people, these diggers and their exploiters. A lot of them were probably exactly the type I'd just described to Giralt. I'd guess most of them had glanced out of the window once the shooting was over, given a grunt, and gone back to bed.

I needed horses. There was a communal stable under a flimsy roof off the main street, but I didn't feel like bartering for mounts, and I didn't have anything much to barter with anyway. When I stepped in there was a young lad sleeping behind a curtain, who pushed back the corner to check who was there. When he saw me his fingers gripped the edge of the fabric, scrunched it good.

'You run this place?' I asked. He nodded, head bobbing rapidly.

'My uncle's,' he said. Scared. Couldn't keep his eyes from me. Couldn't really blame him.

'You know who I am?'

He nodded.

'You killed them folks outside Sav's place.'

'That I did,' I said. 'You don't have anything to fear from me. I don't kill kids. You know that some of them that got themselves killed were soldiers? They must have ridden down from one of the stations and I doubt they need those horses anymore. Want to point them out to me?'

He was brave to come out and show me, but then he probably had to be brave to sleep alone in a stable in a place like Fortunetown.

I ended up with five horses, and most of them were pretty good beasts. Black or brown, a few white socks. I led them back to the house where Tnota and Giralt hadn't wasted any more time. They'd thrown the things they needed into big military packs.

'You can't come back here. Not ever. If there's anything you've left buried, anything you think you might want one day, you need to get it now,' I said.

Giralt sighed and looked back at the wooden building. It wasn't anything special, but I guess it was to him. It wasn't fair. Of course it wasn't. It never was.

'Where to?' Tnota asked.

'Where do we always end up?' I said. 'All roads lead to Valengrad in the end.'

7

The ride south along the Range wasn't comfortable. The horses didn't like me, and the company was even less comfortable than the saddle. The easy camaraderie that Tnota and I should have enjoyed was being squatted on, his relationship with Giralt a blockade between us. Tnota wanted to appease us both, I wanted to focus on the objective at hand, and Giralt wanted his life back and for me to fuck off out of it. I couldn't blame him for that. I'd spent so many years with Tnota, and we'd lived through nightmares together. Giralt knew he could never be a part of that. Ezabeth's ghost had come between Valiya and me the same way.

I took us west, away from the Misery and the supply road that ran along the Range. We followed a disused canal instead. Where laden supply barges should have fed tonnes of cargo up and down between the Range stations there were only ducks and weeds now. Old, abandoned barges littered the banks, some of them home to otters and red geese, others to vagrants. It would have been prime scouring ground back in my Blackwing career, and I would have bet that most of the grubby faces that peered out from the barges had abandoned a contract of service given to them by the citadel.

'What do you want to do when we reach the city?' Tnota asked. He didn't ride well these days. His back was giving him gyp, and a single hand on the reins didn't help. Giralt wasn't much of a rider, but he managed. I was just out of practice, but while you remember these things quick, your thighs and balls remember them slower. Nobody ever reminds you to wrap your tackle up good and proper before getting on a horse, but after a day of feeling like you're being punched in the balls over and over, you remember it quick enough.

'I need to make contact with Captain Klaunus and find out if he's heard from Crowfoot lately,' I said. 'Whatever's coming, I need to be ready to meet it.'

'Never liked Klaunus much,' Tnota said. 'Not after what Valiya found out about him.'

I nodded. It was a poor reflection on Blackwing that of its seven captains, most of us had a stain in our past.

'Tell me everything you know about the man with the dark hair.'

'He gave his name as North,' Tnota said. 'He came to Fortunetown about two months back. Stuck around for a week without doing much, talked to me a couple of times about making a Misery trip. Digging, nothing unusual. I was done with navigating by then. Retired.' He glanced guiltily across at Giralt.

'And then?'

'Then one night he came by the house,' Giralt said. 'And he shoved a pistol in my face, and he had some thugs rough Tnota up. And he said if I didn't come quietly, they'd feed me his kidneys.' He glared at me, as though that were my fault. 'I didn't know why. They took me to a house with a cellar and kept me there. He didn't tell me anything.'

'Then he set up the visits from the boy,' Tnota said. He was morose, hurting over what they'd done to Giralt. Anybody would have been. 'I couldn't do anything. I didn't know if they were watching me, watching the house. Would have got a message to Amaira if I'd been able, but she's been gone a long while.'

64

'Better that she was kept out of it,' I said. That made Tnota chuckle. I arched an eyebrow.

'She isn't some fresh-hatched chick needs shielding from the rain,' he said. 'Not anymore. She toughened up fast, after she made her deal. You should know – you trained her.'

Amaira. Small, bony, foul-mouthed Amaira, who'd wanted so much to be Blackwing, who'd cut a deal with Crowfoot to save my life. I'd done what I could for her. She learned fast, like all kids do. I taught her the sword, the dagger, wrestling, shooting, everything that a teenage girl needs to survive the Range. I tried to carry on teaching her the letters that Valiya had given her, but I taught her about people too. The way their minds worked, their weaknesses, their dreams, the way they make decisions. How to find them. How to silence them without bloodshed, how to make them talk with it. She learned fast, and no matter how much I taught her, in two years it wasn't nearly enough. I wasn't there the day the raven delivered its first message to her, two days before the Crowfall. I was out in the Misery, and those days I only dipped in for a couple of weeks at a time, a month at best. That was before the Always House, before the rains came.

The rain was due now. An old lock keeper's cottage sat dark and soulless along the bank and a glance towards the Misery showed that the poisoned clouds were crawling in. The cottage was bleak and depressing but at least it had a roof. We even managed to lay a fire in the hearth before the first drops fell.

'Always something cosy about being indoors when it's pissing down,' Tnota said, trying to rekindle some of his usual cheer.

'What was it Nenn used to say? "Rain is the spirits' way of telling you it's time to hit the bar."'

We shared a shallow smile, enjoying the warmth of the

memory before the inevitable pang of loss turned it cold.

The rain beat down.

It was all Crowfoot's fault. The rain, the whispers on the wind, the Saplers: he had done this. Not intentionally. It wasn't that he would have been incapable of it, it was just a waste. A waste of power. A ricochet, an accidental side effect of the Crowfall. Whatever the Nameless had done, it was vast, and terrible, and beyond anything that they had tried before.

I didn't understand all of it. Not yet. But the Nameless, their bodies frozen solid in the faraway north, had done what they could to hold back The Sleeper. The Deep Kings would have sunk the world already if they'd raised it from the ocean's depths, and the Nameless had done whatever they'd had to. But in the aftermath, the world was burning. Poison fell from the sky and every year, the crops were smaller. Feebler. Blander, and some plants soaked up the black rain and were no longer edible. Apples were off-limits. Pumpkins were so bitter they were uneatable. Corn grew black on the stalk.

The Nameless had sacrificed much to put The Sleeper back in his icy bed, but it hadn't been enough. Nall had said Crowfoot was brewing some kind of plan, but with Nall himself crippled and dying, the future had never seemed less certain.

As I watched the rain hissing across the darkened land, I thought about what Crowfoot had done to our world. The Misery burned into existence against reality, such abomination that the sky itself tore open and the land boiled and burned. The citizens of Clear and Adrogorsk had melted into monsters beneath the fury of the Heart of the Void. Crowfoot had driven the Deep Kings back, but the cost had been vast. And, given what Nall had told me, it still hadn't been enough.

Real company felt strange. I'd grown accustomed to

hearing nobody but the ghosts, and they're just reflections of what you're thinking anyway. When it got late, I settled myself into a corner. Tnota and Giralt had been separated a long time as those things go. They needed time together without me and I couldn't blame Giralt for his hostility. I gave them some alone time by trying to rest in the cottage's small second room. The reunion was going pretty well from what I heard.

The night was thick when the door opened and Tnota crept in, shutting it quietly behind him. He put a finger to his lips.

'Best keep it down. He's sleeping,' he said. He tried to keep his brutalised face impassive but couldn't fight his grin.

'Nothing keeps you down for long, huh?' I said, but while my smile wasn't quite as wide, it was there. Been a long time since I'd felt one of those on my face. It didn't sit right, like a child's hat being forced onto a head that had outgrown any realistic possibility of fitting into it.

Tnota took a seat opposite me at the table. He was toying with the idea of making a pun, I could see it on his face, but then he decided that he didn't have long, and that business was pressing. He didn't want Giralt to wake up and find him gone. I could read Tnota easier than a book.

'You look worse, Ryhalt,' he said. 'There's black in your veins. And your eyes don't just give off that light. There's some kind of fire in them. Liquid fire, moving. Like I can see into the past, see the world burning in them.'

I could already see where this was going.

'I made a decision, a long while back. We all made a plan.' I bared my right arm for him, showed him the old scars, the ones that I'd cut so deep that no amount of Misery healing could erase them. *BECOME THE ANVIL.* 'We always knew there'd be a price.'

Tnota sat silently. He knew I was right. He knew I was too far gone for it to matter anyway. What could I do now?

Go back to an ordinary life in society? I had changed too much. The damage was already done.

'Damn, but it's good to see you,' I said, and meant it. Out there in my isolation I'd not realised just how much I'd missed him. 'I wish we could just chew over old times, but we have work to do. Someone on our side of the Range wants me dead. The Deep Kings want me dead. Acradius has set himself up as the Deep Emperor, and he's coming for us. It's all connected.'

'We still have the Engine,' Tnota said. He knew I'd not say those words lightly. 'Don't we?'

'With Nall so depleted … I don't think so. Crowfoot had a plan for a weapon that he could use against them, but he's hurting. He sent Nall for me, to get his plan into motion.'

'You won't have heard about Captain Josaf and Captain Linette,' Tnota said. 'I should have mentioned them sooner.'

Josaf had been one of the worst people I'd ever met. A violent, coldhearted killer who would have been hanged for a bunch of crimes far worse than many I'd put men down for, if Crowfoot hadn't given him a raven tattoo. Linette had run a pirate galley before she'd taken on the debt, but she'd had a certain roguish charm. Amaira had liked her. There were seven of us in total, and while the Range had often made hard demands of those that protected it in the shadows, those two had brought their petty cruelties to play more than I liked to think about.

'What did you hear?'

'Don't know details, only that they're dead. And if this North had got you, that would have made three. Maybe someone knows what Crowfoot's going to try, and is taking out his captains to stop him.'

'Maybe,' I said. I felt nothing for their deaths. They'd earned them, and I didn't need their help. What was coming would be easier without them getting in my way.

'Whatever happens, I think that these will be the last days of the Range.'

'I think we know it, Captain,' Tnota said, gesturing to the rain outside. 'The world is burning. Bleeding out. We're just waiting for the death-stroke to finish it off.'

'I'm not your captain anymore, Tnota,' I said.

'You'll always be my captain, Ryhalt,' Tnota said gently. 'Even when you've grown a tail and start breathing fire, you can rely on me. I've been at this too long to give up on you now.'

They were kind words and he meant them. But I knew I couldn't keep asking him to involve himself in these affairs. He wasn't getting any younger, and I didn't need him to navigate for me anymore. He wasn't a fighter and he deserved better than to spend his last years following me around. Doing so had already cost him an arm and a leg. Well, an arm, anyway.

Or maybe, selfishly, I just didn't want him to see what I'd become.

'You asked about Amaira,' Tnota said.

'Yes.'

'And you asked about Maldon.'

'Best to keep track of him.'

'And Dantry.' He ticked them off on his fingers. I didn't say anything. I knew where he was going and I didn't want to go there with him. Tnota could be a cock sometimes. 'Anyone else you want to ask about?'

Of those few of us that had survived the battle around the Grandspire, the only other that I cared for had been Valiya. I hadn't seen her since that day, six years ago, when she left that borrowed house for the last time. She'd chosen to go her own way, and I respected that. It hurt more than digging out the crossbow bolt had, but there was nothing to say. I had no way to contact her, she had no reason to want to contact me, and truth be told I'd only ever caused her pain.

'She'll be doing her thing, trying to control the world, wherever she is,' I said. 'I made the choices that I had to.'

'Not doubting that you did,' Tnota said. 'Nobody could. But you aren't concerned that you might run into her once we reach Valengrad?'

'Is she in Valengrad?' I asked without thinking, then wished that I hadn't.

'Don't know. Haven't seen her since we burned Nenn's body. I had messages from her, sometimes. Don't know how she found out where I was hiding, but she did. She always was too clever by far.'

'What did she say?'

'Not a lot. She told me Amaira said she had to go away for a long time, couple of years back. That was the last any of us saw of the kid. And she passed me info on what the princes were up to a couple of times. But that's about it.'

I tried to still the grinding discomfort that rose when I thought of Amaira, out there, following Crowfoot's orders. She was good: fast, cunning, tough. But she still seemed so young to me, would always seem the little girl that I'd sat with under a table in the dark. Perhaps all parents felt that way about their children. She was not my blood, but if I did one thing right in my life it would be to stand as her father, if, or when, she needed me. I pushed it down, tried to remind myself she had a life of her own to live.

'Good. Whatever she's doing, she'll be doing it well. She's good for the Range. They need people like her to run things.'

Tnota got up, put a hand on my shoulder. It felt unnatural. I'd carried him home a bunch of times when he'd been too ratted to stand, but the familiarity was unfamiliar now. Too close. Even through the swelling and the scuffs and bumps on his face, concern showed through.

'It's alright to be sore about things, sometimes. You don't always got to be made of granite,' he said. He patted me on the shoulder once, then went back towards the other room. Giralt would wake and miss him soon enough.

I saw light through the window. Moving steadily, not rapid and bouncing around but not going slow either. Horsemen with phos lanterns mounted on their horses' tack trotting along the edge of the canal.

The fire had died low and we had no other lights. No reason for whoever it was to come calling. I untied my matchlock's bag and fixed the viewing scope in place. I didn't load, but I sighted on the riders. They wore ordinary civilian clothing, men and women wrapped up against the winter cold. Armed, but on the Range a lack of weapons would have been stranger, and if they were soldiers they were not proclaiming themselves as such. There was no reason to be suspicious of them, none at all, other than that they were riding hard along the canal path at this time of night.

I loaded the matchlock slowly, taking my time, not want-ing to disturb Tnota and Giralt unless I had no choice. I sparked up the match-cord, fixed it into position, got the flash pan primed, the powder and ball loaded. Stoked. Went back to watching. There were five riders in all, three women and two men. Tough-looking people. The world still smelled of rain, and they wouldn't sniff out my match unless they came in close. I watched them carefully through the scope. They glanced towards the old cottage but didn't come any closer, then pressed their horses on, further up the Range. Once they were past I snuffed the match, laid the gun down, and settled back against the wall. If they'd been looking for me they'd have checked out the house, or at least that was my thought. No reason to assume that they were. Just some riders trying to make time through the night.

Sure they were.

8

If you've ever seen a neglectful parent sucking on a wrap of white-leaf while their toddler plays with cutlery on the floor, you'll have some idea how I felt about Valengrad.

The smoke from the factory chimneys was blackening the sky long before she came into view, drifts of pollution suspended like the world's most depressing bunting. The Grandspire thrust high, majestic and domed now with a great shell of black iron that could be opened or closed to manage the acquisition of phos. The Engine sat silent, but there seemed to be something mournful in the curve of the jester's-hat projectors. Their droop seemed too knowing, as if their demise had been communicated to them, and they knew.

The city smelled the same. People. Animals. Industry. Canal water. I almost missed the Misery's tang. People hurried by, busy about their work.

Sometimes I felt that everything I'd done in the last thirty years had been for Valengrad, its stones, its people, but if I was honest, I'd done it all for two little lives that I'd wanted to save more than anything, and a deal that had drawn me one step back from the brink. I wasn't some altruist working to save others. I'd only met a handful of people in my life who were. Ezabeth had burned for it, and Dantry was the most wanted criminal in all the states, so it hadn't got either of them far.

It wasn't until I could make out the citadel that I saw that my initial assessment was wrong. Things were not the same at all. A chunk of the citadel was missing. The western face ended in ragged, broken stonework. We stopped dead in the street and stared at the damage, open-mouthed and horrified. The broken neon letters across the citadel's front read COURA, the letters sputtering weakly.

Unthinkable. My jaw hung open.

'Big Dog says, "What in the fuck could have done that to the citadel?"' Tnota said.

'First time I ever heard your Big Dog ask a question,' I said. 'First time me and him are on the same page.' Tnota just nodded.

Goggles on, dust-mask up, hood over my head, we rode into the city. The guards at the gate saw that we had nothing to trade so they waved us through without much concern. Gate duty is tedious at the best of times, and they had little interest in three old men. I pulled us up to talk to them.

'What happened to the citadel?' I asked.

'No one's saying,' the guard said. He avoided looking at it.

'When did it happen?'

'Two days back. There was a crash in the night, and the west wing was gone.'

He was an older man. He'd lived through Shavada's attack on the wall, and the sky-fires raining down upon the city. And of course, the Misery. The damage to the citadel had still shaken him. We rode on.

'What's the plan?' Tnota asked. He looked grim.

'Set up base. Rooms at an inn. Not a shit-hole. Not The Bell either. Nowhere that we're likely to be recognised.'

'Nobody's going to recognise you these days,' Giralt said. His sour mood had made him start jabbing at me. I hadn't the heart to get pissed at him over it. Didn't blame him, if I was honest.

'But they'd recognise Tnota,' I said. 'I'll hole up. I need you to go shopping for me.'

Pikes was a soldier district and we found a decent-looking inn there which not only seemed free from vermin and bedbugs but boasted an impressive array of ales and spirits. We went for a soldier place because I figured they'd be less likely to care that I was covering my face up, and the small arsenal of weaponry I carried up to our room didn't raise any eyebrows. Part of me had worried that Tnota's name would have been shouted by some old acquaintance on entering, and from there it wouldn't take a genius to equate the six-six man behind him with his old drinking buddy. I stooped low, trying to hide my height. Be less intimidating. The girl who got Tnota to sign his name in her book didn't seem to care who we were, provided that we could pay.

We took adjoining rooms. They were comfortable, the beds springy and the fireplaces freshly laid. I sent Tnota and Giralt shopping while I took a nap. I'd slept little on the journey down from the north and though I hadn't seen any more riders in the night, I'd been on edge the whole time. I lay down and closed my eyes.

I dreamed of Ezabeth. I seldom dreamed of her anymore, and the dreams didn't hurt me the way they once had. Time will numb you to anything. There is nothing that a determined human being cannot come to cope with in time. It doesn't mean that the pain of the loss is gone, or that its embers cease to burn, deep in your core. It just changes. It changes from the incapacitating agony of a gut punch to the solid, deep aching of a broken bone. It becomes familiar. You carry it with you, accepted, never to leave. When Tnota's soft knock brought me back from slumber, the memory came with me, but I left the sting to some other, dreaming, me.

They had done well.

Cosmetics. Coloured powders, but mostly the thick white

74

foundation that victims of rabbit-rash wore to mask their scarring. Spectacles with heavy, face-wrapping lenses shaped like teardrops. I'd seen phos-engineers wearing them, the yellow glass helping to protect their eyes from stray sparks and beams of condensed moonlight. And clothes, too. Some of them were tight – it had been a struggle to find castoffs that would fit me, but Valengrad had a roaring trade in dead men's kit. They'd managed to pick up undergarments, breeches, socks, shirts, waistcoats, and, best of all, new boots. My boots had borne the brunt of the Misery. I felt like a child being presented with birthday gifts, and barely held myself back long enough to sponge myself off with a basin of water before I put them on. The water turned black. Then it steamed. More than just dust and dirt in there.

My sponge-bath was only interrupted by one coughing fit. My lungs and throat felt like they were packed with shards of broken glass. When I wiped my mouth, strings of green-black tar clung to my lips. They carried the taint of the Misery, the familiar stench filling the room. My body was rejecting the Misery's poison as soon as it was able. Either that, or I was dying. In both cases, I had more important things to worry about.

I looked out across the rooftops, past the spires and columns of industrial smoke, to the broken citadel. No signs of fire, no fused stone or warped air that might indicate the aftermath of a magical catastrophe. The Engine and its projectors were far enough from the damage that, through either luck or design, it had not been afflicted. Did it matter, though? Nall was on his way out. I didn't think that we could activate the Engine without him and, from what he'd told me, the Engine wasn't going to protect us from Acradius anyway.

'We need money,' Tnota said, applying the last of the powders. My face felt thick and heavy with the cosmetics.

'You running low?'

'Didn't have a lot to start with, and these rooms aren't cheap. Only had enough for a couple more days in coin.'

'I'll sort something.'

I'd brought no money of my own. I didn't carry it around with me in the Misery for obvious reasons. Unfairly, I'd not even paused to consider it when I sent them out to buy me a disguise. I should have been thinking of them, but I wasn't used to taking others into consideration. Tnota and Giralt hadn't been flush with coin – Giralt had run a business. Everything he had was tied up in the stock I'd made him abandon. Little wonder he didn't look at me as Tnota painted my face an off-white shade that resembled wall plaster.

'We'll get by, Captain. We always do,' Tnota said. 'You're all done. You got less colour than milk, now, but the Big Dog says you're mighty pretty. You don't look normal with all this paint on, but you don't look like something out of the Misery either.'

The room had a mirror. I put the glasses on and checked myself out. I'd have laughed, but I might have cracked the paint.

'Good enough,' I said. I wore a head scarf and turned up the collar of the too-small greatcoat that Tnota had found for me. It was fine in length but the former owner had been far narrower in the chest and my upper arms were squeezed. I enjoyed the discouraging shade of matt brown more than I did the decorative gold banding across the breast.

'What now?' Giralt asked despondently. He stared out into the gathering dusk.

'I need to find out who that guy North was, and who sent him,' I said. 'But first I need to make contact with the resident Blackwing captain.'

I completed my outfit with a wide-brimmed hat that was, surprisingly, slightly too large, and hustled out into the city's gloom. It wasn't safe for me here, not entirely. I didn't think there was much chance of running into anyone who'd recognise me through the paint, but Range Marshal Davandein hated me. I wasn't strictly an outlaw, but we were not friends and she had somehow pinned the blame on me for the devastating attack the Iron Sun had made on her army. I couldn't forgive her for attacking the city, for butchering those poor idiots. Besides, there was my connection to Dantry to think about, and the Office of Urban Security might well decide that – Blackwing or not – I was the old ally most likely to know his whereabouts. I hadn't been in contact with the citadel for years. They probably thought me dead.

I ducked and slunk along shadowed roads and smog-stained streets, to a decent part of town that housed a bad sort of people. Lawyers are the worst. I have a deep hatred of bankers, but they at least pursue their greed with an honest kind of blatancy. The legal district was kept well swept and the wild pigs and dogs were hunted down by appointed wardens. It didn't smell so bad which meant, being Valengrad, it still smelled bad.

Nenn was waiting for me at a street corner.

'You shouldn't be here,' I told her.

'It's my city too,' she said.

'That's not what I mean. You shouldn't be outside the Misery. You don't *exist* outside the Misery.'

'I don't make the rules,' she snapped. She started to walk alongside me, whistling my least favourite folk tune. She seemed all too real to me. Real enough that I could have reached out to poke her in the cheek, which I wouldn't, because if she was real she'd probably bite my hand. 'Maybe you're just imagining me. Maybe all that sludge running through your veins has started getting into your head. You must have known it would.'

'You telling me you're a hallucination?'

'Asking your own madness if you're really experiencing it? You're definitely crazy.'

A broken clock tower loomed ahead of me, a black spire rising from a thick bank of green-tinged smog that rolled down from the glass factory. The tip of the tower had been destroyed by a sky-fire, and nobody had bothered to replace it. The clock itself still worked, sort of. It showed numbers, but they were generally wrong. I approached through the clinging, tacky green mist which clutched at me with long, tendril fingers before they inevitably snapped and returned to the fold. Klaunus' decision to set up residence in this decaying monolith didn't sit well with me. Blackwing relied on informants and the sinister chemical runoff around here hardly ushered them in. But if he wanted to keep prying eyes away then I supposed it had a certain sorcerous charm. And Klaunus was a sorcerer, after all.

The smog ended as abruptly as it had begun, and I stepped clear into a ring of cold air surrounding the clock tower. Nenn hadn't followed me through. Old beds of flowers had shrivelled and died, brown husks on black stalks, their vitality sapped away by toxins and a lack of light. A young man sitting by the doorway startled, disturbing the blanket that he wore around his shoulders. He had the look of a street thug from the Spills, badly inked tattoos across his fingers and beneath his eyes, his hair shaved into a single strip. He wore a sword, badly, but Klaunus had tried to dress him up to look like a doorman. The uniform might have seen better days, but he had a sparkly new timepiece on his wrist and a jewel in one ear. He still wasn't convincing, and I took his measure in a glance. His childhood had been spent stealing, his teenage years running parcels of leaf and pollen, later on, fighting and intimidating. Bad nutrition as a kid meant he'd never be tall or carry much muscle, but he'd learned street-side savagery. Dangerous, unpredictable, a permanently cornered cat. He was proof of the problem with making captains out of the cream; they never really understood the world beneath their feet, and all the real work is done down in the mud.

'I'm here to see Klaunus. He in?' I said. The tough looked me over, didn't like what he saw. I must have weighed twice what he did, but he was clearly used to making a show and a leap over everything. Showing his front, parading his dick. Probably why Klaunus had hired him.

'Yeah? Maybe he doesn't wanna see you. The fuck you think you are?' he asked. Definite Spills accent.

'Blackwing Captain Galharrow,' I said.

He started at my name. Then he nodded a bunch of times.

'Oh, got you, yes sir I got you,' he said eagerly. His head bobbed up and down and the front and bravado melted away to be replaced by something else. Probably not respect. Fear, maybe, if he'd heard the stories about me. Nobody spoke of my brief stint as acting Range Marshal anymore, it was the tales of night-time raids and broken men that lay in my shadow now. Survive the world long enough and inevitably you will be replaced, cast down and despised.

The doorman stepped inside the clock tower, leaving his blanket in a puddle outside. I heard the whine of a charging communicator, then the tapping of the message. After a few moments he returned.

'You can go up,' he said. He flattened himself as he went past. 'Is it true you stopped the sky-fires?' he asked.

'I was there. But it was Major Nenn and her boys stopped the sky-fires,' I said.

'I don't know who that is,' he said.

I sighed as I started up the spiralling cast-iron staircase. Six years ago, everyone in the city knew Nenn's name. She and her Ducks had been popular. Maybe this kid was younger than he looked. Only her name was already flickering, wavering out like a candle flame in the inevitable wind of change. Her hard-won glory would be lost to the night with me.

Klaunus' residence was a cold floor near the top of the clock tower. Maybe some kind of flair for the dramatic had led him to reside here, being one of those sorcerers who took being a sorcerer way too seriously. It wasn't my style, but then it was questionable whether I had any. The staircase creaked and rattled under my weight, loose bolts chuckling at my discomfort.

Klaunus was waiting for me, standing, as was befitting for a meeting of equals. He was six-foot, fair, clean shaven, good bones, but there was a fleshless cast to his face that took away the possibility of his being handsome. He wore a fashionable purple cravat over his white silk shirt, pearl buttons catching the dim light making him entirely over-dressed without company. He'd been a lord-farmer before Crowfoot had offered him a deal and his prestige – if it could be called that – had gone all the way to his head. All Crowfoot's servants had all stared into the void and seen worse things than me, but his eyes went wide all the same.

'I'd given you up for dead,' Klaunus said. 'I thought that I was the last of us.' For an awkward moment I thought that he might try to embrace me.

'The last what?'

'Blackwing,' he said. 'Come in. Drink?'

'I'll pass.'

Klaunus showed me into the room. One wall bore gears, tubes, and tightly strung ropes disappearing into the ceiling as they fed into the phos-driven clock above. The other walls were decorated with pinboards, pamphlets, posters, and handwritten sheets, all connected with pieces of string. Klaunus' underfunded intelligence network. I thought back to how Valiya had run my own network of spies and informants and found his methods disorganised, even if his lodgings indicated an excessive need for cleanliness and order.

Klaunus could be said to be fairly well adjusted compared

to most of us. He was sad, dour even, one of those that regretted his debt the most. We all resented it in one way or another, except maybe Silpur, but Klaunus carried his regret like a cloud around his shoulders.

'You've not heard from the others recently?'

'You don't know, then?' he said. He assumed that I didn't. 'Captain Josaf was found face down in a ditch down near Station Four, a knife in his back. Captain Linette got herself garrotted in a tavern bedroom. Vasilov and Amaira haven't been back for years.'

'Silpur?'

Klaunus was a sorcerer, and a strong one, but a tremor of discomfort passed over his face.

'If I ever meet that creature again it will be too soon. If I hear he's dead too then I'll light a pipe and crack open a good vintage.'

'Have you heard from Crowfoot?' I asked as I took a seat on a couch that had seen better days. Spirits knew how they'd got it up those stairs. Klaunus sat opposite me on a hard, wooden chair.

'Not in eight years. Long before the Crowfall. Have you?' There was yearning in his voice. Desperation, maybe.

'No.'

'I have feared for some time that something terrible happened to him,' Klaunus said bleakly. I knew what he wanted to ask. It was too terrible to say it. Or too hopeful. Maybe both.

'If he were dead,' I said, 'we'd know it. I don't know what would happen to you and I if Crowfoot perished, but I doubt we'd enjoy it. Cold's captains all exploded when the Deep Kings took him out.'

Klaunus nodded. I thought that he looked relieved.

'Then where is he?'

'Weakened,' I said. 'Broken, maybe. Wounded. The Crowfall cost all of the Nameless.'

'Shallowgrave has been active,' Klaunus said. 'You've seen the damage to the citadel? That was his doing. An accident, as far as we can tell, though you can't be too sure of anything where the Nameless are concerned.'

'Shallowgrave took out half the citadel?' I was horrified.

'Trying to send us a gift of some sort, or at least that's how it's being told. Some kind of weapon. But Marshal Davandein has the place sealed up tight and won't even talk to me about it. She's not been friendly to Blackwing for a long time. I think we both know why.'

Klaunus was an ally, but he was also his own man. We both served the crow, but that didn't mean that I could trust him. Valiya had gathered intelligence on him and found his name whispered around a history of pregnant young women, all suffocated. Servants, labourers on his farm. But he was never on hand when they died. Crowfoot chose competent or powerful people to serve him. High morals were considered a disadvantage. Maybe Klaunus knew more about the citadel than he was letting on, or maybe he knew nothing at all. He had his own agenda, his own goals, just as I did. He watched me closely, took in my yellowed eyes, the cosmetic smeared thick over my skin. He could probably smell the Misery on me.

'Where have you been, Galharrow? What have you been doing? They all ask; the other captains, the citadel, even the Office of Urban Security. They all want to know where you went. Nobody's seen you in half a decade and now here you are. Stranger than a blue robin, sounding like you've swallowed a toad. Davandein wants you arrested for working with the mad count.'

That was news to me, but I wasn't surprised. I ran it through my mind, but I didn't think that North was working for the citadel. He'd not been trying to take me in. He'd been looking to put me down.

'Where did Crowfoot send you?' Klaunus asked.

His assumption was wrong, and he was breaching etiquette by asking, if he thought I'd been on a mission.

'Working towards the greater good. I'm sure you've been doing the same here.' I made a dismissive gesture towards his papers and strings. Klaunus' eyes lost some of their welcome, and I regretted doing it. Klaunus wasn't my enemy, and I'd been the one to seek him out.

'Someone tried to take me out, up at Four-Four. A southerner calling himself North – he was quick, skilled, and professional. Linette and Josaf are already down. We're being hunted.'

'A concerted effort against Blackwing?' Klaunus said. His brows drew in. 'Two dead captains is suspicious. A third attempt leads towards conspiracy. North is not a common name. I'll look into it.' He squinted at his wall of papers and strings.

'What have you heard about Linette and Josaf? Any leads?'

'The citadel passed me information about them.' He frowned. 'Josaf took a dagger in the spine, Linette took a wire across the throat,' he said. 'Not shot, not stabbed. That's a hit, not some kind of random accident. I believe you're right. Nobody carries a garrotte without meaning to use it, and she wasn't the kind to let her guard down. There was one lead to Linette's killing. A description of a stranger.'

'That's more than I heard,' I said. 'Anything useful?'

'Not really. One of the staff claims she saw a Darling skulking around the night Linette died.'

'Darlings don't garrotte people. They tear them apart,' I said. 'And there hasn't been a Darling on the Range in a long while. More likely just a child.'

'I thought the same, but you asked what I've heard. I put a Smother-ward on the door before you came in, just in case you were lying about your identity to my doorman. It pays to be careful.'

In a way I was glad that I'd not known about the ward. Klaunus was a Mute, and I know fewer details about a Mute's sorcery than I do about the detail of my own arse, but suffice to say that they could kill with silent precision. Crowfoot liked to indenture sorcerers when he could: Captain Vasilov was a Spinner, and I had no fucking clue what Silpur was, but nobody ought to be able to move as fast as he did.

'I figure I have a new lead for you,' I said. I shared the story about the dark-haired man up at Fortunetown but Klaunus just wrote the information down and pinned it to his wall without any semblance of enthusiasm. He was drained, depleted, and I was disappointed. Had his tower room not indicated a fastidious need to clean, I might have wondered if his lugubrious mood could have pointed to a Sapler taking hold of him, but hiding places for the little shits were few. I'd hoped he might have had some idea who'd set the attack dogs on me. Only he didn't seem to know much of anything, alone and isolated in his tower. He'd had no news about Vasilov, Silpur, or Amaira in a long time. The resident captain in Valengrad was supposed to be the focal point, to keep track of where Crowfoot's hands were and what they were gripping onto. I'd done it myself for the best part of twenty years. Now that there were only five of us left – assuming that the others were all still alive – it seemed more important than ever to coordinate. I had to find someone who had real intelligence to share.

'Another name came up. Winter. You know who that is?'

'Doesn't mean anything to me,' Klaunus said. I nodded. I only knew of Winter's existence because Nall had named him in the Misery. It had been a long shot, but I had so little to go on, every avenue had to be explored.

Klaunus scanned a bunch of his lists and came away shaking his head. 'The citadel is looking for you, but I doubt that Davandein would resort to murderous hirelings. She likes to wave her banners about too much. It's more important that she has her name paraded around in victory than it is to win the victory in the first place. Word on the wind says she intends to marry Grand Prince Vercanti and has designs on succeeding him as the first Marshal-Prince. She just might do it as well, if she can win one big victory. She's talked about retaking Adrogorsk.'

Even after all this time, the name made me flinch.

'Idiocy,' I said.

'I thought you might feel that way,' Klaunus said. Even that didn't bring a smile to his dour face. 'Sometimes I think I'm running an empty mission here. I have little by way of resources. That boy on the door is all I can afford from the pittance the citadel throws me – just enough to keep a foot in the door in case Crowfoot ever returns. But he won't, will he? He might not be dead, but he's done. I can feel it.'

'It never pays to count Crowfoot out,' I said. Something had tugged at my mind. 'That boy on the door. How much do you pay him?'

'Two hundred a week,' Klaunus said bitterly. 'Barely enough to keep him housed. He's got less intuition than a chicken and half the agency. Sitting at the door is about all he's good for.'

'And you didn't give him a timepiece? Or a jewel for his ear?'

Klaunus seemed perplexed by the questions. It had never even occurred to him to see the details. The cream barely take notice of those swirling in the drains below.

'Of course not. He's not my lover, if that's what you're asking. I don't turn my sheets that way.'

'I wasn't. But if you aren't paying him well, and you aren't, then you aren't his only income source. Damn it, Klaunus. He's in someone else's pay right under your nose.'

Klaunus frowned, then took out a piece of paper and began to write down exactly what I'd just told him. He pinned it to the wall, frowning at it as though it were a piece in a greater puzzle. He might be going through the motions, but he was spent. He was no use to me. But that was good, for both of us; he wasn't going to oppose me when it came time to throw back the curtain, either.

I was out of the door in a matter of seconds, clattering down the unstable staircase. Klaunus called something after me but I was already gone. So was the lad, when I got down to the ground. He'd no doubt run straight to Davandein the moment I was through the door. I pushed through the ring of fog that circled the clock tower and found them waiting for me.

9

Two men had just dismounted and tethered their hard-ridden horses to an iron rail. They were the kind of men you notice when you don't want to be noticed yourself, tough, wiry men with short hair and hard eyes. Serious men with serious swords, enough scars between them to show they'd been in a few scrapes, few enough to say they'd come out of them well. They saw me emerge like a revenant through the fog.

'It's been a long time, Captain,' the taller of the two said. He was in his thirties, hair receding into a widow's peak. His shorter friend moved out a few paces.

'It has. Good to see you, Casso,' I said. He'd been on my payroll once, my top Blackwing enforcer. I hadn't seen him since I got lost in the Misery. He'd gone over to the Bright Order and I'd assumed he'd died in Davandein's attack. 'Looks like you found yourself a new line of work.'

'I work for the Office of Urban Security now,' he said. He'd always been a terse, serious man, seldom wearing a smile. That hadn't changed. 'The marshal wants to see you.'

'If I wanted to see the marshal, I know where to find her,' I said. 'Do the smart thing, Casso. Don't make me tell you to fuck off.'

He was calm despite my antagonism. Urban Security are a step above the street watch. Where the latter dealt with petty gangs and swept the beggars off the temple steps, the

Office of Urban Security played the long game, pushing and pulling on behalf of princes and the military. Casso had never had a problem dealing with dangerous men getting tetchy.

'Won't take long,' he said. 'The marshal can be pretty generous. She's mellowed out, isn't that right, Tate?'

'Sure has,' the other man agreed. He was a lumpy sort, hard to tell where flab came to an end and the muscle started. He watched me, arms folded.

'If you ever thought that money motivated me then I guess you weren't paying attention,' I said. 'I'll thank you not to patronise me. We both know that wouldn't end well for anyone.'

'Looks like you've been out in the Misery a long time,' Casso said. 'Looks like it's taking its toll. Isn't doing your skin no good, and your eyes ain't exactly right.'

'And here I thought I was entering a beauty contest.'

Casso didn't smile. He'd grown leaner, harder still in the days since Saravor's attempt to seize power.

'I'm asking nice for old times' sake,' he said calmly. He tucked his thumbs through his belt, shoulders back, confident. 'But don't take my friendliness for fear of you. You were something real special back in the day, but you've been through the hells since and we're all on the same side here. We just need you to answer a few questions.'

I could already imagine the shape of their questions. *Where is Dantry Tanza? When was the last time you saw Dantry Tanza? Why did he destroy the phos mill at Heirengrad? At Snosk? How did he overload the battery coils? What's your involvement with his criminal activities?*

You don't remember? Perhaps a week in the white cells will set your mind straight.

A coughing fit seized me and I hacked some black-and-green nightmare slime into my hand.

'Maybe it ain't fair to beat on a sick man,' Casso said.

'But you don't want to come nice, then we don't have much choice, do we?'

'The moment you touch that hilt, you lose your fucking hand,' I snarled. 'I might look old to you, but when I say I don't go where I don't want to, you better believe I'm telling the truth.'

Tendrils of the ensorcelled fog curled around my feet. Tate mustered forwards alongside Casso. He was ready to go, his hand moving slowly towards his hilt.

'No,' Casso said.

'We have to take him in,' Tate said.

'No. He's right. It wouldn't go easy.' Maybe he had learned something from me after all. 'Is it true, Captain? Are you in league with Count Tanza? He's the most wanted man in the states.'

'I haven't seen Dantry Tanza in six years,' I said. 'I've no idea where he is.'

'More of us will come,' Casso said. 'Now that she knows you're here, Davandein won't stop until she has you. Bringing in Count Tanza is the win she needs to secure her place alongside Vercanti. Maybe then this talk of Adrogorsk will stop. Tanza's dangerous and he's a traitor. Time was, you'd have been hunting him down alongside us.'

'All things change,' I said. 'The world's not what it was.'

'We were just the first to get the message,' Casso said. 'We'll still have you before tomorrow night. You're only delaying, which only makes it harder for you.'

'I'll take my chances.'

Casso nodded slowly. I turned and walked away down a darkened alley. I was glad that he'd learned some sense from me. I didn't exactly like Casso, but I respected him. He was only doing his job and he was right that upon a time I'd have been doing it too. They didn't understand the importance Dantry's work entailed. Innocents had been caught in the crossfire, but if Casso had learned something from me, then I'd learned something from Crowfoot in turn. You can't save everyone.

I headed back to Pikes and checked over my makeup disguise. Meeting Klaunus hadn't given me much of anything, but I was worried over what he'd said about Shallowgrave damaging the citadel. If King Acradius had a new way to strike at the citadel, the last thing we needed was our own wizards doing his work for him. Shallowgrave had always been strange, even by the standards of the Nameless.

I was hungry, so I went down to the bar and added a platter of flatbread and cheese to the tab. The cheese was hard, the bread harder, but after six months of the same three lumps of mutton and pottage, anything different was delicious. When I was done I asked for scrambled egg and bacon. My throat was sore after another round of choking up slime, and simple food seemed like a spirit-sent luxury.

Tnota joined me and ordered a round of beers. I sipped mine slowly. I almost felt afraid of it, but it was small beer, and it would take half a dozen pints to even give me a glow.

'How did it go?'

'Badly,' I said. 'Klaunus has lost his way. I think that losing Crowfoot has cracked him. It's a shame. He was always a prick, but he was powerful once. Remember that den of Brides that tried setting up in Snosk? He shut them down all by himself. It's a shame he won't be much help.'

'So what's the plan?' Tnota said. 'Still want to try to find this Winter character?'

'I do. Whoever he is, Winter's Nall's captain and he managed to track me down to the Misery. He's our best chance of finding out who's trying to take me out.'

'Davandein seems to be eager enough.'

'She might want to talk to me, and she might be swollen with her own importance but her heart's in the right place. Most of it, anyway. She needs the Range to be kept safe, and hurting Crowfoot's people wouldn't help that.'

Davandein wanted to bring me in. The dark-haired man, North, wanted to bring me down, and the Deep Kings shared his sentiment. Maybe I should have been flattered. I was awfully popular.

'What are you going to do?' Tnota asked.

'If this Winter is as good as I think he is then he'll find me, now that the Office of Urban Security knows I'm here. I'm going to check for word from Dantry at the drop-off. I haven't been there in a while.'

'We'll check it in the morning,' Tnota said. He downed the last few mouthfuls of his beer and signalled for more. Drink takes a toll over the years, and Tnota had been paying it as age crept over him. Back when we'd first met, we'd have chugged the suds until dawn and rolled down the street laughing, but those days were long gone.

'No,' I said. 'I'll check it.' I took a deep breath. I'd made my mind up on the way back from the clock tower. 'I want you and Giralt to find a caravan and head west.'

'What? Why?'

I sighed. It was going to be hard to say it. Hard for him, because he wouldn't want to hear it, and hard for me because it meant the end of something that had mattered a lot to me down the years. But I'd thought on it all the way down from Fortunetown, and it was the only thing my conscience allowed.

'You're too old for this, Tnota. You aren't as spry as you were, and what happened back there in Fortunetown – that was my fault. Around me you're in danger, and you've not the constitution for it.'

'Don't get all weepy over me, Ryhalt,' Tnota said. He tried to keep how offended he was from his face, but he'd never been good at wearing masks. 'I always knew the risks that came from riding with you. I never backed out of them before, and I don't plan to now.'

'You rode with me because we got paid, and we had a job to do,' I said. 'But this job is mine and mine alone.'

'Is that what you think?' he said bitterly. 'Just another common mercenary?'

'No,' I said. 'At first maybe. But then you rode with us because you cared for me, and for Nenn, and we all rode for each other. But you've someone else to ride for now, and I can't take you away from him. I had my chance with Ezabeth and I lost it. I had another with Valiya, and I fucked that up too. You and Giralt have something worth keeping, and I can't let that be traded for the small help you can give me. I don't need you to navigate for me, and you don't have any other skills that I can use.'

'You need me,' Tnota said.

'I don't. You're not even another pair of hands,' I said brutally. The words hung like knives between us. It was true: I didn't need Tnota anymore. He couldn't fight, he couldn't charm information out of anyone, and his navigating skills were no longer even equal to my own. And at the same time it was a lie: I needed him very much. But not more than he needed to see something decent at the end of his life.

'So you send us away, and then what?'

I reached into my coat pocket and took out a small parcel that I'd been saving. It wasn't going to be useful for much longer. Tugging open the strings, I showed him a glimpse of what lay inside. Tnota inhaled sharply as he saw the light reflect from the clear, sharp stones.

'Misery diamonds,' I said, drawing the strings tight again. I pushed it across the table towards him. 'A small fortune, if you sell them in the next few days. Enough to get you and Giralt across the states. Enough to take you all the way to Valaigne, if you want to go that far. Giralt can start a new business. You can make a peaceful life for the two of you. But you've only got a few more days to spend them, at best, before they turn to sand, as they always do. Sell them for real money and get out of here. I'll work more easily without the threat that someone might get hold of you and use you against me.'

He was imagining it. A life far from here, leagues away from the cracked and wailing sky. A business for Giralt to run, to give him back something of the life he'd crafted for himself. Retirement from the never-ending war between the Nameless and the Deep Kings. A chance to get off the bottle and make whatever he could of the years that remained to him. He lowered his eyes.

'You don't have to be alone,' he said. But he was wrong.

I pushed the parcel across the table towards him. Indecision warred on Tnota's face, and then he put a hand over mine.

'I'll think about it,' he said. 'How will I know if you manage it? The plan you've given up all these years for?'

'You'll know,' I said, turning my hand and pressing his fingers down around the diamonds. 'Either we'll all end up drudge, or I'll succeed. Those are the only two options left.'

10

Dawn came. Not a good dawn, not an especially important one, just the rising of the sun against Clada's blue shimmer. Down in the street I could hear labourers heading out to look for work as the night people crept on back to their slums.

'These are everywhere,' Tnota said, pushing a piece of paper into my hand. Giralt gave me a more congenial nod than usual. Tnota had clearly shared what I'd told him. I felt glad that his anger towards me had cooled, but it would only take Tnota to refuse to rekindle the flame.

The likeness of my face was pretty well drawn, though I think they'd made me more handsome and younger than I deserved. The ink was smeared – they'd yanked this off the press fast to get them up around the districts. The poster read, *Galharrow, the goblin man! Dangerous! Reward offered for information. Do not approach!*

It had been hastily put together, the type hadn't been properly aligned well on the blocks, but the message was clear enough. It seemed a lot of trouble to go to on the chance I might have some information about Dantry's whereabouts. At the bottom of the paper a single line read *By order of the Office of Urban Security.*

'I have a stronger chin,' I said, handing the paper back to Tnota. Tnota mimicked the sour grimace my portrait was giving and I couldn't help but smile.

94

'You're in trouble,' he said. 'If the city's plastered with these, some gang is going to pick you up even if Urban Security don't.'

I agreed with him, and gave Tnota and Giralt directions to a store down on Slack Row and wrote a list of things I needed on the back of the poster. Matchlock balls, a small sack of powder or, better, premade charges if they had them. Two new knives, a soldier's shovel, two good leather bags. A few other odds and ends, some because they were comforts and some because I needed them.

When they had gone I stood before the mirror and wondered how old that picture must have been. The artwork might have been years old. They'd got my eyes right, only they'd shaded them dark rather than lit from within. My skin had a hard, oily sheen to it now, like I'd been varnished, threads of black and green running through the veins. The change that had come upon me was something nobody had experienced before, six years spent absorbing the broken energy of the damned lands. I'd never exactly melted hearts, but it would take a twisted witch to find anything appealing about me now.

My beard was midway down my chest, my hair was long and brittle. Grey had overtaken any pretence at colour, and the pebbled, cracked skin lay across my wrinkles and raven's feet. I didn't like what I saw. Nobody wants to age, but I looked a lot older than I felt. I set about removing as much hair and beard as I could. Partway through I wondered whether I was trying to make myself resemble that portrait again, but halfway through the cutting is too late to stop.

Once I was painted up like a two-mark actor again it was time to run my second errand. I donned my goggles, tipped the hood up over my goblin face. The day was overcast, and rain was threatening. Nobody would question a hurrying traveller without good cause. As I reached for the door handle another coughing fit struck me, left me doubled over. The hand I pressed over my mouth came away streaked with what looked like black syrup, my throat howled as if flayed by vomiting out acid-soaked gravel. I sat back on the bed, spat out more of the shit, waited for it to pass. Whenever I left the Misery, my body started to reject it. In the past it had meant recovery. Now, I'd gone too deep. Pushed too far. I needed to get back into the Misery before being out of it killed me.

The morning traffic was dying into the miasma of the working day, but somebody had left the phos tubes on, wasting power as they cast the length of the street into dry white light. I kept my eyes away from them. The chance of being noticed was less likely than a freak hurricane blowing in to sweep us all away, but you can't be too careful.

'Surely there's time for a drink?' I heard Nenn whisper, but she wasn't even there. Spirit of Mercy, I really was imagining things. I reminded myself that I'd been isolated for a long, long time. Now that I was around people again, maybe it would shake some of the ghosts out of my head. That was probably it. I definitely wasn't losing my mind.

Scaffolds stood across the damage done to the distant citadel, engineers at work trying to repair the phos tubes that shone their message of COURAGE across the city, trying to reset order against a background of chaos. It was right that they did so. Hope is never broken whilst there is a chance to rebuild.

I made it over to a narrow-fronted shop in Wicks which sold spinning wheels without anyone trying to arrest or stab me. I squinted through the cloudy windows, saw that the shop seemed quiet, and ducked under the low doorway.

A young woman glanced up as I entered. She had a babe in a crib beside her as she worked at a spindle, expertly turning a heap of dyed fleece into thread. She looked up at me as though I were some kind of apparition, which given my painted face and absurdly yellow eyes, I may well have seemed. Her eyes dropped down to the hilt poking out from my belt.

'You don't look the type to be looking for a wheel,' she said.

'In all honesty, I'm not much of a spinner,' I admitted. Rows of shelves along the narrow room held a number of wheels of different woods, different constructions. Clever things: wheels, pedals, needles.

'What are you looking for?'

'The woman who owns this shop. Glauda. She around?'

'She was my aunt,' the woman said. The wheel slowed. 'She died last winter. A fever. This is my shop now.'

Bugger.

'My condolences for your loss,' I said, inclining my head.

'You knew my aunt?'

'We had a business arrangement,' I said. The young woman frowned. Maybe she figured I was there to give her trouble. If she'd inherited the shop, she'd inherited any debts it carried with it. 'Glauda used to receive messages for me. I'm not in these parts much and she would keep my letters until I could collect them. You know anything about that?'

'Oh. I see. You're the captain.' She looked nervous, but then, I had an unnerving look about me.

'That's me.'

'There was a letter for you. It was some months ago, I'm afraid. With all the clutter of the takeover from my aunt's business I can't quite remember what I did with it. I can dig it out for you, though.'

My heart gave a little surge. I hadn't heard from Dantry for a long time. We'd agreed not to communicate unless there was something worth saying. If he'd finally sent me something, then he had to have made a breakthrough.

'I'd be obliged. The courier paid you when he delivered it, I take it?'

'He did. Would you mind watching the shop for a moment? I'll go and find it.'

She rose and lifted the child from the crib and disappeared through the back curtain. The shop didn't seem to care whether I was minding it, didn't seem to notice much about what I was doing at all. I spun a wheel or two, idly, enjoying the fine craftsmanship that let them rotate so cleanly. She must have buried it beneath a stack of paperwork or stuffed it in some secure, forgotten box, she was taking so long.

Glauda had been a decent woman, but she'd been old and her passing didn't surprise me. She'd been an inconspicuous, stable fixture in Valengrad through whom Dantry could send me messages without going through the usual channels. A prudent arrangement, given the trouble he'd been causing.

It occurred to me later than it should have that you don't need to take a baby with you to find a letter. I pushed through the curtain but there was nobody in the kitchen and the back door hung open. I ran up the stairs but the whole fucking house was empty.

I'd chosen Glauda because she knew how to mind her own business. Her niece evidently did not.

I went out the back way. Whoever she'd run to, they'd be coming by road. An alley filled with broken old pieces of wood and lazy snails led through into another that stank of damp. I kicked off a wall and hopped over a six-foot fence, which protested loudly and nearly gave way beneath my weight. I came away with a glove full of splinters and a protest from my back as it mourned my lost youth. There were enough alleys and back turns that I was more confident that I'd soon be lost than I was that anyone would be able to follow me.

Damn it. Dantry had sent something, and it was long gone.

Glancing back over your shoulder's a good habit whether

you're in the Misery, or on supposedly safe ground. When I looked back, I wished that I hadn't.

A wispy rope of phos wormed down the alley towards me like an eel, hissing and sparking with golden-blue power. It was time to run.

I bolted away from the snaking energy, straight into a dead end. I looked back to see the trail of light rounding the corner and swore. I'd never seen phos do this before but I doubted that touching it would be healthy. A weak latch gave in to a good kick and I passed through a backyard into another maze of alleys. A heap of broken old floorboards made a ramp up and over a fence and I cleared it to find myself on a street I didn't recognise. A few startled folk flinched as I splashed down in a calf-deep puddle.

Everything seemed calm here, for the few seconds before the fence that I'd jumped detonated outwards into the road with a bang and the worming power flowed out, a long rope that fizzed and glittered. Nothing that I could fight. I ran on. The phos wasn't fast but it was relentless, following where I went, questing and seeking. People shrieked and cleared out of its way as a dog barked and snapped at it from a safe distance.

At the corner of Ditch Avenue, a wave of stars flickered across my vision and my head swam. I felt the Misery, out beyond the walls, calling to me. Calling me back? Pain shot down through my legs, my arms, and I staggered against the wall of a tobacconist's, knocking potted plants from the window ledge. Ignore the pain, ignore the screaming, stiffening muscle. I tried to run on and got three paces before all the strength left me and I went down again.

Shimmering colour and blinking lights tilted the world. The Misery's sky-song crashed in my ears as nausea rocked me. The old spear wound, dealt to my leg by a drudge during the Siege of Valengrad, caught hold of the shooting pain and wrapped around it. Scarred magic called to scarred blood and bone.

I couldn't outrun the light, not now. I told myself to ignore the pain, that it was just in my mind. Pain only lives in the mind, and sometimes the fight pushes it all out of you and you don't realise you're cut and bleeding until it's over, but this wasn't one of those times. I looked back and the power was nearly upon me. Years ago I'd tackled Darling magic head-on and it hadn't killed me. The Misery steeped within me had rejected and deflected the killing spells. I didn't know whether it would work against this crackling serpent, but I didn't have much else to try. I summoned the Misery-taint within me, felt for the toxic pollution flowing through my veins, ingrained into my essence over years of consuming the worst that the Misery could offer. A thousand vile meals, burning Misery-flesh forced down my throat with all the nightmares and fevers that brought, and I felt for it now as I faced the burning sorcery.

Better to face it as it came at me. Down the street, beyond the phos-eel, stood two figures, so obviously out of place that they could only be playing a major part in my imminent demise.

The smaller of the pair was female, nearly as wide as she was tall, and mostly concealed beneath a long blue cloak. Her hair held as much silver as ash-blond. The hands that protruded from beneath her cloak were gloved, but the glow that emanated from them suggested she was the one sending the light after me. A Spinner is a deadly opponent, but it was the giant beside her that drew my attention.

I am a big man. Six and a half feet tall, and I'd worked hard to put mass on that height. The black-robed thing that stood alongside the Spinner would have left me in the shade. He was eight feet tall or damn close, and there's no man that grows that size naturally. The Spinner could have sat a twin atop her shoulders and looked him in the eye. He had a big, bald head and his face bore ritual scarring across his ice-white cheekbones and jaw, but he appeared entirely unarmed. Weaponry probably didn't matter too much to him. At that size, he *was* a weapon.

The Spinner folded her arms across her chest with a look of satisfaction. The giant's red eyes were disinterested. The light swam through the air towards me and I gritted my teeth.

'Walk with me, Ezabeth,' I hissed as it struck.

Sparks showered outwards, away from me, as if the light were a blade and I the grindstone. I felt a coarse vibration within my body, and the light ground to a halt. It began to coil, bunching up on itself as the Spinner focused harder on me and then with a crash of breaking glass, the phos tubes along the road detonated, razor shards showering down on screaming passersby. The light-worm disappeared in a clap of sheet lightning which washed over me like a warm wind. Down the street the Spinner staggered and fell to her knees, her face a show of consternation. There were questions in her eyes. I didn't feel much inclined to answer them, not unless steel was the answer she was looking for.

I drew my sword, and that prompted the giant to advance on me. His eyes had a reddish cast to them, but there was an uncaring lack of humanity in them that unsettled me more. Skin as smooth and white as marble, he didn't look any more human than I did, but no matter how big he'd grown, if he took a sword through the chest then all that impressive size wouldn't mean a thing. Sometimes big just means an easier target.

I took a chance and struck in at him, thrusting high for the face, but my leg buckled and dropped my step short, leaving my lunge well out of distance. The giant's hand snapped forwards and caught my blade, dragging it aside almost contemptuously. I tried to twist it, but his grip was solid and the blade didn't flinch. I released it and carried on forwards on my screaming leg, delivering a massive right fist to his solar plexus. The giant didn't flinch as he flung my sword away into the gutter with a clang, and struck out with an open hand. My head snapped around, but I rolled with it. Not my first fistfight. I launched upwards, my fist connecting with the giant's jaw, but that was a mistake. It was like punching stone. The impact sent a spear of pain down my arm even as I felt my finger bones crack. One last try, and I swung my left fist at a lower, easier target. This time he caught my fist. You can't catch a fist, especially not one with all my weight behind it. The giant didn't know that, so did it all the same, his huge hand wrapping around mine and buckling the blow. He twisted my arm, locked the joint out, and then his other hand cut down on my exposed forearm.

The hard pain of breaking bone roared within me. Before I could recover, his other fist came around to smash into my chest, launching me across the road. I landed badly, felt something nasty crunch in my hip. The giant moved in to stand above me, as unconcerned by my attempts to rise as he had been by my attacks. He placed a foot on my chest and forced me down into the puddle. No emotion. Nothing on his face save maybe an idle curiosity. I thanked my ribs for all the times they had kept my chest intact before and forgave them for their impending failure. But he didn't strike. Instead he stared down at me with eyes as red as blood. There was no expression in his oversized face, no battle joy, no exultation in the victory. He just kept me pinned there, and waited.

The Spinner joined us, a cluster of young men in red coats behind her.

'How did you do that?' she demanded.

'Easy,' I said, though the foot on my chest made speaking difficult. 'After he hit me, gravity did most of it.' I spat blood where my teeth had cut the inside of my cheek. It was streaked with black.

It took her a moment to get the joke.

'How did you nullify the containment spell?' she demanded.

It wasn't a science that I could explain, and I wouldn't have told her if I could. A face I recognised came to peer down at me. Casso.

'Well done, Spinner Kanalina. You flushed him, just as you said you would.'

'I said I would capture him,' the Spinner said angrily. 'I didn't.'

'All's well that ends well,' my old jackdaw said cheerfully. 'Get him up, boys. Time for him to go see the boss. You should have come easy, Captain. I hate to see it come to this, but I did warn you.'

'Fuck you, you jumped-up little shit,' I spat at him. Childish, maybe, but the anger helped to drive back the pain in my hand, my arm, my hip, my leg. All of me seemed fucking cracked and torn. Casso stared down at me, his cold face unreadable.

'You taught me to make sure that prisoners come quietly,' he said. 'Do you remember?'

He kicked me in the hip, and whatever had been cracked decided it was time to break altogether. I only half caught the shriek, the first half escaping before I controlled it and turned it into a full-body shuddering. Walking was now out of the question, one leg useless and the opposite hip having decided to spend some time apart. It didn't really matter to Casso, because his men were happy to drag me, and my pained moans didn't matter to them either.

11

They tossed my broken body into a cell beneath the citadel. Dungeons conjure images of darkness, walls slick with growths of slime and the weeping of broken prisoners. This one was clean, neat, dry, and somehow worse. Half of the cell was partitioned behind a series of iron bars. The walls were painted starkly white, and an overly intense phos tube highlighted the stains that wouldn't scrub clean in a pale, lifeless light.

After the door clapped shut, I lay panting and trying to retain consciousness. I couldn't quite work through what had just happened. Back at Fortunetown I'd taken a crossbow bolt to the chest and shrugged it off, but that pale monster had smashed me around like I was a rat in the jaws of a terrier. I thought that I'd made myself strong. Strong enough to do what had to be done. I was supposed to be an anvil. The broken bones were saying otherwise. The only consolation as I lay gasping and wheezing was that they would heal. The Misery-taint would do that for me, but it was going to hurt all the while. I would survive, though bones took longer to mend than the soft bits. But the first thing I had to do was make sure they set straight. I had to move fast, before they knitted themselves at some awkward angle.

I couldn't make a fist with either hand and my right forearm was broken, but the break wasn't jagged and the pieces weren't misaligned, so far as I could tell through the immense swelling. The fingers of my left hand weren't in such good shape. I set them against the floor, put my foot down on top of them, and waited for the wave of dizzying pain and nausea to pass. Then I drew up, keeping them trapped as I rose. I pitched forwards and vomited my breakfast over the dusty white floor as searing bright pain rushed through my hand and up my arm. I lay there panting, then looked them over. About as good as they were going to get.

It was hard to think. The pain commanded all of my attention, but I forced myself to focus.

I'd delivered a lot of men to the white cells. I'd recruited men out of them too. The cell was divided into two sections by a row of close-ranked iron bars. In a way I'd been fortunate – most of the white cells were only a couple of feet wide, and the six square feet of space I had were practically luxurious. Once you went into the cells you didn't get out of them unless someone let you out. There were no windows, no sewers, no vents and the floors above were occupied by soldiers. Only fools and madmen tried to break out of the white cells, and no one succeeded.

I pushed my back up against the wall, pressed a hand against the sharp pain where my hip had broken. The stabbing sensation was about all I could think on for a time. There was no way to ease it, no narcotic on hand to dull it. No shift of posture lessened it. It was the kind of hard, cold pain that makes breathing hard. My chest hurt where the huge man's foot – assuming he was a man – had crushed down on it but I didn't think he'd cracked any of my ribs. That was something.

They only left me alone with my pain for a short while. I was glad of the distraction when the door opened and the Spinner stepped through into the area sectioned off by the bars, but even so she left the door open, and a pair of guards lingered outside. The woman looked at me as though she ran a finishing school and I were some dirt-encrusted orphan thrust in front of her.

'You'll excuse me if I don't get up,' I said. Speaking elicited fresh pain.

'You may stay on the floor.' She gestured, and the lumpy Urban Security man, Tate, brought in a heavy wooden chair. He gave me a pleased sneer, then left. She sat.

Spinner Kanalina was a hard-faced, heavyset woman. Her features were elegant without being ostentatious, and only the hints of crow's feet around her eyes and the grey threads amongst the blond hinted at her age. She wore a modest dress that flared towards the knee, and beneath it the high laced boots that had been a staple of Valengrad's fashion for over a decade. She appraised me, taking my measure. She was smart. Sometimes you can tell that about a person without ever having a conversation. Done looking me over, Kanalina opened a satchel and took out a stack of papers and a pen.

'Your name?'

'You know my name.' I coughed. The motion sent another spur of pain through my hip.

'I'd like you to state it, for my record,' she said. She had a rural accent, all the sounds coming from the back of her throat.

'I'm the Goblin Man.'

Spinner Kanalina looked up at me with an unimpressed stare. Definitely something of the school matron about her.

'I am not here to make your life difficult, only to ask you questions,' she said evenly. 'If you seek to make that harder, I can make things harder for you in turn. Do not misunderstand the situation. You are in a deal of trouble. Talking to me may be your best chance of returning to' – and there she didn't quite know what to say – '. . . to whatever life you had.'

She was probably right about that. I'd had better days.

'I'm Ryhalt Galharrow,' I said. 'Blackwing captain. Hero of the Range. Formerly acting Range Marshal during the Siege. Formerly a brigadier serving beneath Range Marshal Venzer. Formerly son of a count. Killer of drudge, and victor against Torolo Mancono. You need me to go on?'

She watched me for a few moments, then simply pursed her lips and went to writing. She might even have been writing all that down. Made me regret having given so much of myself away.

'How do you know Count Dantry Tanza?'

'Haven't seen him for years.' It was true. Not since the night we'd set our plan into motion. Not since we shook on it.

'That isn't what I asked.'

She was shrewd. Direct. In other circumstances, I think that I would have liked her.

'I know him because I met him a long time ago. Before the battle for Valengrad, where I acted as Range Marshal. Hero of the Range. Killer of drudge. Remember that?'

'Hm.' Her pen swished side to side as she wrote. I doubt she believed me. That particular aspect of my past had been buried by those that came after. I'd been forgotten even faster than Nenn. 'How did you meet him?'

There seemed to be no harm in telling her things that could easily be common knowledge. That I'd gone into the Misery and fished him out, that I'd tried to help his sister. That after Ezabeth had been killed we'd lodged together at The Bell for a time. I didn't tell her of rescuing him from Saravor's slaughterhouse beneath the city, but Casso knew all about that, and therefore so did she. Spinner Kanalina didn't need me to give her those details. She was asking easy questions because doing so made giving answers familiar. Established a rapport. Standard interrogation technique.

'When did you last see him?'

'To be honest, I haven't been keeping track of time that

well lately,' I told her. That was true. 'But a long while. Five years.'

'Hm.'

'I don't know where he is, if that's what you're planning to ask.'

'Why do you think Dantry Tanza became an enemy of the state?'

'I didn't know that he has.' That wasn't true. Spinner Kanalina seemed weary of asking me questions already, or maybe it was that I was only giving her the answers that she had expected.

'Three years ago, Dantry Tanza went into the phos mill at Heirengrad and did something that overloaded the battery coils. They exploded. Nobody was killed, but millions of marks' worth of equipment was destroyed. The mill belonged to Prince Herono, a kinsman of Dantry's.'

'I killed the previous Prince Herono, did you know that?' I asked. The position had been filled by a young man of no great ambition who had no mind for matters either military or economic. For all that his aunt had been possessed by Stale's maggot living in her brain, she'd probably still have been a better prince than he was managing to be.

'Why did he destroy the mill?'

'I have no fucking idea. Maybe his mind cracked. Ask your dog Casso.'

Kanalina finished writing down my answer and then fished through her papers. She drew out a missive, written in a familiar hand. I tried to keep my face neutral. She held it up for several seconds.

'We took this from the spinning wheel shop. Fortunately the new owner thought these messages might be between sympathisers and reported it,' she said. 'There's not a great deal in this letter. But it's clear that there were others, and that you've been corresponding with Count Tanza across the years. Doing so with a great deal of secrecy. Why would a man who can survive alone in the Misery be exchanging communications with a saboteur? You were a hero during the war. What changed?'

I chuckled, an unpleasant sensation as it sent fresh pain lancing up through my side.

'During the war? You people can't help but repeat the same mistakes, over and over. You think the war's over? You think that ten years ago the Deep Kings decided that we'd smashed them so hard they might as well give up? That's how we nearly lost everything the last time. You know the biggest change in Valengrad since I left it? A new opera house. A symphony hall over at Willows. Now they broadcast prayer times instead of the reminder to keep on fighting, to keep on living. I'm not the one that fucking changed.'

Spinner Kanalina had stopped writing. She rested her pen on her papers, her hands upon crossed knees.

'When Dantry Tanza destroyed the second mill, at Snosk, we knew the first had been no accident,' she said. 'His research was forbidden by the Council Academia Superior when he started chasing the same nonsense his sister had pursued years before. But he was determined. When he overloaded the coils at Snosk, the ensuing blast killed fifteen Talents working at the mill. Fifteen people murdered, because one obsessed nobleman can't resist trying out his theories.'

I frowned. People died all the time. I was the cause of it as often as not. I'd always known that there would be collateral damage. We were at war. But I hadn't known he'd killed so many. I'd thought Dantry would be more careful. It was an accident, sure enough. Or at least I hoped it had been. For obvious reasons, I couldn't tell the Spinner that.

'I was a Talent at the Snosk mill, before I realised I could do more than simply draw the light into looms,' Kanalina said. That explained her accent. 'There were former colleagues of mine amongst the dead. I could have been amongst them. So you see, Captain, I have forgotten nothing. For me, Dantry Tanza's crimes are all too real.'

'So go and find him,' I said. 'You got nothing on me. I'm a spirits-damned captain of Blackwing. Do you even have the slightest idea what that means? No. You've forgotten, all of you. Crowfall happened, and the black rain started, and you forgot everything that went before. *Everything*. But I'm still fighting. Keeping the mills secure is your business. Not mine.'

She ignored me.

'In this letter, Dantry Tanza mentions something he calls the Anvil. What is it?'

I shrugged.

'Is it a weapon?'

I said nothing. I wanted to see that paper.

Spinner Kanalina narrowed her eyes, trying to read me. Maybe the amber colouring of my own was off-putting, because she couldn't hold my gaze long and I gave her nothing.

'I'll have food and drink delivered. You'll receive medical attention if you decide to help us. You'll need it, and you might lose that arm if you don't get it. Think on what I've asked you. Perhaps it's time to find your conscience, Former-Captain Galharrow.'

She stood up.

'Wait. Tell her this,' I said. 'If Davandein wants to trade information, then she needs to come to me in person. She's already let half the citadel be destroyed. If she wants to know how to stop the rest of it falling, she has to talk to me.'

The door shut, a definitive series of locks sliding and clicking into place signalling that I was well and truly incarcerated. The room was suddenly quiet save for the dry buzz of the phos light. I would have stood up and smashed it, only it was beyond easy reach and the pain in my side wasn't making the idea of jumping up and down seem plausible. An unpleasant numbness had spread down my leg and the flesh around my hip had swollen, the dark shade of ruptured blood vessels beneath the skin. I had to settle for the only darkness I could find. I pressed my eyes closed.

Time does not move in the blankness of the white cells. They were playing nice, because this cell wasn't two feet wide. I'd not always put people in the nice ones. In fact, I'd once argued to convert them all into slots. My captors might have acted like professionals, but by comparison to me they were amateurs.

Nobody returned for what felt like a very long time. At some point I slept, and when I woke somebody had left a plate of cold duck, bean paste, and flatbread beside a cup of water. Thoughts ticked past leaving me with nothing but the pain of broken bones and my own fears. The breaks had settled down to an unpleasant ache. Standing still proved difficult but I could get myself upright. I sat, I coughed, I wiped the blackish slime on the lime-white walls. I thought of Gleck Maldon and how he'd written his thesis in shit across the walls of his cell. His captivity had ended when Prince Herono betrayed him to the drudge and to Shavada. I had to wonder whether my own prospects were any better than his had been.

No. I wouldn't end down here. There was work to do.

I slept again, though I wasn't tired. A plate of cold food and a jug of weak tea appeared. The phos tubes were never dimmed, the blank, sterile light ever present. I managed to hobble around the room, which was a surprise because I'd figured my broken hip was going to keep me down for longer than that. I took off my shirt and examined the black-and-purple bruising that the giant's foot had left across my chest. The discolouration reminded me of the Misery sky, the broken threads of red and blue spiralling amongst the gold and the green. Oddly, I couldn't help but feel that I was missing it. I missed the jagged cracks running through the heavens, the sky's sonorous wail.

Of course I missed it. I'd been soaking the Misery up for years. That was the point, wasn't it? I missed it like a fish misses the water. It was home.

I knew what they were doing, of course. Isolation and silence bring a man around in a way that the urgency of a threat doesn't. They wanted Dantry Tanza badly enough to grab me, but they'd been hunting him for years. A few hours wouldn't make much difference. When the door finally opened and Spinner Kanalina stepped in, I had no idea how long I'd been alone in the cell for. I'd eaten four meals and felt hungry twice, but it could have been two days or four.

Kanalina brought a chair again, and I kept my place on the floor. They hadn't provided me with any furniture save a bucket for shitting in.

'What is that on the walls?' she asked.

'Shit from the Misery,' I shrugged. The wall beside which I most commonly sat was a mess of oily tar smears. Kanalina seemed less fazed than disapproving as she sorted her papers into order and took out her pen.

'I am coming under great pressure to move things along swiftly,' she said eventually.

'Is that a threat?'

'Do you think I can make it otherwise?'

'Well, I guess that makes you my hero then.'

She ignored me and instead began to run through her questions about Dantry Tanza again. Some of them were different. She was trying a new angle, trying to work out if I knew anything about Dantry's foray into light-spinning theory. I made the same unhelpful, terse responses. I could have just stayed silent, but there's something within me that likes to give smart-arsed answers instead.

'What I don't understand is why a mathematician with no ability to spin light would become so interested in working on ideas that even Spinners find difficult to grasp.'

'That must frustrate you.'

Kanalina put her pen down. She was wearing a pair of horn-rimmed glasses, but she removed them now to look at me. I liked her face but it was undeniably sharp in places; a pointed nose, angled brows.

'I have been learning more about you,' she said. 'At first I thought you to be some kind of simple loon, a hermit living out in the Misery. I knew about your Blackwing past, but the rest was true as well. You killed Torolo Mancono in the courthouse, and led the defence of Valengrad, for two days at least. Which makes your betrayal even more disappointing.'

I had nothing to say to that. She tapped the end of her pen against her papers. I stared back, blank faced.

'Did you see the Deep King?' she asked.

'Shavada? I saw him,' I said. It was hard to remember what he'd looked like. I recalled a great darkness, deep black shadows, and the sound of clanking iron but that was it. His presence in my mind had become hazy over time, as though with his passing, reality were trying to erase every trace of his existence. Sometimes, though, when I put my hand against the Misery-sands and felt out into the distance, I could sense the Deep Kings and amongst them, some trace of his being still lingered. Even after the Nameless had torn his heart out and used its power to fuel Nall's Engine, a being of such cosmic importance could not be erased utterly.

'The marshal once told me that we all owe our survival to you and Dantry Tanza's sister.'

'Davandein talks a lot of shit,' I said. 'But she's right about that. Maybe you should go talk to her again and see what she thinks about me being in chains.'

'You were a defender of the states,' Kanalina said. 'What changed?'

'Everything changed,' I said. 'Davandein turned on her own city. Blackwing was reduced to a shadow of its former power. And I realised something. The Engine, the Nameless, the citadel? None of them matter. There's just me. I'm the only one fighting this fucking war the way that it needs to be fought. All I want is to be left alone. Why the fuck do you think I've been living out in the Misery all these years?'

'I don't know. Tell me.'

'I like the solitude.'

'I've been out there, Captain. The ghosts don't rest quietly. If you wanted solitude there are safer places to find it. It's amazing you've survived out there all this time. Alone. How do you do it?'

I raised a bronze-tinted hand, callused, threaded with green and red, old scars stacked atop tattoos for the dead. I turned it in the hard phos light.

'You call this surviving?'

12

Meals had come and gone, and some kind of time had passed. I lost track of how many times I'd eaten, how many times I'd shat in the bucket. I slept too deeply. I began to wonder whether they were putting some kind of tranquilliser in the food, since I was never awake when it arrived. The only person I ever saw was Kanalina, the only possible conversation revolving around what I'd been doing in the Misery, where Dantry Tanza could be found, what he intended to achieve.

It is a dark thing to be locked away with your own thoughts. They revolve, around and around, questioned and uncertain until you begin to doubt what you knew in the first place. We are not made for isolation. The white cells began to take their toll.

No day and no night, only the constant glare of the bright, stale light. When surges of power caused them to flicker I flinched, startled, and stared into them in the hope that perhaps I'd be given a glimpse of what I had lost. But it was a vain hope. Ezabeth was all but gone from the world. I knew how much it had cost her to protect me when Saravor attempted to ascend. She was little spoken of now, more and more a ghost in truth.

My hip was healing. A break like that should have laid me up for months, but somewhere between sixteen and twenty-five meals, I wouldn't have known it had ever happened.

When there's nothing to keep you occupied save your own body there are only two ways to keep entertained. The first would have been degrading, the second was to challenge myself. I challenged myself. It had been years since I'd worked my body as I'd done when I was young. I worked my muscles against my own weight, trying anything I could do alone with no tool but my body to work with. At times I did it to give myself something to concentrate on, at others because I wanted to exhaust myself. My arm was strong again. My fingers were stiff, but the bones no longer ached. I exerted myself until I lay face down in a puddle of sweat and my eyes were finally willing to close.

I woke from some kind of tattered sleep and found myself in the Misery. I wasn't, of course, but it looked like it. Redness, coarse sand, and black rock. A dream, but I knew it was a dream. Nenn sat on a rock, juggling a knife from hand to hand.

'What's happening to me?'

'Fucked if I know. What's happening to me?' she countered. It wasn't helpful.

'You aren't anything,' I said. 'You're just a reflection. You're more me than you are you.'

'We're all each other,' she said. She spun the knife into the air and caught it by the blade as it fell. 'We exist in each other's minds as much as we exist in our own. You think you're alone, but you aren't. I learned that pretty late in life. You taught me that. Just before the – bleurgh.' She mimed yanking her guts out.

'I shouldn't be seeing you here.'

'Maybe you aren't,' she said. 'Like I said before. You're probably just nuts.'

I blinked and the redness, the broken sky, and the Misery stink were gone and there was nothing around me but the blank whiteness of the cell.

Day followed day, or maybe it didn't. The moons might

have stopped their rotations around the earth for all I knew. Nenn came and went, sometimes appearing in the cell between breaths, sometimes waiting for me when I woke, but most of the time the white cell was silent aside from the sounds that I put into it, the grunts, the gasps, the laboured breathing, the hacking cough that brought pain to my chest and tar to my lips. They'd need to rename this place 'the grey cell' with the amount of the stuff now smeared across the walls. Sometimes that pain defeated me, drove me to my knees. Other times it just made me more determined.

When there's nothing to focus upon, the little things begin to take on meaning. I counted the rows of white plastered bricks in the walls. I ordered the beans they gave me into little regiments, used them to re-create famous battles. I began hoarding them, armies of bean soldiers to create bigger engagements. They must have known, somehow, because they began giving me soup instead. Soup made for less tactically satisfying dioramas.

I decided that the crap I'd choked out and wiped on the walls was doing nobody but me a disservice. The old adage that you shouldn't shit where you eat seemed to apply, although since I had to shit in the cell where I ate, there was only so far I could pursue the sentiment. Still, I tried to scrape away the crap I'd smeared onto the walls but in some places it had hardened to something close to stone. In others it seemed to have eaten away at the brick, no longer a smear across the stone but a coloured stain, furrows eaten into the brickwork. If it was capable of doing that to dressed stone, I hated to think what it was doing to my insides.

Day followed day. Or didn't. Who knew? Tick, tock, tick, tock. No chance of a rescue. Nobody except my captors even knew that I was here. And Nenn, maybe, although she was dead, and probably wasn't actually there anyway.

Spinner Kanalina opened the door to find me with my feet up towards the ceiling, doing vertical press-ups against the wall. I'd just hit ninety-three, a personal best. I hit a new personal best every time I tried something. I was putting out numbers I'd never achieved even in the prime of my youth. The Misery-taint within me was responding to the stimulus, changing me. It healed me, and it answered my need for strength. She cared for me, even here in the glaring phos light of a cell.

'How are you able to do that?' Kanalina asked. She stared. I'd stripped to the waist and the hard lines of my copper-toned body were damp with sweat.

'Want me to show you?'

'Your hip was broken,' she said. I kicked against the wall and dropped down onto my feet.

'It got better.'

'It shouldn't have. Not this fast.' She looked me over, and my ego gave a little spurt as she eyed the contours of my body. Age had given my gut a soft padding over the years but that had melted away in a handful of what could have been days, or hours, or weeks. 'You're changing,' she said. 'There's less grey in your hair. Or more black, anyway. What's happening to you?'

'Damned if I know. Maybe this white room agrees with me. Maybe it's all the static in the air.' I rolled my shoulders, flexed muscle I hadn't previously possessed. The changes to my body weren't all natural but it had been many years since I'd been this hardened, this lean.

Kanalina sniffed. She could feel the charge around us too. Like the vibrancy of air before a thunderstorm, the prickling of excitement before a duel.

'Are you one of them?' she asked eventually.

'One of who?'

'The drudge. Did they change you?'

'No.'

'Today is my last day,' she said. She seemed frustrated. She looked at the black and green streaks I'd wiped across the walls, the floor. Did her best not to show any emotion, but couldn't quite hold her face steady. 'I thought you would come around, given enough time. Decide that doing what's right is better than spending the rest of your life in a cell.'

I shrugged, got down on the floor, and began to knock out some press-ups. I began using just one hand, then switched to the other. It was too easy. I pushed myself up onto my fingertips and did them that way instead. Kanalina watched me for a time.

'Do you want to know what happens now?'

'Will it make any difference whether I know or not?' I said without breaking rhythm. Moving this way, holding up my own weight, shouldn't have been this easy.

'You'll be racked,' she said. 'Heinrich Adenauer is the Chief of Urban Security. He'll take over from me, since I can get nothing from you. He prefers the rack. Do you know what the rack does to a person?'

'I've got some idea.'

'Your knees will be torn from their sockets,' she said. 'Arms too. Your feet will break apart. When they rack someone, the remnant left behind never walks again. Barely sits up. Most likely they'll break you, and when you don't give them what they want, they'll cut your throat and cast a skin bag of cracked and broken bones out into the gutter.'

Nothing I didn't already know, though I'd never seen a man racked. In my day it was all hot irons and sharp knives. Those things are mundane, everyday tools that can be turned to black purposes. But when a man has a rack constructed he's making a declaration: he intends to hurt people, formally and often. There were always plenty of spies and sympathisers to send down to the cells but when Venzer was in charge there had been limits. Heinrich Adenauer was no soldier. He'd been Prince Adenauer's natural-born son. I'd met him only once, when he tried to goad Dantry Tanza into a duel to stop him freeing his sister from the Maud. I remembered him as a snivelling little bureaucrat and a turd.

'Your concern is touching,' I grunted. Forty-one, forty-two. 'But really, go fuck yourself.'

Kanalina looked neither impressed nor surprised.

'Have you not wondered why you have been cast into this cell instead of being sent straight to the slots? You're here because someone is protecting you, someone that doesn't want you in pieces. I've done all I can, but they can't protect you indefinitely.'

'Great job of protecting me so far,' I said. 'If it wasn't for your pet monster out there, I'd not be in here at all. Who is this friend?'

'Whoever it is, they've blocked Adenauer's requests to put you on the board so far,' she snapped. 'But today is your final chance, Galharrow. Give me something or I've no choice but to turn you over to Adenauer.'

Fifty-five, fifty-six. Maybe it was true. Maybe I did still have a friend in the citadel. But, more likely, it was just another way to persuade me to give up what I knew. Offer the hope that one day I might make it out of here, give me a glimmer of light. Only Kanalina seemed angry, probably because she hadn't got what she wanted, and she struck me as the kind of woman who usually did.

'Ask them to turn the phos down to clear this static from the air,' I said. I went back to my exercises.

She left me alone with the stoked embers of fear. The white cells were bad, but they had not counted on my familiarity with isolation. Out in the Misery I'd lived for months with nothing but ghosts, and they were worse than silence.

When the door opened the following day, I was ready to fight. Better to try something – anything, however futile it might seem – than to be led meekly to the rack. I'd endured my time in the Misery. I wasn't going to go quietly, to be asked questions I couldn't answer, and certainly not by that bottom-grubber Adenauer. But the soldiers who came to the door held flintlock pistols ready and trained on me. And there were eight of them. Nobody was taking chances with me. Competent men, men who knew how desperate the cells would have made me.

'Turn around, and put your hands behind your back,' one of them said.

'No.'

The soldier didn't look like a cruel man. He looked like someone who has a family, who joined up because it was the right thing to do. But they make them tough on the Range.

'I was told that if you don't, then we're to leave you here,' he said. He shared an uncertain look with his second. 'And to tell you that if you don't, then tomorrow we're to bring you the Fracan's arm.'

My will, clutched tight and hard in my chest all this time, crumpled a little.

'What?'

'I don't know what it means,' the soldier said. 'I'm just following orders.' He must have known that it wasn't exactly an ordinary, or legal, kind of message, and he looked pained to be giving it, but his pistol was aimed steadily. 'My orders were stamped with the marshal's own seal. I'd advise following them. Put them on.'

Tnota was an innocent in all this. He was nothing to the citadel, just an old navigator past his best. I'd hoped that he'd have taken my diamonds and gone west. But, of course, he would have lingered when I didn't return. Maybe eventually, desperate, he would have asked after me at the citadel. They could have been bluffing, but it was a terrible risk to take.

'Where are you taking me?'

'Another cell, on the level above,' the soldier said.

I knew these cells. Above the white cells were the grey, and that must have been where they kept the rack. I looked down at the manacles. They were thick, joined not by a flimsy chain but by a single heavy link. I might have found a new level of strength in the white cells, but I wouldn't break them once they were on. My wrists still bore the scars that drudge ropes had inflicted, years ago.

'Do it,' I said. I turned and presented my wrists. One of the soldiers approached, cautiously, but there was only one way out and it was full of men with pistols. Hurting one innocent soldier wouldn't help me. The irons snapped shut around my wrists like the closing of a coffin lid.

It was the first time in what seemed like a very long time that I had been out of the cell. They walked four ahead of me, four behind, pistol barrels in my back. I couldn't try anything. We climbed the stairs – the only staircase that led up from the white cells – and onto a corridor. Doors with metal grilles housed political prisoners here, the cells intended to keep a man waiting for his death rather than to break his mind. It was quiet. A prison is a rowdy place, full of the jeers and noise of the incarcerated, but a dungeon is different. Those forced to abide in a dungeon know there is no way out save the gallows. We stopped at a thick door.

'In here.'

I was ushered in alone, expecting to find a leering man beside a contraption of wood and rope, ready to crack me apart. But the cell was empty except for a bed of straw and an all-too-familiar shitting bucket. Just an ordinary dungeon room, or at least as ordinary as any cell can be.

The door closed behind me.

'They'll be here for you in the morning,' the lead soldier said through the grille. Their footsteps receded away along the corridor.

I looked around my new temporary home, wondering why the hell they'd have transferred me to this marginally more comfortable accommodation. It wasn't much better, but a bed of straw is better than a cold stone floor. I sat down.

Five minutes later the grille snapped back again and a new face peered in. Guards, more than one.

'Alright there,' he said. He must have dealt with dangerous, condemned men every day, but he grimaced at my appearance. 'It's your lucky day. You're being transferred. On your feet, but don't make any sudden moves. Fuck me, you're an ugly one.'

The door opened up, the men entered. Something wasn't right. But I was still manacled and although these wardens didn't have loaded pistols trained on me, their batons were studded with steel and my hands were firmly locked behind my back. I let them lead me out into the corridor and saw another prisoner, a fierce-looking man, missing an eye, his face covered in gang tattoos. The five badly inked daggers across his forehead were a classless show of front: one for each person he'd killed. The guards shoved him into the cell in my place and slammed the door shut.

'He won't be out of there in a while. You must have done the right thing, in someone's book,' the guard said. 'Not many get up to the brown cells once they're down in the grey, but they've been filling up like mad the last few days. Guess you told them something they wanted.'

I didn't answer. He seemed the kind that liked to talk, but didn't want a conversation. Jailors all tend to come from the same stock. We were halfway up the next stairwell when we met another pair coming down from above, dressed in the black coats of citadel officials. The stairway was too narrow for us to pass easily.

'Hold up,' one of them said, spotting me behind the first guard. 'Is that the prisoner from cell thirty-nine?'

'Yeah,' the guard said. 'What of it?'

'You taking him to cell four?'

'No. Cell fifteen, brown level.'

'We just had to put a real bad one in cell fifteen,' the official said. 'We've orders to move him to four instead.'

'My orders came from the Office of Urban Security, so he's going in cell fifteen,' the guard said, annoyed to be having this conversation on the stairs.

'Ours too,' the official said. She produced a folded piece of paper, showed it to him.

'That's strange,' the warden said. 'My orders only came ten minutes ago.'

'Bloody odd, that,' the official agreed, frowning. 'Maybe there's a mistake, but all the cells are full. Leads have come in so thick the last few days we've bagged half the pollen dealers in the city. But we just put some guy in fifteen, so why don't we stick your guy in cell four and speak to Casso. Get it sorted out?'

'That Casso isn't one to anger,' the guard agreed. 'So if there's shit for it, it's on your shoulders.'

The official shrugged. She had her orders on paper. That was all the protection she really needed.

Cell four was almost comfortable compared to thirty-nine, and positively luxurious compared to the white cells. The white cells didn't have numbers. They were just the white cells. Now I had a bed and a chair, a table, all of them more basic than any you'd find in a barracks. I'd been locked in and sat on the chair for five minutes, when I heard the key turn in the lock again.

13

The uniformed soldier who opened the door was different from the others.

She was short, with a broad round face and the distinctive features and coal-dark hair that marked her as hailing from the distant west, and her face was all seriousness. A heavy bag hung over her shoulder. Her scowl took me in quickly, but any surprise she felt was quickly bitten down.

'You're Ryhalt?' she said. I nodded. 'You're meant to be fifty. You sure?'

'Pretty sure.'

'I guess there's no mistaking that colour on you. Get up. I'm going to take off the shackles. A friend sent me.'

'Who?'

'Winter.'

I didn't know if Winter was a friend or not, but someone had gone to a lot of trouble to get me from the white cells into the brown. The woman removed the pins that held the manacles in place, tossed them onto the table, and offered me the bag.

'Put these on.'

My first change of clothes in however long it had been since they'd thrown me into the glare. Citadel blues, a porter's uniform. I was surprised that they fit me. Not many clothes do.

'You going to turn your back?' I asked.

'On you? No. Hurry. We don't have long.'

'Who are you?'

'You can call me Sang,' she said, and even if it wasn't her real name, it was as good as I was going to get. She had no weapons on her. 'Pull the hat down low and hunch. Look small, if you can.'

Sang led me out of the cell and through an empty guard-room. Somebody should have been at the desk, checking in anybody that wanted access to the cells. I'd checked in enough prisoners down the years, and even though the guard's absence helped my escape I wondered how lax the citadel must have become to employ men who'd leave that important post unattended. We exited the detention block into a central courtyard. It was night – a concept that had held little meaning in the white cells – and the phos lights were all turned off. A few technicians with handheld phos globes or oil lamps were checking cables and tubes, looking to see why they were dead. The shadows were deep, the points of light blinding, and nobody paid any attention to a mismatched pair in uniform crossing to another door.

'Through here. To the west wing,' Sang said.

'There's no way out this way,' I told her.

'There is now.'

She'd brought me out of the cell, so I decided that I could trust her again now. There was nothing for anyone to gain by this ruse if they weren't trying to help me. Winter would have to be trusted.

Sang led me down a corridor, past a couple of old men with rolls of copper wire over their shoulders, hurrying to-wards the lightless yard. They didn't pay me any attention. I thought that we were heading into a barracks, but then I realised: no. No barracks there anymore.

We stepped out again into the night. Huge piles of rubble framed a wide stretch of uneven ground, the remnants of what had once been part of the citadel. A bitter, almond odour hit me in a wave. The air was warmer here, too warm, and it reminded me of the heat that rose from the Misery's sand. Arrayed across the ground were tall, ovular pods, ten feet high, their bumpy surfaces gleaming wetly.

'What are those?'

'Shallowgrave sent them,' Sang said quietly. 'They're supposed to help us.'

'That's what smashed the citadel?'

She nodded.

'We go around them.'

There were twenty of them in four rows of five. They were nearly all identical, and though they were silent and immobile I had the unnerving feeling that they were alive. Only one of them, in the centre, was different. It had split open, the flaccid halves lying where they had fallen.

'What was inside it?'

'The thing that broke you,' she said. 'Come on. Don't linger. They'll know you're missing soon.'

If there were supposed to be any guards around, I didn't see any sign of them. We hurried on past the pods, and as we left them behind, the warmth faded and the night's cold came in. We were two streets from the citadel when a siren rose behind us, keening my disappearance. We hastened on, not running but upping to a steady pace. Sang struggled to keep up with my stride.

'Not that way,' she said.

'I need to get to Pikes.'

'No. Follow me. Your friends are safe.'

We turned down street after street, all of them as familiar to me as the feet that carried me down them. For a moment I thought Sang was taking me to the old Blackwing office, but we went past it and the building was a merchant house now, a neon sign displaying the traders' names. I felt a pang of regret that it had become just another house of commerce. I didn't have any special dislike for traders, I just didn't have any reason to admire them either. We continued into Nook, a reserved, quiet district that boasted no greater claim than that the people who lived there generally just wanted to be left alone. Sang stopped at a nondescript building, unlocked the door, and showed me in.

'The citadel doesn't know about this place,' she said. 'They won't find you here.'

Tnota was waiting for me. I met him in a hug.

'Hells, Ryhalt, but it's good to see you.'

'You too,' I said. He'd not gone west, then, but the citadel didn't have him either. 'Is Giralt safe?'

'He's here. Sleeping. I didn't want to wake him until I was sure.' He looked me over. 'You're different,' he said.

'Different how?'

'You're still the colour of a bent penny. But spirits, Ryhalt. You look young again. What did you do?'

A mirror hung in the hallway. I was frowning as I went to it, but he was right. The lines around my eyes had receded. My cheeks had firmed, losing their sag, and the bags beneath my eyes had smoothed out. I barely recognised the man who stared back. The breaks in my nose had straightened, the grey in my hair was down to a few stray threads. But my eyes – the glow was stronger than ever, the obsidian veins beneath the skin more pronounced. I'd asked the Misery-taint to change me, I'd pushed it to the surface and embraced it, and it had.

'Upstairs,' Sang said. 'Winter is waiting for you.'

I broke my gaze from the stranger in the polished glass. Tnota reached a hand out to touch my arm.

'Ryhalt,' he said quietly. 'You should know, before you go up there. It's her. She's Winter.'

Something hard lodged in my throat. It had been obvious, really. Nobody else could have found me in the Misery or pulled off such a quiet, bloodless jailbreak. The level of planning it had taken must have been immense. Orders for each set of guards, delivered nearly simultaneously. Filling all but one cell. Sabotaging the phos lights outside. It had been planned to the last inch. I found that I'd closed my eyes, and opened them slowly. It was time, I supposed. I was ready. But regenerated youth or not, I didn't want to be seen this way.

I followed Sang up the stairs. She ushered me in, and shut the door behind me.

It was an office, as I'd known it would be. Bookshelves lined the walls. Neat, orderly rows of straight-backed books. A pair of tidy desks, holding a globe, a microscope, and other instruments of investigation. The lights were dim, phos tubes barely glowing. And amidst it all, a woman I'd told myself I'd never see again.

'Hello, Ryhalt,' Valiya said. 'It's been a long time.'

She didn't look so very different from the day she'd walked away, six years ago. The fire in her hair had turned grey. She was thinner, not much left of her now. But the quiet poise, the calmness with which she stood, hands clasped before her, was all Valiya. Six years. We'd gone our separate ways, and it had been for the best. She was still beautiful.

There was part of me that wanted to tell her how often I'd thought of her. Some schoolboy part of me that remembered every long night that we'd worked together wanted her to know, right there and then. But I couldn't find the words, or maybe I didn't have them inside me.

'Valiya,' I said. 'Or Winter, is it now?'

'You may call me Valiya,' she said. Formal. Distant. She gestured that I should sit. 'Would you like some tea?'

I almost laughed. Valiya and her damn, undrinkable tea.

'No,' I said. 'How have you been?'

She shrugged.

'I am as I am. There's always more to be done.'

'It took you a while to get to me.'

'The white cells are unreachable,' she said, sitting at her desk. 'They were designed that way.'

Valiya didn't smile. There was something else about her that was different. I hadn't noticed it at first, but I was not the only one to have changed. Her eyes had no pupils, and her irises reflected light like a mirror. She no longer looked quite human; Winter described her well. There was no warmth in her face, not even for an old friend.

'But you reached me.'

'It was a close thing. I couldn't be sure that my agents would be able to shut the power down on time, and forging the orders took forever. But yes.'

'I should have guessed that Nall would choose you. You were always too clever by half. You're one of his captains, now?'

'His only captain,' she said.

'Your eyes—'

'Yours too. Is that really what you want to talk about?'

I settled down in a chair. The air between us was uncomfortable, and there were questions that I wanted to ask her. *Did you marry again? Why did you make a deal?* But our old closeness was gone. Lost to choice and time and everything else.

'What happened to the others?'

'Nall didn't lose any captains. I was the only one from the start. He always preferred to do his own work. I know about Josaf and Linette, though. Nobody knows who killed them, as far as I've been able to ascertain, but you must assume you are a target.'

'Nall's dying,' I said.

Valiya nodded sadly.

'I know. He reached you then, in the Misery?'

Rain began to fall. The black rain, a light fall that struck too hard against the window, heavier than water ought to be.

'Most of him. He ran into some gillings.' I didn't need to tell her the avatar hadn't returned. She'd known he wouldn't when she sent him to find me. 'The Nameless are broken. The Sleeper may not have risen, but they didn't win the battle. Nall's Engine is the only defence we have left, and Shallowgrave trying to bring down the citadel doesn't help. What happened?'

Valiya frowned.

'It's hard to say. There was a flash of green and a bang louder than the sky-fires, and then the citadel's north wing came down. And the eggs were just there.'

'Eggs?'

'Maybe not the right word for them,' Valiya said. 'But one of them hatched. You've already met the thing that came out. About eight feet tall, milk-white skin, red-eyed and scarred.'

'We're acquainted,' I said, feeling uneasy. I'd wondered what the hell that thing had been. 'Do you know what they are?'

'Yes,' she said. 'Shallowgrave has sent us the Marble Guard.'

For a moment I didn't know what to say. Then I found a smile cracking my face.

'Great. Maybe the Lady of Waves will send us a battalion of mermaids and a kraken too.'

'I'm serious,' Valiya said. My reflection in her mirror-shine eyes and the set of her lips told me she wasn't joking. Her new name fit her well. Valiya had always been driven by her work, but there was a coldness to her that made me wonder how deeply the woman I knew was buried. Her captaincy had changed more than just her appearance.

The Marble Guard were a myth that hailed back to the warrior-heroes of the ancient world, long before there were princes and a republic. When men fought with bronze spears and threw rocks at each other, a deposed king had made a deal with a spirit that had been insulted by the usurper. It gave him twenty warriors, born from the heart of its mountain, warriors that could not be defeated in battle, and with them he retook his kingdom. But the Marble Guard had an insatiable appetite for blood, and he found himself alone in his throne room with his inhuman warriors, his people devoured to sate their thirst. They were a parable, a warning to those that sought power at any cost.

'A children's fable,' I said.

'Myths tend to have a basis in truth,' Valiya said. 'There's a god in your arm and you've stared into the heart of the Misery. Why not this?'

'As long as they're on our side, I guess it doesn't matter.'

'Whatever our side is, anymore,' Valiya said. 'I worked alongside Davandein for a while. Then, after the Crowfall, she pushed me out. She's afraid, and instead of accepting my help she drew inwards. I still have some influence, good people in the citadel who take my counsel and slip it into her ear, but she struggles to trust the Nameless, or those that serve them anymore.'

'I don't blame her.'

'I think that's why Shallowgrave has sent the Marble Guard. He's trying to reassert control. Only one of them has hatched from its shell. We don't know if the others will hatch, or when. They named the one that emerged First, and we expect the rest of them to follow eventually.'

Ancient warriors sent in our time of need. It was a shame the king's story hadn't had a happier ending. First had been a terrible adversary, though. They would be useful when the Deep Kings came. They wouldn't make the difference, not if Acradius held the power of The Sleeper, but we needed all the help we could get.

'It's good to see you,' I said.

Valiya didn't blink.

'Marshal Davandein is planning to launch an expedition

to Adrogorsk. She's building an army a few miles from the Range, but she's keeping her motives close to her chest. My spies have learned nothing, which means she hasn't told anybody. But one of the Lady of Waves' captains paid her a visit, just before she issued the order.'

'Valiya. I know this is important, but can we take a minute to ... It's been six years—'

'I know what you're planning to do,' she said, and that shut me up.

The rain hissed against the window, steady and relentless.

'You know why I have to do it.'

'I know,' she said. 'I knew even before Nall did. Your determination to save Ezabeth is written into your skin.'

Her eyes never left mine. I had imagined this moment over and over, while I was out in the Misery. A reunion, a coming together of two people who'd once had something special and untouched between them. I had never envisaged it like this. Whatever softness had stirred inside me at seeing her again after all this time shifted, cogs and wheels clicking into place to begin turning again. The old flicker of warmth I held for her retreated back into its recess, and the world continued to turn.

'Good,' I said. 'Then you won't get in my way.'

On Valiya's desk, a phos-prism suddenly brightened and began to hum. A communicator. Valiya took hold of a strip of paper that protruded from the box beneath it and slowly drew it out as the tapping arm began to stab at the paper. *Scrape. Dot-scrape-dot. Dot-scrape. Dot-scrape-scrape-dot.*

'Who is it?' I asked.

Dot-scrape-scrape-dot. Dot. Scrape-dot-dot. And then nothing. We waited, but no more came. Not much of a message, but my breath had turned cold in my chest as I worked out its meaning. Valiya's emotionless eyes stared down at the paper.

'Who was that?' I asked again.

'Amaira,' she said.

Blood slowed, cold in my veins. I closed my eyes, my newfound freedom turning to ashes in my mouth.

The message had been simple. *Trapped.*

14

Valiya led me up a staircase to a fourth-floor room that smelled of cold machinery and phos. The lights around the ceiling hummed into life. In the centre of the room, four fat metal cylinders the size of beer kegs sat below a pedestal, connected by wires and tubes.

'What's this?' I asked.

'I need to speak with your master. He can tell us where he sent Amaira.'

'You don't know where she is?'

'Crowfoot sent her on a mission, and she only uses the communicator to tell me that she's still alive. You don't tell people the details of your missions, do you?'

'I guess not. But I can't just pull him out of my arm.'

'You won't have to. I can bring him to us.'

That didn't sound like a good idea. Valiya went to a heavy safe and turned four dials until they clicked. She took out a cloth-wrapped bundle that sat on a bed of ice and brought it to me.

'Attach the wires on the pedestal to this,' she said and gave it to me, then turned away and drew up her sleeves. The parcel didn't have much weight to it so I pulled back the covering and felt a stone lodge in my gut. The cloth was wrapped around the carcass of a hooded raven, a ring of white around its shoulders. It only had one wing. I remembered this bird, though it couldn't be the same one that had followed me around the Misery.

'Where did you get this?'

'It came out of Amaira's arm. It's the one that sent her away. I kept it.'

'Why?'

'I thought it would be useful. And now it is. Attach it to the nodes.'

Atop the pedestal, four thick copper wires arched inwards like the dragon-headed prows of old ships. Each ended with a spring-loaded clip. I wasn't sure about any of this, but Valiya usually knew what she was doing so I spread the cold, delicate wing and attached it to two of the clips. The others took its feet. The maimed bird looked absurd, spread out over the metal plate. This seemed like a terrible idea, but Amaira's message had pushed me to take a risk. She'd learned fast, and I'd have backed her against the best warrior the drudge could throw into her path, but it didn't matter. My girl was in danger.

'I don't see what this can do.'

'Lady Tanza burned Crowfoot's avatar out of your arm with phos, during the Siege,' Valiya said. She didn't meet my eye, tracing her fingers up and down her own forearm. 'It gave me this idea. I just had to work out how to do it. The canisters beneath the pedestal will channel the phos into the bird. The carcass is still part of Crowfoot, so the phos magic will alert him to what we're doing.'

'How can you know it will work?' And not explode or erupt in a spray of defensive power. Messing with Crowfoot's simulacrums had not proven sensible in the past.

Valiya drew back her sleeve, and her fingers flickered lightly over her arm. The flower tattoos that had once sat there were gone. Instead, her skin crawled with numbers, lines, and symbols. Mathematics, physics. She swiped an equation to the side and it tracked across her skin, her fingers sliding a series of numbers into an array of circles. She added lines, which appeared faint and grey, solidified as they performed calculations for her, then faded out to be replaced with answers, answers that Valiya moved into tables that expanded, changed, and were swallowed by an ever more complicated array of figures.

'What is that?' I whispered.

'Nall gave it to me,' she said, switching to her other arm. She glanced between them as if checking her working. 'It accesses everything. The way it all works.'

'The way what works?'

'The universe,' she said, as though it were no more important than the weather.

'Fucking hell,' I said. I had always thought Nall was the best of the Nameless. Perhaps I had been wrong. This wasn't right.

'Put your hand on it,' she said. 'That will force the link. It's Amaira's bird, but you're all joined together through him. Are you ready?'

I'd evaded Crowfoot's notice for years, steeped out in the concealing taint of the Misery. I'd hidden, while the world burned and the black rain fell, and while I'd known that this reunion was coming, I approached it with the relish of a man about to lose a rotten limb to the surgeon's saw. No. I wasn't ready. But the communicator had tapped out its message, and I couldn't set it aside any longer. I let my resolve harden.

'I'm ready,' I said. Valiya swiped the numbers one more time, dotted them, and then drew down her sleeves. I was glad to see her hide them; the numbers disturbed me even more than the mirrors in her eyes. I put a hand on the bird's carcass and Valiya threw a switch.

Phos hummed to life and flowed through the copper pipes. The icy body warmed suddenly, then twitched, spindly legs kicking against the restraints. The smell of wet feathers and phos filled the room, and I felt something flowing out of me and into me at once. A channel, opening.

I saw another place, a vision overlying the room. A hot place, hotter than any man could withstand. A crack in the earth, deep and sheltered, lit by rivulets of glowing orange magma that leaked down the walls or lay in pools on the jagged black rock. Choking smoke filled the air, sulphuric and toxic. I could not see Crowfoot, but I felt him there, his presence vast but at the same time diminished. Hollow.

'Galharrow ...' Crowfoot's voice was a black whisper within the illusion. 'Where have you been, Galharrow?'

There was pain in his voice, the ache so heavy and deep set that I knew it resonated through his entire immortal being. Despite the anger, despite my deep resentment over all he had made me do, how he had used me, I felt his pain. Pain greater than any that I'd known, more than a living man was capable of. The bitter agony of defeat, defeat that came after a thousand long years of toil and strife. The abyss of his shattered pride fell deeper than the cavern into which he had fled.

'My lord,' I said. I was aware of Valiya, aware of the heating bird carcass beneath my fingers. 'Captain Amaira is in trouble. I need to find her. Where is she?'

I had ignored his question. His fury should have shaken my body inside out, but there was so little left to him. Everything that Crowfoot possessed was invested in his foothold in reality, in holding what remained of him together. He was fallen, a broken thing that had once been mightier than the stars. I should not have, but I pitied him.

'Amaira and Vasilov must be protected,' he whispered into my mind. 'I sent them to the place of power where the Nameless fought the Deep Kings. But I am blind. I do not see them. The world is shadowed. I cannot afford to expend power on anything but my existence.'

I remembered that lonely place. Crowfoot's simulacrum

had shown him to me, sitting frozen solid with Nall and Shallowgrave when they gathered to work their magic against the Deep Kings.

'They are gathering my weapon,' Crowfoot's voice came soft. 'They must not fail.'

'I won't let them, lord,' I said.

'If they fail, we have nothing to use against the Deep Kings,' he muttered. 'Find them, and bring back my weapon. Take the Duskland Gate to the top of the world.'

The bird beneath my hand was hot, and I was distantly aware of the smell of charring bone. The second world wavered, and I blinked as though the clouds of toxic smoke stung my eyes.

'The Duskland Gate,' I said. 'It's too dangerous.'

'There is no other way,' Crowfoot said. 'And Galharrow.' I was sure that he was about to tell me not to fuck it up, but instead he gave me a far more chilling command. 'Do not trust the Nameless.'

With a whoosh of flame, he disappeared, and I snatched my hand back from the burning raven's body. Crowfoot was gone.

Valiya had questions, but I needed a minute. I sat in a chair and breathed slowly. I had known the Nameless' battle had cost them all, but I had not imagined the damage had been so great. A wizard's power is like a basin, slowly filling from a dripping tap, the magic building drop by drop over decades. They relinquished it only in the greatest of need, never carelessly. It accumulated too slowly for reckless expenditure. At the height of his power Crowfoot had crafted the Heart of the Void and broken the world. But now he was *empty*. Less than empty. He clung to his existence by threads of will alone. He possessed less power than I did.

It was like learning that your father isn't the terrifying brute that you'd feared through your childhood, seeing him for the first time as a broken old man, wasted by age and fed with a spoon. I had hidden from him for years and seeing him firsthand, so shrunken, was hard.

'It worked, then,' Valiya said solemnly. 'What did you see?'

'I know where Amaira is,' I said. I would not share the truth of my master's condition, not even with her. 'Captain Vasilov is with her. That's good. He's a Spinner. One of the best. But fuck me, they're far. I'm going to need some things if I'm to get her.'

'How many men do you need?'

'As many as you can spare. But they need to be tough. Men who aren't easily surprised, and who won't run when things get strange. The journey is going to be fast, and it's going to be bad.'

Valiya nodded once, the amber glow of my eyes reflected back from the mirror-steel shine in hers.

'You'll have them,' she said.

'I need to ask something of you.'

I had found Giralt in the kitchen while Tnota was taking a nap. The stove hummed softly, warming a pan of water for tea. He stirred the leaves suspiciously. It was the first time we'd spoken since Valiya spirited me out of the cells.

'Say your piece,' he said. 'But I'm making no promises.'

'I need you to stop asking Tnota to abandon me,' I said.

Giralt looked down into the tea, as if looking for something in the brown water. He was a gentle man: calm, steady, but strong. Just the kind of man that Tnota needed.

'I can't do that,' he said. 'As long as he's caught up following you around, he'll run into trouble again and again. You might want him—'

'I know,' I said. 'I agree. He's too old for this work, and he's a hindrance to me. He wants to help, but he can only slow me down.'

Giralt eyed me with suspicion.

'Then why do you want him with you?'

'I don't,' I said. 'But as long as you're telling him it's a choice between you and me, he's going to choose me.'

Giralt threw the wooden spoon down into the pan and turned his back on me, putting his stare into the fire. His shoulders worked up and down. There was a lot he wanted to say. He'd probably rehearsed this conversation over and over during my long periods of absence.

'I know,' he said. 'And it kills me.' He turned around and showed me the tears in his eyes. 'You're taking him from me. He's yours, and I can't win. Whatever we have, whatever we build, you're always there between us.'

And there it was. Whenever I doubted my course, when I hung my head at the things that I'd done, the things I knew I would have to do, it all came back to this. The love that a person holds for another. It's what we live for, what we fight for, and when fate calls to us, what we're prepared to die for. It wasn't my love. It was theirs. But it was worth fighting for just as strong.

I shook my head.

'You've got it all wrong,' I said. 'What Tnota and I have is history. We've shared things that nobody else on this earth has ever seen. I walked beside him for a thousand Misery miles, and every step of my survival was down to him. He walked into every kind of hell you can imagine with me, and I kept the Misery's worst from destroying him. We're blood-bound and spirits know, there's so much love in me for the man that it tears my soul to lose him. But you need to understand the truth. Tnota loves you. It's a different kind of love. Stronger. Better. But the more you tell him to make a choice, the more he's going to choose me.'

'He shouldn't,' Giralt said angrily.

'You aren't giving him a true choice,' I said. 'I see the way you look at each other. Whatever we went through together, what you've built in a few years goes deeper than everything he and I did in over twenty. And because of that, he knows that you'll follow him. You'll wait for him. You'll be here if, or when, he comes back to you. Because you need him, and I don't. As long as you tell him not to choose me, he can have us both.'

Giralt wiped his eyes.

'Do you want me to say that I'm grateful?'

'No,' I said. 'I don't need your forgiveness. I just need you to get your things ready, and prepare to leave the Range tomorrow. Forever. You have the Misery diamond money. Use it and change your story. He'll follow you.'

'And if he doesn't?' Giralt demanded.

'I've walked a thousand miles with him. I know which way his feet turn. Let him make the decision for himself.'

The world was truly broken if I was giving relationship advice. I left him alone then, hoping that I was right, and not sure that I was. But it was all I could do for him.

Choices are made and unmade, and the wheels of life drive us forwards towards an ending that will never be of our making. I hoped that whatever the future held for Tnota, I had steered his dotage towards something more worthwhile than where I was going.

I sat alone on the roof terrace, the wooden boards still slick and pungent with the rain. Somewhere nearby I could hear somebody raving, an unfortunate who for some awful reason had not managed to find shelter before the downpour struck. He cried out about betrayal, about having his heart torn out.

I was dying. As much as my body had changed down in the white cells, regenerating and renewing itself into something of its former warrior-glory, I knew that I was breaking down. The cough was worse than ever, but it went far beyond that. It wasn't the Misery that was killing me, it was its absence. Feeling it soak up into me from the earth,

142

the wind. All that I had consumed lingered within me, volatile and questing through veins and marrow. But like an addict, I'd grown accustomed to getting my fix. I wanted more. Needed to bask in it. I knew, sure as the moons would cross the sky, that I did not belong here, and without the Misery refilling me I would dissolve away into nothing. A slow death, driven by a lack of poison.

I had stood on a Valengrad roof much like this one and watched Ezabeth spin the light, a decade ago now. It was all so long ago. The big events of our lives, the ones that define us, stay to haunt us long after the facts have ceased to be remembered. She'd been incredible, spinning the moons without loom or goggles, using nothing but her own mastery. I'd loved her then, as I'd always loved her, but I'd seen her anew. I'd known, maybe, that she was something else. She was out there still; I had to believe that. But what was she now, after so long in the light, ten years away from our flesh-and-blood world? I knew in my heart that she was no longer the Ezabeth I'd dreamed of, the carefree summer girl who'd catapulted me from boyhood into manhood, any more than I was the youth that had wanted to show her how well I rode a horse. But she was still something, whatever that something was. I was changed, riddled with the black taint of the Misery. Tnota was changed, his arm lost to a matchlock shot and a surgeon's mercy. Valiya was changed, to whatever it was Nall had needed her to be. And Ezabeth was little more than a rare whisper in the light and the memory of a once-lofty ideal. None of us get to be what we wanted. We are, in the end, what the world makes of us. It would have to be enough.

'Tnota is packing his things,' Valiya said. I had not heard her join me. 'He'll leave in the morning.'

'Good,' I said.

'I like it up here,' she said. The city's lights danced in her mirror eyes, the reds, blues, and greens twisting as she scanned the rooftops. The three moons had drawn close together, almost aligned. They'd been circling closer and closer in recent days, forming lines in the sky. 'From above, it looks peaceful, doesn't it?'

I didn't know what to say to her, so I didn't say anything. She came and sat in a chair beside me. Not close enough to touch, but close enough to scent the jasmine that still trailed her. I found I couldn't bear to look out anymore, and my gaze drifted down to the stones. It had been easy out in the Misery. There was nobody to speak to except the ghosts, and when you know that they hold nothing but your regrets, they grow easy to ignore. Valiya was a different kind of ghost. She still resembled the woman that she had been, save that her hair had turned grey, her eyes to steel. There had always been steel in her, though.

'The moons are drawing towards one another,' Valiya said. 'There will be a triple eclipse before long, all three of them, lined up in front of the sun. It only happens once every nine hundred and eighty-two years. We'll get to see it.'

'Doubt we'll see much of anything with the moons blocking out the sun.'

'The moons are just spheres of crystal,' Valiya said. 'The light will pass right through them all. It should be spectacular.'

'I've seen enough odd shit for one lifetime,' I grunted.

'You're angry with me,' Valiya said.

'No. I'm not.'

'You haven't changed as much as you think,' she said. 'You're angry. You don't like what I've done.'

'There's a difference between being angry, and not liking an outcome.'

'I've done a lot of good while you've been away, Ryhalt,' she said. 'I understood why you had to go. Why you had to do what you've done to yourself. But the war didn't end because you went off on a personal crusade.'

'It's not my war,' I said. 'It was never my war. I just have to fight it.'

'But it was mine,' she said. 'Perhaps that was the difference between us.'

'No,' I said. 'That wasn't the difference. Do you really want me to go into it?'

'You're free to think that it was whatever you thought it was,' Valiya said. 'I don't need a man to tell me who I am. We each chose our paths.'

'You're right,' I said. 'If nothing else, we did that.'

We sat and watched the city lights as they winked out or flared into life.

'You want to ask me something,' Valiya said eventually.

'I do?'

'I worked it out. I shouldn't have, but I wanted to know. Why you left. What you're going to attempt.' Her sleeves were drawn down, but I could guess what she meant. I wondered how long that kind of calculation would have taken, or how anyone could have attempted it. The answer was right before me. Valiya would work on something for as long as it needed to be worked upon, and difficulty had never deterred her.

'Fine,' I said. 'Why didn't you come after me?'

Valiya frowned and drew back her sleeve. She played with the numbers, the graphs and charts as they flickered and rolled over her skin. She became engrossed, pushing things aside, bringing in new variables. Eventually she swiped her palm across it all and drew her sleeve back down.

'That's not what I expected,' she said. 'You know why.'

'Do I?'

'Yes,' she said. 'You do. Ezabeth.' The name hung heavy between us in the night. As it always had. 'You were meant to ask me why I dealt with Nall,' she said.

'I can guess why you made your deal,' I said. 'You wanted to fight harder. You wanted to protect the Range. You wanted to be more efficient. I've been away a long time, but I didn't forget who you are, Valiya. Even if you did.'

It was awkward. Painfully awkward, but only for me. Valiya's face remained impassive, calm and serene. I'd barely seen it crease since we'd been reunited. She moved on from hurtful words as though they were nothing but reflections in her mirror-bright eyes.

'I've found a mercenary troop with the right reputation, willing to take good pay without details. They'll be ready to travel tomorrow.'

'And you can get me out of the city?'

'That was never hard.'

'Good. Things are too hot here. Davandein won't stop looking for me, nor will whoever tried to kill me at Fortunetown. It doesn't matter. I can make it work, one way or another, as long as I'm not in the white cells.' I looked at Valiya, maybe hoping to see some of the damage in my own heart reflected back at me. 'There's something that you want to ask me too.'

'No,' she said. 'I know all that I need to.'

'No,' I disagreed. 'You want to know why I didn't come back. Why I was willing to give up everything.'

Valiya smiled, the warmth hitting her face for the first time. Her eyes caught the red letters of the citadel, and for a moment the word COURAGE hung there.

'I've met you, Ryhalt. How can you ever imagine that I wouldn't understand?'

15

'I don't want things to end this way,' Tnota said. He packed the last of the things he'd brought from Fortunetown into a satchel and put it neatly on the table. It wasn't even full. We imagine that in our old age there'll be a big house stuffed with the sentimental litter of our lives, the relics of a well-lived life, but even those don't have so much value, and even when your body is old you don't feel any different than you did when you were young. Wiser, maybe. More cautious, perhaps. But no different where it counts.

'I know,' I said. 'But it's right.'

'Do you remember what I said to you, the day we met?' he asked.

'You said, "Oi, you, heavy fucker, that's my beer."'

'I did,' Tnota grinned. 'And then I promised I'd never guide you a step wrong in the Misery. And I never did.'

'You never did,' I agreed. 'The best navigator in the states. I couldn't have asked for a better man to ride beside me, Tnota. We did some good for people, and you always rose to the task.'

'I'll ride with you some of the way.' He produced a bottle from under his jacket. 'One last drink for the road?'

'I can't,' I said. Awkward. We'd done our share of drinking together over the years, and I needed a clear head today. 'I've never been good at saying good-bye. Don't delay it any longer than we have to.'

We embraced. One last time. Tnota had been a fixture in my life for so long. A steady, stable voice of caution and wisdom no matter what mad risks Nenn wanted to take, and no matter what I tried to persuade him to do. But I couldn't hold on to that mooring post now the storm had blown in. The ships that cling to the dock are the ones that get wrecked and I chose to rise alone on the waves or fall beneath them. I had grown used to my solitude. Ezabeth gone, Nenn gone, and now I cut away the last of them. A final cut to thicken the scar.

'You'll make it,' he said quietly. 'You never let me down either.'

Valiya had readied horses for us, and I mounted up and followed her out into dark and silent streets. I looked back only once, and saw Tnota and Giralt together, watching us ride away. Tnota raised his arm and waved, and I nodded back to him.

I hoped that Tnota and Giralt would find some quiet cottage somewhere where the air was clean and the beer was good. I hoped they would live another thirty years together, their love would grow, and that as the days passed the Misery, the Range, the kidnaps and the Darlings and the cracked and howling sky all passed with them until they seemed little more than a bad dream, seldom remembered.

'Are you alright?' Valiya asked.

'Let's get going,' I said.

'Need a light, mister?' a glimjack yawned a couple of streets on. A kid no more than ten held an unlit lantern, ready to guide late-night travellers for a handful of copper. A dangerous vocation, and those kids were as likely to lead you down an alley full of thugs as they were safely to your door. I threw him a half-mark but turned him down all the same. We knew the way. This had been my city, once.

The mercenaries were meeting us at the Duskland Gate with the supplies that Valiya had arranged. We left

148

Valengrad through the tunnel I'd taken in, back when Saravor controlled the city and Davandein had been approaching with her army. Mostly we travelled in silence.

We passed by Narheim, Crowfoot's old mansion. It had collapsed in on itself when Crowfall struck, burying the vault that lay beneath it. Nobody had tried to scavenge the stone, though the marble gleamed rich and pale under a blue moon. Narheim had always felt wrong, and I doubted anybody had been sad to see it go.

'We need to take a detour on the way,' I said.

About a half mile on from Narheim a stone marker read LENNISGRAD: 150 MILES. I couldn't speak to the accuracy of that, but ten paces from the marker a nondescript track led away into scrubland. Dawn was lightening the horizon. The trail forked down towards some poor farmsteads, but we followed the higher track into woodland instead.

'Paying somebody a visit?'

'No. Retrieving something,' I said.

A great dead tree stood alongside the trail. From there I looked for the stump of an ancient oak, and from there to a wide, flat stone. I tipped it over, exposing a disorderly regiment of things that crawled and wormed their way through the dark. I flicked them away with my boot, knelt down in the damp earth, and began to dig.

'If this turns out to be a bottle of Whitelande brandy then I won't be impressed,' Valiya said. An attempt at levity in the cold.

I shifted earth, shovelling with my hands. Part of me feared that my buried treasure would be gone, but there was no reason anyone would come out here, no reason that anyone would dig up the ground. My fingers scraped a hard, flat surface and not long after I had the lid of the box clear. I hadn't locked it; if anyone had found it, they'd be curious enough to smash the lid open. Inside were a few oddments, precious things I'd stashed before beginning my exile in the

Misery. As I opened the box I found a smile. I picked up a miniature painting, held it up to the half-light.

The artist had captured us well. Nenn, Tnota, and I standing side by side, expressionless. Nenn had commissioned it when she felt her newfound position pulling her away from us, and she'd refused to wear her uniform that day. In some ways the mercenary life had been foisted upon her, but that didn't mean she hadn't been well suited to it. Tnota had tried to dress up for the picture, but he couldn't pull off the finery.

I hadn't come for the memories. I'd left some money – I tossed it to Valiya without opening the purse and rummaged around until I found what I needed. Wrapped in a red velvet rag, a pocket watch. I held it up to the rising light and read the inscription across the back:

Better than you deserve! Gleck.

'We came here for sentiment? Because this could have waited until Amaira was safe,' Valiya said, eyeing the timepiece. It had been a gift, a long, long time ago. I couldn't help but regret what I had to do next.

'Not sentiment,' I said. 'You have your communicator. I have mine.'

I brought the pocket watch down against the flat rock, smashing it completely. I bashed it again a couple of times, made sure it was well and truly ruined. Couldn't help but feel a twinge of regret.

'Why did you do that?'

'Breaking it sends a message to Maldon. Dantry too, assuming they're still together. Tells them to come find me.'

'You think it's time to bring them back?'

'We don't have much choice. It's coming to a head now, whether Dantry's research has taught him what he needs to know or not.'

'The triple eclipse,' Valiya said. 'That's what you mean?'

'That's what I mean,' I said.

I left everything else in the box and buried it again, hid it beneath the stone. Probably wouldn't come back for it, but you never knew. I left the miniature painting behind. One day it would be the only thing that still connected Nenn, Tnota, and me, and its survival seemed important.

The next village we came to was Nejska, where they were well used to dishevelled soldiers passing through. Farm labourers were heading out to the fields with scythes, sickles, and baskets across their shoulders. It was harvest time, then: seasons had meant little to me in the Misery where everything is red, and dust, and inconstant. The labourers were few. Nejska made her living from passing merchants, free companies, soldiers, performers, and anyone else trailing to or from Valengrad. Every other building was an inn, with gaudy bright phos lighting forming elaborate shapes around their trade signs even in the day.

'While you're gone I'll learn more about the man who attacked you in Fortunetown,' Valiya told me. 'I'll speak with Klaunus. He might be able to help.'

'Klaunus is no help to anyone these days. Not even himself, even if he is Blackwing. His spirit's broken,' I said. 'The kindest thing anyone could do for him is put a bullet in his head.'

Valiya's lips tightened. 'There are too many forces at work against you, Ryhalt. Josaf's and Linette's deaths tell me you're all at risk. Klaunus may find that bullet if we don't work down to the bottom of this.'

'Someone set that bastard against me at Fortunetown, that's for sure,' I agreed. 'Klaunus can look after himself. He's holed up tight in his tower, but look out for him, if you can. He's not always been a good man, but we're low on allies. I'd rather not lose any more.'

'The citadel isn't going to forget you that quickly,' she

said. 'After you find Amaira, it won't be safe for you to come back. You know that, don't you?'

'Nowhere is ever safe,' I said. I looked over at her, but she stared ahead with those blank, silver eyes. 'I will find her,' I said. 'I'll bring her home. You know I will.'

'I love that girl,' she said. 'Don't fail her. Don't fail me.'

Country miles passed beneath us. As the hooves clopped through stunted wheat and flatlands of tufted grass I regretted each one.

Torsk was a nothing kind of place. I didn't know anybody that lived there, and they probably had no interest in knowing us. They were timber cutters mostly, although the woodland they harvested made for poor lumber. We didn't enter the village, cutting across a field instead and into the trees along an overgrown path. The thump of axes and the grating of saws sounded distantly. We rode nearly a half hour into the woodland, crossing deer trails as we followed a stream. The trail steepened as we entered the hills, then dipped down into a valley.

Valiya's hired, subtle men were waiting for us, cold and damp with morning dew. They had the look of professionals, already kitted out in light armour and leather, matchlocks stacked in pyramids beside campfires. The supplies that I needed, thick bundles of heavy winter furs, were stowed tight and roped to pack animals. Tents had already been collapsed. Beyond the mercenaries, flanked by rising walls of rock on three sides, lay the Duskland Gate. We went to speak with Sang, who'd led the twenty men out here the day before. She was chatting with the mercenary commander, a heavy man with small eyes and a confident posture.

'Can't say I understand what we're doing out here,' he said. 'You look like you've dipped the Misery once too often.' He didn't seem perturbed by my appearance. He'd seen stranger, if he'd been soldiering long on the Range.

'You all need to follow whatever Galharrow says, exactly

152

as he tells you to do it,' Valiya told him. 'The fee is already with your banking house.'

'The usual payment for any losses suffered?' he asked. Valiya nodded curtly.

'We'll be ready to go in an hour. Just need to get the last of the kit stowed on the beasts.'

I left Sang and the commander to make their final preparations and walked with Valiya to the wide, circular stone below the walls of rock. I could feel the change in the air. Colder. The grass whispered, but there was no wind in the shelter of the hillside.

The Duskland Gate. I'd hoped never to set foot on it again. I'd used it only once before, long ago, before I was Blackwing and the memory had never left me, though I'd tried to drink it away. It was efficient, but only a madman would take this road if the need wasn't desperate. Amaira was trapped. Crowfoot was depleted. My need was desperate enough.

Four humps of earth, each taller than me, were covered with grass and arrayed around a broad stone platform that no plant would approach, flat and smooth except for the carved design that spiralled from the outer edge to the centre in a continuous whirl. I knelt down and traced the tiny pictures that formed the spiral.

'Birds,' Valiya said wearily. 'I'm so sick of birds.' I nodded. 'What are the mounds?'

'Graves, I think,' I said. 'Old graves.'

'Graves above ground?'

'I guess so.'

'So you make the payment and then just ... stand here? That sounds easy enough.' She drew back her sleeve and started to calculate how it worked. I took her by the arm, covering the numbers and diagrams that had started to flow together.

'It won't be easy. It will be awful. Worse than the white

cells. Worse than the Misery. There are some things you don't need to know.'

Valiya was thirsty for the knowledge. I felt a tingling beneath my palm, the magic that inhabited her body itching against the Misery's touch. The taint in me repelled other magic. It did not want to share. Reluctantly Valiya nodded. Alcohol had always been my addiction, but hers was knowledge.

'Be careful, Ryhalt,' she said. 'Bring her back.'

She reached out and laid a hand over the top of mine. I was tired, and the Misery was burning a path through my body, and I didn't want to face the Duskland Gate. That gentle touch dragged at imagined conversations, things that I'd played through my mind a thousand times. I swallowed them down. It makes no sense to tell a woman that you love her and regret your choices when you're still crushed beneath the weight of obligation to another.

'I'll bring her back,' I promised.

There was a disturbance in the camp. The mercenaries stared towards the tree line where a bright light had appeared, small but intense, moving fast. And then I saw it: a snaking rope of phos, sparking blue and gold as it swam through the air.

'They've found us.'

The light was making a line straight for me. It crossed the hundred yards of meadow at pace, blasted aside a trio of stacked matchlocks as it hissed and writhed along the valley.

'It's Kanalina,' Valiya said.

Beyond the rope of light, horsemen cantered out of the trees, a dozen of them in the uniforms of Urban Security men with the Spinner at their head. But running alongside them, black-robed and ice-white-skinned, the giant who'd battered me into pieces kept easy pace.

The phos rope arced towards me, but I'd met this magic once before and I knew it wasn't the threat that it seemed. I raised a hand, felt for the Misery-taint inside me, and pushed out towards it. It was a powerful working, and Kanalina was strong as a Spinner to craft it to find me, but it was nothing compared to the magic that linked me to the whole damn Misery. The light squealed, flexed back on itself with a snap, and disappeared in a sheet-lightning flash. Kanalina fell from her saddle.

'Form up,' I shouted, but the mercenaries were already moving, grabbing their weapons. They didn't know these men, even if they recognised their uniforms, but it was First that commanded their attention. He didn't slow his pace: he charged directly at them.

A mercenary lowered a bayonet in First's direction, but the massive warrior tore the matchlock from her hands and backhanded her away. She flew through the air to break against a boulder. The mercenaries were hardened warriors and the bonds between fighters grow tight. They drew steel and rushed towards the threat. First wasn't slowed, and his fist smashed a man from his feet, breastplate crumpled. He checked a sabre blow with his forearm, which bit into the milky flesh but drew no blood, grabbed the assailant, and tore his head from his shoulders as easily as if he were wringing a bird's neck. Blood splashed over his face and a long tongue snaked out to taste it.

The Marble Guard.

'Shit,' I swore. First sent another two men flying with a sweep of his huge arm. Matchlocks cracked but he didn't slow, looming through the smoke like a creature of legend. Which I guess he was.

The mercenaries were screaming and swinging their swords, fighting and dying and doing little to slow First's approach, but another figure had broken free of the trees. A small man, dark-haired and hunched low over his horse's neck. He charged straight towards us. I drew the pistol from my belt, pointed it at him, and thumbed back the hammer, but he passed First who had been tackled by three men with poleaxes, and came right at us. He leapt down from the saddle without slowing, and I knew him.

He was a Blackwing captain.

'Silpur?'

'Time to go,' he said. Five foot five, slim and hard-faced, he had an ageless quality about him. Despite the urgency of our situation he had a quiet voice, like the lapping of waves on a shore. He was bronze skinned, with eyes greener than spring, and dressed black as a mole. His age was hard to judge, but his appearance said early twenties. He had looked that way for the last thirty years.

'Onto the stone.'

'Help me take that thing down,' I said.

'Time to go,' he said again in his quiet voice. 'First too strong. Better to run.'

I would have argued, but the mercenaries were getting thinned out fast, and the cavalry behind them had started to approach too. They came on nervously, not wanting to get caught up in the fighting, and they didn't need to. I could already see that First was going to win. One of the mercenaries ditched his axe and tried to run but the giant tackled him to the ground. Big fists rose up and then slammed down. Bloodlust was getting the better of the huge creature, and First swung his teeth down into his victim's exposed neck.

'Ryhalt, you have to go,' Valiya said, inhuman eyes stricken.

Staying here was no option. And with First on a rampage, I couldn't leave her behind.

I ran for the nearest pack mule, dragged it over onto the platform. It heaved back on the reins, sensing the wrongness of the place, but we needed it. Silpur brought his horse with us. For all his urgency he looked unconcerned.

'You've done this before?' I asked.

'Lots of times.'

'I have to stay,' Valiya said, 'I can reason with them ...'

I took her around the waist and dragged her with me. She feared the stone, rightly. She'd done her research on the Duskland Gate, and knew what awaited us.

'Put me down!' she protested.

'No,' I said. 'Whatever you do, don't get off the stone.' I dragged her down beside me and put my arms around her, still clutching the reins.

Without a hint of preamble Silpur drew his sword and put it halfway through his horse's neck. The stallion flailed its hooves, but only briefly. Silpur knew his work well and it crashed down, blood spraying the stones and flowing across the ancient carvings. He sheathed the blade and stood motionless, not a hint of emotion showing. Two of the mercenaries ran towards us. There were only five or six left and these two had given up the fight. First bounded after them, blood streaking his face as Kanalina, mounted again, yelled at him. He caught the runners, slammed them together in a meeting of shattering bones, and turned towards us. The mercenary commander had bolted from the fight, running for us now, as though we could protect him any better than his men had.

A flock of starlings wheeled through the ruddy sky above, arcing in their looping, impossible formation. They came down on the burial mounds in their hundreds as the mercenary commander made it panting onto the stone. The starlings' eyes winked redly.

Valiya was shaking.

'Whatever you do,' I repeated, 'don't get off the stone.'

Scared isn't the right word for how I felt. I'd done this before and I felt the fear rising through me, even more afraid than Valiya. I gripped her hard.

There are theories about what the Nameless are. They aren't sorcerers, not like the Spinners, the Mutes, the distant Dryja, or those other people that command magic. Ideas about the Nameless ranged from calling them gods to abominations; all I could say for certain about Crowfoot was that for some fucking reason his magic always seemed to involve birds.

As the horse's blood flowed along the carvings, the starlings rose into the air as one, and then began to swoop around the clearing. A thousand thousand fluttering wings and hard buffets of air battered us. The pack mule brayed in terror, its instincts telling it to run, but there was no direction in which any of us could bolt. I crouched lower, my arms still around Valiya.

The dark birds hurtled faster, faster, far faster than even a diving falcon should have flown. They blurred, no longer birds but streaks of blackness all coalescing together until we were surrounded on all sides by a whirling hurricane of darkness. The cacophony of birds cawing became a single abrasive note as powerful winds whipped around us, tugging at clothing. The mercenary commander screamed. Silpur stood silent.

'Close your eyes and don't listen,' I roared into Valiya's ear, though I don't know if she heard over the roaring of the birds' flight and their screeching song.

Whispers came, soft hisses, but clear across the thunder of the wings. They said black things, dark things. They knew secrets they shouldn't, and reminded us of everything we wished that we weren't.

Valiya gripped tight to me, eyes closed. Doing well.

The rushing of wings intensified, a curtain of darkness all around us, and I saw them, out there in the blackness. Lighter shapes of grey, their limbs overly long, heads distended, orbs of light in the palms of their hands, over their hearts. The Long Men of the Barrows moved within the flow of magic, trying to enter our circle of stone. They came slowly but they knew we were there. They orchestrated the whispers of the dead, indistinct things from the world beyond, or beside, or whatever hell the evil dead lurked in.

'You let them all down.' One of the whispers stood clearer than the others. I gritted my teeth.

'We died for your fucking promotion,' an old comrade whispered from the past.

'Got her killed, didn't you? Got her killed. Even her.'

'You could never stop the patchwork man.'

I pressed my face into Valiya's hair. We keep our fears and our doubts to ourselves and crush them down. The Long Men know them all.

The mercenary commander was panicked beyond restraint. I made a grab for him as he fled the circle and plunged away into oblivion. The grey figures flocked to him the moment he left the stone and then he was gone and the Long Men were back in place, slow and purposeful in their movements. The magic roared around us.

'Davan!' Valiya screamed. 'Davan, don't go out there again, don't go!' She howled it through tears but she clung to me tighter and tighter. 'Davan! Davan, stay here with me, Davan!'

'Ignore it,' I growled. 'It's not real. Ignore it.'

Valiya gripped harder, her nails digging into the back of my neck as she buried her face in my shoulder. She continued to cry out for her lost husband. Her screams took on a pained quality as though someone drove a cold iron into her back but above them I still heard the Long Men whispering that I had failed to keep my promises, failed to stop Ezabeth burning, failed to save Nenn, failed to save anybody. It was all my fault, the blood, the sorrow, the dead children staring at me with empty, soulless eyes. I hadn't been strong enough, hadn't had the guts, hadn't been sober enough to save any of them.

Silpur stood as calmly as if the terrors of death were nothing but a light summer breeze, restraining the mule easily though it must have been five times his weight. He looked content. The black rushing around us built and built, and the whispers grew deeper, seeking out every nightmare that I'd ever felt and every regret I'd ever endured. It was too much, far too much. I was worthless. Nothing had any meaning.

And then it was over, and we were somewhere else.

16

Silence.

Cold crashed into me like a stampeding buffalo, and my teeth began chattering violently as my body responded to the shock. I couldn't draw breath, lungs constricting. I felt my overworked heart do a somersault as it responded to this sudden new, painful stimulus. Had I not been so flushed from the terrors of the Long Men, the shock of it might have stopped me dead there and then.

'S-spirits,' Valiya chattered, prying her eyes open to peer over my shoulder. I held on to her as I surveyed the devastation all around us. We had emerged from the darkness into a new kind of chaos.

I'd seen this landscape before in a raven-induced vision, but not like this. Then, the horizon had been a perfectly flat, empty line in every direction, an endless plain of featureless white ice beneath an endless azure sky. A serene place of power. No longer. Beyond the smooth, flat stone platform on which we still sat, the world was chaos. Great, sharp platforms of torn and tumbled ice rose and fell at vast angles, shattered in jagged discord. Above us, huge chunks of ice hung suspended in the sky, motionless, weightless. Everything was broken. Everything was wrong.

None of that mattered. Only the cold.

Silpur twitched but otherwise seemed unfazed. The mule honked its distress, hooves pawing the ground as the expressionless captain dragged heavy moose fur coats out of the pack on its back and threw them to us. I thrust shaking hands into the sleeves as fast as my cramping, cold-bitten body would go, then wrapped Valiya in one.

'Get your arms in,' I said, pulling the hood up over her head. I had never experienced cold like this. Our breath didn't just steam in the air, it formed crystals on our lips. I had never believed such cold existed.

'You are Galharrow,' Silpur said, drawing out thick mittens and throwing them to me. He stared, overly intent, like a love-struck youth seeing his first possible dalliance.

'We've met before,' I said through chattering teeth. 'A few times.' He didn't seem to register my words, his green-eyed stare unblinking. Our past encounters had been infrequent but there were three things I always reminded myself of. First: his seeming nonchalance didn't mean he wasn't paying attention. Second: he shouldn't be treated like other people. Third: never to turn my back to him. If ever Crowfoot decided I'd outlived my usefulness, he'd send Silpur to deal with me.

'Who is that?' he asked.

'Winter,' I said. I had never trusted Silpur. He didn't need to know Valiya's true name.

'Not the woman.' He indicated a frozen body lying on the ice nearby, or at least, a tangle of frozen guts, bones, and skin that had recently been a person. Probably, anyway.

'I don't know.'

'Probably Captain Vasilov. Always was weak. Left the circle.'

The winter furs were keeping the worst of the wind from my body and head, but my hands were still like ice inside my gloves. The air hurt to breathe. The stone circle beneath us was glazed with translucent ice and the birds on this platform were different.

'It's not Vasilov,' I said. The little skin I could make out was fair, and Vasilov was Fracan. Silpur shrugged. He probably didn't remember Vasilov either. Silpur had a boyish face that might have tickled a girl's fancy, except for those big, staring, unblinking eyes. There was nothing appealing in the deadness that looked out of those.

'It's midday here,' Valiya said. We'd lost time, or maybe gained it. Time moves differently when you travel through death.

'Time to move,' Silpur said.

A powerful wind howled between the jagged thrusts of ice in the shattered place of power. The ice plain had been broken, smashed beyond the natural laws that bound us to the world. Great shards of ice had been hurled upwards, torn from the ground finding invisible, unconnected purchase on the air. Valiya looked up at the floating islands, unreadable. She shook her head, then knelt beside the tangle that had probably once been a person.

'This happened because he left the stone?'

'I'd guess so. There's a reason the boss doesn't send us through the Duskland Gate very often.' I watched Silpur walk away. Most of us didn't use the stone often, anyway. There were no normal people amongst the Blackwing captains, but he was the strangest of all.

Valiya shivered, drew her furs more tightly around her shoulders. She still shook.

'Poor Sang,' she said quietly.

'Maybe they'll take her prisoner,' I said, but it was a bleak hope. Faint words of comfort. First had gone into a blood-crazed rage. He hadn't been looking to take anyone captive. Sang's only chance would have been to hide. Maybe that would have protected her.

'Where are we?' Valiya asked, teeth clacking together. 'Spirits, Ryhalt. We won't last long out here. We have to find shelter.'

'We need to go that way.' I pointed after Silpur.

'What's that way?'

'That's where we'll find Amaira.' I struggled to find the right words. 'And something else.'

I felt it in my chest. It was the Misery, and it was Crowfoot, and some of it was me. But they were all linked together, all one now. We were part of a whole. Like called to like. The Misery-taint glowed within me, reaching for the magic that I felt in the air all around me. I reached out and pushed aside a shard of ice that hung suspended in the air. It floated away, slowed, and came to a stop a foot above the ground.

The mule's legs buckled and it collapsed onto its side, hooves scrabbling. Maybe it was the shock of the cold, or the horrors it had experienced as we passed through the Duskland Gate. Its eyes rolled madly in its head, and then it lay still, a last breath steaming from its muzzle. There was nothing that could be done for it. We rifled through the packs, picking out anything that might be of use. My feet were losing feeling, and I covered them with big moosehide slippers. I found an extra coat and put it over Valiya. She was skinny. The coat was made for a fighting man and it wasn't hard to get her into it. There was no food to carry.

Nothing for leagues around us but broken ice. I took a longsword that had been strapped to the mule's baggage. I doubted there'd be anything to use it on here in this broken, desolate place, but a tool's worth taking. Valiya bent and hefted her bundle.

'Let's get moving.'

We caught up with Silpur. He was moving fast, climbing the rising planes of ice and sliding down those that descended. Valiya struggled along beside me, taking my hand when a shelf was too high to pull herself up. The going wasn't easy, the peaks and troughs deep, as if the ice plain had been a massive dinner plate and someone had brought a vast hammer down upon it. Narrow ravines sometimes separated the planes but nothing that we couldn't step over. Footing was treacherous, the unbroken ice smooth and slick. Several times we slithered back down a platform that proved too steep and had to find another way around and our hands and feet took the worst of the cold. The rise and fall of the ice planes sheltered us from the howling wind, the smallest of mercies.

Silpur stopped at the peak of one of the rises and waited for us to join him. I pulled Valiya up the last difficult climb and we looked down into a perfect circle of flat ice, a mile wide. Millions of cracks radiated out from the epicentre, linking and blending into each other, and a pale blue light glowed upwards through them. There was a hum in the air, a static charge. A remnant of whatever had happened here. As I looked up, beyond the floating icebergs, I realised with a dark, sinking feeling, what I was seeing.

A crack in the sky.

'Fucking hells,' Valiya swore. It took a lot to make Valiya swear. This was a lot.

'He's done it again,' I said. 'Broken the world *again*.'

'No other choice,' Silpur said. He paid the crack in the sky no attention at all. Nothing seemed to faze him, not the cold, not the floating masses of ice above us, nothing. He scarcely seemed human, which was rich coming from me. He pointed towards the centre of the devastation where he'd spotted something on the ice plain. He had better eyes than mine. It was small, just a dark lump of something – but where else would we go except to the centre? I'd been into the heart of the Misery and survived it, but I struggled to remember much of what I'd seen there. Some of it had been real, and some of it hadn't, or at least I hoped not. I'd emerged with nothing but the knowledge I needed to take Saravor down and three words hacked into my arm. I didn't want to contemplate what I'd left behind.

'People have been this way,' Valiya said, her voice caught and tossed by the wind. The broken ice was scuffed and marked by their passage, floating shards of ice had been pushed aside in the making of a path, forming a corridor around us. Here and there was an actual footprint, following the same line that we had. Perhaps they were fossils of Amaira's passage, but there seemed to be too many.

I looked up at that terrible crack, through which soft white light spilled down into our reality. Three threads of equal length radiated out, perfect in their symmetry, imperfect in their existence.

Distance was hard to judge in the endless white. It took longer to reach the dark little lump than I had imagined, and every time I stepped over a crack I expected the cold blue light to scorch me, but it was a quiet, silent thing that gave no response to our passage.

In the centre of the devastation a body sat, cross-legged, wrapped in heavy cloaks, frozen solid. I put an arm around Valiya's shoulders at the sight. It was Nall – or one of his avatars, at least.

'The master's friend,' Silpur said. 'He is dead. We go on.'

'Wait,' I said through the scarf that I'd wrapped over my mouth. It had already hardened with ice. Valiya stood back as I approached and knelt before the body. I couldn't tell what she was thinking. The eyes are so important. We communicate more with them than we realise, and hers gave back nothing but reflections.

Nall's body looked similar to the avatar that had reached me in the Misery, but older, greyer, even less meat on its bones. The skin was blue-grey, hard. The heavy folds of its frozen cloak hung forwards as it hunched against the cold, but I saw inside them and icy breath caught in my throat. I pulled the fabric back to get a better look, and it cracked like glass. I felt inside, confirmed that my eyes weren't playing tricks on me.

Nall's rib cage had splayed open. There was a gaping cavity where his heart should have been.

The heart of a wizard is a terrible thing. At the height of the Siege, Crowfoot and the other Nameless had broken Shavada apart and used his magic to power the Engine. Before him, it had been Songlope, another of the Nameless murdered for their magic. I'd seen his heart deep within the Engine. Nall was broken, almost destroyed, but I had thought that he had been struck down in the silent battle of wills against the Deep Kings and The Sleeper, not destroyed by the other Nameless. I stared into the hard-frozen chest cavity.

There was likely a perfectly insane explanation. Maybe when Nall's power had been broken, his heart had burst out of his chest. Why not? What did I know of the Nameless' magic, after all?

Do not trust your master, Nall had told me.

Do not trust the Nameless, Crowfoot had said.

Back in Valengrad, sitting on the roof of Valiya's hide-away, I'd heard a man screaming that his heart had been torn out. A victim of the black rain. Nall had told me to listen to the rain. The rain that brought madness, visions, and burning pain. And something else. The rain knew what had happened here. The rain remembered.

Do not trust your master. The words had a sudden new resonance which raised hard, dark questions in my mind. I pulled the cloak back around his chest as best I could. There would be a time to share what I'd learned with Valiya – as his captain, she deserved to know – but it was not now. My feet had lost all feeling, and despite the thick mittens, my hands weren't faring much better.

'Crowfoot sat here,' Silpur said. He had no interest in Nall's body, and instead stood on a patch of ice where cracks radiated outwards in cobweb lines.

'And Shallowgrave over there,' I said, noting a similar

pattern. Three points of a triangle. Only the Lady of Waves had been absent. The Nameless had worked in concert for a mutual goal: survival. Why had the Lady been absent? They were not truly allies. They had their own goals, their own agendas. It was only in the hours of desperation that they came together – or in Nall's case, apart.

'We go down,' Silpur said. 'As they did.'

'Down?' I asked. He pointed.

One of the cracks was wider and deeper than the others, the same wavering blue light emanating from it. Pegs had been driven into the ground, and three heavy, knotted ropes trailed down into the glow. The ice around the rim was scuffed and it looked like a peg had torn free and broken a chunk of ice away with it.

'You think Amaira went down there?' Valiya asked.

Silpur didn't answer, busy testing the rope, feeling its weight. I knelt and put my hand to the faint blue light. It was warm, welcoming. As the colour flowed across my fingers I felt something in my chest loosen. The cough that had been building relented and settled back down. I looked down into the depths. The light was no more intense down there, if it was even light at all. The crack in the earth looked to fall a long, long way.

'There's something down there,' I said. 'I felt it, when I saw this place before. Something old. Older than the Nameless. Frozen for more than a thousand years.'

'What is it?'

'I don't know.' I didn't think that I wanted to. 'But it looks like Amaira and Vasilov went down there.'

'But there are three ropes,' Valiya said. 'And it looks like there were four at some point. Were they alone?' Good question.

'We must descend,' Silpur said.

'I don't know if I can,' Valiya said, looking cautiously over the edge. Valiya was amongst the most capable people that I'd ever met, but her strength was better suited to re-ordering the world than to mountaineering. The climb over the ice plates had already been hard enough, and there was no telling how deep that pit went. A young, fit man would have found it gruelling.

'If you stay up here you'll freeze,' I said. I tried one of the ropes. The iron peg had been driven firmly into the ice and it seemed strong. 'Hold on to me. I'll carry you down.'

'I may not weigh as little as you think,' Valiya said. I shook my head. Everyone thinks they're heavier than they are.

'I'm stronger than I look. And you're stronger than you know.'

The sky gave a forlorn little squeal. It wasn't the howling roar of the cracks in the Misery, but the tear here was small.

Silpur was already on his way. He slithered over the edge and disappeared, the rope going taut.

'Are you sure about this?' Valiya asked.

'Trust me. I can carry us both.'

'Will the rope take the weight? Without meaning any offence, you have to weigh more than three hundred pounds. You've more muscle on you than I've ever seen.'

It was a stupid thing to feel a spur of pride in. The Misery had altered me in the white cells, it wasn't my doing.

'We'll have to hope so. There's no other option.'

Valiya climbed onto my back and put her arms around my neck. It wasn't dignified, but I barely noticed her weight. I took off my belt, made it into a loop, and then tied it around her wrists. I didn't know how long the descent was and if her strength gave out, she could hang on it, painful though that would be. I hadn't climbed anything like this in a long time, but it was what it was. We'd not achieve anything sitting around up here, and Amaira's message was still burned in my mind. I'd have climbed down into the hells for that kid. I was glad that Silpur had gone first. We'd heard no scream from him plummeting to his death, though I doubted that he would have screamed even if his rope gave out.

'Ready?'

'I'm ready,' Valiya said in my ear.

I pulled the rope tight, slithered over the edge and we began to descend. The blue light absorbed us, insubstantial and gentle. Spirits, but I'd grown strong in the cells. My arms barely protested at their burden. My feet scuffed for purchase against the sheer ice wall as I began to walk us down, step by difficult step. Valiya clung fiercely to me, legs wrapping my waist, suspended out over the void. I moved slowly at first, making sure that each step was secure before taking the next, but there was little purchase on the ice. It wasn't entirely smooth, but I didn't put much faith in the few gritty protrusions. It was easier just to use my arms. Hand over hand, down and down. Valiya clung tight as I upped the pace, her arms locked around my neck. We were down ten feet, then twenty, more, motes of blue floating in the air like dandelion seeds.

'It's fine,' I said. 'It's not hard.' And it wasn't. I had never been this strong. Had never known that anyone could be this strong. Maybe they couldn't. It occurred to me that I was, thanks to the Misery's influence, possibly the strongest man that had ever lived. I could have done this all day.

The ice had other ideas.

There was a sharp cracking sound from above and the rope gave a lurch. Just a couple of inches, but I suddenly knew with a horrible certainty that the peg was going to break free. I should have made Valiya calculate whether it would take our combined weight. I should have gone alone first. I should have—

'Ryhalt!' Valiya cried, 'Move!'

I looked down and still couldn't see the bottom of the shaft. I swung a hand down, then the other, faster and faster and faster. A groaning sound came from above, stabbed through with the tinkling of splintering glass. Hand over hand over hand over hand over hand and my heart thundered in my chest. The groaning grew louder. Maybe it would have held Valiya alone. Maybe none of the ropes would have held me. The ice couldn't take both of us together, that was certain.

'Grab the rope,' I said, stopping. I leaned forwards so that Valiya could get her hands onto it. 'Don't let go,' I said. 'Whatever you do, hold on to it. Take your legs off me.'

'What are you doing?' she said.

'Hold on,' I said as she took her own weight on the rope and uncoupled her legs. 'I'm sorry.'

There was no time to think, to calculate. It was act now or we would both fall. The rope couldn't hold my weight, and there was still nothing but murky blueness beneath us. We would fall and be smashed apart. I couldn't allow that.

I reached inside, felt for the Misery within me, and let go.

Valiya's sudden shriek disappeared in the rush of air. I fell, and then the blue haze cleared and I saw Silpur looking up at me for two seconds of hurtling descent before I met the ground with a crash.

I should have been pulverised but the Misery roared through me. I felt her sending fire through my bones, absorbing, gripping, taking hold of the immense impact. Shards of floor-ice sprayed out around me as my body shuddered and strained with the terrible force. It screamed through me, hammered through bone and organs, vibrating in my skull and roaring in my ears. It was a vast power, and it was going to shake me apart.

I roared, and the energy released all around me. Silpur was knocked from his feet, pencil-line cracks shooting up the ice cavern's walls. The hard, black ice beneath me shattered into a mosaic of a thousand jagged pieces.

I was alive. Alive, and whole and unbroken, and for a few moments I felt the black Misery-power coursing through me. I was invincible. I had saved her. The exultation of the power flowed through me, and then, from above came a crunch, and a scream.

Valiya fell as the ice holding the peg gave way. She didn't have Misery-strength, but the magic was still awake, fierce and dark within me. I saw her shadow falling through the blue and instinct took over.

I willed strength into my legs, demanded it from the blaze of power that had awakened within me, and jumped for a spur three feet up. I kicked off it to reach another, higher, then another, hurling myself up with everything I had. Six feet up, ten, fifteen, each jump bringing me higher, higher than should have been possible. And then as she hurtled down towards me, out.

We met in midair and I grabbed her tight. I carried her across the gulf, slammed into the wall, shards of ice flying as I slid down against it, Valiya clutched against me. We hit the ground hard.

The light dimmed, all the warning that I got, and I pressed Valiya down onto the ice and covered her with my body.

A block of broken ice, torn from the lip of the crevasse, hit me with the force of a sledgehammer ... and shattered. Misery-energy writhed as it held me together, the blue-stained air around us filled with fragments of falling ice. I lay over Valiya, shaking as the magic sought to protect us from what should have been a second death in the space of ten seconds. The amber glow from my eyes blazed hotter, reflecting back at me from Valiya's mirror-shine eyes. I gritted my teeth as threads of pain slowly spread across the skin and muscle, then sucked in a huge, cold breath. I rolled from her and lay on my back, expecting the damage to break through the barrier of magic in my flesh.

It didn't come. I breathed in, and the drifting blue light entered me. Calming. Soothing. An ally.

I tried to rise and collapsed face-first onto the ice. I hadn't enough energy left to lift my arm. New threads of black split and ran wider beneath my skin. My whole body was taut and stiff as the darkness took hold and cold spurs of pain moved across it. I couldn't even muster the energy to groan.

'That was impossible,' Silpur said, picking himself up. He only looked at me, failing to consider, or care about, Valiya. 'Should be dead. Like that man.'

I focused on my neck, which was screaming that I'd fucked it beyond all endurance, and slowly, slowly managed to turn my head to look. A mangled wreck of splattered human lay beside a coiled rope. He was shattered and split open with the impact and putrid black ichor had leaked from the broken skin. No smell, not in this cold, but the rot was plain to see. My body was trembling, my mind whirled with strands of the Misery's chaos, but I'd seen those damn rotten insides before. Only one of my enemies changed men that way.

Saravor.

17

It felt like a long time before I found the strength to sit. My head rang as if an alarm bell had been trapped inside and the rest of me felt worse than if I'd run flat-out for fifty miles. The Misery's power had saved me, but it had taken from me too. My darkened hands shook as I forced myself up from the ice.

Silpur was poking about at the remains of whoever had fallen before us, but Valiya was in pain. She was shaking, and the terror of the fall hummed through her. The impact of meeting me in the air and the following crash back down to earth had hit her hard, and she clutched her shoulder. Metallic tears slithered down her cheeks, rivers of mercury. For a time I could do nothing but sit and listen.

'Where does it hurt?' I asked eventually.

'Everywhere,' she breathed, strained as she fought for breath. I tried to fight my own pain down. She was in shock. She needed me calm.

'I need you with me. Need you strong for Amaira,' I said. 'Be specific. I need to check how badly you're hurt.' There would be time for kind words and gentleness later, but I'd treated injuries before. Bleeding wounds first, broken bones second, and hope that I wouldn't find anything worse.

'I feel like I've been trampled by a cavalry regiment,' she whispered, wincing. 'My shoulder doesn't feel right.'

'I need to check to see if anything is broken,' I said. 'I'll have to put my hands on you to do it.'

'Of course,' she said. 'How are you still alive? I thought that I'd lost you.'

'Six years of Misery-poison,' I said. That's what I figured anyway. I didn't know how it worked.

'Your eyes are so bright,' she said quietly. I snapped my fingers in front of her face a few times.

'Stay with me. Don't get lost in the pain. Tell me if what I do hurts. Think of Amaira. There's no telling how long we have to reach her.'

I started with Valiya's head, then felt around her neck, but nothing was amiss. Her left shoulder had taken a great wrench and it didn't feel right.

'Hurts a lot?' I said. Valiya nodded, sinking teeth into her lower lip. I felt around some more. Dislocated. 'Your arm's come out of its socket. I can fix it, but it will hurt.' I continued my examination. Her hips had taken a wrench, probably from being swung around as we landed. I looked for Silpur. He was kneeling beside the broken body and the coil of rope abandoned beside it. We weren't the only ones betrayed by the ice. I was about to ask him to hold Valiya still for me, but the thought of him putting his hands on her didn't thrill me. 'Do you trust me?'

'I always have,' she said. 'You've done this before?'

'A few times. It happens all the time to soldiers in training. It's going to hurt, but only for a moment. The pain will lessen. Try to stay still.'

I wasn't a surgeon, but I'd tended my share of battlefield wounds. I just hoped I had enough strength and precision to do what was needed. I put my foot beneath Valiya's armpit to keep her still, then pulled on her forearm, slowly but with increasing pressure. Valiya went stiff, her eyes pressing closed. She balled her right fist, beat it on the ground. Slowly, slowly, and then there was a sliding sensation and

175

the bone found its rightful place. She gasped and opened her eyes. I'd been wrong to write those eyes off as inhuman. I could see her suffering written in them, and I hated the pain that shone there. I felt along her shoulder to make sure that everything was as it was supposed to be.

'All good now,' I said, trying to give her a smile. She tried flexing her arm, her fingers. Everything seemed to be in working order. We'd been damn lucky. Aside from increasingly yellow eyes, I'd come away without a scratch. I looked around at the shards of ice that littered the cavern floor. Together, they must have weighed as much as a horse. I shouldn't have survived the fall, or the impact after.

It was this place. I could feel the bluish essence all around me, gliding around me like fireside warmth. First had smashed me around, but we'd been in Valengrad, away from the Misery's embrace. Whatever this place was, it was similar. I was stronger here. Whatever power had smashed the ice plain, it was kin to the Misery's pollution. I was steeped in it, and that had made me stronger.

BECOME THE ANVIL.

Valiya's head seemed to be clearing, and I got her to sit up against a wall as I took proper stock of our surroundings. We were at the edge of a cavern in the ice, a frozen ceiling stretching high above. Pillars of ice, too square to be natural formations, kept it from crashing down on us. I didn't know what it was, but it was old. Very old. Sometimes you just know. The cavern extended off into a deeper, midnight-blue haze. I got up to join Silpur. The old spear wound in my leg had awakened. A tonne of ice hadn't scratched me, but that old complaint still made me limp.

'Killed these before,' he said, indicating the fallen man. His rope lay beside what was left of him. Where he'd broken open there was brown-black rot, lesions, and sores on his insides. I was glad that the cold locked back the stench. I'd smelled it too many times before.

176

'A fixed man,' I said. 'One of Saravor's puppets. You know about Saravor. I sent you a dossier on him.'

'Got it, yes,' Silpur said. 'Insides are rotten.'

'He's been fixed up by Saravor at some point in the past. I guess that the rot has spread through him. It seems we're not the only ones with an interest in finding whatever Crowfoot has down here. But Saravor should be dead. I thought the Grandspire had burned him out of existence.'

'Just a figurehead. The grey children,' Silpur said. 'Fought them once.'

'When?'

Silpur blinked for the first time since he'd charged up to us. Tried to remember.

'Shanasti was queen,' he said.

That was impossible. Shanasti had been the last queen of Dortmark some four hundred years ago. Silpur was bad at remembering things. He regularly forgot who I was, and if he was more than four centuries old then he'd also forgotten whatever he knew about conversational skills, or compassion. But since we were bathed in the blue light of mystical devastation, and I'd just survived falling eighty feet without a scratch, there didn't seem much point in bringing up any doubts I had about how long he'd been around.

'Where there was one, we'll find more,' I said. 'Saravor would hardly send one man alone out here. Wonder how they got here.'

'The Duskland Gate,' Silpur said. 'No other way.'

It was plausible. Saravor had come into possession of The Taran Codex, written by one of the Nameless, long dead. What he'd learned from it could only be guessed at. Dantry Tanza had translated some of it, and he'd refused to write down any of what he'd learned.

My longsword had survived the landing, thankfully. I had a feeling that I was going to need it. The dead man had a sword belt, but his weapon was gone. I helped Valiya up by her good arm.

'We need to get going,' she said. 'Every minute we waste here increases the chance that Amaira won't make it out of here.' She dusted shards of ice from the thick fur cloak.

'You want a weapon?' I asked, offering her my dagger.

'I have a weapon,' she said. 'You.'

I gave her a smile that I didn't feel. I looked down at the back of my hand and saw two black threads connect to one another beneath the skin. The exertion of Misery-power had furthered the spread of corruption.

'I'll take it anyway.' She tucked it into a pocket of her coat.

We started farther into the cavern. I didn't want to think about how we were going to get out of there again. When Amaira had said she was trapped, we'd only been able to guess at what she meant. Now I was beginning to understand. Ascending the ropes seemed like a very bad idea. Valiya wouldn't be able to make the climb by herself, especially not after dislocating her arm, and I didn't want to risk my weight on the rope again either. We'd have to find some other way. If there was one.

The cavern floor was perfectly smooth, too smooth to be natural. The blue incandescence gave us plenty of light to see by, and it was much warmer down here than it had been above, in the wind. For a moment I thought that I heard a voice, whispering my name, familiar but metallic, hollow. I looked around, but there was nothing there.

'Look at this.' Valiya beckoned me over to one of the pillars. The surface had been carved with rows of images, scenes depicting something that had happened long ago. I'd seen similar carvings on ancient columns in Karnun, the weathered remnants of civilisations that had collapsed in days of legend. The carvings depicted figures in profile, at work, carrying loads or dragging sleds. Some drew water, others were dressed as warriors with bundles of spears on their shoulders and primitive shields on their arms.

'They aren't human,' Valiya said. 'Look at their faces.'

'Either that, or the artist wasn't very good,' I said, but that wasn't the case. Plenty of the details were startling in their accuracy, down to the rings on the workers' fingers. The figures' eyes were overly large on noseless faces. Short, stubby horns pointed back from their brows.

'They look like drudge,' Valiya said. Maybe it was just because I had Saravor on my mind, but they reminded me of the glimpse I'd had of the grey children in their true form, revealed by Crowfoot's magic in Valengrad's sewers. 'It's a story,' she said. 'It scrolls all around the pillar. Look, they were building something.'

'We don't have time for history,' I said. 'Come on. We need to find Amaira.'

'They were building something, but then it was torn down. See here, where the buildings are being destroyed. What's this?'

In one of the carvings something huge loomed over a city, smashing down towers. Six-legged, a huge maw filled with fangs. Valiya continued around.

'The people were being destroyed. They sent envoys across the sea, to beg the help of some kind of great serpent. Six children, to beg the snake to help them. The snake and the destroyer fought.' She tried to peer higher up the column. 'I can't see any farther.'

Six children. A disturbingly familiar number. The number that had appeared when Maldon and Saravor had fought in my mind.

'It doesn't matter. It's just a myth,' I said. 'Come on.'

Silpur had already gone on ahead. At the far end of the cavern, a great doorway was framed as if with pillars and a lintel, though they were all cut from the ice.

'I don't trust Silpur,' Valiya said. 'It's like he's not all here with us.'

'I know,' I said. 'But he's utterly loyal to Crowfoot. We don't have to like him, and we can't expect any compassion from him, but his devotion isn't built solely through fear or debt like the rest of the Blackwing captains. He's a fanatic. As long as we're doing what Crowfoot needs, we can trust him.'

Carved ice warriors flanked the door, horned and round eyed, looked down on us as we passed through into a tunnel that sloped down, the walls decorated with friezes like those on the pillars. Despite the bone-deep weariness, hunger began to strike a gong in my stomach, but we had nothing to eat. I thought of all the meat on the mule and wished that I'd had the foresight to carve a few pieces to bring with us. Raw flesh wasn't appetising, but I'd consumed far worse in the Misery.

The tunnel turned sharply to the left and we lost sight of Silpur. It turned again, then again. We were spiralling downwards into the ice. The friezes were more of the same that we'd seen before but covered the walls from floor to ceiling, odd-shaped people at work, life-sized. They were gathered around pyramids, looking up at mightier figures at their peaks – gods, I supposed. The gods did not resemble the people. They were geometric shapes, clouds, fire, or other nonphysical things. The friezes showed supplicants honouring their deities, prisoners dragged to the altars, knives slicing out hearts.

'They practised soul magic,' Valiya said. 'Just like the Deep Kings. Spirit of Mercy, where are we? How old is all this?'

Silpur reappeared around the corner, a finger pressed to his lips. He drew his sword, slowly, making no sound, then beckoned for us to follow. I drew my own and went after.

The corridor opened out into another broad cavern, just

as smooth and pillared as the previous one. But there were things here, human and imperfect in the blue stillness. Three bodies lay where they'd collapsed. No sign of anything moving or living. I hurried to them, fearing what I'd find, but none of them were the right size or shape for a slim young woman hitting twenty. They were burly men, or at least, they had been before being burned to a crisp. They were blackened, turned nearly to charcoal. A pair of matchlocks lay nearby, barrels warped by heat, and there was a long burn-scar in the ice in front of them. I recognised the blast pattern.

'Vasilov's doing,' I said. Silpur nodded.

'Must have been.'

The charred bodies had to be more of Saravor's fixed men, but there wasn't enough of them left to examine to be sure. The intense heat of Vasilov's sorcery had burned them away. He was as good a Spinner as they came and I was glad he was with Amaira. I'd taught her what I could about putting a sword through a man, but a Battle Spinner of Vasilov's calibre was worth a whole battalion, until his canisters ran out. He'd not be able to spin a thing down here when they did.

'Let's move,' I said. We went faster now, ignoring the carvings in the ice, and I limped as fast as I was able to. Lost works of art didn't matter, but the one at the doorway on the far side covered the entire wall with a single vast and unmissable picture. To the left, the six-legged destroyer was wrapped in conflict with a dragon-headed serpent, six tiny children looking up from below. To the right, a vast tidal wave swept towards a city, rows of short-horned figures cowering away from their impending destruction. Their gods were numbered amongst them, geometry, fire, and clouds.

'They asked the serpent for help, and the battle sank their world,' Valiya said. Even with the urgency of finding

Amaira hot around us, she couldn't help but want to know. 'Spirits. I think that— Ryhalt. Their gods fought and lost. They all drowned. The Deep Kings ...'

I heard it again. My name, spoken in that hard, iron-tinged resonance. I blinked and looked around, feeling as though a hand had reached into my chest and clamped around my heart. There was nobody else there but Valiya and Silpur, but I felt a presence. Speaking to me, through the cracks in the world. Ezabeth. Or what was left of her. It couldn't be more than imagination. We were in a place of gods and demons, and there was no moonlight down here.

Silpur pointed up, above the gigantic snake and the beast that it fought. I couldn't make out what he was showing me at first, but then, I caught it. An innocuous little carving, almost like it had been scratched into the ice as an afterthought. A tiny bird, wheeling high above the titans. Silpur's unblinking eyes turned to us. He smiled.

'Four thousand years,' he said. 'The war continues.'

'We're not here for ancient history,' I said. 'Hurry.'

More burn-scars decorated the walls as we went down, the murals carved into the ice had melted and distorted. We found another four bodies, two of them fused together. They'd pursued Amaira and Vasilov and paid a heavy price for it.

Then, echoing along the tunnel, a sound. Tapping. We continued towards it, and the tunnel opened out again, and I gestured that Valiya should stay back and peered around the corner, looking out into a cavern almost identical to those we'd seen before. There were people ahead of us.

There were ten of them. Wrapped up in furs, they had packs of supplies and materials stacked in a ring. They were formed up in front of a hole in the ice wall, not the smooth, sculpted passageways we'd encountered but a rough, mostly circular hole, big enough to crawl into but not much more. They had firearms on their shoulders, blades and hammers

182

at their belts. One of them went unarmed, a young woman whose cranium seemed too large for the rest of her head, bald except for a ring of grey hair that became black at the nape of her neck. She had the look of the Karnari, pale, fierce, and she wore their traditional tribal charms, animal skulls and feathers, on a series of strings around her neck. A shaman. What they were doing around the hole wasn't clear, but they were fixated on it, paying no attention to anything else. None of them were moving, just staring towards it. Waiting.

Trapped.

They didn't speak. Didn't do anything. Still as statues, they had to be more of Saravor's fixed creatures. There were a lot of them. More than Silpur and I would be able to deal with.

'Ryhalt, look,' Valiya whispered. 'What's that in the ice?'

It couldn't be seen clearly. A vast, dark shadow, deep behind the translucent, icy wall. I knew what it was. I'd felt its presence once, that first time Crowfoot showed me the place of power. I'd seen it carved in the ice halls above us, seen its downfall as it fought the Earth Serpent. Just a shadow, but here it lay, sealed away for thousands of years where it had fallen. The destroyer of worlds, an ice fiend, dead for millennia and yet still its power echoed through the chambers, casting the blue light. A primeval, ancient thing of immeasurable power, a beast from a forgotten world. The shadow we could make out could only be a tiny part of it.

On the other side of the cavern, there was a crack in the ceiling. Three arms of equal length, perfect in their symmetry, imperfect in their existence. An exact mirror to the tear in the sky, far above. The damage had penetrated the ice. A beam of gentler white light within the blue descended to the icy floor where it met another crack, an exact mirror of that above it. And in that light, a figure.

'Do you see her?' I whispered. My heart wanted to shatter within my chest.

'I don't see anybody,' Valiya said.

It was Ezabeth, and it was not Ezabeth. She had the same stature, small and slight, and her face bore the scars that had made her. But she was changed. There was a hardness to her, her eyes blank and white, her upright posture no longer the determined set of a woman of purpose, but something colder. Ezabeth had never lacked for confidence, but she hadn't been arrogant. I'd seen such arrogance only in a handful of immortals.

Her hair was fire, a bright cascade flickering across her shoulders.

'Ryhalt,' she said, though her lips did not move. She looked squarely at me. My knees wanted to buckle. The force of the word was greater than the impact of falling down the shaft and the Misery-taint in me swarmed like a cloud of hornets.

'What are you seeing?' Valiya asked.

'You are the Ryhalt that I remember,' Ezabeth's voice echoed in my mind, and I felt her words flowing to me on a wave of the broken world's magic. The tear brought all worlds closer together.

'Is it really you?' I asked.

'What is and what is not is undecided,' the voice said. 'I have been waiting for you.'

'Ezabeth,' I said, and it emerged as a moan. The burning figure's head rotated slightly.

'I am nobody,' she said. 'But I remember that name.'

I shivered.

'You are Ezabeth Tanza,' I said.

'Something of me was. A long time ago. But she is gone. She told me to wait for you. But I have been a long time in the light. Much of what I was is lost to me. But I remember you.'

184

I closed my eyes, not wanting to see her. Not wanting to hear the awful things that she was saying. Things that I'd felt as she slipped further and further away from me and into the light. As she diminished over the years, fading further and further from memory.

'I promised I would save her,' I said.

'I do not remember,' the apparition spoke silently into my mind. 'The night is dark. The time draws near. The darkness grows greater every day. I am gone, but I am still here. You must know the truth of what happened here.'

'Tell me,' I said.

'I do not remember,' she said. 'But the sky remembers. Ask the sky what happened to me.'

'It can't all be for nothing,' I growled. 'Everything I've done. Everything I've become. Years of planning. It can't all be for nothing.'

'What is real and what is not real is undecided,' she said again. 'I am weary. The part of me that remembers is glad to have seen you again.'

'Ezabeth ...'

The figure shimmered in its silent fire. It stood looking at me without emotion, without care. Nall's words came back to me. *You understand that humanity is the key, don't you?* But there was no humanity left. Ezabeth had burned herself from one existence into another, and it had claimed her. Ten years in the light, burning in the fire. She wasn't my Ezabeth anymore. But then, we were all changed, and I was hardly the man that she had loved, however briefly, in those frantic, bloody days of the Siege.

She stood still, bathed in the light of the crack above. The crack that mirrored the new tear that Crowfoot had put in the sky.

'Ryhalt,' a voice said, and this time it was a real woman's voice. Valiya. I shook my head and felt something break away. A connection from one world to the next. Ezabeth

185

remained, but she was no longer looking at me, only towards the shadow in the ice.

'Are you alright?' Valiya placed a hand on my arm, but I shook it off. I wasn't alright. I didn't think that I'd ever be alright again.

'They're moving,' Silpur said.

18

'You kill two,' Silpur said. And then he padded away silently into the cavern, moving swiftly to one of the vast carved pillars, a curved sword in each hand. I didn't have time to drag him back, to plan. He wouldn't have cared if I'd tried.

'You can't fight that many,' Valiya said.

'I survived falling down that shaft,' I said. But the weariness had set in deep and I could still feel the Misery-taint thrumming through me.

'You're in no state to fight,' she said. She drew back her sleeve. She'd plotted tables and graphs, and an anatomical drawing of a man right out of a university textbook sat proud amongst them. 'You're barely able to stand.'

'Amaira's cornered in there,' I said. 'I don't have a choice.'

I closed my eyes for a moment, feeling for the drifting energy in the air. I tried to breathe it in, to get back something of what the Misery had taken from me when it saved me. Focused on my bad leg, asked it to remember how to work properly.

Two of the fixed men had primed their matchlocks, trails of smoke drifting upwards in the still air. They approached the hole cautiously. The shaman stood well back from it all, her bulbous head looking too heavy for her slender neck. She had to be the leader. I didn't know much about the Karnari witch-shaman. I'd only spent a little time amongst them, and they were savages who preferred to stick to their traditions over accepting civilisation. They still ate their own dead. She would be dangerous, though. The men with the primed weapons looked inside the hole, then one of them hunkered down and began to crawl inside. He disappeared into the darkness, a red trail in his wake as he bled from the eyes.

The tunnel lit up with a bang as something detonated. The fixed man tumbled out making animal sounds. His clothes and hair smoked and his face was red and burned, but he picked himself up. I could smell the phos in the air, but that blast had been feeble by any Spinner's standards. The shaman snapped an order, her voice deep and harsh, and the second man padded towards the hole.

Amaira and Vasilov were in there and Vasilov was running low on phos. If he'd had any more, that would have been a killing blast, like the ones that had finished the dead men we'd passed. As quietly as I was able, I limped to the nearest pillar. I gave Valiya one last look, and she nodded.

From the hole, a brief flash and the crack of a matchlock shot bounced around the cavern. The shaman fluttered her hands and gave orders and the men took out powder charges and ramrods and began to load. She had sensed weakness. She was sending them in for the kill.

Silpur moved before I was ready. He came out behind a pillar, silent as a ghost and his sword erupted from the chest of a startled man. He looked down at it as the bright, bloody steel punched through him, then made a grab for it as it slithered back through. Silpur advanced on the next of them, walking, not charging. The nearest man brought his matchlock around like a club but he fared no better and went down gargling blood from one hole in his throat and another from the slash in his groin. Silpur struck at them without emotion, no haste as he passed between them, devastating speed when he struck.

I didn't have his finesse. I held my sword to my shoulder and charged.

It wasn't much of a charge. Bright flashes of Misery-skies ripped through my mind and the world lurched. My legs buckled beneath me and I crashed down to my knees with a curse, flickers and flares of light shredding my vision.

Not now, not now!

Men spun, saw me, abandoned their half-loaded firearms, and drew steel. I forced myself back to my feet, starbursts of pain spearing up my legs. The fixed men closed in warily. Even if I was already half beaten to death, I still looked like something from the second hell, eyes ablaze and teeth bared. The oddity of my appearance checked them only for a moment; they had the numbers and three of them began to fan out around me.

I took a forwards, warding guard, and started to back away. So much for my charge.

Silpur had cut his way through another two men but was being pressed by men with bayonets plugged into their matchlocks, and two of those are more than a match for a swordsman, no matter how good he is. My lips drew back in fury. That fucking arrogant shit had got us killed. The shaman had a knife in her hand but ran it back and forth across her palm, slicing shallow cuts. She smeared the blood across her face, and began to sing.

No time to listen to her song. The first man came in, swinging at my hands, the only target he had with my sword point stuck out like that. I snapped them back, struck right back at his, but my step was short and he made it away. Another came in, and as his blade came down I swung a wild parry, snapping it aside. The shivering lights in my head redirected themselves: a sudden burst of energy stole through me and my enemy wasn't prepared for my lunge, or to die, but both of them happened.

The thrust had left me vulnerable. A sword arced down and in desperation I threw my arm up in front of my head. The impact was mostly deflected by the thick moosefur coat, but not entirely. Some of the edge bit through. There was no pain, not with the rush on me, and my attacker had to scamper back out of my longer sword's reach. The cut barely bled, and what trickled from my sleeve was sluggish, steaming, black. The disorientation was gone. The energy that rippled through me was warm. Laughing.

Moving, moving, keep on moving. I couldn't pause, couldn't stop or I'd give them the ground that they needed. Circle around, get them walking into each other, hope that one of them tripped.

The noise that the shaman was making rose, driven high from the back of the throat, undulating up and down. The air got heavier as she emanated magic in primitive, tangled pulses. The Misery-taint in me rebelled against it, but only weakly. It wasn't being directed towards me. She'd seen that I was the lesser threat and went for Silpur.

I'd been wrong about the bayonets. Somehow Silpur had got past one of them and taken a man's arm off and now he parried a bayonet thrust down and hammered a sword into the man's head. Effortless, efficient, exquisite swordsmanship. But the shaman had him in her sights, blood spitting from her teeth as she wove her tribal sorcery around him. Silpur tried to advance on her but he stumbled and crashed down, his legs failing. He looked down at them in puzzlement, wondering why they weren't working for a moment, then back to the shaman. The man whose arm he'd taken off was picking himself up, dragging a heavy dirk from his belt. Tracks of blood wept from his eyes.

Another sweep of my sword drove my assailants back again, but keeping the weapon moving between them was stripping the fight from my already exhausted muscles. One of the men feinted and I whirled the sword through the air to push him back again and that cost me. The blade stopped its spinning and the point sank towards the ground. My chest was heaving, my leg almost ready to give way.

Amaira burst from the hole in the ice. Dusk-skinned, hair like night, and taller than I remembered, she sped towards the men who had their blades to me. She came in low, cutting through the first man in moments, turning his sword aside on her buckler and slashing him once, twice, a third time and then turning to the last. I summoned what final strength I had and made to part him down the centre, but he managed to parry it aside. The distraction was all Amaira needed to drive her sword through his back. He went down silently.

Somehow Silpur was on his feet again and the rest of the fixed men were all on the floor too. A few last gasps from dying men, and then it was all over. Somehow that pale, green-eyed shit had taken out six armed men. I let the sword fall from my fingers and slumped down onto my knees.

There was a time when Amaira would have thrown herself into my arms, but childhood had passed. The woman who stood before me was somebody else now. She was still narrow and the bones in her cheeks were hard, angular panes and her nose would always belie her heritage, but her eyes said it all. I'd left her as a child, and now she was a woman. A deadly woman, at that. She looked me over for wounds.

'Just in time, Captain-Sir,' she said with the hint of a smile, and maybe she hadn't changed as much as I'd feared.

'Took your time, you mean,' I said.

'I know,' she said. 'But I meant you, of course. Thank you.' The smile died away. 'Vasilov's shot.'

She glanced towards Valiya, sorrow beyond her years passing over her face, then hurried back to the tunnel while I took a look at Silpur. He was covered in blood, but none of it was his. I turned to the Karnari shaman. There was a knife in her back. My knife. Valiya leaned against one of the pillars, trying to wipe the blood from her hands onto the furs, scrubbing at them over and over.

'It's alright,' I said. 'Good work.'

She shook her head, a troubled look on her face. It was probably the first time she'd ever hurt somebody. Knowing that she'd had to wouldn't make a difference. I crouched beside the shaman's body, and was not surprised when her eyes slowly opened, beads of blood welling at their corners. It wasn't the woman who looked out at me.

'You usher forth the day of your own destruction,' a dry, corpse voice hissed from unmoving lips. Saravor, speaking through the dead.

'Seems to me that we're winning,' I said.

'Look around you. Look at the breaks in the world,' it whispered. 'Does this look like victory? If Crowfoot empowers his weapon and unleashes it on the Misery, what then? How far would he go not to lose?'

'You're an altruist now, is that it? Fighting to save the rest of us?' I spat. 'You'll understand my doubts about that.'

'What victory lies in being an emperor of dust?' Saravor hissed. 'The sky is broken. The black rain maddens the world. Crops fail, creatures rise in the dark. The Nameless war with each other, your Bright Lady fades to nothing and the Deep Emperor comes with The Sleeper at his call. Can you honestly claim, Galharrow, that you chose the right side?'

I stared down at the twin tracks of blood running down the shaman's cheeks.

'I choose to be my own side,' I said.

'This world belonged to the grey children long before your kind walked it,' Saravor breathed. 'They understand the price of Crowfoot's betrayal. Look for me, Galharrow, when the moons align. The children will not allow the raven to tear the world apart simply to be the last one standing before the sky rips apart and unmakes us all.'

The blood flow stopped, and the eyes rolled up behind closing lids.

'Your own side,' Silpur repeated. His unblinking green eyes gave me a sterile, pointed gaze. For him, there was the crow and nothing else. I let him stare.

Blackwing Captain Vasilov had served his time well. He'd come into Crowfoot's service around the time of the Siege of Valengrad, and he was a rarity amongst the Nameless' servants. Well adjusted to social situations, admired and loved by the soldiery, he even brought princes and the cream to his side with his easy manner and handsome smile. On top of all that he was a Spinner of considerable strength. His complexion marked him as Fracan, and Vasilov was probably not the name he'd been born with. He'd spent most of his time working around the states, rooting out the seeds of Bride lairs and cultists where his manners, charm, and wit were put to best use. He was comely, good natured, and in a really bad way. He held a lead box that he wouldn't relinquish.

Amaira helped him out of the tunnel and Valiya made him a bed out of things she'd dragged from the fixed men's packs. He was sheened with sweat, and there was a hole in his side where a matchlock ball had punched right through him. I helped the women to cut strips of bandage and stuff the wounds front and back, and Vasilov put up with what must have been considerable agony with grim stoicism, but the sweat ran from him in rivers. He'd seen enough injuries in his time to know the truth. He must have known he was done for.

'We didn't think help was coming,' Amaira said, 'And we couldn't spare much phos for a longer message.' She wiped sweat from Vasilov's brow. There was fondness between them, friendship. She talked to distract herself. 'Been stuck in that hole for nearly three days. After we cut the tunnel, we were nearly out of phos canisters. It was the worst kind of luck. We'd gone to try to read the friezes while we waited for Crowfoot to tell us how to get home when the witch and her men came on us. They cornered us here, and we had no way out.'

'How did you get down here?' Valiya asked.

Amaira looked up at her sadly. She saw what had become of Valiya's eyes and couldn't keep the sorrow from her face. She looked back to Vasilov's wounds, though they couldn't have been an easier sight.

'There's a stairway in the chamber above that leads to the surface.' She indicated a door on the far side of the cavern.

'You used the Duskland Gate to get here?' I said.

'You know any other way to this place? We're a thousand miles and an ocean away from any other living people. Saravor's men must have used it too,' she said.

'We can use it again if we climb out.'

'You have beasts with you?' Amaira asked. I shook my head, and her expression crumpled to darkness. 'Then no,' she said. 'We can't.'

'I should try to stitch Vasilov's wounds,' Valiya interrupted. She and Amaira shared a look. Amaira took my hand.

'Walk with me,' she said, and led me away from the other captains. We walked across the hall to Ezabeth's ghost, immobile and uncaring under the crack in the world. The spirit didn't notice us, seemingly engrossed with some flames running up and down her arm.

'You see her?' she asked.

'Yes. You can too?'

'Of course. But Vasilov can't. I don't know why I can. Maybe because he doesn't remember her. That's all that's left of her, isn't it? Memory. Her time's running out. When she appeared to us that day in the courtroom, she seemed so strong.'

'The others can't see her either, but Valiya saw her once.'

'Perhaps she chooses not to. I don't know. Do you still dream about her?'

'Sometimes. But it's not the same, and they're just dreams. Back then she was asking me for help. I don't think that she's there anymore. Not as she was.' It was painful to look at Ezabeth, or what had been Ezabeth, long ago. I didn't want to talk about her. Amaira took that moment to put her arms around me, and there was warmth in her arms, and comfort, but not much.

'I'm glad he sent you.'

'We can't use the Duskland Gate to get back,' I said.

'We can, if we find something to sacrifice,' she said. 'The gates are powered by the dead. Something has to draw the Long Men out. Look around you. Do you see anything living here?'

'Why would Crowfoot send you here with no way back?'

'We had animals with us,' Amaira said. 'But they went wild and broke free when the Long Men came out of the barrows. If I'd tried to hold them they'd have pulled me in after them.'

Ezabeth's ghost stood on its tiptoes and turned a lazy circle. Lost and trapped beneath a world-bridging crack in the sky. Forever, or until she faded from memory altogether.

'I hope you got what you came here for,' I said.

'We got it,' Amaira said quietly. 'It's in that box Vasilov has. He used up most of the canisters we'd brought burning the hole through the ice. After that we had to use an axe. But we got through, and cut what we could away.'

'What is it?'

'Same thing it always is,' she said. 'The fossilised heart of the ice fiend. It's always a heart, isn't it?' She shivered. 'Try not to touch it, Captain-Sir. You'll see things you don't want to see. Things from the age when that thing walked the earth. Nothing you'll want to remember.'

'And that's Crowfoot's weapon?'

'Not on its own,' she said. 'It's a vessel, the same way

that Saravor used Shavada's Eye as a vessel for soul magic, only that was part of a Deep King and the thing in the ice ... it's so much more. The same type of thing the Deep Kings tried to raise from the ocean. Its capacity to absorb magic is a million times greater than theirs. The Deep Kings might be immortals, but the ice fiend in there is something worse. This heart is why the Nameless are sending Davandein to Adrogorsk. They think they can use it there, somehow. The master didn't tell me how.'

'I don't like where this is going,' I said. Amaira didn't either.

There was a hiss across the chamber. We hurried back. Silpur drew back his sleeve, displaying the raven tattooed across his forearm. Except that it didn't look like any raven that I'd ever seen: featherless, with batlike wings and an elongated beak.

'Tourniquet,' Amaira said, stripping off her belt, but Silpur put out a hand to hold her off. The raven came slowly, a sickly, withered thing missing half of its feathers and barely able to force itself free. A tiny shred of Crowfoot's power, or at least it would have been, if he'd had anything left. Silpur didn't even flinch as it ripped through the flesh of his arm. It spoke to Silpur only, in a language that I'd never heard in all my long years in Valengrad, where every culture under the sun came together. I had never seen Crowfoot's avatar emerge from anybody else before, and his usual rage was subdued, withered in the feeble creature's throat. We watched the shrivelled thing give its instructions. There was no anger in them, and Silpur stared blank-eyed, asking no questions, only nodding occasionally to show that he understood. When the withered bird had delivered its message, it collapsed, and smoke drifted from its burned-out eyes.

'Time to go.' Silpur said.

'We can't move Vasilov yet. The wound will tear open.

He's in no condition to travel,' Valiya said. Silpur's green eyes seemed somehow less human than her silvered ones.

'Time to go.'

19

There were a dozen questions still unanswered, but the sooner we got out of there, the better. I had guessed what Crowfoot's message said. I didn't need to ask Silpur. I just had to follow where Crowfoot's chain of thought would have gone, what would have suited his needs best. I knew the master better than I knew myself, maybe. It was a chilling thought but despite his potentially vast powers, Crowfoot was simple. Take everything. Give nothing. Win at all costs, refuse any compromise. If I wanted to know how he thought, I only had to watch a carrion bird.

I couldn't look at Vasilov, though. He was injured. Weak. Expendable.

I needed time to rest and Silpur allowed that we could take an hour. He didn't help with Vasilov at all, just sat down on one of the fixed men's packs and stared straight forwards, his hands on his knees. Motionless as a statue. How long, I wondered, had he been doing Crowfoot's bidding? How many people had he killed, how many missions had he undertaken in my master's never-ending war? How casually he'd accepted the master's demands. How little he cared for what they entailed. The Blackwing records said Captain Narada had been the one to convey the Heart of the Void out to what had become the Endless Devoid, the centre of the Misery. She must have known what she was doing, must have suspected how many lives Crowfoot's weapon would take. I wondered whether she'd been like Silpur, as dry and free from outward emotion as a stone, or whether she'd regretted what she was doing. I guess that her deal had been important enough to her to go through with it. Or maybe she'd just been weak.

There was no weakness in Silpur.

The hour passed to grunts of discomfort and pain. The cut on my arm had healed even before I looked at it, drawing in the motes of blue light. I watched the semblance of Ezabeth, tried to talk to her more than once, but she didn't notice me again. Years ago, I told her that if it took me a hundred years, I'd see her free of the light. Looking at her here, eaten away by pain and time and the split between our worlds, I had to wonder if fate would make a liar of me in that too.

'I lived without you this long,' I said quietly. 'I'll see you again soon. When it matters.' I gave her a salute, but she was too busy watching flame drip between her fingers.

I left her behind. I was no use to her here, and she was no use to me either.

'Time to go,' Silpur said. I was feeling a little recovered, certainly not back to my former strength but I could walk around easily enough and I had enough in me to assist Amaira in getting Vasilov to his feet. He couldn't walk easily, and it was going to be a long way for a badly wounded man. Amaira led us towards the stairway.

'You look like shit, Ryhalt,' she said. 'I didn't even recognise you at first. You look younger too. Like young shit.'

'Language,' I grunted at her. She gave me that old catch-me-if-you-can grin, insolent, wild but now that she had matured there was a depth to it that said that I wouldn't catch her, and her wildness was a choice, not a lack of up-bringing. She'd have turned heads in any playhouse, but she was strong with it, hardened and fierce. Smart, resilient, and powerful; I was proud of what she'd grown into, even if I could claim only a fraction of the responsibility for shaping her.

We went through into another of the chambers, no longer giving a damn what crap the ancient people had carved onto the ice. I could feel the presence of the monstrosity in the ice, dead but still simmering with old, terrible magic. I wanted to be away from it as soon as possible. Silpur carried the box that contained the fragment of its heart and walked ahead of us, frequently outpacing us all as Vasilov winced and grimaced. The gunshot hadn't killed him outright, but it didn't look good.

We all knew. We didn't have to say it, but we knew.

It would have been helpful if Crowfoot had informed us that there was a way down here that didn't involve falling nearly a hundred feet and surviving only due to years of eating Misery-magic into myself, but wizards are arseholes. We left everything that we didn't need at the foot of the stairs. The portable communicator that Amaira had brought with her was worth a small fortune, but that joined swords, emptied phos canisters, and all the other crap that wasn't needed for the ascent. We were all drained, exhausted, and only Silpur still looked fresh. He didn't remove his swords, seemingly as full of energy now as he had been when he swung down on the rope. Implacable, resolute, uncaring.

'You can open the Duskland Gate?' I asked him.

'It will open,' he said. Like I'd asked about the weather. Like it was nothing.

The stairway spiralled around, up and up it went, and with each step Vasilov clenched his teeth. I'd been hurt that badly before, and worse, and understood what he was going through. Poor bastard. It didn't seem fair.

'We'll get you the best surgeon money can buy back in Valengrad,' I said. 'You'll have matching scars front and back.' He tried to offer me a smile, but it turned into a groan halfway through, and his eyes pressed tight.

I was lying, of course. We all knew that I was lying. Even if he didn't bleed out, even if by some miracle the lead ball hadn't mangled his insides, we knew he wasn't going to make it home. Amaira and I carried a weight far greater than his body, and he knew it too.

Up, and up, and up. The creatures that had cut these steps had made them even, precise, every one the same. This had been a holy place to them, the tomb of a great and terrible enemy. The destroyer. The ice fiend. I'd heard stories – ridiculous, nonsensical stories – about the world serpents, snakes the size of castles that were said to drive the magic of the world, turning in everlasting circles, far away on some other landmass across seas which only braggarts pretended to have sailed. Perhaps they were true. If they were, I'd have liked to have seen one.

Or, having felt the presence of the ice fiend, maybe not.

At last, the stairs ended. My legs were roaring at me, the old spear wound was sending whips of pain up and down the bone. A fall of broken ice obscured part of the entrance, and we had to climb up over it, but then we emerged out into the freezing wind. I could see the epicentre beneath the crack in the sky, could see the Duskland Gate a half mile away, a pale patch of dark stone, oddly apart from the jumbled, shattered ice plateaus. If we'd only known about it, we'd have saved ourselves a horrific ordeal and things might have gone faster and easier. If we'd been there sooner, maybe Vasilov wouldn't have torn pieces of cloth holding his insides inside. It was our destination, and it was our only option, but my heart hung heavy at what we had to do.

Silpur stalked on ahead of us, leaving us to carry Vasilov the last of the distance. The ice wasn't so badly broken here, but it still wasn't easy going. We slipped and slid our way over to the dead mule's body. As we drew near to the stone platform, I released Vasilov and went to Valiya. She looked as tired as I was feeling, but I suspected that I looked a damn sight worse. The further we went from the blue light, the worse I felt. I put an arm around Valiya's shoulders, leaned in, and whispered into her ear.

'Don't interfere,' I said.

'We have to get home,' she said through chattering teeth.

'We will,' I said. 'Leave it to me.'

'The world has asked too much of you already,' she said. 'And you've asked more of it still. When does this end? The loss, the pain – when does it all become worth it?'

'I don't know,' I said. 'I'll tell you when we get there. But we will get there.'

We walked onto the dark stone of the Duskland Gate. Birdlike shapes looked up beneath the film of clear ice that glazed it. The Duskland Gates had always been an awful place to tread; even the first desperate time that I'd sought out Crowfoot and asked him to give me a deal, the gate had filled me with dread. This time, it was worse.

Death. It was the Long Men of the Barrows that caused the magic, the trapped, screaming, evil souls of the spite-filled dead that let the world flex and bend and transported us from one gate to the next. The platform was like a beacon, blasting death out like a trumpet, calling to them. The first time I'd crossed through, I'd tried to use a rabbit. The Long Men hadn't cared for it. Horses worked, and I'd read in one of the annals that pigs were even better. Perhaps the soul of a horse was worth more than that of a rabbit. The Long Men seemed to think so. When they answered, when death surrounded us entirely, we crossed over. Death is the great displacer. It is the same everywhere, and thus all places are one to death. Or something like that. On every previous journey I'd done the smart thing and brought animals for the journey out and the journey back. But the sacrificial mule had already fallen over dead, and I didn't have any-thing else left to sacrifice.

Vasilov was glad to collapse onto the hard platform. His bandages were soaked through with blood, his dark skin had taken on a greyish tinge, and there was growing fever in his eyes. He looked up, past the floating blocks of hanging ice, to where Rioque was reddening the sky as the light began to fade. Dusk was upon us – appropriate. He squinted hard at the moon and began to draw power. Threads of red light trailed his fingers. I'd seen Ezabeth do something similar once, but where she had drawn dozens of threads, one after the other as fast as she might comb her hair, Vasilov drew each one as if with great effort. I still had the Talent's goggles that I'd used to hide the glow from my eyes, and I gave them to him. He grimaced through a thank-you, and his efforts sped up.

'Prepare to leave,' Silpur said. He turned his back on the rest of us and looked out towards the crack in the sky.

Vasilov's fingers glowed as he absorbed the phos. He could charge himself with a little. No human body could hold a huge amount, that was what the canisters were for, but he drew what he could. It was wasted effort, but it hadn't clicked in his mind yet. Vasilov was badly injured, very likely dying. It was a shame, but there was no other way. He wasn't going to make it anyway.

Vasilov put his fingers against his wound and there was a bright phos-flare beneath them. He gasped and collapsed back on the plinth, panting at the pain. He'd seared his wound closed. It seemed a needless pain to go through. Even if he managed to seal the wound, infection was almost certain to kill him.

It struck me suddenly, howling through me like the icy wind passing between the jutting planes of ice. I'd been a fool. Crowfoot wouldn't sacrifice one of his captains. Not so easily, not if he didn't have to, not even if one of them was dying. He'd eke out every last minute of service that he could. Amaira, Silpur, Vasilov, and I all belonged to him, and he didn't cast away his tools.

Valiya did not belong to him.

Do not trust your master.

I stood up slowly and moved to stand in front of Valiya. My rasping, Misery-burned voice dropped lower than usual.

'What did Crowfoot tell you to do?' I growled. Silpur met my stare, his wide green eyes as empty of feeling as the frozen world was empty of life.

'Time to go,' he whispered.

'All of us?' I said. 'Or all of *his*?'

I looked from Vasilov to Silpur.

'Give me the box.'

'Spill the blood,' Silpur said. He was staring directly at Valiya. 'Open the gate.'

Valiya and Amaira understood in that instant. Amaira swung around to stand in front of Valiya, both of us blocking her from Silpur. My sword had seemed a needless weight to carry, but by the spirits I needed it now. *Stupid, Galharrow! Get bright!* There was no scenario in which abandoning your sword made sense.

'Someone must die,' Silpur said. His hiss was colder than the air.

'He thought it would be me,' Vasilov said, propping himself up on his arm. 'Didn't you, Galharrow?'

I didn't look down at him. I kept my eyes on Silpur and the swords at his belt. He was faster than a striking greatcat. He only needed a second to open the gate. Icy wind whistled through the broken ice around us.

'We'll find another way,' I said.

'We don't have time,' Vasilov said. He dragged a strand of light from the air. 'We have the fiend's heart. It has to be delivered to the Lady of Waves' agent at the citadel. Acradius has been preparing to march on Valengrad ever since he merged with The Sleeper. We have to get to Adrogorsk and empower the weapon.' He coughed, clutching at his bloody side as pain shook him.

The sky groaned, a languid, mournful sound of despair. Silpur stared directly at me. He would try to open the gate. He would do whatever he had to. It was his way. I wondered in that moment what difference there was between Silpur's service of Crowfoot and the drudge's mindless subservience to the Deep Kings.

'Why at Adrogorsk?'

'The fiend's heart is just a vessel,' Vasilov said. 'But I can empower it when the moons align. A triple eclipse will align over Adrogorsk's ruins.' The pain hit him again and he fought for breath. 'The light will refract over and over, magnifying its power. For ten seconds I'll be able to spin more power into the fiend's heart than all the mills in Dortmark produce in five hundred years. The ice fiend was the embodiment of pure destruction. It's the weapon that Crowfoot needs.'

'That the Nameless need,' Valiya corrected him.

'That we all need,' I said.

'One must die,' Silpur said. 'Gate must open. Orders were clear.'

'That isn't happening,' Amaira said. 'There has to be another way. You don't get the final say on this just because the bird came out of your arm.'

'You are captains,' Silpur said, his brow creasing. Puzzled. He didn't understand.

Vasilov drew more and more phos from the air. He panted and gasped, and I realised with cold dread that Silpur wasn't the only one that was armed. Lights danced along Vasilov's fingers and ran through his veins as the power filled him again, smoking from his skin. The desire to survive is powerful.

'We'll think of something else,' I said. 'You aren't touching Valiya and Vasilov is dying, even if he doesn't care to fucking admit it. Crowfoot isn't in his right mind anymore, if he ever was. We've all seen that. We're his captains. We have to take care of things for him until his power starts to return. That doesn't involve killing innocent people to get what we want. Once that starts, there's no reason for any of this. There's nothing left to save.'

'It was never about saving anything, Galharrow,' Vasilov said. The light he was absorbing was giving him strength, raw power drawn from the sky. 'It's about winning.'

'Not at any cost.'

'At all costs,' Silpur said.

'No.'

Silpur and Vasilov stared at me as though I'd just shat on their god. Amaira tensed. The platform began to feel very crowded.

Silpur drew a sword and advanced. He moved fast, weaving like a snake, looking for a way around us. He was driven in his mission and he followed his orders to the letter. He didn't want to kill Amaira or me, but that didn't mean he couldn't disable us. The curved blade in his hand rolled in flickering eights, little windmills slicing the air. Valiya's fingers clutched the back of my coat tight.

I would not let her be taken. Not by Crowfoot, not for a weapon, not for anything. I summoned up the black Misery-power, forcing it to the surface, trying to drive it into my muscles, my skin. It buzzed with welcome. Blood vessels burst and lights danced in my eyes.

'Get out of the way, Galharrow,' Vasilov coughed. Phos blossomed on his outstretched palm, a sharp, narrow dagger of light.

Silpur came on and Amaira went in. She was fast, nearly as fast as he was and though he had a clear thrust straight into her, he held back. His orders were to keep the captains alive and he couldn't break them. Like a fucking drudge. Amaira lunged for his sword hand, got her fingers around it, and tried to close to throw him down. But Silpur was just as tough, hard as stone and had centuries of experience to fall back on. He rolled his hand, twisted and Amaira cried out as he locked her arm. A knee slammed into her guts but she held on. Silpur struck with his knee again, and again, and then he turned her wrist and drove her face down onto the stone. But he'd lost his grip on the sword as they grappled and I stooped to grab it.

Like a fool.

I looked back as Vasilov saw his opening and launched his light-dagger at Valiya, no longer shielded by my Misery-tainted body.

My arm snapped out and I caught the flaring stiletto of energy midflight.

The Misery objected to the foreign magic. It bucked, writhed, no longer a perfect spike of energy but a twisting, hissing snake. But I held it, and it couldn't burn me. I was bigger than this little magic. Vasilov's eyes widened; those cocky Spinners had it too easy. No wonder they came as arrogant as the cream.

'Stand down!' I roared, but Vasilov drew up another, smaller spearhead, perspiration running in rivers onto his chest. He'd fought hard. He'd protected Amaira. He'd been given a shit hand and told to play the stooge. I pitied him. But he'd crossed a line that I couldn't allow. He tried to cast another phos-blast at Valiya.

I hurled the light back at him and it exploded through his chest. Blood spattered across the stone.

Ice rose up in a storm around the Duskland Gate, circling and rushing around us. It rose higher, taking the light as Vasilov's blood ran across the carvings, feeding the rock, summoning the Long Men. I spun towards Silpur, sword in hand, but he sheathed his. Valiya sheltered behind me.

'Lost your bloodlust?' I shouted over the roaring wind. He looked from me to Vasilov. The Spinner was already dead.

Means nothing now, he mouthed, all interest in Valiya gone. For him, that was how easy this was. There was a task, and he'd done what he could to achieve it. He bore no grudges, didn't even look to Amaira as she dizzily picked herself up. He looked out at the shattered ice as the swirling chaos blocked out sight of anything, the ice planes and the tear in the sky disappearing in the raging wind. Out there I saw the flickering, humanoid shapes picked out in light, crawling towards us through the flurry. They were insubstantial, glowing shapes, but from their heads a pair of stubby horns jutted backwards.

'Someone had to die,' I shouted. 'Valiya is more useful to Crowfoot. I need her. Vasilov wouldn't even have made it through the journey. You understand that, don't you?'

'Need her why?' Silpur asked.

You never could do the hard things, one of the Long Men whispered into my mind.

'She knows things. Things that we need. Four Blackwing captains alone isn't enough. If we're going to win this war and stop the Deep Kings from breaking the Range, we all need to work together. I can't beat them alone. And neither can you.'

Silpur watched me, unblinking.

'Vasilov was his.'

'He was. And now there are three of us and we have to serve the master the best we can. Make peace. It was a desperate situation. And I was wrong.'

I offered him my hand. Sparks of light, threads of black, worked beneath my copper skin. Silpur considered it.

'You were wrong,' he said.

'I did what I had to. Crowfoot is the master, and he knows much. But he doesn't see through our eyes. He doesn't know exactly where we are and what we have to do. He chose us because he thinks we're the ones who can get the job done. Vasilov had served his time. He was no more use.

I'm many things, Silpur. I'm a soldier, and I'm a captain, and maybe I'm weak. I may not be as lethal as you are or as young as Amaira, but I serve, and I'm loyal.'

You never keep your promises, the Long Men whispered.

'Serve the master,' Silpur said. He reached out and took my wrist and we shook.

I did not let go.

'I'm one other thing,' I said. 'I'm a liar.'

I threw my weight backwards and our arms locked out. He was strong for a man of his size, but he was short and I was big, he was slight and I was heavy, and whatever power Crowfoot had given him, the Misery had turned me into something else. He lurched as I swung him around, eyes never blinking as they locked on me. I spun us around, him at arm's length and his feet left the floor. I turned, spinning like a hammer-thrower. Silpur dug his nails in but my skin was slick with sweat between us and centripetal force is a powerful thing. I roared as I let go.

Silpur sailed out, off the platform and out into the blizzard, becoming an indistinct shadow. The wind screamed and the Long Men swarmed towards him. His sword came out, he thrashed left and right as the glowing figures drew in, no skill, just frantic, panicked slashes in the ice blaze.

We love you, bringer of death, the Long Men whispered. And then darkness swept in around us.

20

The Duskland Gate spat us back out into silence, save for the rustling of the wind through the trees. I counted us over. Me, Valiya, Amaira. Three survivors, and everyone seemed whole.

'You alright?' I asked. Valiya nodded, shaken. Amaira gave me half of a smile and a two-fingered salute.

'All in one piece,' she said. 'Poor Vasilov. He wasn't a bad man.'

'No,' I agreed. 'He did his duty.'

'You seem to have forgotten yours.' She mimed Silpur's flight out into the Duskland.

'Never,' I said. 'I know what has to be done. But I'll not burn the world for it.'

She considered me, then nodded and tugged the heavy black box from Vasilov's death grasp.

Two more Blackwing captains, gone, and this time by my own hand. The thought left me cold. The world was no poorer place without Silpur in it, but I was doing the enemy's work for them.

The ravine had changed. More than a day had passed since we left – here, at least. Rows of graves had been dug, sticks serving as posts to mark where the dead lay. I counted twenty-one. One for every mercenary, and another for Sang. The bodies of dead horses and mules had been dragged to the other side of the ravine and left to rot. Carrion birds were having a feast.

'That thing killed everybody,' I said.

There was a crack from above, and the hilt of the sword in my belt went spinning away, shot clean off. There was no cover, nowhere to run to. A lone figure sat halfway up the valley's side, a smoking pistol in one hand, another long-barrelled weapon in the other. The dark-haired man who'd brought men to kill me at Fortunetown. North.

'Thought you could hit a falcon mid-dive,' I said. There was no point running. He smiled, his eyes hidden behind lenses of blackened glass. A coughing fit suddenly struck me, and I tried to keep my eyes on him as he began to slither down towards us.

'You think I missed? Pretty good disarming shot if I did, neh?' He kept his second weapon trained on me.

'He only has one shot left,' I said to Amaira as the coughing had subsided. 'He's fast as lightning but you can take him.'

'She bloody well can't,' he said. He had that pricey sword at his belt, more pistols, and we had shit all except a heavy metal box and whatever strength the climb across the ice planes had left us with. 'If I wanted you downed or even winged, I'd have done it already. You're a tough old thing, neh? Do you have the fiend's heart?'

'What do you know about it?' Amaira snapped.

'You're not the only ones with connections to those above,' he said, a sardonic smile hovering over a pointed chin. He stood a dozen paces away and put his pistols through his belt. They weren't any less dangerous where he'd just put them. 'You must be Captain Amaira. And this must be Winter. A pleasure to meet you all. My name is North. You're to accompany me.'

'Not trying to end me, this time?' I asked.

'What can I say? I've mellowed. The Lady of Waves

perceived you as a threat to the Range. Nobody should be out there soaking up those toxins, or helping the mad count destroy phos mills. She'll get to you later, but for now, the Nameless seem to want us to work together. Nobody gives a shit about Dantry Tanza anymore anyway, and Marshal Davandein would be furious if I killed you.'

Do not trust the Nameless.

'You're one of the Lady of Waves' captains.'

'At your service. Well, not exactly. At your back, maybe? I know what you have there. I'm to convey you to the citadel.'

'My last trip there didn't go well,' I said.

'I can imagine,' North smiled. 'But it's not really a request. If you refuse to come with me sensibly, I'll shoot your knees out and send some men to carry you. The marshal thought that a greeting party of one would be better than a few dozen men to march you there.'

'If you go back there, it's the rack,' Valiya said. She was right, although I wondered if they had a big enough one to pull me apart. I'd survived worse.

'Times have changed in the month you've been gone. The Lady doesn't care about a few exploded phos mills anymore. It's all about Adrogorsk now, and she needs you to find it.'

'She wants me to find Adrogorsk for her?'

'That's the size of it.'

'Tell her to get a navigator,' I said.

'They've tried,' North said. 'But they can't find it. It's moved. Or gone. But you – you could find it, couldn't you, Galharrow? Crowfoot wants you to take the fiend's heart there. Yes, the Lady of Waves has explained the Nameless' plan to me in magnificent detail. We're all on the same side. Funny how things work out, neh?'

'So that's it? We're supposed to be friends now?' I said. North inclined his head towards me.

'Friends might be pushing it. I won't shoot you right

now though, that will have to be a start. Shall we be getting along? We'll have to walk, and rain's due. None of us want to be caught out in that.'

I conferred with Valiya and Amaira. He was right that he could shoot our legs out, and there wasn't much that any of us could do about it. He wasn't going to let any of us close enough to rush him. And the heart did need to be delivered. North was one of the Lady of Waves' captains. That made him ruthless, competent but ultimately, maybe, our side.

'The truth is, without the citadel's help, Crowfoot's weapon isn't going to be deployed,' Valiya said. 'If it's to stop King Acradius, then we need a Spinner.'

'Not just a Spinner,' Amaira said. 'Vasilov said it would take a phos loom big enough to handle the sudden rush of power. The kind of lenses they have in the floors of the Grandspire. We can't get that stuff out there without Davandein's help. We need her on our side.'

'You really think she's forgotten about Dantry?' I asked.

'No, not for a moment,' Valiya said. 'But this is bigger. This isn't just a few broken mills. This is the Range we're talking about. She'll see the bigger picture, for now at least.'

'I wish that I trusted Davandein's decision making as much as you do,' I said. But I didn't see that I had a whole lot of choice in the matter.

Nenn rode beside us. Or at least, she kind of drifted alongside us as if there were a horse underneath her. Nobody else saw her. She chattered on about putting chillies into beer and how she was planning to climb the Obsidian Mountains at the Misery's northern edge. She stayed for longer than she had before and was quite content to gabble on to herself. I did my best to ignore her, and instead examined the black veins under my skin. They'd grown thicker, harder since I fell down the chasm shaft. They ran across my palms now, bled into my fingernails. I was tired. So damn tired that I could have used a week in bed. My stomach hadn't forgotten how hungry I was, either, and I drifted in and out of the conversation.

North filled us in. He kept a good distance to be certain that none of us were going to make any sudden moves, but we were ragged, dotted with scrapes and scabs and at the end of our strength. I wasn't doing any better than Valiya, and only Amaira's youth kept her striding along easily. Kids are indestructible, never-ending energy letting them blaze ahead no matter what.

The drudge had raised a new army on their side of the Misery, and it was ready to start moving. Our scouts never went that far, but we had it from the Nameless. The Lady of Waves was awake for once, risen from her usual slumber and passing us information. They were all putting their gamble on empowering the fiend's heart at Adrogorsk before Acradius could get close enough to Valengrad to take out Nall's Engine. All of that was being kept from the populace, but North seemed to assume we were as well informed as he was. It seemed all too reminiscent of the Heart of the Void for my liking. Crowfoot's last ultimate weapon had shattered the sky and brought the Misery into the world. Nobody could be feeling good about that, and I didn't like to think how the sky would take a second impact of that kind, or of the results for the world if it had to.

As we drew closer, I could feel the Misery, away beyond the horizon. She reached out to me. Her presence quested into my mind, spreading through the black veins beneath my skin. She urged me to return, longing, morose. I was a piece lost from the game board, and the game wasn't as much fun without me. She loomed vast, full of promise, and part of me quested back towards her, searching for her embrace. I would change and change again, she told me, and I would welcome it.

An army was camped out beyond the walls. Davandein

had raised troops, a huge force. I'd never seen so many men in one encampment. Good. We'd need them.

I tried to get a better read on North. We didn't mention the fact that he'd tried to kill me, or that he'd badly mistreated people that I cared about. I considered asking if he'd been the one to take out Linette and Josaf, but there was no point to that kind of discussion: he had no reason to tell me the truth, and I had no power to pull it from him. That he was one of the Lady's captains was troubling. Had his decision to strike at me been his choice, or her order? He talked cheerfully enough, though, confident, relaxed. All in a day's work for a captain. I toyed with the idea of taking him out now, because I knew that one day I was going to have to, but I was in no condition for it. Every part of me found a way to ache as we made the slow journey back to the city.

'Red geese,' North said after the walls came into sight. The brickwork was still pitted and scarred from the cannon fire that Davandein's army had put into them. Overhead, a V of scarlet birds passed by. North drew one of his pistols, squinted, and fired it off with a crack. One of the geese fell away from the formation and spiralled downwards. An impossible shot, really, but we were all impossible people in one way or another and I'd given up being amazed by pretty much anything. Maybe he was showing off, or maybe it was a warning.

We stopped at the gates. North told the sergeants to fetch an escort, and shortly after we were led to the citadel.

Suffice to say, I did not like the escort that came to meet us.

Sixteen oversized, bone-white figures in thick black robes advanced silently down the street, red-eyed, hard-boned and staring. They didn't seem to have any more interest in us than they did in the other people on the street, which meant that they noted everyone, appraising them the same

215

way that I would look at spits of meat on a street vendor's grill.

Spinner Kanalina rode at their head.

'Back again,' she said. 'I didn't think you'd be coming.'

'Pleasure's all mine,' I said. Kanalina looked to the box in Amaira's hands.

'Is that it?' she said, a new reverence in her voice.

'It is,' Amaira said.

'It's so small.'

'You try carrying it,' Amaira answered. Kanalina nodded.

'Captain North, if you could take it from here. The Lady will be pleased to know it has arrived safely.' We didn't have any capacity to argue the point. Amaira pried the cold lead away from her palms and North held on to it like he'd been given a box containing eternal life rather than the long-frozen heart of a nightmare.

'Welcome back, Captain. And Winter, if I'm not mistaken. The marshal is waiting for you. Let's go.'

People cleared the way for us. There were soldiers everywhere, not just in black citadel uniforms but mercenaries in garish reds and yellows, blues and greens. The army camp lay outside the city, but plenty of the recruits seemed to have found their way into the city. The last time I'd known Davandein to raise an army, it had not gone well for us. They scurried away from the eight-foot-tall warriors.

'Are they all out of their eggs now?' I asked.

'Nearly. Seventeen so far, and more daily,' Kanalina said. She didn't seem nervous around them. Perhaps she should have been. They responded easily to her directions. I didn't think that First was amongst them; he had been slightly bigger if my memory served, but they all looked identical except for varying degrees of ritual scarring across their sharp cheekbones and hairless jawlines.

A man was pinning up Missing Person posters on a corner, for a friend disappeared two days before. His posters were not the only ones showing the crudely drawn faces of loved ones. When he saw the Marble Guard approaching, he paled and hurried away.

They gave us time to take a bath and clean up before being presented to the marshal. It had only been a day to us, but the Duskland Gate had stolen time. They didn't have any clothes that would fit me so I ended up wearing my tattered stuff, still stained from sweat and snagged from the ice. We weren't being treated as prisoners, despite the escorts. We were honoured guests. Sort of. A servant waited outside the room with a pair of Davadein's Drakes, her personal guard. She'd rebuilt their numbers in the years since she reclaimed power. I sent the servant off to bring me food. When I'd eaten the whole platter, I coughed up black shit, then sent him off to find me more. A few turkey legs hadn't been enough. I could have eaten a whole flock.

Amaira had got herself cleaned up and joined me in the sitting room. She looked well enough, other than being underfed and in need of a haircut. Her clothes had been in worse shape than mine, but they'd found her some uniform breeches, a shirt, and a jacket that fit her well enough. They'd let her have a standard-issue sword as well.

'I'm sorry about Vasilov,' I said when we sat down before the fire.

'So am I,' she said, and meant it. 'He and Linette were the good ones. We're running low on friends, Ryhalt.' Her eyes took a fierce light. 'We should have just killed Silpur.'

'Maybe. If there was one bastard out there that might survive the Long Men it was probably him. He's trapped up there, regardless. He won't be bothering us again. Were you and Vasilov close?'

'We'd been stuffed up together in that hole for nearly three days, as near as I can tell,' Amaira said. 'He seemed like a decent enough sort, for a Blackwing captain.' She looked me over critically, looking at the scaly pebbling along my cheeks, the metallic sheen to my skin, and the undying light in my eyes. 'We crossed a line, Ryhalt,' she said.

'It had to be crossed.'

'Crowfoot will know he lost two more captains.'

'He will. But he can't do anything about it. You saw what came out of Silpur's arm. Crowfoot's power is broken. He doesn't have anything left. Whatever happened during the Crowfall, he lost everything. Nall too. The Lady of Waves and Shallowgrave will be running the show now. Crowfoot's just a whisper.'

'Like Ezabeth,' Amaira said.

'I'm not sure she's even that much, now,' I said. Amaira felt the pain in my words and came to sit beside me, an arm across my shoulder the way that Nenn used to do. I'd helped to raise Amaira as a kid, but she was grown now, fighting her own battles without complaint. She'd grown up strong. Something to be grateful for.

'So,' Amaira said, changing the subject. Her eyes took on a knowing gleam that had never been there as a child. 'How do you feel about seeing Valiya again?'

'She's different,' I said.

'Well, obviously she's different,' Amaira said. 'We're all different, aren't we. That's not what I'm asking you. The silver hair suits her, don't you think?'

I gave Amaira a frown, but she just laughed at me behind her hand and I flushed, which probably looked pretty weird through my copper skin.

'It's been a long time,' I said. 'I'm still glad that we have her on our side.'

As if talking about her had summoned her, Valiya joined us. She looked troubled, which was difficult for somebody with mirrors for eyes, but easy for someone who'd been through our ordeal.

'What's wrong?'

'I don't know,' she said. She drew back a sleeve and traced her fingers up and down the numbers. Swiped them across, aggressively, started digging her nails against the skin. I went to her and took hold of her wrist. Long red welts tracked across the numbers and lines that moved, swirling and changing. 'I can't control them anymore,' she said. 'They're moving too fast. I can't read them. Can't understand them. None of it makes any sense anymore. Like this one.' She stabbed her finger at an equation that would have baffled the professors of mathematics at the university. 'It's wrong. The numbers don't add up.'

I ushered her into a chair.

'The world is reeling,' I said. 'Maybe that's it.' But she shook her head and stared at the numbers flowing together and dissipating into nothing across her skin.

'Put it away,' Amaira said gently.

'But I need it,' Valiya said desperately. 'It was the deal. I can help with this. Nall told me that I had to be part of it, whatever was to come. That I have to see it out to the end. He gave me this. As my weapon. But it's all wrong. There's a key to it all. There has to be a way to win.'

Amaira drew Valiya's sleeve down.

'You're still you, whether you have the key or not,' she said gently. 'We're going to win. Of course we are. It will all have been worth it, in the end.'

Amaira and I shared a look. I could only think of one reason that Nall's gift might be starting to falter, and she knew it too. Valiya must have, if she was honest with herself. The Nameless didn't make mistakes. Not often.

21

The ghost that wasn't Nenn, but thought that it was Nenn, joined me for the walk up to the roof. Range Marshal Davandein liked to meet people there, because it put her on top of things. She'd summoned us one by one, and I went last. She stood alone on the roof, her clutter of attendants unusually absent. She still dressed like she was striking a new fashion, half uniform and half ball gown.

'They'd told me it was bad,' Davandein said. 'Should I trust you, looking like that?'

'You can choose to trust me or not,' I said. 'It's all one to me.'

'Gurling Stracht had the same look,' she said. 'But he picked it up over forty years in the Misery. You've done this to yourself deliberately. Haven't you?'

'I don't like to leave things to chance.'

'Why did you do it? What madness made you do this to yourself?'

'I decided to find my own way through the war.'

Davandein played with one of the many delicate, priceless rings that sparkled on her fingers.

'You've been in there since we crushed the Bright Order, and you navigate the Misery alone. Whatever you've done to yourself, you've learned some new tricks.' Her intelligence was good.

'You're planning to march on Adrogorsk,' I said.

Davandein was calm. I'd seen her in a rage, I'd seen her desperate, and I'd seen her make a terrible decision that had cost a lot of innocent people everything they had. But today, at the seat of her power, there was a cool stillness about her.

'The Lady of Waves ordered it three weeks ago. Shallowgrave has sent the Marble Guard to support us.'

I wasn't convinced that that was a good thing.

'You've spoken with the Lady directly?'

Davandein took a deep breath.

'I have. I understand now, Galharrow. I understand what they are, and I know that we don't have a choice. She gave me a glimpse of what she can see, knowledge carried through the clouds, deposited back into the sea. The Deep Kings have amassed a new army of warriors. A new breed of drudge, stronger, harder. Many thousands of them, drawn from all corners of their empire. But Acradius holds the power of something they call "The Sleeper." Power beyond anything we've seen before.'

Davandein turned to the crenellations and placed her hands on the wall. She stared out across the wasteland, the craters that the Engine had punched into the earth a reminder of the power it had taken to stop them ten years ago.

'The Engine can't stop it.'

'The Lady does not believe so.'

'I know the plan that the Lady has given you,' I said. 'Take the fiend's heart to Adrogorsk, and empower it during the eclipse. It's a bold move. But that much phos causes a problem. The backlash paradox means we can't use it. The more phos you expend, the greater the backlash – it's how Nall's Engine works. So what can we use it for?'

'We can't,' Davandein said. 'But the Nameless can.'

'And do what with it?' I said angrily. 'Another Heart of the Void? The sky is shattered, and the rain sends men mad. Even the geese are trying to eat us. What the fuck do we have to gain by unleashing that kind of power again?'

'These thoughts have kept me awake long into the night,' Davandein said wearily. 'And every time, I come to the same conclusion. We can't win without the Nameless, and this is their play. We have no means to combat King Acradius, the Deep Kings that he rules, or The Sleeper without them.'

'And you think it will be enough? Crowfoot is fucked. Nall is fucked, and I don't trust the two that remain.'

'It will have to be enough!' Davandein snapped. 'I won't give up the Range. I won't flee across the sea and leave the people of Dortmark to burn. And this conversation is point-less, because neither will you. We may not always see eye to eye, Galharrow, but we've never been at cross purposes. Not in the end.'

That was pretty rich given that she'd been prepared to stick me on a rack only a few days ago – although a month seemed to have passed in my absence. Davandein's view of reality always suited her own purposes.

I had a lot of anger for Davandein. I would have seen her replaced, deposed, maybe even hanged for leading that attack against Valengrad. She'd done what she thought necessary to keep the Range safe, and she'd been completely, and irreversibly, wrong, but for all her pride, all her ambition, Davandein was a soldier.

'Shallowgrave's monster wiped out twenty-one good people trying to bring me in.'

'The Guardians can be ... difficult to restrain. There have been a lot of disappearances since they started to hatch. Adenauer sent them because he serves the law, but the casualties were ... regrettable.'

That was one way to put it. Valiya's woman, Sang, had numbered amongst them. Collateral damage to the Nameless. They cared nothing for us, not even for each other's minions. Each playing their own, long, games.

'And you've managed to lose Adrogorsk.'

Davandein laughed.

'It was a fixed point in the Misery, as you know. But not anymore.'

'It's still a fixed point,' I said. 'It's the land around it that changed, when the Crowfall took place. Most of the Misery changes over hours. Around there, it shifts in minutes.'

'The Lady of Waves says that the triple eclipse will peak directly over the ruins,' she said. 'All three moons will align before the sun, the vast spheres of crystal filtering the light. The power they offer will give ten seconds of godhood to the Spinner that can draw it. The heart has to be there.'

Of course it did.

I'd fought at Adrogorsk, thirty years ago when I was still young and naïve enough to believe that there was glory to be won in killing over broken stone and fallen rock. The beginning of my failure, the start of my disgrace. One of my footmen had been honoured to carry my banner there, a great flag of red, the silver fist of my house gleaming upon it. Damn, but that kid had been proud to be the one to bear it. He'd fallen in the fighting, and in my despair I'd torn it into pieces. It was there that my pride had begun to crumble.

Where else would it end?

'The Deep Kings will try to stop us.'

'They will. They'll send everything they have,' Davandein agreed. There was fire in her belly. This was her moment. Even if she'd managed to advance her position, her legacy would always be tainted by the massacre she'd presided over. She had an opportunity to lead the charge that would wipe that black mark from her past. 'I've raised sixty thousand men. The biggest, best trained, best equipped army that Dortmark has ever put into the field. I have artillery, I have Spinners, and I have the heart. But it doesn't matter if I can raise ten times that number if I can't get them to Adrogorsk.'

Fate turns, and turns, and her cogs and wheels grind the future inexorably into place. I almost smiled.

'I'll do it,' I said. 'But I'll want something in return.'

'If you get us there and it works, I'll make you a prince,' Davandein said easily. I smiled. The thought of me as a prince, surrounded by courtly hangers-on and fawning servants, had a certain appeal to it, if only because I could dismiss them all and watch their faces. Nenn's shadow seemed to agree because she was mimicking a stately walk around the roof, giving dainty, rolling waves to imaginary supplicants.

'I only want a pardon for Dantry Tanza. And he gets his lands back.'

'The man is a criminal,' she said. 'A saboteur and a killer.'

'That's my offer. I'll take his pardon with me today, or you can find someone else to navigate to Adrogorsk for you.'

Davandein laughed.

'You're an arrogant, overserious prick, Galharrow. Fine. The ink will be dry before you leave, but tell me one thing first. If you want him pardoned, then you must know why he's been causing so much destruction.'

'I do.'

'And will you tell me?'

'No.'

Davandein shook her head.

'I suppose the world wouldn't be right if you weren't still keeping secrets from me. Go on then. And Galharrow.' She paused. 'I like Captain Amaira. Keep her safe.'

Davandein offered me accommodation at the citadel, but I preferred to keep to myself and didn't want to start feeling locked in. I'd grown used to having my own space, out there in the dust, so I headed back to Valiya's safehouse.

I got to sleep at last, or to try to at least. When I closed my eyes, bright lights danced across them and I heard whispers, coming to me across the distance. The Misery. I had a conversation with the Iron Goat, Marshal Venzer himself, at one point, but later I couldn't remember whether I'd really been talking to him or if it had been a rambling dream. I didn't recall the conversation.

It had been a month since we'd left Valengrad, even if it had only seemed a day. I seemed to be hungry enough to eat a month's worth of rations. I got through a whole string of blood sausage and half a loaf of bread, smeared with thick, grainy mustard. I could barely taste it through the Misery-taint that never left my mouth, but my belly welcomed it and as I ate I felt my mind growing clearer. The little lights that winked and glimmered at the edges of my vision receded. Even Nenn had gone away for a while.

Valiya scarcely picked her way through a single sausage. She kept scratching at her arms, trying to get the numbers to work the way that she thought they should. She was always trying to order the world to her liking, and it wouldn't do what she wanted.

'Stop doing that. Please. You'll hurt yourself,' I told her.

'What's wrong with them?' she asked. 'How can we win if we don't have any answers?'

'We can win,' I said. I did a rare thing then. I knelt beside her chair and put my arms around her, but it was like embracing a statue. Her skin was cold, limbs tensed hard as if against an unwanted attack. I'd let some of my guard down, but hers was tight as a fortress.

'Let me go, please,' she said quietly. An uncomfortable moment for both of us. She pushed away from me and left the room. I looked across at Amaira. She may not even have been twenty – her exact age had never quite been clear – but there was understanding in the look that she gave me.

'Come on,' I said, wanting to avoid her gaze. 'We've an appointment to keep.'

Amaira smeared white plaster makeup over my face and fitted the teardrop-shaped goggles into place. I could almost have passed for human again. We raided Valiya's small armoury and headed out into the day.

'It's not easy for her,' she said.

'None of this is easy.'

'That's not what I mean and you know it,' Amaira said. 'Wait a moment. Let me just go in here. Feels like an age since I had sweets.' She ducked inside a sugar shop. Someone had put up a poster outside: *Reward for information on death of Finnea Stiegan, bitten and beaten. Six hundred marks.* It was a paltry amount of money, but plenty if you lived day to day. That information would have found its way to my desk, back when I was taking care of this place. I wondered if Klaunus had it up on his wall of strings and notes. I knew I should go to see him, to involve him in what was coming, but he'd let me down once already, and I had someone more important to see.

Amaira emerged with a jar of ice drizzled with red syrup. She offered me a wooden spoonful of sugary ice.

'I'm good, thanks,' I said. She smiled happily and shovelled it into her mouth. I'd made Amaira a weapon, in some ways by mistake and some ways by choice, and it was easy to forget that she was barely more than a girl.

'Love this stuff,' she said brightly. 'But where were we? Oh, yes. Valiya. You being back makes all this that much harder for her.'

'She's grieving,' I said. 'For Sang, and for Nall. She knows he's dying.'

'Of course,' she said. 'But that's not all it is, and you know it. Bloody hell, Captain-Sir, but you refuse to see what's right in front of you. Tell me this: why do you think Valiya went to Nall for a deal?'

'It's just her way,' I said. 'She wants something badly enough, she'll go whatever distance is needed.' Something

Amaira had said struck me. 'Wait a moment. She went to him?'

'Yup.'

I frowned. Wordlessly I reached for the jar of ice and shovelled some in my mouth. It was unpleasantly cold, cloyingly sweet. Sucking on it saved me from having to say anything for a while.

'I don't understand,' I said. 'Even for Valiya, that's extreme. The Nameless take far more than they give, even if she can now map out the way a duck flies on her arm. Why would she do that to herself?'

'Make herself inhumanly strange, you mean?' Amaira said. 'Yeah, why would she do that?'

A parent-child relationship is hard to change, especially with the time that had passed, but sometimes I wanted to remind Amaira that I was older, wiser and knew better about everything than she did. I didn't, of course, and I didn't like her suggestion.

'Not everything is about me,' I sighed.

'Not for most people,' Amaira said. 'But can you honestly say you've not dedicated your life to the love you hold for a woman?'

We turned a corner and I was glad to see the familiar, misshapen timbers of The Bell on the street ahead, ending the conversation. I'd lived there once, for a bit, after the Siege. Nenn, Tnota and I had practically held the bar in place for a number of years. There was little to recommend it other than that the beer was cheap and they kept the barrels sealed so the chances of finding a happily drowned mouse in your pint were even lower. I found a toad once, spirits alone know how it had got there. I'd always suspected Nenn's hand in it.

Midday meant that there were only regulars on the benches, and regulars knew well enough not to poke about in anyone else's business, even when someone as refreshing to look at as Amaira wandered in. She'd been fortunate enough to grow up to be beautiful, and in some ways that would bless her life. People would do things for her, think well of her for no other reason, and welcome her into conversation. Men would fall in love with her as easy as falling over. But good looks carried a second edge. She'd attract attention from every drunk, men in authority would seek to coax her into bed, and she'd go to sleep some nights asking herself whether people liked her for anything more than wide eyes and fine cheekbones. I thought of Amaira as a daughter, and in some ways wished she'd grown up to be plainer. A striking appearance wasn't necessarily an advantage for a Blackwing captain.

The people we were meeting were settled in at a corner table, killing time. A well-groomed man of forty, yellow hair that fell halfway down his chest framing a pale, narrow face. He was reading a book of philosophy. He looked handsome in a subtle but well-cut jacket of midnight blue, the slashed sleeves showing silver cloth beneath, and seemed entirely out of place amongst the midday drinkers in The Bell. Beside him, an undignified boy was scratching something into the table with a knife that he probably shouldn't have been, given that he had a bandana all the way down to the end of his nose. The blind kid looked up as we sat down.

'I'd offer you wine, but I'm afraid I only have the one glass,' Dantry Tanza said, putting his book down. He held his hands out apologetically. 'I had to bring it with me. They don't have glasses here, and a tin cup spoils the flavour.'

'The Bell's wine doesn't have any flavour,' I said. I couldn't keep a smile from my face.

'I brought the wine too,' Dantry said. 'I've been paying them to let me sit here all day for the last two weeks. I was beginning to think you weren't coming.'

When I'd first met Dantry, out near Cold's Crater, he'd seemed younger than his years should have allowed. Since then we'd been through a thing or two, and maturity was sitting well with him. Time in Saravor's dungeon had beaten the optimism out of him, and while I'd never have wished that imprisonment on anyone, a little cynicism is good for the soul. He looked healthy. Flourishing. Being the most wanted criminal in the Dortmark states had suited him.

'You weren't worried that the Office of Urban Security were going to come pick you up?'

'They'd never think to find me here,' Dantry said easily. Maybe not all of his optimism had gone. 'Nobody knows who I am down here anyway. Do you like the longer hair? It's a disguise.'

'You look like an actor,' I said. Was it a compliment? Probably not.

'You've not yet introduced me to your companion,' Dantry said.

'Captain Amaira,' she said. 'You don't remember me? I brought you soup.'

Dantry double-blinked at her. His face softened. Lightened. Took back some of that lost youth.

'Well, good grief,' he said. 'You've changed so much. How wonderful to see you again. It's been such a long time. You've, erm, changed so much.'

'Oh, balls, not again,' Maldon muttered.

And I saw in that moment, with a dreadful sinking feeling, that Dantry Tanza had just fallen head over heels in love with a woman half his age, who had absolutely no interest in him whatsoever. She would no doubt mock his stumbling words and make sure he knew that she was about business and nothing else.

'Thank you, I think,' Amaira blushed. 'I like your new hair.'

Double balls. Time to change the subject and get on with business.

'Things are moving fast,' I said. I handed Dantry an

envelope. 'You're pardoned. Keep this with you at all times. I have a copy kept safe in case you lose it, but there's another in the citadel's archive, and a fourth at the courthouse. They can't touch you now, not legally. Congratulations. You're an ordinary citizen again.'

'Well, there's a pity,' Dantry said. 'I rather enjoyed being a man of mystery.'

'What happened at the Snosk mill?' I asked. 'I heard that people died.'

'My fault,' Maldon said. He was drinking what looked to be the The Bell's strongest beer through a hollow reed. I had expected some kind of explanation from Dantry that it had been an accident. Maldon's glib acceptance of what he'd done sent a jolt of anger through me.

'What did you do?'

'It was an error,' Dantry said. He, at least, had the dignity to look pained.

'I miscalculated the backlash,' Maldon said. 'You know how it works. When phos is used, there's a backlash, getting bigger and bigger the more phos that's burned. My calculation was off. But that's why we've been working at this for the last six years, isn't it? Trying to get the numbers right. It's been a bloody nightmare travelling with this fop. Do you know how many times he bathes? *Every day*. And who ends up having to heat the water?'

'It's to maintain the pretence that you're my servant. But I'm no cruel overlord. You've gone off to conduct your fair share of "essential tasks," and before you start, I have absolutely no interest in knowing what horrible things you've been getting up to,' Dantry said airily, but there was a spark of humour in his eyes. 'We *did* try to overload the Snosk mill. The Talents were supposed to be out taking their daily walk around the compound. They don't treat them well down at Snosk, Ryhalt. They're literally chained to the benches. We'd made the calculations for the detonation and the backlash, so that we could take the readings. It was going to be big. I even timed it for the Talents to be as far from the mill as possible. We didn't know some of them had been left inside, though. The ones who were too far gone for it to matter, I suppose. It's on my head.'

I'd wanted an explanation, and I'd had one. Mistakes happened all the time, and I couldn't blame Dantry for it any more than I could blame myself for leading a poor retreat from Adrogorsk. My mistakes had cost a lot more lives than Dantry's miscalculation.

'Not your fault,' Maldon said. 'I'll take the blame. They can hang me for it if they want to.'

'Probably not a satisfactory outcome there for them or for you,' I said. But however serious the incident at Snosk had been, however much damage Dantry had done as he travelled the republic testing his calculations and theories, it was only preamble.

'Tell me then,' I said. I took a deep breath. 'Will it work?'

Dantry turned his wineglass in his hand.

'No.'

I was not deterred. I didn't agree.

'Why not?'

'The backlashes have been hard to measure, but they still weren't enough. Getting into the phos reserves within Nall's Engine was always going to be hard, but even with everything that they've built up there in the last ten years ... What the Taran Codex said about the Nameless – I'm sorry, Ryhalt. It's not enough.'

'But the theory is sound? It can be done, if we have enough power?'

'Providing that Taran was right, then yes. The theory has always been sound.'

'Good,' I said. 'So imagine that we had a hundred Nall's Engines. All their backlashes going back on each other. Would that work?'

'It might,' Dantry said. 'But there's not enough power to do that in all the states.'

My smile cracked the heavy paint on my face.

'Not yet.'

22

Nenn and Marshal Venzer had never met when they were alive, but they sat opposite each other playing, somehow, two entirely different games that bled into one. Nenn was playing tiles, which she'd not been especially good at, but she had been excellent at cheating, so she'd won more often than not anyway. Marshal Venzer was playing a game called Stop, which was only popular amongst the cream, in part because it took three years to learn the most basic rules, and the rulebook was only sold at Lennisgrad University. As far as I could tell, Venzer had successfully stacked his stones around the centre of the board, while Nenn had at least three tiles resting on her knee beneath the table so it was anyone's guess who was going to win. Nenn was drunk, but Venzer had a noose around his neck so that seemed pretty even too.

'Ryhalt. Ryhalt!'

I blinked back and Valiya had my attention again. We were back at her place. Dantry and Maldon were moving their bags up to another of the guest rooms. With me and Amaira taking up the better ones, space was tight and they were going to have to share.

'What?'

'Are you even paying attention? Check the list. It's everything that I think we'll need.'

Valiya had regained her composure. She'd thrown herself

back into her work as a distraction from the meaningless confusion crawling over her arms. She scratched at them without looking as she pointed at items on the list.

'There's too much on here,' I said. 'I don't need all that stuff. Why would I need three tents?'

'It's not just for you,' she said. 'You get one. I'll share with Amaira. Dantry and Maldon can share too, they've been rooming together long enough.'

'I'm not sharing with Nenn,' I said. Valiya's mouth made a hard, tight line.

'You won't have to,' she said gently. 'Nenn doesn't need a tent.'

'You can be the one to tell her that,' I said with a laugh, and then I shook my head. Something was confusing me. The Misery's draw was growing stronger all the time. I let its presence brush against my mind, but I drew back at the briefest of touches. No point wallowing in it when I couldn't be out there.

'Wait,' I said. 'I don't need three. Just two. I'll take Maldon and Dantry, but the rest of you are staying here, where it's safe.'

'Absolutely not,' Valiya said. 'Don't be absurd. This is the most important expedition of our lifetimes. Of course we're going.'

'No,' I said. 'You and Amaira have never been out in the Misery. You don't know what you're saying. And I want you both here, away from whatever happens.'

'We should be there,' she said firmly.

Nenn cackled and placed two of her tiles on top of Venzer's carefully arrayed stones. They wobbled and fell off. Venzer nodded as though it were a thoughtful, well-played move. His turn was going to take up to thirty minutes. Nenn mimed pouring herself another drink, then sat there not-drinking from the invisible cup in her hand.

'Do you know the story of Captain Narada?' I asked.

'No,' Valiya said.

'You wouldn't,' I agreed. 'Narada was a Blackwing captain, ninety years ago. Crowfoot gave her the responsibility of deploying the Heart of the Void against the drudge. Nobody knows what happened, and do you know why? Because the weapon was at the epicentre. The Misery was created and everyone within the killing zone burned up, or got twisted into whatever they became. I don't know what kind of weapon Crowfoot thinks that he can make out of the fiend's heart, but I have a horrible suspicion that it's not going to be entirely dissimilar. It worked once for him, didn't it?'

Valiya stared at me.

'You believe he'd unleash that again?' she asked.

'You know he would,' I said. 'Any of the Nameless would. These are desperate times. They'll employ whatever measures they can to ensure they survive.'

'But you're still going.' She made it a statement.

'I've been preparing for this for six years,' I said, holding my hand up. The black-veined skin across my knuckles had taken on a rough, pebbled texture. Like a lizard, I thought. I wanted to laugh.

'You're not well, Ryhalt,' Valiya said. 'You need us. Your friends. Whatever happens, we're going to drive the Deep Kings back again, as we have before.'

'It's just a cough,' I said. I felt unusually light of heart, which should probably have told me that something wasn't quite right. I didn't feel sick. I felt hungry, and I felt like it was time to get out into the Misery again. I missed my Always House. Those lumps of mutton would be boiling away in the stew and I could dig out that cigarillo from between the floorboards and sit on the porch.

'How much liquorice does one person need?' Valiya asked.

'We have to get there within eleven days or we'll get hit

by the rain,' I said. 'Three roots per day would do most people.' I refused to acknowledge that they were coming. I could argue the point, but neither Valiya nor Amaira had ever been very good at doing what they were told. Short of tying them up, there wasn't any way I could stop them. I was suddenly glad that I'd sent Tnota away before he had to make this choice. I'd never have stopped him. Nenn either. I glanced over to where she rocked back on her chair, dancing to a tune that only she could hear to try to distract Venzer from her attempts to slide a tile into a better, illegal, position.

I knew she wasn't real. It was just nice to pretend sometimes.

'There's been an attack on the citadel,' Valiya said, waking me. 'They want us right away.'

'An attack? By whom?'

'I don't know. We need to get over there now.'

We had our shit together in thirty seconds and were out the door. Two hours before dawn. The phos tubes were mostly dormant and the city was as close to dark as it ever got. We accompanied the citadel sergeant who'd been sent to get us.

'When?'

'Less than an hour ago,' the sergeant said. 'Armed men tried to fight their way in. They were stopped.'

'Who?' I asked.

'I don't know. There's a prisoner. He'll only speak to you.'

We went in by the main gate. With half the citadel demolished, security was much weaker. I saw flawlessly white-skinned Guardians posted at important doors, standing immobile, red eyes watching. Soldiers were out in force, matchlocks on their shoulders and the whole place was lit up like midday.

Davandein met us, with Captain North at her side. I wasn't thrilled to see him.

'What's the short of it?'

'Ten men tried to break in through the damaged wing,' she said. 'Nine armsmen, one sorcerer. We think they were trying to reach the containment chamber where the artefact is being kept.'

'Cultists?'

'That's what you're here to tell us.'

The bodies had been laid out in the courtyard. Heavily armoured men in full harness, packing guns, grenadoes, and keen-edged swords. They were dressed for war, and had brought it against the citadel. I looked down at the first man. His breastplate had been staved in. I could see the maker's stamp near the armour's rim, and knew from experience that that steel could have taken my best swing with a sledgehammer and come away only mildly dented. The second man's head had been removed entirely. The third was missing both of his arms.

'They didn't fare so well.'

'The Guardians brought them to heel in a corridor,' Davandein said. 'First took down the sorcerer. We have him alive in the grey cells. For now, at least. He's badly injured.'

'These men aren't going to do much talking,' Valiya said. 'Have you asked the prisoner anything yet?'

'He'll only talk to you,' Davandein said. 'Kanalina has him bound in a light-field. He won't be able to hurt you. But time is short. We can't risk getting close enough to tend him, and First got overly enthused and did some damage that isn't going to heal. We're on a clock.'

'You notice that these marble things seem to get "overly enthused" whenever there's violence to be done?' I asked.

'They're living weapons like nothing in my arsenal,' Davandein said. 'They're very efficient.' I grunted at that.

'The difference between the other weapons in your

arsenal and these creatures is that you're in control of the rest of your arsenal,' I said. 'Don't overestimate how much you can rely on these things to do what you want. I've learned better than to trust gifts sent by the Nameless.'

'Shallowgrave sent them to serve,' she said.

'I hope you're right. Take us to the prisoner.'

'He's not a pretty sight,' North said. 'But I don't think that he was that pretty before First took a chunk out of him. He's a freak, and a dangerous one.'

'What class of sorcerer is he?' Valiya asked.

'We don't know. He had some killing spells at his disposal and dropped a dozen men before First took him out. Magic bounced off him like it was nothing. Those Marble Guardians are really something, neh?'

I ignored North because I didn't like him. I was not built to forgive and forget. It wasn't just that he'd tried to kill me up at Fortunetown. He'd mistreated Tnota and Giralt too, and even working for the Nameless there are some lines that should never be crossed. For everything that Crowfoot, and to some extent Nall, had put me through over the years, I'd never had to use innocent civilians as bait. When you start hurting your own side, the purpose of having sides at all grows dim. The Lady of Waves was seldom heard from, her mind drifting in slumber through the oceans, but she had just as great a capacity for cruelty as the rest of the Nameless.

We headed down towards the cells. Davandein stopped at the top of the stairs. She didn't want to get close to a sorcerer.

'Don't take any risks, Galharrow,' she said. 'I need you when we march out. We all need you. You're too valuable to lose. If you smell anything that you don't like, I want you out of there.'

Her concern was infinitely touching.

'You can fuck off as well,' I said to North.

'I should hear the interrogation too, neh?' he said.

'You'll fuck right off back up the stairs,' I said. 'I don't trust you, North. I don't like anything about you, and if I'm going to pry information from a sorcerer I sure as shit don't want you at my back.'

North's usual relaxed countenance wavered, and his mouth set in a hard line, but he stopped following me.

'I want you to stay back too,' I said to Valiya. 'I can do this alone.'

'I'd rather be there,' she said.

'And I'd rather you were safe. If I have to worry about you in there with him, then I can't do my job. I'm better alone.' I put a hand on her arm and the magic in her skin tingled faintly against my palm. Nearly gone. She was tense, muscles rigid. But my appeal to getting the job done worked, and she relented.

Spinner Kanalina and First were waiting for me at the entrance to a cell. First had a big white finger in his mouth, worrying away at something lodged between his teeth. His skin was clean, but his black robe was dark and sticky. Kanalina had a heavy canister harness across her shoulders, and light smoked from her skin. She was maintaining her working, a slow, steady expulsion of phos. It would only last until her canisters ran out. The prisoner was on a clock. The *Range Officer's Manual* was quite explicit that no enemy sorcerer could be contained without continuous binding. The recommendation was to interrogate and then put them down. Judging by the string of black gristle that First pulled from his teeth, that was likely to be sooner rather than later. He watched me with emotionless, scarlet eyes.

'What can you tell me about him?' I asked at the door.

'Not much,' Kanalina said. 'He's wrapped up in a phos-matrix. Nothing should get through it. He's an odd one alright. Whatever I asked him, he demanded to speak to you. And I asked him *hard*.'

'I bet you did,' I said. I didn't like Kanalina. And definitely not First. I bore pretty strong grudges against people that had tried to hurt me.

I opened the door and stepped inside, quickly closing it behind me.

'Well, well,' the misshapen lump of charred and twisted flesh hissed from beyond the light-matrix. 'I didn't expect you to get here before my body expires. But you always do like to surprise me.' The mocking tone died away into a bubbling, coughing sound. A double helix of bright gold energy rotated slowly around him, a cage of light.

I don't know what I had expected. Some sort of Darling, maybe, or a sorcerer turned to the Cult of the Deep. I had not expected Saravor in person.

'I wasn't expecting you back so soon,' I said.

Six years ago, Saravor had nearly unmade Shavada's Eye in his bid to unleash the power of ten thousand souls and ascend to the power of the Nameless. He'd failed. Nenn had cut his hand away, and the Grandspire had blasted him from the roof in fury of light. No ordinary body could have withstood that power, not even for a moment, but Saravor's body was anything but normal. He had been freakish before that day, and the light had not left him unscathed.

He sat slumped up against the corner, and although he was naked, the concept did not seem to have the same meaning that it would to the rest of us. Much of him was blackened and charred, his skin hardened like boiled leather. The stiff plates of burned skin were riven with cracks, through which gleaming, wet, red fluid peeked out. One of his eyes was missing altogether, and the socket it should have inhabited was warped and filled with a fleshy growth. The hand that Nenn had cut from him was still missing, the end raggedly cauterised. A great chunk of flesh had been torn from Saravor's neck and shoulder. Teeth marks sat raggedly in the skin, meat and white bone exposed. First had been hungry.

240

The grey children were missing. When I'd last seen him, some of them had been fused into his body, but they were gone now. Instead he was a living wound, all of him burned and misshapen, but his left foot had just two toes. They were unscathed by the fire, and not his original toes – however original any of his parts had been – but there was an unhealthy greenish tinge where they joined the blackened flesh. He'd tried to rebuild himself, probably many times over the years. And he had failed. Some damage is simply too great to heal.

Saravor coughed and black-tinged blood ran from his lips.

'I am dying, Galharrow,' he said.

'Good.'

'I have lost track of the years. How many lives I have lived. What do you think lies for us beyond this life? The welcoming arms of a mothering spirit? It would be a pleasant fantasy to maintain, would it not? That it doesn't all end when the flesh gives out.'

I sat down on a stool. He was a dangerous thing, but bound in light and slowly drowning in his own sluggish blood, he wasn't a threat.

'What did you hope to achieve?' I asked.

'I told you, didn't I?' he said. 'I told you, at the top of the world: the grey children will not allow Crowfoot to unleash his weapon. He must be stopped before he can destroy everything.'

'Are you them?' I asked. 'Are they you?'

'The lines have been blurred for a long time,' Saravor said. His one eye was unfocused, the life slowly draining from it. 'I was a man once. Not this patchwork mess I've become. A real man, with a body of his own and a life. But the body fades. They showed me how to grow, to change. To endure. They were merciful, in their way. But they abandoned me in the end. We are not so different, you and I.'

Saravor reached up to probe the wound, and did not like

what he found. The pain would have been unbearable for an ordinary man. His collarbone peeked out at me through the rent flesh.

'We're nothing like each other,' I said.

'Don't kid yourself, Galharrow,' he said. 'We've both been tools, have we not? Do you really believe that the world is better off in Crowfoot's hands than in those of the grey children?'

'Yes,' I said. 'Because he put his faith in me. And the children put their faith in you. When you get to the very top, maybe they're all the same. But it's the methods that matter.'

'Methods, not results?' Saravor croaked. 'Always so fucking sure of yourself. What happens if your mad plan succeeds? A second Heart of the Void in the Misery won't just tear the sky there. The cracks will widen, spread, flow all the way across the world. Strike a castle wall with one cannonade and the stones crack and crumble. Another volley and it all comes down. Who is the hero then, Galharrow?'

He chuckled at that and blood ran down his chest.

'The Deep Kings have to be stopped,' I said. 'You know what they're capable of. King Acradius took part of The Sleeper's power and bound the others beneath him. They love nothing, not even each other.'

'Betrayal?' Saravor chuckled. It seemed to cost him. 'You don't understand, do you, Galharrow? Where is Nall, now? What happened to him? The triple eclipse comes, but do you really think that with so much power on the table, your master is the only one with designs to use it? Cooperating nicely now, aren't they, the Nameless. Shallowgrave wakes his greatest warriors from a millennium of sleep, the Lady of Waves has risen to take command directly. Crowfall sent his own to get the heart. The sky knows the depth of their treachery, Galharrow. You should ask it sometime.'

'What do you mean?' But Saravor had lost his focus.

He looked at his remaining hand, blackened and charred, fingers twisting in grotesque, warped spirals.

'This body,' he said. 'Which parts of it were me, back at the beginning? Any of it? I don't remember anymore. If you replace yourself piece by piece, when do you cease being you and become something that you've created? If you create yourself, does that make you your own god?'

I saw him slipping away, turning inwards as death drew near. Bitterness welled within me. I wanted to have been the one that destroyed him, for what he had done to me. To Nenn. To so many innocents in Valengrad. To have his throat torn out by a monster seemed too small a punishment for such monumental crimes.

'You had the Taran Codex,' I said. 'If you really want to stop Crowfoot, tell me what else I can do to break Acradius' union with The Sleeper.'

Saravor blinked and focused on me, an effort. Blood was beginning to dribble from his lips.

'Why should I care, now? My game is done. It's left to you to scramble to survive.' He smiled at me. It was a twisted thing, ivory-yellow teeth behind warped and blackened lips. 'You played the game well, Galharrow. I thought the Taran Codex held every answer, but I was wrong. Tell me one thing, before I go.' He choked, spat a jet of blood into the light where it fizzed and evaporated into oily steam. 'I had your woman, the major. She belonged to me. I should have won. How did you take her from me?'

I stood up.

'That was your mistake,' I said. 'She wasn't mine. She wasn't yours either. She never belonged to anybody. If you'd understood that, maybe you could have chosen a different path. Power isn't about forcing people into your control. It comes when people choose to follow.'

Saravor clutched at his chest. Then his hand struck out towards me. A blast of power leapt from his hand, but the lightning helix swirled to intercept it and it ricocheted back into him, punching through his chest.

'Had to try ... to even the ... score ... before I go,' he coughed, the smile not leaving his ruined face. 'I'm going ... I'm going ...'

Saravor's one eye rolled upwards in his head. The body sagged forwards into the helix and the light flared. Flames leapt up, flesh melted and dripped and the stench of burning, rotten meat filled the cell. Slowly the body's own weight carried it forwards into the growing flames. I stood and watched until all of him was gone, the last of him burned into nothing.

There is a moment when you see your enemy defeated and feel a surge of loss against the triumph. For ten years I'd wanted to see Saravor's corpse. He'd put me through the hells, and others besides. He'd been a monster, malicious, filled with spite and hatred. His passing was cause enough for a good bottle of Whitelande brandy. One more obstacle removed. But we build ourselves through the minds of those that surround us and judge ourselves as much by our enemies as by our friends. Somehow, as his body burned away, I felt diminished.

I thought of all the hatred that I felt for Saravor, the ways in which I'd pictured this moment. Putting a sword through his neck, a dagger in his eye, hanging him from the Heckle Gate, or far, far worse when I let anger take hold of me. I had no forgiveness in me for him, and he had been unrepentant. But perhaps at the last, his motives had been pure. It was a frightening thought to consider that we might be on the wrong side of the war.

23

I felt strangely subdued as I went through the legwork in the aftermath of the attack. Saravor had given me nothing. The bodies of the men he'd brought were as I'd expected: rotten through and through on the inside. The Marble Guardians were hovering closer to them than I liked the look of, so I had them taken to an industrial furnace for disposal. Their hunger did not inspire me with confidence.

I walked back with Valiya. She was still scratching at her arms.

'One enemy down,' she said.

'It's something,' I said. 'But Saravor isn't the real enemy. They're coming across the Misery with an army, wizards, and a weapon that can break our last defence.'

'It's not like you to be the defeatist,' Valiya asked.

'No,' I said. 'Never that. I'm just looking at the odds and measuring how long they are.'

'I understand,' she said. She watched the road as we walked, eyes downcast. 'The army is nearly ready to move out. Davandein wants to make a start as soon as possible. North has fresh orders from the Lady of Waves and the Nameless want everything in place as soon as possible.'

'We'll be ready,' I said. 'After the next rains, we can go. You still haven't thought better of it?'

'There's nowhere else for me to go,' she said. 'Everything I care about will happen there.'

We'd won a victory, of sorts. Some soldiers had been killed, but soldiers will always get killed sooner or later, and removing Saravor from the game was big. He'd nearly fucked everything up in the frozen land. Knowing that I didn't have to look over my shoulder for his fixed men was a weight from my shoulders, but they were only the start of the burden that I carried. Valiya was morose, dispirited. She'd been distant ever since we were reunited. I'd remembered her small, mocking smile all through my Misery exile. I missed it now.

'We should celebrate,' I said. 'Come on. I know a place. They have actual crab meat, all the way from the coast.'

'We're hardly dressed for dinner,' she said.

'What does that matter?'

'They'll take one look at us and tell us to get back to the Misery,' she said. 'You're made of metal and I've mirrors for eyes. What respectable place is going to accept us?'

'I never said it was respectable,' I said. 'Come on. No arguments.'

I didn't get the smile that I was looking for, but she went along with it nonetheless.

Valengrad was a long, long way from the sea. Despite that, the Salt Shaker did indeed serve a variety of animals that had been brought all the way from the coast. It was potluck what was still alive in their tanks, and better luck yet if you could pull them out without getting your fingers nipped. There were no private tables; guests sat at long rows of benches, shoulder to shoulder, while the waiting staff brought jugs of beer. It was not a place of gentility and culture, even if it was offering exotic cuisine. There was a rough-and-ready approach that I'd always appreciated.

'This is an … interesting place,' Valiya said, sitting opposite me across the table. The wood had been carved with the names of people who'd eaten there and underneath it they'd listed how many dishes they'd managed to get through.

Nenn's name was there somewhere, down the table.

'It's not the best place in the city,' I said. I felt suddenly ashamed for bringing her here. I'd thought that, being a busy, beer-fuelled kind of place, we'd blend in better than at some kind of fine-dining eatery where a couple of lines of pureed lamb kidneys drizzled across half a lonely onion was somehow considered impressive. Everyone else here was too busy drinking the taste of the crab out of their mouth to give us much of a second look, but when you take a woman someplace, you're telling her what you think of her. Maybe I'd misjudged it.

'No, I like it,' Valiya said. 'It reminds me of home. By the sea. What should we eat to celebrate the demise of an enemy?'

'I tend to go with whatever they're prepared to get out of the tank for me,' I said. 'It's been a long time since I've eaten here. Or anywhere.'

The serving girl came to take our order.

'You don't have any wine, do you?' Valiya asked. The waitress shook her head. 'Beer it is then.'

'Just water for me,' I said.

I'd never known Valiya to drink, and she wasn't good at it. She'd make a single pint of beer last the entire night, but that wasn't a bad thing. I no longer felt that urgent need to guzzle it down as I once had. If my time in the Misery had done one thing good for me, it had allowed me to end that old addiction. I couldn't say that I felt any better for it. Some dead sealife arrived, probably not crab but it looked like it had once lived in a shell. It wasn't particularly good, but there was bread and butter to go with it and I wasn't fussy. I couldn't tell if Valiya was enjoying herself or just playing along to keep me happy.

For a time, we spoke of small things. How far we thought Tnota and Giralt might have got inland, how well Amaira had taken to her new life, and how Dantry had spent

247

breakfast getting his words muddled up around her. I should probably have a word with him.

'Amaira told me what you saw, in the ice caves,' she said. The lightness of my mood deepened, and an edge of discomfort settled in between us.

'We all saw a lot of things down there we'd probably rather not,' I said.

'I'm talking about Ezabeth,' Valiya said.

'I know.'

'I've not been honest with you,' Valiya said. She looked away. 'I saw her. In the ice cavern. I could see her, beneath the crack.'

I stopped with a forkful of probably-not crab meat to my mouth. Put it back down on the plate.

'Why would you do that?'

'I don't know,' she said. But she did know. We both knew that she knew. She took a big swig from her mug. 'I panicked. I didn't know what to say. There you were, back after all that time, and there she was as well. I only saw her once, when she saved us. But ...'

I felt cold all over.

'But what?'

'It wasn't my place,' she said, anger or frustration hardening her words. 'She was there for you. She's always there for you. I'm not part of whatever you shared. I never will be. Even in all that, I was an intruder. She'll always hold your heart.'

It had been ten years. Ten years, and it was still raw.

'She always will,' I said. I could only be honest. 'You understand, I guess. You've known what it's like to lose someone.'

'I do,' Valiya agreed. 'But at least that was clean. Davan died, and he was gone. I wasn't faced with him lingering on.' She gave me a look that said that she understood. She hesitated a moment and then reached out and put her hand,

248

small and bony, over the back of my scarred knuckles.

'When you lose someone, it's always hard,' I said. 'I'm not asking for special allowances. Ten years is a long time. Let's say that she'd lived, that we'd won properly. That I hadn't let her down. I've imagined it, often enough. Maybe we'd have been happy together. But when I saw her under that crack in the world ... it wasn't her. Not really. Not anymore.'

'She came for you,' Valiya said gently. 'Through death. Through the light. Through another world.'

'I know,' I said. 'And I'll be there when she needs me.'

Valiya smiled sadly at me.

A growling rose outside, like the groan of a huge, ancient door that hadn't moved for centuries. We locked eyes in sudden alarm, put down our cups, and headed outside into the chill. The sound filled the night, issuing from the sky. And then it heaved and the cracks, immobile and locked into place since the day they'd torn across the sky, *flexed*.

'What in the hells is happening?' Valiya breathed.

The light beyond the cracks boiled and steamed, and I thought that maybe this was it. Maybe this was the end of the world. If those fractures tore open then there was no saying what would happen. I stood powerless, waiting for annihilation. I wanted to take Valiya's hand, but she had walked a few steps farther, her arms held up before her.

'Oh, no,' she said.

Dark clouds boiled from the cracks, flooding the sky. They rolled out in every direction at speed, shadowing the land. Valiya began to walk towards the wall and I called to her to come back, but she wasn't listening.

The wind struck just before the clouds rolled over the city, a driving gale. The people who had emerged to stare screamed and fell head over heels across the street. The gust rocked me but I stayed upright as Valiya grabbed hold of a hobbling post. The sky snarled above us, the wind roared, and then the rain hit. It came down like a wall, a sudden, blazing torrent that gleamed like beads of obsidian in the phos light. It barely registered before I was soaked through, and then my skin began to burn.

Screams rose even above the rush of the rain and the dirge of the wind. Through the lenses of my goggles I saw Valiya collapse. I ran to her and scooped her up. She twitched and convulsed, eyes rolling around in her skull and foam spitting from her lips as a fit took her. My Misery-hardened skin fought back against the pain. The water soaked through my clothes in moments, but I ran back to the Salt Shaker and forced my way back in through the luckier patrons who were trying to drag a fallen man back in through the door. There were others out there, lying in the road, far more than I could help. Far more than I could do anything for. They crawled, howling as if beset by clouds of hornets, blind and groping for shelter.

The rain had not been due for another eight days. Lights danced before my eyes, twisted images flashed through my mind.

I got Valiya over to the bar and punched a hole straight through the side of a beer keg. I doused her in it, showering the dark liquid over her exposed face and hands, then upended it over myself. The keg ran out and I went for the next. The barman glanced from his stock and then to me in a fleeting moment of horror, but he was a better man than that and began to do the same for the others who had been dragged inside. Shrieking came from beyond the windows, as the rain began to flood the unfortunates' minds with twisted, rippling images.

I was not immune, and they were upon me.

I staggered and fell against the bar, shattering glasses and sending dirty plates and fish bones across the floor. I saw a face before me, familiar, sad and weary, but Nall's eyes were hard and focused. They stared into me as I tried to shake him from my mind. I was dimly aware that the floor had risen to meet me. Nall's face disappeared. I saw the place of power, not broken this time but serene, the sky unbroken above it. Three figures sat hunched and frozen in the ice, and a fourth stood alongside them. Ezabeth, caught in light, wisps of flame playing along her arms and brow. She was shouting at them, angry. Ice cracked and fell away as Crowfoot's twisted head turned to look at her.

Shooting stars obliterated everything. I was hurtling, faster and faster through the rain's mad visions. I felt the black, lightless silence at the bottom of the deepest ocean and below me, buried under a mile of silt and stone, a vast and terrible presence stirring. I saw the streams of magic, wavering like weeds as they flowed away. The thing down there was too big. Too terrifying, and yet familiar.

My mother leaned over me, snapping and scolding. My trouser leg was torn, white-linen knees stained with grass where my brother and I had scrapped and rolled around. There were visitors coming, what had I been thinking?

Liquid in my face, the familiar taste of poorly aged brandy. The sparkling lights crackled and shimmered at the edges of my vision as the bar came back into view. The rain continued to hiss outside and my skin burned, raw and bitten. Nall's image remained imprinted on my vision, staring at me. It began to fade, and as it did it gave me a final, slow, nod. Then it was gone.

I crawled over to Valiya. Her body shook.

'Do you have a bath?' I asked the barman as he carried bottles to and from the casualties that had been rescued. Some people had run outside and hauled in more, and they too needed treating.

'No,' he said and hurried on.

Wherever my wet clothes touched me was like being under a tattooist's needle. We needed to get out of them and dry. I dragged Valiya over to the stove where chowder was bubbling over, heaved the heavy pan aside and went and got hold of a stout woman who hadn't been as dumb as us and had stayed inside.

'My friend over there needs to get dry. Cut her out of her clothes and put her in this.' I passed her my trench coat, which I'd left on a peg when I came in. The woman had the look of a mother who'd had to do much worse for many children, and she went to it quickly.

Valiya's modesty mattered, but mine didn't. I stripped down to my smalls and stood awkwardly, looking odd in Misery-golden skin and plaster-white powder. I drew more than one worried look, but there was worse than my appearance to be concerned about.

The sky had torn and sent out the maddening rain. Early. How many people had been caught outside in the sudden downpour? The aftereffects of the vision lingered in my mind. Nall's eyes, sorrowful. Knowing. I'd seen him die twice before. But this was different. Final. When Cold had died, he'd exploded, and his passing had driven a hole into the earth so deeply that not even the Misery could wipe it away.

Nall was gone, and the sky had felt it even more deeply.

We had lost one of the Nameless.

It was unthinkable. All my life, there had been four. Crowfoot, working away behind the scenes, twisting and manipulating. The Lady of Waves, guarding the oceans and punishing any of the Deep Kings' minions that tried to raise a sail. Shallowgrave, dark and hidden and emerging only in the deep of night. And Nall, who had given us his Engine to keep us safe, who had walked amongst us in a thousand ordinary, unassuming guises. The Deep Kings had always outnumbered our protectors. Now they were even fewer, and we were lost.

When Cold had died, his captains had died with him. Horror assailed me twice over – but Valiya was still alive. I hadn't known what would happen if this came to pass. Had chosen not to consider it. But she hadn't exploded. She still breathed. That was something.

After twenty tense minutes, the rain abated. It could have gone on forever. There were no rules now. Water the colour of night ran through the gutters and nobody dared to venture outside. I looked out of the window. A body lay twitching in the middle of the street. We had not been able to save everybody.

Valiya woke as the rain abated. She stared at me with wide, silver eyes. And then her brow drew in, her mouth opened wide, and she let out a despairing sob. I pulled her to me and let her bury her face in my chest as she wept for the passing of a legend. I held her there for a long time, saying nothing, having no words for what had just transpired.

'I saw it all,' she said.

'Saw what?'

'The Crowfall,' she said. 'I know what they did.'

She didn't say any more, and I knew that I couldn't ask. I'd seen the start of it too, I thought. Ezabeth, standing over the Nameless, berating them. I could have smiled if I hadn't been stung, and afraid, and mourning the death of a god.

When Valiya pulled away, my chest was streaked with lines of gleaming mercury. They ran down Valiya's hollow cheeks like the branches of winter trees. When she opened her eyes again, they were blue, beautiful, and human. She drew back her sleeve to look at her arms. The numbers had stopped moving. They were static, locked into figures of impossible complexity. Valiya stared at them, eyes working across from left to right. New letters appeared there now, written in the silver that had been in her eyes. She pressed her arm against her chest, hiding it from me.

'What is it?' I asked.

'It's a final message,' she said. 'From Nall. His last thought.'

'What did he say?'

She shook her head.

'I know my role now,' Valiya said. 'I know what I have to do.' She wiped a smear of silver from her face onto the sleeve of my coat and spoke between gritted teeth. Her eyes had never shown more determination. 'Nall is gone,' she said. 'But we can still win. You and me, Ryhalt. It's not over yet.'

24

In times of crisis, Valengrad pulls together. Those unfortunate enough to have been outside when the rain hit found strangers opening their doors to them. But the Maud was still overwhelmed by the unfortunates carried to its doors.

Davandein's sixty thousand men had fared far worse.

They had their waxed tents and had been coping with the rain as it swept the land every eleven days for years. Routine creates security. But they'd been drilling when the rain struck, a mile from their camp, and thousands had been unable to find shelter.

Some were dead. Others were completely, utterly mad. I stood alongside Davandein as we looked out at the makeshift field hospital, a vast canvas canopy packed with weeping, jabbering men.

'The greatest army the city-states of Dortmark has ever raised,' she said bitterly. 'The best soldiers money can buy, turned to nursing twenty thousand gibbering wrecks.' She was pale, and her jaw was clenched.

'Some of them will recover,' I said. 'At least we can hope so.'

'And then what, Galharrow? Do we venture out in the hope that the rain doesn't come again? We've taken a massive blow from that one fall of rain. What do we do, walk out into the Misery and hope that the weather stays on our side?' She shook her head in anger as if trying to eject her bitter thoughts. 'It's not even the enemy striking at us. It's the bloody sky itself. Is this what it looks like? The end of the world? Is that the edge we stand upon?'

'We always stood at the end of the world,' I said. 'That's what makes this so important. We're the last defence, Marshal. We always have been.'

We walked down into the hospital. The canvas was all heavy, wax-treated tarpaulin that would keep the rain off when it inevitably came to torment us again. Inside, men and women, proud soldiers and camp followers, were tied down to their cots. Their comrades had done what they could to lessen their pain and had padded the ropes with cloth, but those that struggled against them still scraped their skin raw. Some lay staring upwards, immobile, mouthing silent words. Other cried, or gibbered, or begged.

'I don't want to see,' a young gunner whispered over and over. 'I don't want to see. Take it away. Take it away.' His face was scratched and blistered from exposure to the rain.

'He tore my heart out,' a woman said, trying to claw at her chest. 'Give it back! Give my heart back!'

'Don't listen to her, she's mad,' someone said. It took me a moment to realise that he wasn't speaking to us but arguing with the empty air beside him. 'What does she know? Nothing. Ignore her. She's lying.'

'The Sleeper,' an older man croaked. 'It's coming. Surrender to it. Surrender to the Kings.'

'Is there any hope for them?' Davandein asked.

'I don't know.' I didn't.

We walked through the rows of cots. It was important that Davandein be seen here. Not for the patients – they didn't know her anymore – but for those treating them. It showed that she cared, that she knew their plight. Compassion builds loyalty, and she needed that.

The sheer scale of it was horrifying. I'd defended Valengrad with fewer men than now wept and spouted nonsense.

I spotted something beneath one of the beds, a small, clay-like figure no bigger than my finger. A Sapler. I pulled it out and stamped on it. The orderlies checked for the little monstrosities daily, but they sensed the despair and it drew them, or they formed out of air, or however they got there. Davandein was right. The world was ending. Even if we could stop the Deep Kings, how could we survive when the sky itself tore down everything that we tried to build?

'My plan won't work,' Davandein said.

'No,' I said. 'One storm like that out in the Misery and the army will die on its feet. They'd never make it to Adrogorsk. We'd be asking them to walk into death.'

'Then we're lost,' Davandein said. 'We have the Nameless' weapon but we can't empower it.'

'We can,' I said. 'We will.'

'How?'

It didn't look good. But there were few choices left to us.

'We need covered wagons,' I said. 'Animals don't care about the rain. It only affects people. Wagons with tarpaulin covers, so that if the rain hits, we can shelter inside. One wagon per dozen people.'

'We'd need five thousand of them,' Davandein said in horror. 'Even if we had the means – and we don't – then a wagon train that long would crawl.'

'I'll take whoever we can outfit,' I said. 'If needs be, it will be me, Captain Amaira, Captain Klaunus, and a Spinner to work the loom during the eclipse. Winter will insist on coming with us. And I want every soldier you can outfit.'

Davandein's expression resolved into something harder. She forced her despair aside, soldier that she was.

'I'll put people on it right away. But it won't be many. Maybe not enough to handle the Misery.'

'I've survived longer in the Misery than you can even dream of, Marshal,' I said. 'I'll worry about the Misery.'

'And what if the Deep Kings get their warriors to

Adrogorsk ahead of you? You need soldiers.' She nodded to herself. A desperate plan, but all we had. 'I'm sending the Marble Guard with you, and anyone else that I can muster.'

'I don't like them,' I said. 'I don't trust them.'

'When the Nameless send us weapons, we're better off not turning our noses up at them. They aren't like us, it's true. But they're each worth a score of soldiers. You couldn't ask for better protection, and the rain doesn't affect them at all. They endured the whole storm. You'll take them, because this mission is more important than what you do or don't like. I've Spinners to send with you as well.'

'Fine,' I said. 'I'll take the Guardians and all the Spinners and soldiers you can muster. I want your best.'

'Very well. Captain North will accompany you as well,' Davandein said.

'I don't trust him either.'

'He's the one who brought us the eclipse-loom schematic from the Lady of Waves. You'll need him. He says the Deep Kings have an army of ninety thousand drudge about to enter the Misery.'

I might not like it, but I needed that loom.

'I have some idea of what Crowfoot intends,' I said. I was interrupted by a heaving in my chest. More Misery slime made its way out of me. Davandein looked on with voiceless eyes. 'Some of it,' I continued, when it passed. 'But the Lady of Waves and Shallowgrave – they're unknown quantities to me. They want to empower the fiend's heart, but what then? Which of them gets to use it? I worry, Marshal. I fear their apparent unity isn't what it seems. We give them the power of the eclipse, bound into a fossilised heart, and then what?'

Davandein shifted uneasily. Her face was grim.

'Then we learn whether we were right to trust them.'

'The Deep Kings won't wait around to let us. We both know that. I don't want to get to Adrogorsk and find them waiting for us. I doubt even the Guardians could cut a path through that many drudge.'

Davandein nodded.

'I'll have the wagons rigged for you. How long do you need to get ready?'

'The eclipse won't wait on us,' I said. 'We'll go tomorrow morning. I'll meet your people at Station Three-Four. That's the best point to head out from.'

As we passed by, one of the patients tried to sit up.

'Ryhalt,' she said. 'I'm so sorry I have to do this. I'm sorry I can't wait for you. I can't hold on anymore. I have to let go.'

Her voice had a hollow, metallic echo to it. A lump rose up in my throat, hardening, constricting.

'How do you know my name?' I asked.

'We have to act now,' she said. 'Whatever it takes, whatever it costs. What are you waiting for?'

She wasn't speaking to me anymore. She stared off down the endless rows of beds, and then she began to laugh, struggling and thrashing against her bonds. Her cries set off a series of groans and sobs from the nearby patients until the whole place was ringing with their madness. It had been nothing. Maybe I had misheard.

Nenn and Venzer knelt on the other side of the bed and began rolling cigarillos. Strange that they could be so calm when everyone around them seemed to be going crazy.

'We go tomorrow,' I said. Valiya nodded without looking up. She'd laid out schematics across the table and I looked them over. It was the loom that we'd be dragging across the Misery, unique in its design. The pages themselves had a strangely metallic sheen. The Lady of Waves had designed them to be indestructible.

I poured myself a cup of water and sat opposite her.

'You don't have to come,' I said.

'We've been over this before. There's really no option.'

'I don't want you to come,' I said.

Valiya looked up from the metallic paper.

'You'll need all the help you can get,' she said. 'Did Davandein agree?'

'She's sending the Marble Guard with us. And North.'

'We knew that she'd insist on the former, and I feared the latter,' she said. 'It can't be avoided. Who is she sending to work the loom?'

'Kanalina,' I said. 'I don't like her either.'

'She's good enough,' Valiya said. 'She follows orders. And she didn't rack you when she had the chance.'

'Maybe I just don't like other people,' I said. 'Where's Dantry?'

'He's upstairs,' Maldon said, emerging from the wine cellar with a bottle in hand. 'He's with Amaira.'

I felt a moment of intense unease. Valiya studied her shiny papers with unnecessary intensity. Maldon gave me a shit-eating grin from beneath the scarf that covered the hole in his face.

'What are they doing?'

Maldon began to make perverse hip-thrusting motions around the room.

'Stop that,' Valiya said. 'He's telling her about the Misery. What to expect out there.'

'I taught her about the Misery when I was training her,' I said with a frown.

'Oh. Then I don't know what they're doing. Ryhalt,' Valiya called to me as I started for the stair. 'No.'

'No what?'

'No, you're not going to check what they're doing. If Amaira wants to pretend that she needs Dantry to tell her all about the Misery, then she's quite welcome to his wisdom. Isn't she.' She did not make it a question.

'You shouldn't come with us,' Maldon suddenly said to

Valiya. 'Tell her, Ryhalt. Tell her that she needs to stay here.'

'I'm going,' Valiya said.

'You can argue with her if you want,' I said. It would be a losing battle for him, just as it had been for me.

'We've a mission. You've no role to play in it,' Maldon said. 'I'm necessary. Dantry is necessary. Ryhalt is essential. But you aren't. You're a distraction.'

'I have a role to play,' Valiya said. 'I know what I'm needed for. I'm as necessary to this as any of you. It was Nall's last message.'

'Really?' Maldon snorted. 'And what's that?'

'You'll just have to trust me,' Valiya said. 'I'll not get in the way.'

'You get in the way just by being around,' Maldon said. 'You make Ryhalt all confused. And he can't be confused when we get there.'

'Leave it,' I warned him. 'Go and drink your wine and stop bothering the adults.'

'That's low,' Maldon said. He turned his back and headed off to be someplace else, but as he went he snapped his fingers and the phos tubes all died.

'Put those back on!' I called after him, but he didn't bother. 'That little shit,' I grumbled as I headed down into the cellar to crank the primer and get the lights going again. A few turns of the handle and the phos-flow re-engaged and the place got back to brightness.

I got back to the workroom to see Amaira and Dantry coming down the stairs.

'Was that Maldon again?' Dantry asked. I raised one annoyed eyebrow in his direction, but he didn't seem to grasp that I was more annoyed with him than I was with the small, extremely annoying immortal. Amaira looked happier than she had any right to, given that we were heading to the end of the world in the morning.

I looked around at this strange little family. We'd spent six years apart from one another, doing the things that needed doing, and now without any time to rest and get to know one another again, to learn how we'd changed over those years, we were being thrust straight back into the skweam's jaws. Had I been able to choose, I would have left them all here. I would have sent them west, far away, to lands where they'd never heard of Deep Kings and the hearts of ice fiends were nothing but stories with which to frighten children.

'Get ready,' I said. 'Tomorrow we step back into hell.'

25

A subdued procession travelled alone with their thoughts, heading north along the supply road and up to Station Three-Four. The longhorns drawing the wagons couldn't keep pace with the tireless Guardians, whose long legs and steady march saw them pull ahead frequently. They said nothing, but they understood my orders and were always waiting for us at the arranged overnight stops. They had no need of shelter. Since they emerged from their pods, the Guardians seemed to have no need of anything. On the first night they stood outside Station Three-One in ordered rows around the box that contained the ice fiend's heart, long glaives resting on their shoulders, waiting to start moving again the next day. Their weapons were engraved with ancient sigils, and nobody knew where they had come from. I didn't doubt that a sweep of one of those glaives would cut through horses three at a time. The Guardians unnerved me, but nobody doubted that they would be effective. The box that the shred of heart had been stored in was a huge thing of black iron, and the Guardians allowed nobody near it. Not even me.

We stood on the edge of the Misery and looked out into madness.

The cracks in the sky had broadened and splintered. New branches spread in jagged, delicate paths. Rays, called god-lights when they spilled through clouds, fell from the heavens across the Misery's black-and-red expanse, spot-lights falling to the bleak and dangerous stage below. The sky crowed, squealing with restless torment.

I was just as restless to get back out there. This was my land. Vast, sprawling, more fickle than luck – but mine.

'Just waiting on the soldiers, neh?' Captain North said. He'd tied his long hair back in a tail, but he'd chosen to forgo any armour. My own was stowed on one of the wagons. I'd been able to claim it from a man of my size who'd been struck down by the rain. It was a lucky fit; not many suits of lobstered steel were made for men of my size. But while North wasn't wearing harness, he'd acquired a new weapon: an eight-foot-long spear, the shaft black and inscribed with oceanic sigils, tipped with a head of what looked like jade. There was something unsettling about the weapon. It seemed oddly familiar, though I'd never seen its like before.

'They'll be here shortly,' I said. The dawn had risen cold, the Misery-taint blowing towards us from the east. 'That spear. What is it?'

'Your master isn't the only one who bestows gifts,' North said. I didn't like his smile. 'The Lady looks out for her captains. She crafted this from the crystal gardens on Pyre. It'll bring down the worst monster the Misery can offer.'

'Shame she didn't send more,' I said.

'Captain Klaunus is coming with the soldiers?' North asked. I nodded.

'Should be.' I turned to meet his eye. 'When we're out there, you're going to do what I say. You get that? The moment I think you're doing anything but what you're told, I'll send you walking into a field of razor grass. I don't like you, North. Don't forget that when the time comes you get sick of being told what to do. This is my expedition.'

'You're the navigator, neh?' he said easily. 'But it's the Nameless' plan we're following here. When we get to Adrogorsk, I'm setting the loom up. I don't have any tender feelings for you either, but we both need this to work. The alternative doesn't bear thinking about.'

'Tell me this: you tried to kill me at Fortunetown. How long before you try it again?'

North shook his head. Smirked.

'I'm a captain, Galharrow,' he said. 'We put down monsters. That's always been the job, hasn't it? But whatever it is you've made yourself into, you're nothing compared to what's coming. One fishes for minnows to pass the time, but only while the leviathans sleep.'

'And Captain Linette? Josaf? What did they do to anger the Lady?'

'I've plenty of blood on my hands,' he said easily, 'but none of it theirs.'

I found it hard to believe that; but North was so blasé about having tried to kill me at Fortunetown, it seemed strange for him to get coy about that. I could not forgive him for what he'd done to Tnota and Giralt. We might be on the same side now, but when this was over, all bets were off.

I looked over the people that I'd brought with me. The last hope for Dortmark. For humanity. Valiya, Dantry, Amaira, Maldon. People of rare and unusual talent. They were both the people I wanted by my side most, and the people that I wanted as far from it as possible.

The soldiers arrived two hours later than planned. Davandein's people had done well to mobilise in time, and that spoke of their quality.

'How many do we have?' I asked General Kazna as she drew her mount in. I'd known Kazna back when we were both brigadiers. Her career had gone somewhat better than mine. She was wiry, her narrow face pocked from Misery-worm, her armour scuffed and dented from a history of service. Her hair had gone grey a decade ago, but streaks of indigo dye running through it were a regimental reminder of time she'd spent serving overseas, fighting the savages in Karnun. She was a professional, a varied career behind her and soldier running through her to the core. She gave no indication what she made of me.

'Nearly a thousand,' she said. 'They're the best the citadel has. Veterans to a man. We've three hundred gunners, a hundred archers and the rest are mostly cavalry. I've a handful of engineers, and the Spinners.'

We lived in a world of powder and shot, but archers trained from childhood could still put out four times the rate of fire of a gunner. I'd have taken any number of archers over gunners any day, but it took years to train a man to learn the bow, and just weeks to learn the matchlock.

There were ten Battle Spinners, including Kanalina, and they'd loaded their first wagon with phos canisters. The second carried the loom, deconstructed into its parts and dragged by a team of six big longhorns. The iron mountings were thick and heavy, and the huge focusing lenses must have weighed a tonne apiece. The Marble Guard would be needed to construct it, under North's supervision, when we got there. They'd brought two additional navigators as backup, but they wouldn't be able to find Adrogorsk, not the way the Misery shifted around it now. A way home in case I got myself killed, maybe.

'You're late,' I said to Kanalina when she stepped down from the wagon. 'Where's Klaunus?'

She ushered me to walk a few steps away from the others with her.

'He's not coming,' she said. Her face was hard, rigid as a statue. 'He's dead.'

'Dead?'

'Suicide,' she said grimly. 'Looks like he took a pistol up to the top of that clock tower of his and blew a hole in the side of his head.'

Klaunus had not been a friend, but he had been a

Blackwing captain. His death was a blow to Crowfoot's plans. I shook my head.

'You're sure he did himself?'

'The door was locked and bolted from the inside, and there's no other way out of that tower unless someone killed him and then jumped out of a five-storey window,' Kanalina said. 'I had to burn the locks off. He was lying across his desk with a spent gun in his hand.' She shook her head. 'The selfish bastard!'

Another captain gone, just when we needed him most. I had sensed his despair. I understood it. Perhaps I should have done more for him. I had killed Silpur and Vasilov. Klaunus had shot himself in the head. Amaira and I were the only Blackwing captains left now.

'I've known stronger men to take that path,' I said, thinking of my old friend and commander, Venzer. He was over on the roof of a nearby house chasing birds. 'Better not to speak ill of the dead. His powers would have been useful out there, but we'll manage without. Keep this between us, it won't do anything for morale.'

Kanalina nodded sombrely. She caught sight of Maldon. He was bored, having to pretend that he was as blind as the scarf around his face made out, so he was deliberately asking childish questions to which he already knew the answers.

'What is that child doing here?' Kanalina asked.

'He's how I navigate,' I said. 'Don't worry. He's used to it.' It was the best excuse I'd been able to come up with to explain why Maldon had to accompany us.

'You can't be serious?' she breathed. 'You take a child into the Misery with you?'

'Hard times call for hard methods,' I said. That was true, even if I was lying, but the disgust in her eyes was difficult to stomach all the same. I'd given everything for this. My body, my position, even my reputation. It didn't matter. I told myself it didn't matter.

*

I felt the world change beneath me as I put my foot onto the Misery's grit. Her welcome flowed up through my boot, filling me, a chorus of greeting at my return. Like a drink of iced water on a summer's day, she passed all the way through, filling me, flooding the tiny particles that made up my body, greeting the magic she'd put into me like a long-lost daughter, exultant in reunification. Pains that I'd been trying to ignore evaporated, and a weariness in my soul grew light and heady. I walked into her clutches, breathing in her beautiful, exotic scent.

'Good to have you back with us, Captain,' Nenn said. 'Where are we headed?'

'Adrogorsk,' I said. 'Where else? That's where this whole long journey began, isn't it? It was never going to end anywhere else.'

'Think you'll do a better job than last time?' Betch asked. Nenn's beau leaned one arm on her shoulder. The thin, straight line of the knife blade's cut across his throat glowed red in Rioque's crimson rays.

'We can only try,' I said.

'Got you something to commemorate the journey,' Nenn said. I raised an eyebrow as she handed me a canteen – the kind soldiers carried, wide-necked, fat bodied – but made of silver. An inscription on it read *Always with you, boss*. I unscrewed the cap and gave it a sniff – brandy.

'I never drink anymore,' I said.

'Never's a long time,' she said with a grin.

Nenn and Betch faded into the wind as Valiya rode towards me. As I stowed the canteen away in my coat, I was caught by the way her hair caught the colours of the sky, a halo of indigo and violet. I blinked and the effect was gone. Valiya gave me a halfhearted smile but said nothing, only focused on matching the horse's gait with her hips. She was not a natural rider, but it wasn't the sway of the animal's back that was bothering her. 'It gets easier after a while,' I said. 'Don't break out the liquorice yet. The longer you can leave it, the better you'll do.'

'I've lived beside the Misery for so long,' she said. 'I never knew what it was like to step into it. I can feel it soaking into me. In my nose, in my eyes, my gums. Spirit of Mercy, it's like winter cold getting into your bones.'

'You get used to it, eventually,' I said, although that wasn't true. You couldn't get used to the Misery, not without changing. That, I had come to understand, was what she was: the essence of change. For change to occur to a subject, there has to be a reason, but the Misery was reason without subject. She twisted everything, made it different, a random, uncontrolled sluice into alteration. I could have written a philosophy book about it, but without living the way that I had, drawing the Misery into me day by day, I doubt that anybody could have understood.

The wagons rolled out onto the sands. The journey began.

I knew, with a roaring through my bones, the very moment Deep King Acradius entered the Misery.

The best of our scholars couldn't say what the Deep Kings were. Their origins were known only through fragmented legend. They had been subjugated by the Nameless, or something else, something worse, and imprisoned beneath the ocean. They lingered there, trapped, isolated, powerless, and entombed for uncounted generations. Then they had risen, they had conquered, and their power was a match for the Nameless who supposedly watched over us. Behemoths. Gods. They compared to a man as a man does to an ant. I had come face-to-face with King Shavada, in the heart of Nall's Engine. He had been darkness bound into something greater, but his mere presence had driven me to my knees. He had not even noticed I was there.

Emperor Acradius was so much more than Shavada had been.

If I was an ant, and Shavada had been a man, then Acradius was a mountain. His mind slammed into me and the Misery braced my legs and kept me upright as I felt a howling gale all around me, the screaming, roaring wind of ten thousand shrieking souls. I saw a second world, the shadow-world that lurks behind the first, but the Misery rose to bolster my spine, and the storm was nothing but a storm.

The mountain saw me. Gazed into me. Baleful, glaring, so filled with his endlessness that to be the focus of that titanic stare was to feel the weight of the ocean above, and the darkness of it below. But ant or man, he felt my presence as surely as I felt his. We were separated by hundreds of miles, across shifting, inconstant, and corrupted planes of sand and stone, but he knew. He knew, and he saw me as an enemy. Something worth fighting.

You have my brother's heart, he said to me. Not in words, but in knowledge. It passed through the gulf of distance between us to hammer like falling millstones against my mind. As vast as he was, he was not just one entity. I felt that outsider, something that lurked around his edges, a mould creeping inwards, consuming. Acradius was not simply a Deep King. He was bound up with some small essence of The Sleeper and it surged towards the heart we carried in the iron box. Its kin.

This is my land, I replied. *Do you understand what I have become?*

A rush of dark presence surrounded me, whirred and snarled across hundreds of tormented miles. I was not afraid. Not here, walking within the loving arms of my mother.

You are abomination, Acradius whispered. *A mouthpiece for that which cannot be controlled. A vent for its flaw. You belong to the shattered sky.*

Then you know that I must stop you, I told him.

I know you will try, Acradius said. *But I see you, mortal instrument. Your leaders have betrayed you and fight bitter wars amongst themselves. They scramble for scraps of power, that they might take them and flee before my might. It will not avail them. All will submit. All will be ruled.*

'Tell him to fuck off,' Nenn said helpfully.

I stopped you once before, I said, and let the Misery flow within me. I showed him what I was, what I had become. *And I'll stop you again.* The Misery drove deeper through my mind, angry at his presence, and with a snap she drove him out. The howling wind vanished, the shadow-lands faded. It was as easy as that, only the sharp chemical-metal taste remaining around my mouth.

'Ryhalt!' Amaira said, shaking my shoulder. I had not been aware of her. I felt hot wetness on my lips, reached up and wiped away the blood that ran from my nose.

'I'm fine,' I said. Amaira mopped my face. I saw that the Marble Guardians were watching me with a disconcerting level of intensity. Or rather, they were watching the bloody handkerchief that Amaira stuffed back into a pocket.

'Is it affecting you that much?' she asked.

I looked down at the beautiful lights that shimmered beneath the sand, that sailed in the sky. I liked it here.

'It doesn't affect me at all,' I said. I smiled at her. 'It's home.'

Close to the Range, the navigation was easy. I pressed a hand to the ground, read how she'd changed and chose our direction. It was a wonder that nobody else was able to do it.

The usual way to sleep in the Misery is two people, back to back, with a third watching over you. The carpenters who had put the wagons together had been clever. The tarps that covered the wooden frames were thick as sole leather, and it would take a determined predator to get through, and it wouldn't be quiet. No gillings were going to chew their way through that, although I knew that we weren't going to see any gillings. They had grown rarer year by year, where once they'd been amongst the most numerous of the Misery's nasties, and I sensed none nearby. I sat outside the wagon I was supposed to share with Dantry, Maldon, and three of the Battle Spinners. I wasn't tired, so I sat and stared at the trembling sky, letting the Misery's wonders soak into me as I steadily smoked my way through a cigar. Now I was back in the Misery, the hacking cough had dissipated and my chest felt clean again. I didn't even feel like I was dying.

The soldiers had formed their wagons into a defensive ring. There were no sounds of chatter, singing, or levity within that circle. The first day in the Misery was always hard, but it was only going to get harder, and they all knew it. The Marble Guard walked the perimeter, tireless sentries. Sleep was irrelevant to them.

Nenn, Venzer, and Betch sat opposite me. Ghosts of my regret. Shadows of my guilt. At times I'd forgotten that that was all they were. I could recognise that, distantly, only it didn't seem terribly important that I did so. They didn't speak tonight. Just sat and stared at me. Watching.

Nenn, my courageous, kill-hungry warrior. She'd lived harder than anyone, killed faster, loved better. She hadn't always made the best decisions, but that only put her down there with the rest of us. But spirits, she'd been loyal, and brave, and there was nobody that I could have trusted my life with more, no matter how I'd hurt her. It was my fault that she'd lost her nose. We were fighting a pack of limber-men that had stumbled onto us in the Misery and I swung my sword back over my shoulder, and she turned around and the point went right into her face. That shit happened sometimes, in the middle of a melee. She may have known it was my sword that took it, but in the press and the pain, probably not. We'd got her patched up, headed back to the Range, and she'd never spoken of how it happened. Like a coward, neither had I.

Range Marshal Venzer, the Iron Goat, had been old before I got to the Range but he'd had a soft spot for me. Maybe he'd seen something in me that reminded him of his own distant youth, or maybe he'd just liked that I'd been determined. We hadn't always seen eye to eye, but there was always respect there. He'd been a mentor of sorts, even if I hadn't always followed his advice, and I'd been willing to learn from him, although I rarely did. He'd taken his own life when he saw that there was no hope. And there hadn't been, and I couldn't blame him for it, but I would always regret that I couldn't keep him standing.

I had not known Betch well. He'd loved my friend. He'd died a hero. We'd been prisoners, deep in the enemy camp, and his foot had been twisted up beyond any possibility of walking out of there. I'd cut his throat, and he'd faced it bravely. But of the three, his was the hardest burden to bear. Nenn had gone out fighting, and she'd saved us all. Venzer had lived eighty years and was honoured as a hero. But Betch had been a lowly captain, out in the Misery because he loved Nenn. He'd deserved better than my knife.

Shadows of the past, watching me. Judging me. They were not unfamiliar.

It was late enough that everyone else was either asleep or made out of stone, so I got up and began to walk from the camp. First watched me as I headed out into the night. The Guardians were all essentially identical, but I could tell him from the rest. Of all of them, he was the only one that looked at us like we were living things. Marginally more human than the rest. I preferred the ones that were clearly nothing like us. It made them easier to tolerate. But he watched, and he said nothing, and he did not follow.

I stopped, cut a shallow gash across my arm and let the blood drip into the sand. Put a little of myself back into it, from which I'd taken so much. A waypoint.

I used the Misery to speed my pace. I had read the sand, I knew what lay nearby and there was a creature here. A long, worm-like thing that was burrowing slowly beneath the rock. It never ate. It never drank. It simply was. It wasn't dangerous. There were things like the worm in the Misery that won't threaten you. Nobody besides me would even have known that it existed. I found the point where it was trying, poorly, to circumnavigate a stretch of black, charcoal-delicate boulders. It was blind, without senses of any kind that we would have recognised, and I dug it up, its tube-like body as wide as my palm. I'd found these before. It wasn't possible to kill them, not really. Chop them apart and all the parts just kept going.

The only way to consume it was to eat it alive.

There are some things that you wish that you could forget. The first time I'd ever eaten one, I'd felt that way. I'd wanted to get the taste of it out of my mouth, the memory of the writhing, wriggling flesh against my gums, my throat, the way bits of it kept on moving even in my gut. But that day was long, long past. The physical sensations I could ignore. They didn't matter. Instead, as I gorged on the pulpy white flesh, I felt the bond with the Misery intensifying. Shimmering inside me, empowering me, repairing and changing me. I could have laughed, but I was slick with the brown, sludgy stuff that came out of the worm if you bit through the wrong tube inside it, and that wasn't funny. Was it funny? I giggled to myself. Oh, but I'd missed this.

It burned. It burned and stung my mouth, my throat, and then my gut. I felt as though I'd been stabbed and doubled over. A mouthful of churned, maggot-white flesh fell unswallowed from my mouth and I retched, then clapped my hands over my lips and pressed my eyes tight. I had to keep it down. I had to keep hold of what it gave me. Forget everything else. Forget what it was doing to me, forget the growing, hissing presence of the Misery in my mind. None of that mattered. I had to do this.

Had to do this.

Had to do this.

I'd been doing it for years, focused so intently on the goal before me that I could excuse anything. Anything at all. Even this nightmare. In the brief moments of lucid clarity, I knew what I had become.

I was laughing. I didn't know that I was laughing. My mother scolded me as I stuffed more of the shuffling worm-flesh into my mouth, but she was comical, and I hadn't listened to her when she was alive anyway. I wasn't finished with this feast yet. There were hours until dawn, and I'd been away too long.

26

I knew that not all of them were real. Amaira, Nenn, Dantry, and Venzer were all real, of course. But there were others travelling with me that I knew to be shadows. Torolo Mancono followed us, crying that he'd been betrayed. My old friend Gleck Maldon was there, but he was a child now, blind and full of anger, and that didn't make a whistle of sense. Shadows of the past, washing through my mind with the colours and the glare of the god-lights. I stopped talking to them when I didn't have to. I began to worry that Valiya was really the woman that I'd once loved, and not some figment of my imagination, and somehow I'd let her come out here with me. And I saw Ezabeth, flaming hair and blank face, glowing beneath the god-lights that fell from the cracks in the sky above us.

A horde of skin-shedders found us, undetected, while I was distracted watching a trio of ghostly women dance in a circle. The Guardians tore into them and broke them into pieces. The Misery had never felt safer.

My companions tried to speak to me. My friends. Or so they called themselves. Had they really been friends, all this time? They weren't the Misery. They weren't part of me.

When night fell, I went out, looking for a pool of the black, oily liquid that sometimes forms in the Misery, or the creatures that crawled through the grit. I found a series of tracks – small, clawed feet. But dozens of them, maybe more. They were gilling tracks, imprinted all over one another, almost as if they'd been walking in a line. The idea seemed grimly comical. I hadn't seen any gillings in the past year, and no mention of them but for the one which had fed on Nall. As much as I hated the little bastards, I disliked the idea of them flocking even more. I would have killed and eaten one if I could, but the prints were old and the gillings, wherever they were going, were long gone.

I found something that had been half-eaten by something else, and I finished it off. Strange, that I'd once found the consumption of these things repulsive.

Ezabeth stood beneath one of the god-lights, watching me. I hunched my shoulders against her accusatory stare and chewed doggedly on a string of sinew.

'You go too far,' she said.

I kept on chewing. The tough meat caught between my teeth, tingled against my gums.

'Ryhalt,' she said, and my name caused me to stop. I picked at a string of gristle, pulled it free, and spat it into the dirt.

'What?'

'You're losing yourself,' she said. Her voice was hollow, an echo in a cavern of iron.

'That's rich, coming from you,' I said.

'I am nobody,' she said.

'You're Ezabeth Tanza,' I said. I didn't want to have that conversation again, and she didn't rise to it.

'You're letting go,' she said. 'But in the wrong direction. All this waste. This power around us. It's not all you need. Humanity is the key.'

I'd heard that before somewhere, but it felt like a long time ago now and I couldn't place it. I put down the leg that I'd been eating and turned to face her. She didn't look like my Ezabeth anymore. She was something unworldly, something harder, something that reminded me too much of the Nameless. Distant. Flames danced playfully at the hem of her dress, around her fingers.

'Is that what you did?' I asked. 'You let go?'

'I had to,' she said. 'We wouldn't be here if I'd not. But it's cloudy. I don't remember very much of it.'

'And I should ask the sky, is that it?' I said bitterly. I looked up at the spread of violent white lights breaking the red sky apart. 'Tell me, sky,' I said. 'Tell me the answers. Tell me what you did to my Ezabeth.'

The sky had fallen silent. It had nothing to say to me. In a moment of weakness I reached out for her. She no longer reached for me as she once had, and my fingers slid through her image, light playing across my fingers. Two worlds, one corporeal, one of aether, that could never touch.

'Don't let go,' she said. 'Not yet. There are those that still need you.'

The light from the crack began to fade, the ray in which Ezabeth stood diminished, fading away until she too was gone and I sat alone with the remains of something that should never have existed. I laughed at it then, laughed until I couldn't remember why I was laughing, and made my way back to the wagons.

You're trying to reach the focal point, Deep Emperor Acradius whispered into my mind with the crashing of an avalanche.

A vision of a great black palanquin filled my mind, borne on the shoulders of dozens of drudge. They wore robes of high office, crowns, gowns sewn with glittering jewels. Great kings shouldered the burden alongside revered warriors, paint-stained artists, a lavishly tattooed high-courtesan: the elites of the east bore their god across the sands in praise-filled steps.

'So are you,' I said.

What do you hope to accomplish, creature of the Misery?

Acradius' thought rumbled through me. *I bring a legion. I bring The Sleeper's wrath. Even alone, I could scrub you from the earth.*

'But you're still afraid,' I said.

Fear no longer exists within us, Acradius told me. *I am beyond such things. I am the power of the ocean's dark. I am the fury of the storm. You stand close to ascension yourself. I could give it to you. All you have to do is bring me the ice fiend's heart and fall to your knees and I will give you that rebirth. Immortality is not beyond you. You only have to reach for it, and you will find my hand open.*

'I will meet you at Adrogorsk. That is where this will end,' I said. 'It's where it began.'

Twenty thousand swift-riders will greet you there, Acradius said. *You have nothing to bring against us, and you will not live to empower the heart. My riders will take the city before the moons align and your master is broken and powerless against me. If there is anything left of him, tell him. He should know that his plans are futile. Not even my own kind could stand against me. This world is mine again.*

Someone was shaking my arm. I blinked, and the palanquin vanished from my sight. Red-and-grey Misery-sands and cracked, broken rocks filled the horizon. I shook Dantry's arm away. On his left, Amaira watched me with concern.

'You were talking to yourself again,' Dantry said. His face was drawn. The Misery did not sit comfortably around him.

'No,' I said. I did not try to explain. The Deep King's voice echoed on in my head. *This world is mine again.*

Dantry and Amaira shared a look and he put a hand on her arm. A gesture too intimate for the Misery, too intimate for a man his age and a woman of hers. There was nothing that I could say. They would do what they would do, and I couldn't claim I'd ever understood the workings of the heart. Their closeness only made what was coming all the sadder. I knew the wrench that came with finding the thing that meant most to you and having it torn away in the moment of victory.

'Captain Galharrow? Are we still on course?' Spinner Kanalina called to me. She did it every couple of hours. I couldn't blame her. Betch and Nenn kept trying to distract me, to pull us off in some other direction. Arseholes.

I swung down from my horse and read the earth. Let myself sink into it, felt out through the gullies and cracks between places. There was something big over to the east, stamping huge feet as it pecked at the sand. I sent it a nudge of thought, pushed it away. The path I'd chosen would take us well clear of it.

'We're on course,' I said. 'Another three days and we should see the towers.'

'Good,' Kanalina said, as she always did. She was brief with her words. She had an astrolabe in her hands and turned back to looking up at the moons. Over the days their orbits had brought them closer and closer together. Great spheres of crystal, breaking the light, casting it back at us in blue, gold, and red. The Spinners we'd brought with us chattered away, excited at the purity of the phos they spun from the air. They kept apart from me and mine, as we did from the Guardians. Captain North rode alone. We were allies, a common purpose between us, but the divides showed in the distance between us and the sides of the wagons we chose to ride on.

I knelt and quietly drew a knife, slashed a shallow cut in my forearm. Drops of heavy, blackish blood fell to bind me into the Misery's sand. Set me there, as much as I was anywhere.

'I'm looking forwards to it,' Maldon said, riding up to me. 'What are you doing?' Of all of us, the Spinners avoided him the most. They didn't understand why I'd insisted that a child accompany us, but they knew something was wrong with him. He might have looked ten years old, but there was something in the way he spoke that set an adult on edge. I ignored his question and tucked the knife away.

'Looking forwards to what?'

'To finishing this,' he said.

'Everything has to come to an end,' I said. Maldon nodded solemnly. He tipped a hip-flask of brandy to his lips, then paused and brought it away without drinking.

'We made some mistakes,' he said.

'Mistakes happen,' I said. We rode in silence for a little while, but there was something heavy on his mind. He wasn't one to spread his heart for others to see but, given time, the truth worked its way free of his lips.

'I'm sorry,' he said. 'About the Talents. It was my fault that they died. I got carried away. I should have been more careful at the mill. They didn't need to die.'

'No,' I said. 'They probably didn't. But you don't need to talk to me about casualties in war. Not where we're going.'

'They weren't warriors.'

'No. But they were in the war nonetheless.'

I doubt that gave him much comfort.

'Have you been back to Adrogorsk since it happened?'

'No,' I said. 'But the men that died there did so under my command. Died for my bad decisions, and because I was out of my depth.'

'They were soldiers. They knew the risks,' Maldon said. 'And they've been bones for thirty years. What I did was careless. I was impatient to prove the theory. I wanted to know if it was true.'

'Did you know that they were inside when you caused the backlash?' I asked. I had not wanted to know the truth of it.

'I knew,' Maldon said. 'And I did it anyway. I didn't care.'

'But you care now.'

'No,' Maldon said. 'That's not it. I didn't care about them

281

at all. I don't care about them now. I don't care about any-thing, Ryhalt. This body, what Shavada did to me – I don't feel anything for anyone. I don't love anything. They took that from me.'

I felt no anger towards him. Life and death, living and loving, how could I expect something like Maldon to experi-ence them the way that we did? His body was practically indestructible, and even his attempts to end his existence had proved futile. But he was broken, trapped in an endless childhood, eyeless and so different from everyone else he might ever meet. It was a cruel and bleak fate for a man who had once been a hero to the Range.

'They took something from all of us,' I said. I looked down at the twin flowers on my arm, tiny and lost amidst the skulls. 'It's why we're doing this. I know why I'm here. Who I'm doing this for. But tell me, Gleck. If there's noth-ing in the world for you, then why are you here?'

'Because I want to win,' Maldon said, heat in his voice. 'You don't have to get your victory to win. You only have to stop someone else getting theirs. They left me hate. That much, I can still hold to.'

I reached down and laid a hand on Maldon's shoulder. He flinched at the unexpected touch, and though he trembled, didn't brush it away. For a moment, he could have been an actual child, frightened, desperate and in need of a father's hand. Ridiculous, really. He was older than I was, but maybe our hearts never stop craving the security of our youngest days.

'We'll win,' I said. 'We'll win if we have to end the whole fucking world to do it.'

Maldon shrugged my hand away and gave one of his bitter, Darling laughs.

'That's what they don't realise, isn't it?' he said. 'You'd never end the world. Not while your children are still living in it.'

That hit me like a bucket of iced water over my shoulders.

'My children died,' I said. 'You know that.'

'Oh, I know that they died,' he said. 'And I know that right after, you went to the Duskland Gate and sought Crowfoot out. You don't like to tell it that way. You like to make out that Crowfoot came to you and offered you a deal. But I know you better than that. He didn't come to you, did he? You went to him.'

'So what?' I said.

'So there's only one thing that you would have bargained your life away for,' he said. 'That's you all over. You do whatever you want, but you never do it for yourself. You hate yourself too much for that. It's why you couldn't take Valiya's love. It's why you cling to the memory of a dead woman, a woman you couldn't have. It was safe to love Ezabeth. She was never really within reach.'

Painful words, but words hurt the most when there's an undercurrent of truth to them. I had loved Ezabeth as much as I'd ever loved anything. More, maybe. I hadn't loved my children. Not really, not as I should have. I'd barely paid them a moment's thought when they were alive.

'That's all dead and in the past now,' I said.

Maldon laughed.

'If that were the past then we wouldn't be out here, riding towards the Deep Emperor and his army,' he said. 'I know. I feel him too. They're all one, the Deep Kings, though they think they're individuals. The remnant of Shavada in me feels Acradius approaching. Don't worry. I won't tell the others. They aren't as hell-bent on destruction as I am, and if they knew what we're going up against they'd probably turn tail and run. They'd look for some other way to end this. But this is the last chance, isn't it? The most absurd and terrible gamble we'll ever take. And we'll take it, because somewhere out there, Crowfoot brought your children back. Didn't he?'

I sighed. I had never told another living soul what I'd traded myself away for. What I'd done countless awful things to people for, why I'd followed orders that, if I'd believed in it, I'd have said were as close to evil as things got.

'Their souls,' I said finally. 'He took my children's souls and put them into bodies that would have been stillborn, so that they might get a chance to live. I don't know where. I don't know who they are, what their names became. They might not have survived infancy for all I know. But I gave them a chance. They'll never know me, never know anything of who they could have been. That doesn't matter. It was enough to give them a chance.'

'How do you know that he actually did it?' Maldon asked.

'I don't,' I said. 'Maybe everything I've done has been for a lie. Maybe he gave me this raven's mark and spun me a sweet story. It's not like I didn't wonder, from time to time. But it was a chance, and that was worth more than I was.'

We rode along in silence for a while, the wind pushing a film of fine sand around the horses' hooves, the wagons creaking as they ground ahead across the uneven ground.

'I'm glad that you shared it with me,' Maldon said eventually. 'Before you won't be able to.'

'What do you mean?'

'You're slipping,' he said. 'You know that, don't you?'

But I'd lost interest in the conversation. A legion marched alongside the route ahead, aethereal bodies dressed in the uniforms of thirty years ago, weapons shouldered. The Third Battalion, warriors I'd led at Adrogorsk, making the final journey with me once again. I raised my fingers to my brow in a salute, and as I passed each man or woman they returned it. My men, back to watch our advance into oblivion.

'What's real isn't fixed,' I said. 'Not for much longer.'

*

A set of stairs, smooth cut stone, rose up over nothing, and at their peak, an archway ushered into someplace else.

Sometimes the Misery is simple. There are things that will try to eat you, although they're not really hungry. There are big piles of sand and rock, and there are chasms and seas of grass that want your blood. The sky is torn, and it makes a lot of odd noises, but you get used to that. The bad magic, the left-behind waste of apocalypse, ebbs steadily into you, turning your gums sour and your nostrils raw. But even though those things are strange, they come to be familiar.

I signalled that the column should stop.

The door stood out from everything, like a rook in a dovecote. I felt it pulling at me, tendrils of thought reaching out to brush against my arms and shoulders, drawing me towards it. My horse, who didn't like me to begin with, whickered in discomfort.

'What is it?' Amaira asked. She was riding point with me. I knew what it was. I'd been seeing it for the past two years.

'It's a tomb,' I said.

I signalled a halt and the wagon train drew up behind us.

The archway was stone, pale, the grey pillars as wide as old oaks. Unadorned, smooth. A triangular flight of steps led up towards it growing narrower as they ascended, where it hung suspended ten feet above the ground. Through the portal: darkness.

'Remember that spiral stair we found?' Nenn asked. 'That was a fucking mess.'

'We lost Jennin there,' I said.

'Here?' Amaira asked. She hadn't been listening to Nenn and thought I was talking about the archway.

'No. The spiral stair,' I said.

'What stair?'

Nenn rolled her eyes, and Betch shook his head.

We'd run into the spiral stair fifteen years back now. Riding a mission, we'd seen a solid, straight line ascending skywards on the horizon. We'd found a winding stairway, the kind that castle designers had been so fond of a few centuries ago, but detached from any castle that had once housed it. It stretched up, up into the air. I'd sent Jennin up to get a look at the lie of the land. Down near the base, someone had carved 'privy' into one of the steps, an arrow pointing up. Jennin had gone up, braving the gusting wind, and then she hadn't come back down. After a while we'd shouted, and still she hadn't come back. Nenn and I went up after her. We'd climbed twenty feet when I saw the word 'privy' and that same arrow in the stone. I'd stopped, and then down came Jennin.

'There's a great view up there,' she'd said. She'd gone down past us, and we'd headed after her. But when we reached the ground, Jennin wasn't there. There was no other way that she could have gone, so back up we went. Down she came again, commenting on the view, and I took her arm and tried to lead her back down, but my fingers slipped and after she went on around the corner, she didn't make the ground again. I tried to get her back a bunch of times, but she'd crossed over. If I'd stepped over the privy stone, I suspect I'd have joined her there, endlessly descending, lost to an error in space and time. For all I knew, she was still there, checking the view and coming down to meet us, over and over.

The Misery had more than one way of making you its own. The archway was dangerous. It had appeared to me time and again, asking me to enter.

I dismounted and knelt on the rock. I quested outwards, thinking I knew the Misery well enough. I could feel the general directions of Cold's Crater, of the ruins of Adrogorsk and Clear and of course, the Endless Devoid where I'd cut my fate into my arm. But this door was not a fixed point.

It was something different. The earth told me nothing, and the Misery lay silent. It was as if she didn't want me to know how she felt about it. Hid it from me.

'We should go around it,' Valiya said.

'Agreed,' I said. 'Let's take a wide berth.'

'What do you think's through there?' Amaira asked.

'It won't be anything good,' I said. 'Maybe nothing at all.'

'What are they doing?' North asked.

The Marble Guardians had lined up near to the doorway. They bowed their heads as one, which I took to mean that they were communing in their silent way, and then Seventh stepped out of line.

'Hold back,' I said, but for the first time, a Guardian ignored my order and began ascending the stairs. 'What does it think that it's doing?' I muttered. The broad steps were easy for the Guardian's oversized legs. It reached the top of the stairway, and tried to step through.

There was a howl, the same cry that the sky was so fond of emitting, and a rush of air ripped through the doorway. The Guardian was lifted from its feet and bounced down the stairs, pale limbs cracking against the steps until it rolled into the sand at their base. A cold light had grown in the doorway, but it died away quickly.

'Told you it was bad,' I said. 'Let's get on.'

The Guardian picked itself up, apparently unharmed by its bone-breaking fall. It would take more than that to stop one of them.

Something worth remembering.

27

Two miles on, the door loomed ahead of us again.

'What happened?' North said. He squinted at the pale grey stone, then turned a frown in my direction. 'Misery getting the better of you?'

'We're going in circles,' General Kazna growled. She glared at me as though I were doing it on purpose.

We'd left it behind an hour ago, but somehow we seemed to be right back where we'd started. The landscape around us was all the same, red and black, sand and dust. There was no sign of wagons passing by here, but we could have come at it from any of three hundred and sixty degrees.

'It might not be the same door,' I said.

North snorted, unimpressed.

'The Nameless have put their faith in us, Captain,' he said. 'We're working their will here. Get your shit in order.'

I rode on away from them.

'It's the same door,' Valiya said as she joined me. 'It's exactly the same.'

'I know,' I said. I didn't think that I'd been turned around, hadn't sensed anything shifting beneath us. But here we were.

'What does it mean?'

'Means I've fucked up,' I said. 'Hasn't happened in a long time, but I guess that I still can. It doesn't matter. We've not lost much time. I'll just take a new reading and we can go on.'

I was distracted momentarily by the singing of a choir of children. Valiya didn't seem to hear it, but I joined in with them as I put my palms onto the sand. The Misery's poisons tickled as they contacted my skin, bled upwards into me, but so slowly. Slower than they ever had before, but also clearer, more obvious to me than the air passing into my lungs. I felt ahead and around us, breathing myself out into some vaster space. I felt Adrogorsk, its tall, square towers still off to what was currently the northwest. The same direction I'd felt it before. Just as far as it had been before. I must have let myself slip, had let the Misery loop us around. The door stared down at us, dark and empty.

'Look here,' Valiya said. She pointed at some marks in the dirt a little way off. 'What are these?'

'Gilling tracks,' I said. Little three-clawed feet, like chubby bird-prints, overlapping each other as if they had been walking in a line. There were a lot of them.

'Should we be worried?'

'We're in the Misery,' I said. 'We should always be worried. But they're only gillings, wherever they've gone. We've seen worse.' I found a smile, pressed it onto my face. 'General Kazna is annoyed at you for taking over the camp organisation. And organising the grooms. And the way you've reordered the ammunition carts. And the latrine-digging duty. She fumes about it when you're not around.'

'Well,' Valiya said, arching an eyebrow. 'She hasn't told me to stop.'

'She probably knows you wouldn't.'

'Are you coping, Ryhalt?'

Valiya's question took me by surprise. We'd not talked much as we crossed the dunes. Since Nall passed from the world she'd been reserved, looking inward. The Misery didn't seem to be affecting her as badly as it had some of the others, but she'd not been out here before. It was never easy for anyone, except maybe me.

'It's this way,' I said. 'We've still two hours of light left and we need to push on.'

'That's not an answer,' she said. 'I know what you have to do. I know what Crowfoot is asking of us all. But I need to know if you're coping.'

I shrugged. I would, or I wouldn't, and talking about it wasn't going to make the slightest bit of difference.

'You know where we're headed now?' North asked. He was cross with me, but there was a hint of worry behind the snark.

'Carry on straight,' I said. 'Leave the navigating to me. You can take a turn if I fuck it up again.'

The wagons lurched forwards. The longhorns pulling the wagon on which the heart's iron box rested were always at their happiest when they were moving. Their primitive brains seemed to think that doing so would take them away from the burden they dragged. I'd noticed that those at the back of the team had lost some of the hair on their hind-quarters, and the leathery skin beneath looked raw. The Spinners were taking turns driving the wagon, but nobody wanted to be near to the ice fiend's heart for long.

I knelt against the dirt and put my hands against it.

You'll let me through, I told the Misery. *Wherever this door leads, I don't need it. I've done what I had to. Taken everything I need. I'm strong enough without it.*

Not strong enough, she whispered back. *Not until you understand.* Or maybe that was just my imagination.

I sat beside the fire and watched the flames dance in careless waves.

'You're keeping something from me,' Amaira said. She looked fierce in the firelight, black hair bound back, cheekbones sharp beneath her skin. Dantry sat close to her, saying nothing. He was always present around her now. I didn't like it.

'There are things you don't need to know,' I said. 'I have to keep you safe.'

'Look around you, Ryhalt,' she said. 'We're as deep in the Misery as we can get. Nothing is safe out here.'

'You'll just have to trust me,' I said.

Amaira did not blink as she stared at me.

'There was a time that you would have told me,' she said. But she was wrong. Dantry knew the plan. Maldon knew the plan. A crazed, impossible plan formed from pain and desperation. But I'd kept it from Amaira. That had always hurt. I let the fire crackle an answer in my stead.

A lone figure stood a little way from the camp we'd made within the circle of wagons, outside the perimeter. Valiya stared upwards towards the three moons, clustered in a line as they edged closer day by day towards the triple eclipse. The red, gold, and blue cast scintillating colours across the silver of her hair.

'You should go to her,' Amaira said. She spoke with the confidence of command. I'd made that natural confidence part of her, taught her how to give orders veiled as advice. She was turning my own tricks back on me now.

'I don't know what there is left to say,' I said.

'It doesn't matter what it is that you say,' Amaira told me. 'It only matters that you say something.'

'It's too late for that to be worth anything,' I said.

'No,' Amaira told me. Not even twenty and she had all the confidence that I'd been so assured of at that age. The world takes us, little by little, dream by dream unpicked until you reach the hard stone at the bottom and realise there was never anything else anyway. The illusion of possibility is a trick played on the young. Amaira reached out and took my hand. 'It's never too late. Not for you. Not for her. Not for any of us. Look at that brave, courageous woman, Ryhalt. What's she doing out here? What does she bring to the battle? She's no warrior, no tactician. She has

291

no magic. Yes, she may have practically taken over half the running of things, but that's not why she came. Nall's passing stripped her of her advantages, and this isn't her world. She's here because she still has some measure of hope for you. Even if you can't understand it, you need to respect it.'

'It's too late for that,' I said.

Amaira slapped me hard in the face. She winced and pulled back her hand, shaking at the sting. Her blow hadn't even turned my head, and I'd barely felt it.

'I'm not saying I don't deserve that,' I said. 'But don't do it again.'

'Never. Too. Late.' Amaira snapped the words at me, then rose, brushed the sand from her breeches, and stalked away to take out her frustration on the Spinners.

'She's right, you know,' Dantry said. 'There's always time.'

'Time for what?' I asked. I could feel my own bitterness rising like bile, hot and scalding as it hissed in my throat. I'd been this way a thousand times, usually dead-drunk and shuffling my own failures around like game cards.

'For whatever it is that you want,' he said. 'Can I offer you some advice?'

'Everyone else has. Why not you too?'

'You loved my sister,' he said. 'For whatever short time you loved her, you knew right then that there was something else. Something other than' – and he gestured around us – 'whatever this is supposed to be. Do you remember it?'

'It was ten years ago,' I said.

'And you recall it clearer than the dawn,' he said. 'Humour me. Tell me how it felt.'

There is a part of you that never gets old, never fades, never dies. It's not memory; those warp, twist, and turn and become their own stories in your mind, but the feeling remains. It is that that I clung to.

'It felt real,' I said. 'It felt like there was a point to all of

292

this. It felt like I'd found something that I could hold in my chest and not let go. I felt that I was winning. That after everything that had happened, even if we were going to die, I had what I needed.'

'And then you lost it,' he said gently.

'I lost it. We only got to say it once. Once, in a whole lifetime. And then she was dead.'

'If you had heard it a hundred times more,' Dantry said, 'or a thousand, or if every star had been shining the words down upon you, would that have made it more real? If it's said more often does that give it more worth?'

'I don't know.'

'What you're saying only works in the reverse, doesn't it?' Dantry said. He wore bird's feet around his eyes, his beard was full and nobody would have thought him a boy anymore, but there was energy in his voice. For everything that had happened to him, the fear and the torture he had endured at Saravor's hands, his light had not died. It burned as bright as ever. 'Let me speak plainly. I love Amaira. I feel it hard, right here.' He put a hand to his chest, too high, where most people think their heart is.

'Dantry. I'll say this just once. Amaira is not for you.'

'Or what?' Dantry said. 'You'd beat me? Kill me? Try, Ryhalt. I don't know how long I'd last against you, but it would be worth it, just to know if she felt the same. And that's the point, isn't it?'

'You really think that you love her? You barely know her.'

'There's no "think" about it,' he said. He laughed, an alien sound in the Misery. 'Listen to someone who's better at this than you are, even if your self-absorption makes it hard to accept that. Some love grows like fruit on a tree, growing slowly as it soaks up the earth. But sometimes it just takes you, and there's nothing you, or I, or anyone else can do about it. It's a storm. It's an ocean wave, swamping you. If you love someone, it's not about the time spent. It's about what you had in the moments that you had it. Nothing lasts forever. Not even the Nameless.'

'Not even the world,' I said. I sighed and reached out my hand, then thought better of it and pulled on a glove. The second time I offered it, Dantry shook it. It was as much of a blessing as I was prepared to give him.

'Don't cock it up,' I said. 'You know, you're wiser than a pup like you should be.'

Dantry smiled as he got up to follow Amaira.

'And you're less stubborn than an old grouch like you ought to be.'

As he walked away to stop Amaira from fighting with one of the Spinners who had failed to tie down one of the tarpaulins, Torolo Mancono sat down beside me. Blood was running from the rent in his neck where I'd bitten his throat out.

'You're in a bad mood today,' he said.

'You can fuck right off,' I said, shaking my head to try to clear him from it. I looked over to Valiya, standing alone, where I had put her, watching the stars, which I couldn't give her. In another life. In another world. But not this one.

This one was about to end.

I'd known what I had to do all along. Dantry's words played in my mind, and I watched the way he and Amaira walked together, spoke aside from the others, found subtle, gentle ways to touch when nobody was looking. Her, helping him tie a knot. Him, lifting her up onto the wagon bed when there was a perfectly good step. It shouldn't have worked. He was much too old for her. But it was what it was, and maybe we all had a right to take whatever we could get from this existence.

I caught a scent of something on the air then. A foul, sewerage smell, wet drains clogged with rotting meat. There were plenty of foul things in the Misery, and they all had their own acrid, chemical tang, but I knew that one all too clearly. I sprang to my feet, looking all around for signs of threat, but the soldiers were going about their duties, alert but without tension.

'Saravor's here,' I growled. 'He's changed something. Someone. He's here ...'

'Saravor is dead, Ryhalt,' Nenn said. 'You saw him die. Remember?'

'But I thought ...' I shook my head. I'd seen him burn up in that double helix of phos energy, but the smell had been so sharp. So close. It was gone now but it had seemed so clear. I shook my head.

'Don't worry,' she said. 'It's just your mind playing tricks on you.'

We travelled onwards. The beasts pulling the heart wagon were getting weaker, sicker. One of our navigators disappeared. Whether he decided to take his chances alone or something silently took him beneath the sand, nobody knew.

The world rotated around me, and my balance pitched as though I'd been hitting the rum since daybreak. Black roaring filled my ears and a dark wind roared and billowed around me. The black iron palanquin filled my mind, so cold that its chill reached across the twisted miles and wrapped itself around my mind.

You have been foolish to defy me, Son of the Misery, Deep King Acradius said softly. Soft as an avalanche. Soft as the collision of planets. *What can you hope to achieve with your pitiful band of mortals?*

'You wouldn't waste your divine breath on me if you didn't think that I can beat you,' I said. I tasted blood in my mouth and the black oil of the Misery as it bled from my gums. I spat. But through Acradius' mind, I saw them.

They marched in their thousands. Drudge warriors,

corpse-blue-skinned and heavily armoured, spears on their shoulders and shields on their arms. The banners of the Deep Kings flowed long and bright. A huge host, bearing down on us, ready to destroy.

Look back to the west that you value so greatly, Acradius thundered. Loud as summer rain. Loud as a lover's caress. *Your gods have failed you. Where are they now? Cowering in their roosts, on their islands, in their graves beneath the earth. They send their ancient warriors to protect you because they fear to come themselves. Give yourself over to me. You cannot harness the power of the moons without destroying yourselves. Or have they sent you blindly into the storm?*

I pressed myself back up from the sand as friendly hands sought to right me. I pushed them away, my vision still filled with stars and swirling grit.

'It wouldn't matter if I stood here alone,' I said. 'It wouldn't matter if I was the last man alive. You'll find me beneath the walls of Adrogorsk.' I wiped slime and blood from my lips and stared into that black palanquin, stared past the iron and the cold to the swirling shadow that lurked beyond. 'Bring your vassal Kings. Bring your drudge. Bring everything you fucking have, your whole damn empire if you need it. Bring it all. I'll be waiting for you.'

Acradius' laughter echoed in my mind as he retreated from it.

You won't even make it that far.

'What's that?' Kanalina cried, her eyes on the sky.

Something big and black was coming at us from the east, cutting through the sky on vast, shadowed wings. Long in the body, a pair of scorpion tails trailing out behind it like rudders. Its flight was going to bring it right at us. A trail of black smoke stained the sky in its wake.

A Shantar.

I knelt and pressed a hand to the Misery, questing

outwards, seeking to know what it was. I'd seen the flying things in Misery before but only at a distance and they'd never bothered me, not in six years. But as I let my senses flow through toxic sand and poisoned air, I felt twin essences combined. It was of the Misery, but it was something else besides. Taint upon taint, darkness twined with even deeper darkness.

Acradius.

'Spirits preserve us,' Kanalina intoned, grabbing the charm at her throat. 'Spinners, prepare to engage. Maximum range, all canisters.'

The soldiers fell out from the wagons, priming their slow match, stuffing balls and tamping them down into the barrels as the officers bellowed orders. I doubted their weapons were going to be much use.

The creature sped towards us, black and glistening, the sun at its back, its speed astonishing. I saw horned snouts and burning pits for eyes, razor teeth in three gaping maws, half a dozen long legs that ended in a splay of talons, a dual row of spines protruding from its back as it skimmed the sand, oily smoke in its wake.

'Engage!' Kanalina yelled.

The Spinners drew phos, but the Shantar came in far faster than they'd anticipated, its size masking its speed until it came in close. Skimming the sand it raced in towards us, jaws stretched wide. Kanalina let fly a blast of light as matchlocks cracked, but the devil swerved away and raced through the group, then up, arcing away again into the sky. I heard the screams, looked up to see two of the Spinners caught in its claws, and then it squeezed and pieces of them tumbled through the sky. The smoke it left in its wake stank like hot tar.

North drew his pistols, fired shots one after the other, but they seemed pitiful things compared to the huge, skyborne beast. Gunners discharged their weapons after it, but if they scored even one hit the beast didn't slow. I ran to Valiya.

'Get under the wagons,' I told her. 'Stay there.' She knew that this wasn't her fight, and she did as I'd asked.

'What is that?' Amaira asked. She had her blades out, but there was little that any of us could do against it on the ground.

'A Shantar,' I said. My teeth were gritted hard. 'A creature from the earliest days of the Misery.'

'You can't drive it away?'

'It's not just the Misery,' I hissed. 'It's Acradius.'

I felt his presence within it as it scored a smoking trail through the sky. The black iron palanquin was imprinted upon it, forcing it to obey. To hunt for me. I felt a surge of fury. This thing, whatever it was, did not belong to Acradius. *It was mine.* The Misery belonged to me. The Deep Kings sought to take even that from me.

The Shantar was coming around for another pass. The remaining Spinners had formed up, and now their canisters whined as they drew energy. Phos smoked from their skin as they overloaded themselves.

'Loose!' Kanalina screeched, and a volley of light-spheres blazed out into the sky. But the Shantar was faster than its forty-foot length suggested, and it twisted in flight, dropping, and the orbs detonated harmlessly in the air amidst the black trail in the sky. The devil corrected its flight with a drive of black wings and a sweep of its tail, and then it was coming for us again.

'Hope you have that spear handy,' I said to North. 'Now would be the time.'

North ran for the wagons.

'Loose!' Kanalina ordered, but only three of the Spinners obeyed her, the others throwing themselves flat as the beast roared past. Two of the phos-blasts struck the Shantar head-on, detonating in clouds of sparkling light, and it wavered but still came on. A slash of its claws and a lash of its tails as it passed and there were more screams, blood in the air and dying men and women on the ground. It was targeting our sorcerers. Kanalina picked herself up from the dust, terror in her eyes as the Shantar arced away into the sky again. Matchlocks roared as the soldiers poured fire towards it but it was too fast and their shot was no more effective against it than the smoke that flowed from their barrels.

'It's going for the Spinners,' I said. 'Acradius is trying to take them down. Get them under cover.'

'Do something!' Kanalina demanded, and I thought that she was speaking to me, but then I realised that she was commanding the Marble Guard. They stood without fear, impassive, red eyes turning to the blood pooling around the decapitated Spinners. As if tearing their eyes from it were agony, they swung in chilling unison to watch the creature come around for a third pass.

'Get those culverins up here!' General Kazna yelled. Her sabre was out as she screamed orders, getting men to form lines, but there were no drills against an airborne enemy.

North was back with his jade-tipped spear. I felt a tug of recognition at seeing it again, something about it too familiar, but there was no time to consider it as winged death swooped low again. My sword was in my hand but down here it was going to be about as effective against the Shantar as bad language.

The voice of a thousand years of suffering and hatred screeched nails across a slate in my mind.

How little you grasp your insignificance, Acradius whispered. The Shantar screeched in unison with the thought, possessed, taken by the Deep Emperor's power. *You think the Misery serves you, but I turn even your own weapons against you.* The beast in the sky sped across the sand.

None of the Spinners faced it on its third approach. They ran for cover as it swooped in, and sensing easier prey, the

Shantar swerved from the fleeing figures towards the Marble Guard. That proved to be a mistake. Half of them readied their glaives like javelins, and as the Shantar came closer they threw. Their glaives were not made for throwing. They were polearms, more axe than spear, but the Guardians propelled them with the force of a hurricane. Not one missed, the wide blades punching deep,and with a reptilian bellow of rage, it arced upwards. The weapons fell away, some from the force of the sudden lurch upwards through the air, some as the beast tore them away with its fangs. It crested in its flight, hanging suspended for a moment.

A many-sided dome of light encased the Shantar. Kanalina and the Spinners were working, splays of lightning crackling between them. The light-dome abruptly contracted around it, then detonated in a roar of intense heat. I looked away, momentarily blinded by the blast, light filling my eyes. With a crash, the Shantar hit the ground, the leathery wings blazing with flame, and now we didn't just face a devil, we faced a devil that was on fire.

Sometimes your luck's just not in.

The Marble Guard who'd retained their weapons advanced on it. The three heads hissed and snapped, talons raking the earth, barbed tails arching overhead. And then in a fury of claws and jaws it lunged for them. The Guardians moved silently, but they were fast, as fast as I remembered First being when I'd tried to stop him smashing me to pieces, and they moved as a single cohesive unit. Glaives lanced up to pierce the Shantar's body, or cut shallow slices through its thick, smoking hide, but the smouldering creature was no easy prey. The Shantar caught one of the Guardians in its jaws and ripped it in half, another fell silently as a tail-sting punched through its shoulder. The Guardian's pale white flesh blackened in seconds, sloughing away to nothing. It fought on, half-dissolved, until a snapping mouth tore away its head.

'Use that damn spear,' I told North. He hung back to let the Guardians fight, as I did.

'I can't waste it,' he snapped at me. 'Get in there. Use that monster blood of yours.'

'Against that thing?'

'Ah, you can take it,' Nenn said.

'The Galharrow I knew would have been first into the fight,' Venzer agreed.

Another two Guardians had fallen, but one of the Shantar's heads had been half-severed, lolling on its neck, still hissing and spitting. The devil's hide bubbled like liquid tar, jets of smoke pluming and reeking as a dark cloud swirled around the battle. I heard Dantry's horrified gasp, and saw Amaira circling around, trying to get in with her sword. She flung herself back as a scorpion tail lashed around in an arc, barely avoiding it, losing her sword. She tore a spiked grenadoe from her belt, ripped out a spark cord, and made to throw.

The Shantar surged forwards, smashing a pair of men aside, and there before it: Dantry, charging recklessly, madly to Amaira's aid. A piece of an armsman knocked him flat, and the Shantar strode forwards, its smoking belly passing over him as it sought upright prey.

Amaira hesitated. The grenadoe was a good bet for bringing the Shantar down. The fast-burn fuse reached the ball of spike-studded iron. But the Shantar was over Dantry. Too near. With a shriek she hurled it back, away into the Misery-sand. The blast rang out, kicking sand and grit into the air.

She had chosen to save him, even with death casting its shadow over him. Saved him, maybe killed us. I readied my sword. It was the one I'd taken from my drudge captors, long ago, and it had never failed me. I was going to have to go in against it, but I doubted that even my Misery-hardened skin would take a blow from one of those claws, not even here where I was strongest. The Misery had made me proof against the likes of Kanalina's sorcery, had hardened me against falling ice, but that thing could tear my head off with one bite. For all my Misery corruption, I'd never be as strong as I wanted to be.

A pair of culverins, small cannon, roared and the Shantar reeled back as the powerful balls smashed into it. It staggered, bellowing, one of its heads blown clean away. It turned from Dantry and rushed the gunners, far too fast, and was on them in moments. Black claws swept the guns aside, tossed the brave gunners into the air. They bought their distraction with their lives.

Kanalina and her surviving Spinners gripped hands, working together in unison, their phos canisters detonating as they blew through all of their remaining power. A thundering series of explosions lit the devil up from the inside and the Shantar's rib cage detonated outwards, spraying viscous black liquid across those gunners who'd escaped its talons. They screamed, flesh and armour dissolving in the creature's toxins as its remaining tail lashed left and right, tearing a wagon's canvas to shreds, but finally the last remaining head made a few savage snaps and the devil was done. The fire in its eye pits flickered and died, and then the bones of its huge, burned-away wings sagged down to the Misery-sand.

The snarls died away, the explosions drifted aside on the wind. Gun smoke flowed across the sand in pale wisps. Quiet returned to the Misery.

Dantry huddled over Amaira, who was coughing in the smoke that billowed from the creature's body, waving it from her face. My chest unclenched, the pit of my stomach falling away. I thought I'd lost her. Lost them both. Though the air stank, and oily, Misery-tainted smoke blew around them, they still found their moment of purity as they clung to one another.

I remembered how that had felt. Another lifetime ago, it

seemed now. I knew it was important. It just wasn't for me. Instead, another pressure played against my mind.

The Shantar's corpse called to me. I felt its draw, a sudden lurching pull at something deep in my core. The Misery insisted. Demanded. My mind filled with a shadow-filled haze as I staggered towards the scene of the battle. The sand and rock had been tossed and gouged by the creature's huge claws. Of the twenty Guardians, seven lay torn and broken, their corpses bloodless. The remaining warriors had reclaimed their thrown weapons, but showed no emotion, no remorse. Their eyes had returned to the blood pooling around the dead Spinners, tongues snaking across lips. Hungry.

They knew nothing of hunger. Not as I did.

'This is not a good idea,' Nenn said. 'You probably need to think about this.'

'The opportunity is too good to waste,' I told her. 'Besides. The Bell serves worse.'

'I'm a ghost, and even I think this is stupid,' Nenn argued. 'People are watching you. You aren't thinkin' straight.'

Her words played at the shadowed edges of my mind, but the Shantar was too pure, too exquisite to waste. This thing was ninety years old, and it had been born in the Misery's most primal days. I stood before the Shantar's splayed rib cage and there, inside, I saw the mangled remains of its heart giving its last feeble twitches. The creature's skin still bubbled and smoked, oily foulness filling the air. It was beginning to dissolve, its essence returning to the Misery that had made it. That heart held so much power, so much essence for change. With it, I could be closer to the Misery than ever before. So much stronger. I needed this. I had to.

'No, Ryhalt,' Valiya said, coming to stand behind me. Her arms encircled me, as she whispered, 'Not this. It's too much for you.'

She laid a hand over mine, pushing it down. I blinked at her.

'You don't understand,' I said quietly. My voice shook. 'There's so much power here.'

'I understand,' she said gently. 'But not yet. Not now. Not unless the need is utterly desperate.'

I shook my head. The need was all too desperate. She just didn't see it yet.

I looked back to Dantry and Amaira, for whom the rest of the world had ceased to exist. If I could not protect them one way, I would another, and now I knew what I would do.

28

That same fucking door.

'Lady's Name,' North snapped when we rounded a dune and it came into sight again. 'What is this, Captain Gal-harrow? What do you like about this bloody thing so much?'

I stared at the grey stone, the wind tugging at my coat-tails. I shook my head. I didn't know.

'Set the camp,' I said. 'Something's going wrong. We'll wait out the night and see what we can do in the morning.'

'Time's running out,' North said briskly. 'We've only three days before we have to be at Adrogorsk. Two, to set up in time to spin from the eclipse.'

'We'll be there,' I snapped. 'This isn't like following a map. This is the opposite of following a fucking map. I'll figure it out. Go and organise the camp and leave me to think.'

The wagons were formed into their usual defensive circle, the iron box containing the ice fiend's heart in the centre. After it was uncoupled, one of the longhorns sank down onto the sand and refused to get up again. The others wouldn't feed. I left them all to it, went to the foot of the doorway, and looked up at the empty dark beyond. I took off my sword belt and put it down on the sand, smoothed a little patch for myself, then sat cross-legged at the foot of the steps. The dark archway stared down at me, empty, a portal into nothing.

'I don't like North,' Nenn said, slumping down beside me. 'He's a prick. I don't trust him.'

'I don't trust any of them,' I said. 'They're all just pawns. None of them understand what will happen if Crowfoot manages to detonate the fiend's heart. They think that the Nameless mean to save us. People will convince themselves of anything if it serves their purposes. Ironic, isn't it, that Saravor saw it more clearly than any of them.'

'I'll keep an eye on North for you,' Nenn said. 'Got your back, just like always.'

'You always had my back,' I said. 'I miss you, Nenn. Even after all this time. I miss you.'

'I didn't go anywhere,' she laughed. 'I'd still drink you under the table.'

'No,' I said. 'You aren't anything. Not really. There are times that I think you're so real I could touch you, and then sometimes, like now, I know what you are. You're just a shadow. Just a ghost. A reflection of my guilt and nothing else.'

'I dunno about that,' Nenn said. 'You don't have shit to feel guilty about where I'm concerned. I got to die with a sword in my hand, and I got to live and to love. Life's not a race towards the deathbed, hoping that you'll get to snooze off peacefully without knowing it. Me, I was glad to look it full in the face. Better to go out doing something that matters.'

'Then you should have gone out drunk, fucking Betch, and spitting in some nobleman's eye.'

'That would have been good!' Nenn laughed. 'What about you? You ready for it?'

'I've been ready for a long time,' I said. 'Much as anyone can be. Maybe you can't truly ready yourself to die. What's it like, on the other side? Anything that we'd hoped for?'

'No idea,' Nenn shrugged. 'I'm stuck here with you, aren't I?' She flicked her head towards the silent stone doorway. 'What do you reckon that's all about?'

'I don't know,' I said. 'Never heard of it before. Maybe it's new.'

'New or old,' Nenn mused. 'Don't you want to have a look at what's on the other side?'

'Not even slightly.'

'But you're going to anyway, aren't you?'

I scowled, but it seemed my guilt was more honest with me than I was with myself.

'I don't think she'll let us pass until I do,' I said. 'The Misery isn't speaking to me. But she's bringing me back here. What do you think she wants?'

'What do any of us want?' Nenn asked. 'To live. To endure. To make something our own. So you're going in?'

'Not yet. If I'm going to walk in there, I want something in return.'

Amaira and Dantry sat close together around a small, private campfire. Even here, amidst all the poison, the monsters, the endless shifting of the world, they remained together. The way that she laughed at his joke, which probably wasn't funny. The way that he reached out to push back a strand of hair that probably didn't need moving. That look that said that they understood one another somehow, that they had opened their souls and found something of themselves there in the reflection. For a moment, the beauty of it stopped me dead.

'Enough to make you want to throw up, isn't it?' Maldon asked, but his words lacked their usual venom. He was toying with something long, black, and slightly curved. It took me a moment to realise what it was.

'You shouldn't have taken that,' I said. It was a stinger from one of the Shantar's tails. At one end, a venom sack throbbed like an obsidian testicle. I felt the tug of longing for it, tried to fight it down.

'Figured it might be useful as a weapon,' he said. He made little jabbing motions in the air.

'Get rid of it,' I said. 'I don't want to be around it. Valiya's right. I may be twisted all to the hells, but who knows what changes that thing would make to me.'

'You wouldn't want to eat it, that's for sure,' Maldon said. Just being in its proximity, I could smell the toxicity of the venom. 'Maybe you can use it on Dantry if his hands start wandering. Or I've a garrotte you can get him with if you want to do it quiet. At least that would stop him reciting that awful poetry to her.'

I sat rigid for a moment. Cold rose through marrow, through stiff muscle.

'A garrotte?'

'Somewhere,' he said, running a finger along the back of the stinger's curve. 'I think you knew, deep down. You just didn't want to.'

Maybe he was right. Maybe I'd chosen not to look at those deaths all too closely.

Linette, her throat sliced through with a wire, a report of a Darling at the scene. Josaf, a knife in the back. Klaunus, locked alone in a tower, protected with Smother-wards. What was it that Kanalina had said? *There's no other way out of that tower unless someone killed him and then jumped out of a five-storey window.* Which, I realised, was exactly what the indestructible little bastard had done.

'Why?'

'You know why,' he said. 'For the endgame. To be the last pieces left standing when the time comes. They would have tried to stop us. You're many things, Galharrow, but you don't have a murderer's soul. You know it was necessary. But you don't have the stomach for raw-blooded murder.'

He was wrong. I'd murdered Silpur on the Duskland Gate.

Maldon pointed the stinger towards me. 'She has to understand. Amaira. She has to be willing to let everything else go. You need to tell her. And Dantry needs to be

308

reminded of his role. I didn't throw myself out of a tower for nothing.'

It was brutal. It was true. Amaira had become an unknown quantity. She served Crowfoot, but she served me too. Our purposes had been tightly bound, tighter than the close of a wolverine's jaws. I thought that I could have predicted her every move, but Dantry had taken away the surety that I'd held about her.

I sighed. What I had to do wasn't fair, but they'd made the decision for me. I rose.

'One more thing,' he said. 'Winter.'

I turned back to him.

'Valiya? What of her?'

'You and Amaira are not the only captains out here.'

'She knows the plan,' I said. 'And so did Nall. Now he's gone. She's not fighting for the Nameless anymore. She's fighting for the rest of us. When the hour comes, she won't be standing in our path.'

'Sure you aren't as blind about her as Amaira is about Dantry?'

It wasn't worth arguing with him over something he'd imagined. I left Maldon to play with his stinger and went to do what had to be done.

'Figured out how to get us past that damned archway yet?' Amaira asked as I invaded their private world. She looked tired, but hale. They had more energy than the rest of us, less affected by the Misery. Maybe just distracted from it.

'I have some ideas. Come with me while I take a reading,' I said. 'Both of you. There's something you have to under-stand.'

I led them away from the camp, walking ahead of them. Amaira was worried about me, I could see it in the way she moved, the way she chewed her lower lip. I led them farther from the camp, up a low rise of scree. Further, down into a gully of rocks, out again and onto a broad, flat stretch of sand. Far enough from the camp that there was no chance of anyone hearing, not even the Spinners if they played their clever tricks on us. You can never be too careful around a sorcerer.

'You've been teaching Valiya about the loom?' I said as I turned abruptly on my heel.

'I have,' Dantry said. 'She's a fast learner. Why?'

'I wanted to make sure we had another of our people who understands how to operate it, if needs be,' I said. 'We're too reliant on individuals out here. You, me, Maldon. Too much resting on too few shoulders.'

'Spreading the bets in case we lose someone?' Dantry said. The playfulness with which he'd been teasing Amaira dissipated. 'I understand. I've talked her through all of the schematics. If I wake up to find a gilling's got to me, she'll still be able to go on. We're not reliant on North.'

'Good,' I said, although I didn't think we'd see any gillings out here. 'I want us to be able to run this show using only our people, if it comes to it.'

'What do you mean, "our people"?' Amaira asked. 'We're all our people out here.'

'No,' I said. 'We aren't.'

'What do you mean?'

Something was crawling beneath the sand nearby. My head snapped around to it, a coursing hound sensing game. I grabbed it, tore it from the earth. Something with legs, long as my forearm. Its faces pleaded with me as I tore away its heads and bit down.

'Spirits above, stop!' Amaira gasped. She moved towards me but Dantry took hold of her and held her back. She could have broken free of him had she wanted to; he was no match for her physically. But she let herself be restrained, and in that there was respect and love too. I chewed at the carapace, crunching it between my teeth, sucking at the sizzling ichor inside. It burned in my mouth, scalded my throat, but that wasn't worse than the shame of seeing the look in Amaira's eyes. Horror; disgust; confusion. 'Stop it!' she shouted again.

I sucked the last of the grub-flesh from the carapace and let the rest fall to the sand. I met her look as I cleaned my lips.

'So,' I said. 'Now you understand.'

'This is what you've done to yourself? To change your-self this way? Hells, Ryhalt, why?'

'Because I had to,' I said. 'I made a choice, a long time ago. All or nothing. But I chose both. This is what I am now.'

'Is this what you brought us out here to show us? Now, when we're so close to the end?' Dantry asked hotly. He knew, of course. I'd told him the plan years ago and he'd been working towards it all this time for me. Had become a wanted man to test the theory. To see if it would work. His arms were around Amaira now, comforting rather than restraining. She was a tough thing, but she leaned into him.

'No,' I said. 'This was just chance. But we're so close to the end now. I need to take everything that I can. You can understand that, I hope.'

'What are you talking about?' Amaira snapped. 'Dantry? Tell me what's going on.'

'Not yet,' I said, before he could speak. 'Tell her later. In an hour, maybe. But not yet. I did say "our people," and I meant it. There are sides out here. You see that, don't you?'

'I see us, trying to get a weapon in place to stop the Deep Kings, and I see Acradius howling across the Misery towards us,' Amaira barked. 'You're not thinking straight. This ... these toxins are burning at your mind. We've all seen it. You're getting paranoid, seeing ghosts everywhere. We're all in this together.'

'No,' I said. 'And we haven't been since the beginning.'

'What do you mean, "we"?' Amaira said, her dark eyes bowing in a frown.

I could feel the fresh Misery-energy soaking into me from the creature that I had consumed. A hot, venomous burn spreading through my veins, moving slowly through my limbs as I absorbed it. Beneath my boots, the land exulted.

'Whose mission is this, Amaira?' I asked. 'Is it Crowfoot's? He sent you to get the weapon. The Lady of Waves? She's running the show back at the citadel. Shallowgrave? He's sent his monsters to watch over us, but he took out half the citadel to do so. There's more than one war going on here. The Nameless are spent, depleted, divided. Weak. How long can any of them stand?'

'What are you saying?'

'They will each try to claim the power in the heart for themselves,' I said. 'Crowfoot wants to use it as another weapon. He only cares about beating the Deep Kings. His victory is all that matters. You've spoken to him. You know that.'

Amaira held my gaze but didn't say anything. Her face was dark with storm clouds. The fingers of her right hand brushed the raven's mark on her left forearm, maybe unconsciously.

'We serve the master,' she said. 'We made that deal. We'll deal with other threats if we have to, but the Nameless are allies.'

'Do you think the Lady of Waves will give up her chance at this much power?' I asked. 'She's vanity, spite, and little more. Shallowgrave ... who in the hells knows what he wants?'

'So we stop them,' Amaira said hotly. 'Blackwing answers only to Crowfoot. This is his plan. We'll see it through, and they'd better not get in our way. But I think that you're wrong. The Nameless may be petty and jealous, but they work together.'

312

'Do they?' I asked. 'Linette and Josaf were murdered. North tried to kill me. Klaunus is dead. Someone doesn't want any Blackwing captains present when the moons align.'

'North?' Amaira said immediately. 'You think the Lady would go that far?'

'She'd go further.' I looked at Dantry. 'But it wasn't her. Was it?'

Amaira looked from me, then to Dantry. She read the lines of his face, the shadows around his eyes. She saw something there that she'd never seen before. I saw the threads of creeping doubt.

'There's something you haven't told me,' she said. 'Dantry? What is it?'

'Tell her,' I said. 'Tell her where Maldon was going on his "essential tasks." What you decided that he should do. Who he should kill.'

'Galharrow,' Dantry hissed, his eyes taking a new and dangerous fire. 'Why do this now?'

'You ran at the Shantar like an idiot. Ran straight at death.' I turned to Amaira, thrusting a finger. 'And you could have killed it and saved lives, but you held back. Because of him. Because you're besotted and dreaming. Men died because you didn't do your duty.'

Dantry glared. I'd never seen such fury in his eyes before. The youthful energy that had always wrapped around him sloughed away. Beneath it, a tired, weary man. 'You take this from me now,' he said, a new edge of cold in his voice, sharper than frost. 'Here. With nothing else. You try to take this from me, after all these years. I'm doing it for *her*. But I was doing it for you too.'

The shivering energy of the Misery creature still filled me. Compassion was a distant afterthought, a kite blown away on a hard wind. There was no place for softness out here. Doubt on Amaira's face. Anguish. I'd upended her world.

Without the creature's crackling dark flowing through me, I could not have borne it.

'Get yourselves bright. Remember the task. That's all that's left to us. Don't stay out here too long. The land's going to shift again soon.'

'You lied to me,' I heard Amaira say as I stalked away. Her voice cracked. 'Linette was my friend.' I asked the Misery not to move too soon, left them to the hard truth. I looked beyond the camp, to where the archway hung, suspended over the sand on its impossible stair.

I wore my hypocrisy like an overcoat. I'd broken my friends, taken something beautiful from them in the name of duty. All the while, I'd been avoiding my own. Duty to Valengrad, duty to Crowfoot, duty to the people who needed me. My duty to the Misery. She was asking something of me, and I owed it to her, to all off them, to see it done. If I could bear to break my friends' hearts, then I had to endure this too.

I glanced back at the busy preparations in the camp, soldiers ensuring that everything was covered and lashed down in case the rain hit us again. Valiya stood atop a box, orchestrating. Kazna left her to it.

'Here,' Nenn said, handing me my sword belt. I buckled it on, before wondering how Nenn had managed to pick it up. She was just a ghost after all, and ghosts can touch your mind but nothing else. But Nenn had disappeared off to wherever ghosts go when they're not bothering me. Just a trick of my imagination after all.

I blinked and shook my head to clear it. I wasn't oblivious. I knew that the Misery's influence was doing things to my mind. I just needed a few more days, and it would all be over. But for now, I had to do what she was asking of me.

Soldiers gave me nervous salutes as I passed them. They were good men and women, well used to the Misery's ways, but they hadn't seen anything like me before. To put their trust in someone so clearly different was difficult for them. I nodded back but didn't engage in conversation. They didn't want me around their fires. Smiles were hard enough to come by without me interfering.

I walked past the ring of covered wagons and approached the floating archway.

I placed my foot onto the first step without a word to anyone and something echoed through me, a drop of water falling into an underground lake, a ripple in the silence. It took an effort to push myself up onto the next. There was weight above me, grinding down on my shoulders. It said, *no*. But I'd shouldered heavier burdens, and I climbed one step at a time. Seventh had made it look easy, and that said something about the power lurking in the Guardians' alabaster bodies. I heard shouts from the camp, Valiya and North calling my name, but I ignored them and reached the top. From there I saw there was more than simple darkness beyond the archway. Another stairway led down into a cavern that couldn't possibly exist, a tunnel that led away into the empty air beyond. The steps were rough things, scraped rather than cut, and a foul, grave-rot odour hung on dry air.

I glanced back at Valiya, running towards me. I shook my head at her, raised a hand palm out to say *Stop*. She only slowed at the foot of the stairway. Captain North began yelling, others joining him. When I was sure she would stay there, I stepped through into the gloom.

No wind. No blast back through the doorway. The cavern did not reject me as it had the Guardian. I was permitted to pass.

The impossible tunnel descended into somewhere else. There was a glow down there, a pale, cold whiteness. It reminded me of the light in the Endless Devoid, bright and flat, fluid but dead. The broken sky's wailing faded behind me as I descended into the glare.

The steps went on, and on into the milky glow. I began to take them two at a time.

At first the sound of my boots on the stones were the only break in the stillness, but then I caught a murmur at the edge of my awareness. Singing. Children's voices, caught together in careless, lazy verse.

The night is dark, the night is cold.

It figured.

Down, and down, and down. I thought of the stair where I'd lost Jennin. If I backtracked now, would the dark speck of the entrance ever get any closer? Stairs weren't to be trusted in the Misery. Too late for that now. I pushed on. The Misery had wanted me to come here, had refused to let me pass until I played her game. She had even taken my bargain to secure it.

I drew nearer to something. I didn't know what, but I felt it rise about me. The sensation of arms around my shoulders grew gradually, until I felt the embrace. Welcoming me, or holding me back? It could have been either, but whatever ghostly hug I'd been caught in, it hadn't the weight to bring me down or drive me away. It was not the Misery that I was accustomed to. The same, but different. Older, maybe even stronger. Strong enough that it could put itself into my path, repeatedly, forcing itself through, even against its own changeable nature.

The stairs came to an end. I stepped out into a busy market, shadows long at the beginning of dusk.

The people were familiar, and they were not familiar. The fashions were nothing I recognised. The people were my countrymen, the same colouration, the same eyes, but nobody had worn pantaloons of that type for a century. A troop of soldiers marched with harquebuses shouldered, antique hand-cannons long since overtaken by matchlocks.

They moved in well-ordered regiments, marching to the familiar barking of the squawks. Merchants and towns-people moved from stall to stall, taking quick steps and driving quicker bargains. Children were arrayed on a stage, voices spiralling in time to their teacher's conducting. I had spent so long on the Range that I'd forgotten places like this existed. Places where life went on as normal, where hagglers haggled and singers sang, and life went on day after day without a cracked and broken sky. Overhead, white clouds drifted across an impossible blue.

A pair of enterprising young men approached me, all smiles and bright eyes, but the trays of soldier-trap goods they carried were thrust prominently before them. Trinkets to ward off misfortune, erotic pamphlets, remedies for blisters, none of which did the job they were supposed to.

'Long journey, friend?' one of them asked me. I guess he saw me as a soldier from the road. There were a lot of soldiers about. The market seemed to be stuffed full of them.

'Long enough,' I said.

'I'm not surprised. The roads are a mess, the governors take no care,' he said brightly. 'Must be you've need for a spot of refreshment?' He fished around on the jumble on his tray for a small flask of amber liquid. But I had frozen. I caught his hand, and he looked at me fearfully.

'What did you say?' I asked.

'A spot of refreshment?'

'No. Before that.'

'Well, it's true, isn't it? The governors don't look after the roads, do they?'

I let him go and pushed him away. I blinked and shook my head. What was I doing here? Was any of this even real? Maybe the others were right. Maybe this was the price that I paid for the Misery-poison I'd allowed into my veins.

I delved further into the market. Beyond the stalls, a wagon sat alone and uncared for. A huge sarcophagus of black iron rested on the wagon's sagging bed. From inside it, whispers tried to reach towards me. No words, but a greeting. Impossible, but then, what meaning did that word have for me now? I'd seen too many impossibilities to consider the term relevant anymore.

'Hot cakes going fast!' a man with a loaded tray brayed. 'Going fast! Only seventy-four left!' He handed out steaming buns, took back money. 'Seventy-three, seventy-two ...'

A sultry young woman, eyes dark as coal and lips red as winter berries began to sidle along the edge of the crowd, beautiful and sensual in a way that turned the stomach. She wore a one-shouldered robe, the kind that hadn't been worn by working girls in my lifetime, but everyone knew as shorthand for prostitutes anyway. She spotted me, lifted an eyebrow, noting that I'd been paying attention. I retreated back towards the children, a sudden fear on me. They sang a new song now:

> Chop, chop, chop the wood,
> Make it break and splinter,
> If you don't stack it on the lee side,
> It'll be no use come winter.

'You're out of time again!' the teacher snapped at one of the children, a lad bearing a furious scowl. The child clenched his fists and threw an apple core at the teacher, who brandished a cane in response.

'He's a good boy, just don't anger him,' an apologetic sister said in appeasement, trying to calm the red-faced kid.

I staggered. I'd heard these words before. Many times. I knew them all. A young soldier caught me by the shoulder.

'Whoa there!' he said. 'Looks like you need to take a rest, sir. Maybe take a seat?'

'I'm fine,' I said, not knowing whether I spoke to a real man or a hallucination. This was all a lie. None of it was real, none of it existed. I was going Misery-crazy, not just imagining my old, dead friends, but now whole towns of people. The prostitute sidled up alongside us.

'Evening, master,' she said, her voice low and sultry. 'Care for a good time?'

I clapped my hands over my ears and shut my eyes. When I opened them again, night had turned and undone itself, and dawn was breaking on the horizon. The people were gone, but a pair of figures sat on the edge of the load-bearing wagon. A spectacularly handsome young man who looked like he never used his looks for anything good, and a woman much too young for the crow tattoo that covered most of her face. He looked small, frightened. She looked resolved, but so sad.

Blackwing Captain Narada. Here she sat as the dawn broke, ninety years ago, before there was a Misery. I knew what lay inside that huge iron coffin. The name of this no-where town didn't matter. The people in the market were nothing, just echoes of the past, voicing the same sentiments that the gillings uttered, over and over, stripped out of time and pressed into the voices of the unmade.

'Help me open it,' Narada said, and she and the young man pried away the lid, letting it fall away with a clang. They settled down again on the edge of the wagon, fingers steaming gently, turning rotten and green where they'd touched the iron.

The sky above began to buckle and twist. This was it. The moment that the Heart of the Void had been unleashed. The birth of the Misery. A woman, dressed in too many rings and second-best silks, staggered into the square and caught my arm to keep upright, just as the first crack began to tear through the sky.

'Spirits be merciful,' she whispered. There was terror on her powdered face. 'The Nameless have betrayed us.' She stared upwards, mouthing silent words. 'Death comes.'

The howling of the sky rose to a shimmering roar, and then everything turned to bright whiteness. And then it was gone.

I stood in a rough, damp cavern with a low ceiling. The town, gone. The market, nowhere. The people, disappeared. The shadows were deep around the edges, but the cavern was barely bigger than a tavern's common room. I had barely stepped inside it, the pale tunnel stretching back up behind me. The sloped, uneven floor was covered with the shells of things that should have lived in the sea, and some things that should not. Floating without support of any kind, something for which I had no name emitted the sickly light that illuminated the cavern. The size of a horse chestnut, its light the colour of a desert sunset.

It was not the Heart of the Void. Not entirely. But it had been part of it. A tiny fragment of a voidling's heart, blasted here when Crowfoot had enacted his plan. Its fury had been spent nearly a century ago, but some dark energy lingered inside it still. There is power inside every heart, whether it be wizard, fiend, voidling, or man, but this thing had nowhere to expend it, no direction in which to continue. It was paralysed by its own actions, and its own agony at what it had done.

The Misery had brought me here to pay witness, to observe what it had been forced to do. The obliteration of the cities of Clear and Adrogorsk, the destruction of a million lives. Repeatedly the land had forced the dark archway into my path, maybe seeing that in our newfound bond, finally, finally, someone might understand.

I understood. It wanted what we all quest for, what I'd been seeking ever since I'd cost those brave people their lives in the rout from Adrogorsk. What I'd needed ever since I'd stood in the courthouse, with Torolo Mancono's blood running down my face. What I'd drowned beneath drink after drink when I'd learned that my wife and children were gone.

It wanted to be forgiven.

The Misery had no mind of its own. It was change, unbridled and rampant, a constant shifting miasma of possibilities. But here, the last vestige of the weapon that had created it had built a sanctum and wrapped itself in memory. It could not release that memory, maybe didn't even know what it was. Guilt is a powerful thing. It wraps you, weighs you down, breaks your connection to the truth of the world, and yet, we cannot relinquish it, because in letting go we betray those that we failed. The ghosts of the Misery were not just my guilt. They were the Heart of the Void's bleed-through, its aching loneliness and desire to relinquish the pain of what it had done. That Crowfoot had made it do. And in our coupling, it had found an outlet. A way to feel that which had plagued it for ninety long years.

'Is this what you want?'

Ezabeth had appeared before me, caught in a beam of light that filtered through a crack in the ceiling. Flames licked at her feet and hands.

'No,' I said. 'None of this was ever what I wanted. But we don't get to have a summer. You told me that.'

'You know how this will end,' she whispered, her words rolling like steel. 'With torment and death.'

'We'll see.'

I reached out, reverently, and closed my hand around the point of light. I felt its heat, not some gentle summer heat but the hot cough of contagion and sickness, brought forth from the throat, heavy around the eyes. The Misery inside me sizzled. This wasn't just her power: this was her maker. And in turn, she was mine.

'You are already too far gone to do this,' Ezabeth said. 'Whatever power you hold, you're just one man alone.'

'No,' I said. 'Never alone. You taught me that.'

The light flowed along my wrist, my arm, my elbow, and then on into my chest. I felt it within me. A sense of cold, a sense of endless anguish at what had been done in its name. My fingers buzzed where I'd touched it, but the sensation was not unpleasant. I was its keeper: I would guard this secret, this guilt. I would carry it for both of us, if that was what it needed. That was the deal we made.

I went back to the stairs and headed upwards, back towards the light.

She had been leading me here, all these long years. Every lover wishes to offer you their heart. The Misery had given me hers.

29

When I stepped from the archway, the world had changed.

The towers of Adrogorsk rose from the dust like the fangs of a deep-sea fish, less than a mile to the north. It was daytime, a moonless sky indicating early morning, and the towers were red and gold beneath the rising warmth of the sun. Narrow, crooked, warped and fused where stone had melted and run in the wake of the Heart of the Void, they remained as a reminder that great minds and strong hands had worked here to create something of beauty.

There was nothing beautiful about what remained of the city. The spires were a stark testament to their own demise, vast gravestones for the hundreds of thousands who had died here, spearing the sky in search of a vengeance that would never be fulfilled.

I had been a brigadier when I first came here. A sharp uniform, polished buttons, moon insignia on my shoulder displaying a rank that I was both proud of and chafing at the bit to surpass. What a fool I'd been. I returned here now, the commander of nothing.

The soldiers were already mobilised and heading out towards the city, wagons rattling and beasts lowing. Valiya stood at the foot of the stair, looking up. Her face was drawn, arms clutching a shawl around her shoulders, though it wasn't cold.

'I knew you'd return,' she said. 'When the land began to change around us. I knew.'

'It worked,' I said.

'It worked,' she agreed. 'What lay beyond the portal?'

'Memory,' I said. 'Guilt. Regret. The usual things you find out here.'

'A price, then.'

'There's always a price.' I looked up at the cracks in the sky, wide and flaring. Rioque was passing by one of them, its image distorted, like looking through your own fingers when you hold them in front of one eye. Like sadness, hope, or understanding, the cracks were both real and they weren't. A truth, but only in our minds.

Valiya turned away and walked to our horses. She'd brought mine, saddled and ready for the last mile into the city. I helped her up onto hers, then swung up onto my own. Not so easy as it had once been. I was bigger, heavier, and the horse didn't like me at all. We rode towards Adrogorsk. I caught Dantry watching me with bitter eyes, a weight of heart about him that sloped his shoulders and stole the handsomeness from his face. Amaira rode on the other side of the column, staring straight ahead, adrift.

It had been necessary to break them apart. I needed them both. I found that I kept repeating that to myself, even as I refused to meet Dantry's eyes.

Adrogorsk had been a great city, once. Not in my lifetime. Not for ninety years. Not since the Heart of the Void. She was a ruin in every mortal's living memory, a testament to something that had once been teeming with commerce, art, and culture. In her shattered bones lay the proof, if proof had ever been needed, that there was nothing that the Nameless wouldn't sacrifice to survive.

A long boulevard ran towards what had once been the Garden Gate, wreathed in creepers and baskets of flowers so that it glowed with colour. There is, perhaps, nothing that silences the heart more than fallen giants. The people of Adrogorsk had been proud of the warrior-queens that had once battled with bronze for their fertile lands, erecting great stone statues along the route, towering wonders of the world. Only plinths remained now. Feet endured and in some lucky cases, ankles. Inscriptions ran around the bases of what had once been the greatest sculptures in the known world. They were written in Elgin, a language that had passed from common knowledge long before Crowfoot's weapon had torn them down, but Maldon knew it. He translated them happily.

'Here stands Shinestra, Queen of the World! View her Majesty and despair!' He looked to another. 'Here stands Vinova, Queen of the World! Her beauty entrances, her strength destroys!' He laughed. People don't laugh in the Misery, not if they have sense. Maldon didn't care, or maybe just didn't have any sense. Soldiers cast him worried looks as they marched by with shouldered pikes. Maldon had a scarf over his face, so they knew he wasn't reading it, and they knew more about Darlings than most. I told him to cut it out, as soldiers began to line the way.

There were legions of them. Some faces I recognised, many I didn't. Their uniforms were thirty years out of date, their weapons things of the past, and they formed ranks to either side of the cracked and broken road-stones, aethereal, strands of vapour curling away from them. Ghosts of my past. People who'd died on the walls, or beneath them, or during the hellish retreat back to the Range. Some still carried the wounds that had laid them out, others looked fresh and healthy. A man saluted with a handless wrist, jagged bone protruding from the stump.

'Sir,' he said.

'Carry on, Private,' I said.

'Who are you talking to?' Valiya asked.

'You don't see them?' I said. I looked out across the ranks, where ghosts stretched back across the desert plain. Rank after rank of ghostly troopers with aethereal weapons stood silent. Watching me pass. I shuddered.

'I don't see anyone,' Valiya said.

'There are thousands of them,' I said. My voice had fallen to a whisper. 'Far more than I had at Adrogorsk. Hundreds of thousands.'

Familiar faces mingled with the unremembered. Nenn had taken a position in the ranks, one of the few not standing at anything like attention. She was surrounded by her Ducks, the brave cavalry we'd led out to the crystal forest. Some of those who'd died in defence of Valengrad's walls stood alongside them, and here and there a man I'd hired personally and taken out onto the sands in pursuit of bounties. A young face spurred a memory, long forgotten, of making a young man stand sentry duty all night because he'd kicked sand over my freshly polished boots. Another, a man I'd sent to carry a message up to the wall just before a Darling's killing spell had torn across the ramparts. So many dead. All my doing. My fault.

Mine, the Misery pulsed through me. Not as a word, but a sense of possession. Of claim on me. On them. I pressed my eyes tight and hoped that they would be gone when I opened them again, but they weren't. I have always said that the Misery's ghosts were nothing but reflections of our own guilt, that if we have souls at all then they go some-where else entirely. But with thousands of pairs of spectral eyes following me, now I wasn't so sure.

As we approached the crumbled city walls the Third Battalion, my own men, stood shoulder to shoulder as they had when I'd ordered them to form ranks and fight the rearguard action. They turned to face me with easy smiles, bringing their fingers to their heads in salute. I had not seen their final, heroic stand. I didn't deserve their respect.

'You go on, sir,' Major Gil said as I passed him by. 'We'll

buy you the time. You do what needs to be done.'

I stopped for a moment and looked at him, at the exposed bone of his scalp. He did not look at me directly. He was speaking the words of another place, another day. Just an echo, but one that bit hard all the same. Gil had been ten years older than me then, an old soldier, but that had been thirty years ago. He looked so young to me now. They all did: these children of the Misery.

'You shouldn't have had to die for me,' I said. The first apology I'd ever made to them.

'You didn't do wrong by us, sir,' Gil said. 'You may have been a stuck-up little arsehole, but you were our stuck-up arsehole. We're still here, if you need us.'

I nodded to him, though I wished they would just dissipate. The Misery could have shown me their deaths, but somehow their respect was worse.

The world spun around me, and my balance pitched as though I'd been hitting the rum since daybreak. A roaring sounded in my ears as a dark wind roared and billowed and the black iron palanquin filled my thoughts, so cold as it reached across the twisted miles and wrapped itself around my mind.

Reaching the city will avail you nothing, Son of the Misery, Deep King Acradius said softly. Soft as an avalanche. Soft as the collision of planets. *Bring my brother's heart to me and you shall be spared. Your allies shall wear my mark. None of you need die in futility.*

'You wouldn't waste your divine breath on me if you didn't think that I could beat you,' I said. I tasted blood and Misery-oil as it bled from my gums. I spat. But I still saw them.

They marched in their tens of thousands. Drudge warriors, ghost-skinned and heavily armoured, spears on their shoulders and shields on their arms. The banners of the Deep Emperor flowed long and bright above them. Beyond

327

that huge host, I sensed another driving will. Older, far older even than Acradius. The Sleeper, biding its time.

He meant to intimidate me, to show the strength of the warriors he commanded, but Acradius had misjudged my own abilities. I knew the Misery, I knew her currents and channels, the way the power flowed and changed. And I saw that Acradius' power was stretched thin, thin as paper, just like the Nameless. He clung to existence in the face of The Sleeper's influence and desire to dominate him. He fought down the Deep Kings he had enthralled by a tether of will alone. He should have swept us from the board, but he was as neutered as Crowfoot, as the Lady of Waves, as any of them.

I laughed against the grit and dust and Acradius' fury blazed from red to white. Hotter than a forge, hotter than the sun. No mortal had mocked him before. Not in all his long millennia.

I will keep you alive. Alive for ten thousand years, flayed and pinned to the city walls, Acradius echoed from his iron tomb. *My swiftest riders go ahead of my host. Twenty thousand of my finest warriors will bring you to me in chains.*

'But you can't ride with them,' I said. 'It's taking all your strength to maintain control.'

You will never understand control, Acradius whispered. *I am legions.*

The vision shifted, altering to show me a second force of drudge. A vast contingent, driving their mounts hard. Thick, white skin, unarmoured but carrying bows and lances, draped in long kaftans. They rode a leaner breed of hurks, rugged, horned creatures, whipping their mounts bloody in their headlong charge across the Misery. An umbilical cord of black energy drove the riders onwards, trying to forge a link between Acradius and Adrogorsk that forced the Misery's changes out of their path. The magic pooled and centred around a throne-like chair, borne aloft by beasts of burden. Upon decayed velvet cushions, surrounded by gold and glittering stones, the desiccated, embalmed body of a long-dead sorcerer acted as the focal point for the riders' magic, a tether point between Adrogorsk and Acradius, a bead sliding inexorably along a wire. They had no need of navigators, the corpse-link driving a boundless charge along Acradius' corridor of thought. The swift-riders left dying, exhausted mounts in their wake on the dust-clouded track, twitching feebly. They were giving everything to reach Adrogorsk before the moons could align.

They marched in their thousands. Drudge warriors, corpse-blue-skinned and heavily armoured, spears on their shoulders and shields on their arms. The banners of the Deep Kings flowed long and bright. A huge host, bearing down on us, ready to destroy.

Do you not comprehend the powers I command? Acradius thundered. Loud as winter snow. Hard as a mother's love. *Your masters cower. They hold nothing. Their day is over, all of their schemes and pawns have achieved nothing. But I am the cosmos. I am the world. I cannot betray my worshippers, for I am all. Give yourself over to me. Save your people, and make them something greater than they have ever known. Their fate rests within your hands.*

Inch by inch, I raised myself from the dirt as his presence clamoured and bit.

I forced him back. Repeated words that I'd spoken to him once before.

'The rain's about to hit,' someone said, her voice distant.

'It wouldn't matter if I stood here alone,' I said. 'It wouldn't matter if I was the last man alive. You'll find me beneath the walls of Adrogorsk.'

I scraped the sand from my hands and thrust my fury against him, beyond the blackness, the cold and the evil that sought to twist me to his will.

'Bring your vassal Kings. Bring your drudge. Bring everything you fucking have, your whole damn empire if you need it. Bring it all. We'll be waiting for you.'

30

The sky boomed hollow with thunder and a purple curtain swept across the Misery towards us.

The city gates were a yawning, empty maw. Nothing organic had survived the Heart of the Void, and the soldiers rattled the wagons through, lashing the longhorns' flanks to urge them on. The walls were pitted and scarred where drudge siege engines and spells had gouged chunks from the fused stone, but they still stood firm. Adrogorsk had been built to last. Beyond the walls the buildings still stood as they once had, even if they were twisted, melted things.

It was all so familiar.

'We need shelter,' Valiya said, all too aware of the effects of the rain.

'Where should we take the loom, Captain?' General Kazna asked.

'Kanalina wants it at the highest point in the city. That's the sky-bath at the palace if I remember right, but for now just find a building and get inside.'

'Can you direct the quartermaster to some suitable stores? I want our ammunition unloaded into the dry as soon as possible.'

I shook my head.

'It's been thirty years, General, and the city was full of men, gun smoke and bad sorcery the last time I was here. I remember the sky-bath because I can see it from here.' I had to shout over the growls from the rushing clouds and pointed towards the palace, the tallest structure still standing. A tower rose from its domed roof, flattening out at the top in a shallow dish.

The general fired off orders. Get the moisture extractors set up, find a decent building for a powder store, identify latrines, secure a perimeter, corral the animals. The messengers dispersed with well-practised haste. Their oilcloth cloaks would keep off a light fall, but not for long. The first drops sizzled across us, stinging where they found bare skin.

'Everyone find somewhere to hole up,' I shouted, unnecessarily. The soldiers weren't stupid, and they'd seen the effects of the rain on their comrades firsthand.

Valiya, Maldon, and I ducked through a door that had been half covered by a melted wall. The room beyond was dark, half-melted, the roof sloping down to the floor. Sand and grit had gathered in the corners over the years, but the bones lay undisturbed, three distinctly separate skeletons visible in the dim light. Tattered shreds of old clothing, belt buckles, and tin buttons lay amongst the human detritus.

'This place is a tomb,' Maldon said.

'We probably used this to house some of the wounded brought down from the walls,' I said.

'And when you evacuated the city you left them behind?' Valiya asked.

I knelt beside the bones and picked up a scuffed brass pocket watch. It had run down long ago, the hands frozen in a final moment. Outside the black rain built to its full force, hissing as it doused the streets.

'We left the dead,' I said. 'And those whose injuries were so great that they couldn't be moved had earned a quick death from their officers. The drudge were going to claim the city. A quick knife was preferable to being taken. Mindworms, or being turned into drudge – nobody wanted that.' I brushed my fingers along the top of a skull. Maybe I'd known this soldier. Maybe I'd shared a drink or a laugh with them before the flames of war engulfed us. Nothing there now but bones and scraps of the past. We are all nothing, come the end.

There was nothing more to say. We sat, as far from the door as the sloping roof allowed, and waited for the sky to exhaust itself.

'What will you do, Galharrow?' Venzer asked me. It was just the two of us, alone now in the dark, watching one another, cross-legged on the floor. I tossed a stone from hand to hand, or maybe it was a finger bone. It was hard to tell in the gloom.

'When?'

'When you have to,' he said. 'When Crowfoot's weapon is primed. When the power of the moons has been gathered and spun, and you stand before his new world-ending weapon.'

'I'll do what has to be done,' I said.

'What has to be, or what you want to be done?' Venzer's head flopped to the side, sagging on a broken neck that couldn't hold it upright. His half-mouth of teeth had been worn down by time, but his eyes were bright.

'I've learned,' I said slowly, 'that those can be one and the same.'

'Blackwing, Blackwing, all the captains have flown away,' Venzer said. His head slumped forwards, chin against his chest. He took it in both hands and held it upright. 'What happened to them, I wonder? Who killed Linette, Klaunus, Josaf, and Vasilov? Where is Silpur, the master's attack dog? Why isn't he here to pull the trigger?'

'I did what I had to do.'

'Would they agree?'

'Most of them can't,' I said. 'They didn't have the strength to do what is needed. I don't know how Linette and Josaf died, but in the final moments they would have buckled. I'm not sorry they're gone. I don't trust anyone else. Only me. At the end, the decision will be mine.'

'And what of Amaira, Crowfoot's new little crow? You let the count tell her. Let her into your little conspiracy. But what will she do, when the moment of your betrayal comes? Where will her loyalty lie, I wonder?'

'Leave me to worry about Amaira.'

'And have you done enough to be sure you can do it?' Venzer asked. 'Are you really strong enough to pull it off?'

'Not yet,' I said. I nodded at him. 'But I will be. Yes, sir. You can count on me.'

We lost two men to the rain, fools who'd run out to grab something, hoping that their cloaks would protect them. They convulsed, lost in the memories it forced upon them. Nall's memories. I could hear their gibbering shrieks two streets across as I oversaw the unloading of the loom's components. The settings were thick pieces of iron, woven with intricate lattices of silver and copper wire. The lenses were wrapped up as bulky parcels which the Marble Guardians had to be entrusted to move, as they were far heavier than our biggest men could reasonably manage.

The wagon on which the ice fiend's heart had been brought was a grim sight. The planks had warped, blackened, and the whorls in the wood had the look of gaping, screaming mouths. The longhorns that had been drawing it had been swapped out repeatedly, but even those that had only dragged it for a couple of days had some kind of sickness in their hindquarters, their fur melting away and fat yellow boils spreading across their skin. They'd been in proximity to the fiend's heart for too long. Even through the box's lead panels, the exposure had taken effect.

I found myself standing by it with North on the opposite side of the wagon, leaning on that jade-headed spear. The

Guardian, First, stood close by, watching the cargo.

'You want to be the one to carry it up there, be my guest,' I said. 'I'd rather not get near the damn thing if I don't have to.'

As I looked at them, North with his eyes hidden behind the darkened lenses of his glasses, First with eyes the colour of blood, it did not escape my notice that I'd had to fight both of these servants of the Nameless in recent days. We had a common purpose now, but I didn't like them. North gave a 'hmph' and sauntered away; he wasn't planning on doing any heavy lifting. The box wasn't large, but there were a lot of steps up to the sky-bath, and its weight went beyond its size.

First turned his gaze from the box to me. The Guardians were impassive things, seemingly disinterested in the world around them unless there was blood in the air, but First was looking at me with a different kind of expression. Had I thought it possible, I'd have sworn he was trying to keep back a smile.

'Captain Galharrow,' a runner said. 'General Kazna wants you up on the sky-bath.'

I groaned inwardly at the prospect of those steps, and again for the perilous ascent.

The old palace was the most defensible structure still standing in the city. The queens of Adrogorsk had wanted their visitors awed, and a deep moat surrounded it, spanned by three broad bridges. Stagnant black rainwater, slick and oily with Misery-pollutants, still half-filled it. A good deal of sand had blown into the moat over the years, making the liquid thick. Quicksand. I didn't fancy anyone's chances if they fell in. The moat was not intended as any kind of defence; once upon a time leisure craft would have given the queens a gentle trip around their great works. Half-fallen statues still lined the banks, generations of rulers brought low by Nameless magic and the ravages of the Misery. The toxins in the half-water would probably have eaten through any punts that tried to pole around it now.

The sky-bath topped the roof of a palace that had once housed Adrogorsk's elite. Where better to enjoy a warm communal bath than ten storeys above the ground? By Adrogorsk's standards, ten storeys had been low. Many of her towers had stretched to twice that height, spires of luxury for a class of nobility that had made Dortmark's princes seem like paupers. The lavish gardens that had once surrounded the palace were now dust-grounds and sandpits. An open-air staircase led up the side of the palace, crumpled lead pipes still clinging to the wall alongside it, which gave something to hold on to now as the railing had been torn away by the Heart of the Void. Ten storeys was no Grandspire staircase, but it was enough to get me sweating and set the old spear wound in my thigh pulsing.

The bath itself had been a pool, a little more than waist deep for the average nobleman, and its round basin covered most of the rooftop. The drains were open and the rainwater that had gathered had all poured away, but dirty red streaks coloured the smooth, sloping marble. General Kazna and her officers were gathered on the lip that surrounded the bath, looking east. Amaira leaned against a wall. She was drained of all colour, dust in her hair. She wouldn't meet my eye.

'I would like your assessment of the city's defences, Galharrow,' Kazna said. 'And how best to employ the forces we have available.'

I nodded. I had expected as much. From the palace roof we had a good view of most of the wall, except where the thin, twisted spires obscured it.

'There are five major entry points through the outer wall,' Nenn said helpfully. 'The two main gates, which are broad enough to drive wagons through, the aft gate, which you can't, and the two breaches where the drudge managed to bring large sections of the wall down. But there are a dozen other, smaller tunnels they bored through with sorcery.'

I pointed to them as she named them.

'Well?' Kazna asked.

'You heard her,' I said. Kazna and the officers shared looks that I didn't like and I scowled at them. Nenn was a major, and I didn't take disrespect to her lightly. She rolled her eyes.

'You tell them, if they ain't going to listen to me,' she said. I shook my head wearily. Her assessment had been as good as anyone's. I repeated exactly what Nenn had just told them, and this time they paid attention.

'You said an advance party of drudge are on their way,' Kazna said. 'How long before they arrive?'

'I'd guess two days,' I said. 'But it could be less. It could be more.'

'We only have to hold the ruins until Spinner Kanalina has completed her task,' Kazna said, more for the benefit of the officers than for me. I wondered whether they could hear the hopelessness in her voice. She was putting a brave chin on it, but my assessment was deeply dispiriting. 'After that we'll abandon whatever we can and ride hard for the Range. The drudge will be weary after their forced march. We shall be rested, and should be able to stay well ahead of them.' She glanced up at the sky as though the orbits of the moons told her the proximity of the eclipse. 'Three days. That's how long we need to hold out here. How many are we facing in the drudge's advance force?'

'You don't want to know,' I said.

The officers were tough. They'd each ranged in the Misery more than once, and they had the lines around their eyes to show it. Their uniforms were armour, their weapons were practical. No delicate orchids these. I still knew my answer was going to hurt.

337

'I can't plan the defence if I don't know what I'm up against,' Kazna said.

'I don't have an accurate count,' I said. 'But if I were to guess? Twenty thousand.'

Faces paled, greyed, greened. Amaira looked at me now. Her eyes were dark, her mouth a pursed, hard line.

'Spirits of Fucking Mercy, we're outnumbered twenty to one and that's just the advance force? How are we going to hold against twenty thousand?' a tough old Fracan man snarled.

'You all knew this mission was dangerous,' Kazna said. She pushed back strands of grey and indigo hair from her face. 'It's the Misery after all.' Her voice was firm. 'Let us prepare.'

The discussions were subdued. I lingered at the edge, listening, half paying attention and half watching a detachment of the Third Battalion marching through the dusty former gardens. They all looked up at me, expectant, and I gave them a salute. It felt good to see my men again.

I blinked and the Third wavered and disappeared from view. Only Amaira and Kazna remained, the officers heading away down the stairs.

'Twenty thousand,' the general said. 'How long have you known?'

'Not long,' I said.

'We can't hold the city against that many.'

I could have given her false hope. I could have lied. She might have respected me more for it.

'I know.'

Kazna shook her head, leaned against the wall that led around the edge of the roof. Amaira balled her fists and struck me a fair punch to the chest.

'This was always a suicide mission,' she said. 'Wasn't it?'

I debated telling her. She didn't need to know the truth, but in the end I decided that certainty was more useful than desperate hope. Resignation can bring despair, or it can offer resolve. Harder choices become easier. Resources can be spent differently. It was a practical decision to tell them, not a fair one. None of it was fair on anyone.

'Even if Kanalina spins the light, Adrogorsk won't survive,' I said. 'The Misery might not survive. The Range? Dortmark? I don't know. We're not just here to charge some battery coils. We're here to power a weapon. Look around. You've seen the work of the Nameless' weapons. You've breathed it in. Our job is to hold long enough that we get to see that end. You must have known, Amaira. Crowfoot uses us, however he needs to.'

Kazna nodded. She stared out to the east as though she might pierce through the heat haze on the horizon, stare all the way through the Misery to Old Dhojara, the subjugated kingdoms of the Deep Kings.

'But we won't live that long,' she said. 'That will be all, Captains.'

My battalion crowded the streets. They nodded to me as I passed, or saluted. I kept them on their toes, wasn't afraid of giving them a midnight kit inspection, or turfing them out to run three miles around the barracks. They admired me for that, I thought. Not to my face, and not in the gossip I heard behind whispered hands in the officers' mess, but deep down they knew it was for the best. This was war, and look where it had brought them all. They'd be glad of those late-night runs when the drudge arrived. *If* they arrived. They probably wouldn't. Adrogorsk wasn't worth squat.

'Get that pike sharpened,' I said to a man who was too busy inspecting the arrow buried in his arm to notice that he'd let his weapon falter.

'Of course, Brigadier,' he said smartly, giving me the appropriate salute. A pair of women began to busily see to their weapons. I couldn't help but laugh as I strode between them along these old, familiar streets. Their own bones lay at their feet, and what an absurd thing that was. I had a good mind to tell them to clear them up.

'They were good lads,' Nenn said, falling in alongside me. 'Good lasses.'

'They were,' I said. 'They are, I guess.'

'Does it hurt? Seeing them here?'

'In all honesty, I'm not entirely sure where we are, what we're doing or who you are,' I told her. 'It's all getting fuzzy. There's more than just me in here, now. I'm not the Misery. Not yet. But I couldn't tell you where I end, and she begins.'

'Wasn't that always the plan?'

'I don't know,' I told her. 'I don't know what the point of any of it was anymore.'

We walked on. Nenn joined in chastising my men, though she'd barely been ten years old when they went into the ground. They didn't seem to mind. She chewed aethereal blacksap which now seemed to come in the shape of chillies, and offered me some. I'd never liked the stuff because of the oily dark stains it put on your teeth, but my teeth, jagged and, as I probed with my tongue, in some cases serrated, were hardly a show. I took some and chewed as we walked. It had a gritty, bitter flavour.

'Never understood why you liked this shit,' I said.

'I didn't,' she said. 'It just used to really wind you up.' She spat. 'It's not as much fun when you join in.'

'I'm not even surprised.'

'You do know,' Nenn said. 'You think you don't, but you do.'

'Know what?'

'Why you're doing this. All of this.' She gestured around us. 'If you dig down deep enough it's still there. It will always be there.'

340

'You're even more annoying dead than you were alive,' I said.

'Nah,' she replied, spitting the rest of the blacksap at some unfortunate ghosts who were trying to hide their tile game from me. 'I'm more or less the same.' She put a hand on my shoulder and turned me. 'You understand, don't you? You're here for her. But we're here for you too. Not just me, and Betch and Venzer. All of us. We're here, when you need us.'

I shook her off, shook my head. She wasn't even real. I needed more ghosts like I needed another spear through my leg – which was what I was probably going to get if I didn't find North and make some kind of peace with him. Failing that I'd just have to take him out. He wasn't important to the equation. A pragmatic part of my mind told me that a quick jab with a stiletto might make everything just that bit easier.

I found Valiya moving rain-sodden sand about with a shovel in the palace grounds. She heard me coming, whirled about, and brandished the spade like she might do me an injury with it. The pain on her face cut through the ghosts and sent them back to wherever they went when they weren't trying to drive me mad. She didn't try to mask it. She was exhausted. We all were. It wasn't just the trek through the Misery, it was the losses and the constant uncertainty of the future. That anxiety gnawed at you, whittling you down. Valiya's hair couldn't turn any greyer, but her face had.

'There's soldiers that can do whatever it is you're doing,' I said. I wasn't sure why I'd sought her out. I didn't know what her role was here. She believed that she had some part to play in all this, but she wasn't in charge of the loom, couldn't spin, and wasn't a fighter. Maybe the echo of Nall's fight lingered on in her, even though her eyes had bled silver and her calculations stopped flowing. She had some kind of a part to play in things to come, but what it might be, I didn't know. I looked at the sand she was shovelling. 'What are you doing?'

'Covering the manholes that lead down into the sewers,' she said.

'Why?'

'I'll show you.'

She shovelled a couple more loads of sand onto the pile, then produced a map. Trust Valiya to have a street map of Adrogorsk. She led me along, looking for something marked on the paper, stopped before a huge temple with colonnades at the front. My first time here, some of the soldiers had set up a field hospital inside. Valiya watched her step carefully, but the old sewer entrance was easily visible.

'Don't panic,' she said. 'And don't tell anyone about this. There's nothing that we can do other than cover the holes and I fear we'd have desertions if they knew.'

I heard the voices before we reached the hole. High and whining, a babble of nonsense.

'Seventy-three, seventy-two.'

'He's a good boy, just don't anger him.'

'Evening, master, care for a good time?'

I peered down into the darkness beneath the street. By the little light that reached down into the darkness, I could make out movement. Squirming, wriggling movement. There must have been thousands of them. Gillings by the spirits-damned score. The tracks we'd seen, their absence out in the Misery, they'd come here in tubby scarlet legions and now they clustered together beneath Adrogorsk's streets.

'Fucking gillings,' I said. 'Been looking for these little shits for months. I guess they knew they were coming here before we did.'

'What are they doing here?' Valiya asked. She was un-afraid. The gillings weren't able to clamber out and it was a six-foot drop to the writhing mass below.

'Crowfoot is coming,' I said. 'They can feel it. When I was lost in the Misery, they flocked to the hooded raven. Called him "father," once. They're drawn to him. Like us, they're here for the end.'

Valiya went to one of the half-melted buildings and found a broad, flat drip of stone that had broken away under its own weight. Her hands were scuffed and nicked from dragging slabs around in other places. She laboured under its weight, trying to roll it into place, and I just stood there and watched, wondering why she was bothering. She gave me a scalding look. 'You could help?'

'It's pointless,' I said. 'They found their way in there, and it's not like they can climb out.'

'They might,' she said harshly. She got the slab up onto its uneven side and began rolling it over towards the hole.

'They won't,' I said. It didn't seem important. I peered down into the wriggling mass of misshapen, fat little bodies. 'Why bother?'

'Because it's something I can do,' she said with a sigh. She lost control of the stone and it fell back on its side. Valiya bent over, trying to pry it upright again, but it probably weighed more than she did. I heard one of her fingernails break against it as she clawed for purchase. I don't know why that moved me, but it did. I reached down and lifted the stone up with one hand, taking hers in the other. Her hand was small, unreasonably small and pale in my copper-hued talons. The nails that had turned black a long time ago were looking suspiciously like claws, more so than ever since we'd re-entered the Misery. I looked down at Valiya's far smaller hand, the veins blue beneath the skin, the bones stark.

'You don't have to keep going,' I said. 'You've done enough. You can leave the rest to me.'

Valiya just shook her head. I couldn't read her expression. I wasn't so good at grasping the nuance anymore.

343

'You really must be losing your mind if you think I will quit,' she said. 'Cover it, then heap some sand on it.'

I did what she asked, although it was a waste of time. Valiya's map showed that the sewers around the palace's island had at least two dozen entrances. It would take a team of determined men a full day to cover them all, and the gillings would still get out if they wanted to and there'd be bugger-all we could do about it. They seemed happy enough down there in the dark, though, chattering their endless, whimsical nonsense.

'I don't do it because it's essential, Ryhalt,' Valiya said as I finished piling the bone-dust atop the stone. 'I do it because I can.'

I looked at her, and something inside me cracked, a frozen waterfall pushed by the glacier that consumes it.

'I can send you back,' I said.

'What do you mean?

'I can send you back. To the Range. If you want to go. To live.'

Valiya glared at me.

'How?'

'It's complicated,' I said. 'My blood. Sand. All this polluted magic around us. They're all tied up together, now. But I think that I have enough of the Misery's essence in me to send someone back. Just one. If I can save someone, just one person – it should be you.'

Valiya turned her back to me.

'You never truly let go, did you?'

'I know,' I said. 'I struggle to feel it. I struggle to feel anything, now. I know what I've become, Valiya. I've delved into hate, and rage, and selfishness. I've tasted what it means to be Nameless, or a Deep King, and that kind of contact leaves scars on your mind. But mostly I've drunk from the Misery, and the taste never quite goes away. My mind plays so many tricks on me, I don't know who's dead

344

and who's alive anymore. Are you real? Were any of the friends I saw along the way there? It's all broken up inside me. I don't even know who I am, sometimes.'

Valiya took my absurd, clawed hand in hers and looked up at me with eyes that were no longer silver, but carried far more reflection than they had before. There was a spark of me, deep inside, that rebelled and kicked within my rib cage, that tried to reach outside me. But I no longer remembered or understood what it was.

'No. Nall gave me a final command before he was gone. I'll not abandon it now. Or you. There's something else I found while I was walking around looking for something to do,' Valiya said. 'Come.'

We didn't have long. The swift-riders were closing fast. Whatever plans we put in place, there was no real chance of holding against twenty thousand drudge and I knew it. We were all pretty fucked if they made it, unless I came up with something pretty spectacular. But Valiya's fingers, though I could barely feel them through the pebbled skin of my own, drew me on anyway. She led me across the broad, moat-spanning bridges to a building close to the palace. I recognised it in some way. We'd used it as ... an armoury? No. A store of some kind. The memory was thirty years old, and hazy. She drew me inside.

The Spirit of Mercy alone knew what had made Valiya enter that particular building, but something must have guided her. Maybe just luck. Blind, pointless luck. I felt a smile trying to fight its way onto my face, awkward now that my teeth didn't really fit a human mouth properly. I hadn't seen this in decades. A mark of pride. A mark of shame.

But mine.

Around the walls we'd retired the banners of the lords who had fallen in the defence. It was a mausoleum to the colours of those that had not come home. Their bones lay out there amongst the melted ruins, long picked clean, long ago bleached by the sun, stained red now by the rain. I saw the arms of houses that had died during the rout, symbols of bygone men whose names were no longer spoken. The general's banner hung limp, a field of jade with three rampant, golden horses. He'd stood with the men, against an assault on a breach in the walls, and had died for it. They had all died for it, heroes every one. Dead heroes.

On the floor, four tattered pieces of dusty red cloth lay where I'd dropped them, thirty years before. My banner. My own colours. A single silver fist on a field of scarlet. In the hour before we abandoned Adrogorsk to the approaching Deep Kings, I'd brought it here and torn it apart. I'd been so angry. Angry at the drudge, but furious at the dead men whose colours looked back at me now. I'd been twenty years old and they'd left so many lives in my hands. I'd been so full of fury.

'I forgot myself here,' I murmured into the dust and gloom, lifting a shred of banner from the floor. 'This is where the man I'd been ended. Where Ryhalt Galharrow began.'

'You know who you are,' Valiya said. 'You're the same good man you've always been.'

I let the fabric trail through my fingers.

'You knew this was mine,' I said. 'Why did you show it to me?'

'Because I need you to remember,' she said. 'I need you to know who you are.'

'I know what I am,' I said. I tossed the fragment of the past back into the dust. 'The world doesn't. But I do.'

31

'Has the Misery taken your mind? Attack twenty thousand drudge?'

The eyes on me were disbelieving. It was raining again, a second downpour in just two days. The soldiers huddled in the ruins of twisted buildings as the black hissed down around them. I faced Kazna, Kanalina, North, First, and the officers in an empty chamber on the fourth floor of the palace. A strange Command Council, misfits and veterans side by side.

'We can't hold the city,' I said. 'There are no gates. There are holes in the walls. We have five light cannon, and our gunners will barely dent the numbers that the drudge can put against us. They'll be here in two days, and when they arrive, they'll pour through the walls like smoke.'

'We've all held tough spots before, Captain,' Kazna reminded me.

'Not like this,' I said. 'We couldn't hold against five thousand. We certainly couldn't hold against ten. Twenty will wash us aside in less than an hour. If we defend here, we fail.'

'So you want us to head out into the Misery and attack the drudge head-on? That's madness,' North said. I'd rather he hadn't been there. He was a thorn in my hand, an irksome splinter.

'Not head-on. We can't break them or rout them. But we

can stop them reaching Adrogorsk. If we strike out at them, we can buy the time that the Spinners need to enact the Nameless' plan before Acradius arrives.'

There was grumbling amongst the officers, but Kazna rested a curled finger against her lip, thinking. Her eyes were narrowed, her back straight. She wasn't a big woman, but her mood set the tone in the room. Gradually the officers subsided into silence, even North.

'I'm willing to hear you out,' she said.

'The drudge aren't navigating their way here,' I said. 'Adrogorsk shifts and hides from them just as it did from us. But there are some things even the Misery can't resist. The swift-riders are guided by Acradius. He's ploughing them a furrow, straight through the Misery.'

'Then we need to fortify,' Kanalina said. 'Defend the walls.'

'Come.'

I beckoned her over to where Valiya and I stood at the window, and reluctantly she crossed to us. Amaira still wasn't talking to me, but North and First followed. The huge Guardian unnerved me more than his brethren. He seemed more human by the day, red eyes watchful. I didn't turn my back on either of them.

I gestured out towards the city walls, broken and jutting like the rotting teeth of a drunk.

'The city walls have more holes in them than a beggar's shirt,' I said. 'And we have fourteen Guardians, six Spinners, and a thousand men.'

'The best men on the Range,' one of the officers grunted.

'The best. But still only a thousand of them.' I threw a careless, clawed hand out towards the walls. My voice sounded like gravel going through a grinder. 'By my count there are sixteen holes in the city walls that the drudge could get through, including the three gates. We have no hope of holding them all. The Guardians might be worth a hundred men each in a pitched battle, but the drudge aren't going to line up to fight. They only need to reach the loom and destroy it, and Acradius knows that. He'll sacrifice ten thousand warriors just to breach the walls. Once they're in, we can't stop them.'

'The palace is defensible,' Kanalina said. 'We can hold the bridges. Nothing could make it through that moat.'

'How long for, and against how many drudge?' I asked.

'We can hold.'

'No,' North said. He frowned, resigned. 'We can't. Not against those numbers. We can put three hundred men at each bridge, but the bridges are sixty feet across, neh?'

I'd not expected support from North, but I'd take it from any quarter.

'Not only that, but we'd be surrounded and trapped,' I agreed. 'And if they've brought Darlings, they'll cut our men to pieces in the middle of a bridge. Acradius is going to throw everything he has at us.'

'How did you scout them?' North asked.

'There are things you don't need to know,' I said. 'You trusted me this far. Trust me on this.'

Nenn was trying to work out how to take two of Venzer's tiles using a piece from a different game. For a moment I was absorbed in the game, and nudged one of her pieces into place when Venzer wasn't looking. Nenn thought it was hilarious and Venzer managed to fall backwards out of the window in shock at seeing his king suddenly surrounded.

'Are you even listening?' Kanalina snapped. I blinked and refocused on her.

'What?'

'I said, what then?' Kanalina demanded.

'We take the fight to them,' I said. 'We choose the ground. We choose how to attack, and what. And we break their advance. We divert them and let the Misery take them somewhere else.'

'You want to go for their navigators,' North said. He was much sharper than he had any right to be.

'Yes, but they aren't using astrolabes or navigators that we'd recognise,' I said. 'Acradius has locked himself onto Adrogorsk. It's a fixed point, and he has a ribbon of power stretching across the Misery, making a crow-flight line straight here. They have an old cadaver, the mummified body of a sorcerer. Spirits alone know where they found it, but it's pointing them right in our direction. If we can destroy it, maybe the Misery itself will stop them.'

'How many drudge do we need to go through to get to it?' North asked. I met his eye.

'A lot. But they're riding in a column, spread thin. An ambush is our best shot at destroying the thing that's guiding them.'

'And if we destroy it?' North said.

'Then anyone still alive runs,' I replied. 'And hope to the spirits that the drudge are too tired to chase us down.'

'That is not the Lady's plan,' North growled.

'I bet it isn't.'

'Enough,' Kazna snapped. 'You can parade your feathers and work out whose sword is longest later. Your plan makes sense. We can't stop twenty thousand drudge. We've assessed the defences. We have neither the men nor the walls to stop them. But the Misery could.'

'I could,' Nenn put in, helpful as ever. Marshal Venzer had climbed back onto the windowsill, but his neck was still broken, and his head lolled awkwardly to one side.

'I'll lead our attack force to intercept them, and I can take us there fast. What the drudge cover in two days, I can navigate in less than one. The farther from the city we strike the better,' I told them. 'I want the Guardians and nine hundred men. And I want the Spinners. They can cloak us until we're ready to strike.'

'I need to stay here to spin the light,' Kanalina said. 'I'll need some measure of protection.'

'Kanalina and fifty men stay,' Kazna said. 'The rest of us go.'

'I stay.'

Heads turned in First's direction. His voice was awkward, the grinding of millstones. A voice that had never been used before.

'You'll follow orders,' Kazna said.

'I stay,' First repeated. 'Guardians go. I stay.'

There wasn't much that any of us could say to that. It wasn't as though we could force him.

'I'm not attacking twenty thousand bloody drudge!' one of the officers snapped. 'That's not just a suicide mission, it's utter madness.'

'This has been madness from the start,' I said. 'Attack is our best chance of surviving it. I'll lead out at dusk. The swift-riders won't stop by night. Not when they're this close. We'll hit them at dawn. Whatever spirits you need to pray to, I suggest you pray hard.'

The Guardians didn't need to discuss anything. When the time came to move, they were gathered outside Adrogorsk's walls, their glaives shouldered, staring out to the east. Our tired men rode out of the city in columns. There were no wagons, no tents. If the rain hit us out there, it was all over. But the sky was cloudless, and in war, sometimes you have to trust to luck. Two of the Spinners joined me, one tall, the other with an old web of burns beneath one eye. She seemed too young to be out here. Ripples of colour seemed to wash over the sand, a sheen of iridescent, flowing oil. I blinked at them until they went away or, at least, stopped demanding my attention.

'Not riding with your friends?' I asked.

'We're to keep you alive,' the tall woman said. Her name

was Dovroi. The scarred woman was Spinner Vurtna. 'If we succeed then you're our only way back, so Kazna has given orders that you're not to engage in the fighting.' Dovroi shook her head.

I looked around.

'Where are the other Spinners?'

'There have been desertions. The other Spinners and the navigators took what they could carry and rode west. What they thought was west, anyway.'

'They deserted?' I said. The word always carried an acrid taste.

Dovroi nodded. Vurtna kept her distance from me, preferring the ice-skinned Guardians for company. I wondered how many of our soldiers had chosen to go with them.

I could hear an old marching song drifting out from the gaps in the walls. Some of the boys from the Third Battalion were having a good old time at least.

I pressed my hand into the Misery-sand and listened. I sensed the enemy, felt the heavy black tether that drew them on to us. It was rancid, sick with the soul-essence of the Deep Kings' magic. Even to me, steeped in Misery-pollution, it felt corrupt. I tried to shake it off as I drew my knife. I bared a forearm, made a shallow cut, and squeezed blood from the wound. It was dark, thick, and sluggish as it dripped onto the sand. The Misery felt it, absorbed it. A waypoint, to bring us back. I hoped we were going to need it.

Dantry rode out on a black charger, armoured in gleaming black steel. He looked like the cadaver of a fairy-tale prince, golden hair around bog-corpse skin.

'You should stay here,' I said.

'Everyone else is going,' he said, shadow and frost in his voice. 'Don't ask me to sit back. Because I won't. I'm not yours to command, Ryhalt.'

'You're still angry with me,' I said.

'Angry? No.'

'Then what?'

He sighed, not for my benefit, just a dry expulsion of spirit.

'It was all for nothing,' he said. 'Even if we succeed. Look at what they've made of us. Look at what we've done. What was the point in any of it, if this is who we have to be? We're no better than the Deep Kings. Murderers. Warlords. Assassins. We're everything we're supposed to be fighting against.'

He kicked his horse along the column, emptiness trailing in his wake. I mounted, and led my band out into the night. The cut in my arm healed over in minutes.

Acradius' invisible leash ploughed through whatever the Misery shifted in front of it. Patches of razor grass had shrivelled and shrunk away from it, and even banks of rock and sand had been driven aside. Acradius' road, cut slowly by invisible forces, defied even the Misery. Whatever my link to her, not even I had that kind of power to alter her. Questing out, I found a gully, shallow slopes rising to the height of a castle wall around it for a stretch of cracked and broken rock a third of a mile long. The leash had forced sand and rock aside, creating a road to hurry the riders along. They would pass right below us.

We rode quickly and without chatter. Each man and woman prayed to whatever spirits they favoured, checked their lucky amulets, adjusted straps that didn't need adjusting. They knew the mission, and it was simple: destroy the corpse. The night was lit by Eala, a waxy golden light upon us as we pressed on.

As we rode I let my mother braid my hair. I'd never had long hair before, and her rocking chair was oddly silent as she focused on it, working the threads and strands. I'd missed her touch so much down the years. It was comforting to sit with her in her parlour. I knew that I couldn't be in her parlour, because I was riding a horse through the Misery, but it was good to be there all the same.

In the quiet of the rising dawn, we took up positions and made final preparations.

I found Amaira. She sat alone, tending to her weapons, the scraping of the whetstone against her blade a quiet squeaking in the calm morning air.

'I want you with me,' I said. 'On the ridge.'

She glanced up at me, then frowned as though irritated with herself for noting my presence.

'No,' she said.

'No?'

'No. I'm going in with the cavalry.'

I sat down beside her.

'I don't want to risk you. One more sword won't make any more difference. Even one as sharp as yours.'

She stopped her grinding, tested the edge with a finger. Not satisfied, she went back to it.

'I used to idolise you,' she said. 'No, that's not right. I trusted you. Trusted you like I'd never been able to trust anybody. I always knew you'd come for me. Always knew you'd do what you had to. Was I a fool?'

'I don't understand,' I said.

Amaira grunted, tossed the whetstone aside. Stared towards the horizon, wrapped her arms around her knees.

'I'm going to die today,' she said. 'We're all going to die today. And I could have died in love. You took that from me. You burned the best thing I'd ever found.' She looked at me then. 'For her.'

'Stay on the ridge with me,' I said. 'Don't die. There's time for reparations, if that's what you want.'

'Captain Linette was my friend,' she said. 'You deceived me. All of you deceived me.'

I hadn't known, but there was no point setting her right about that now. I wasn't there to bring more conflict. I knew, the sensation of quicksand all around me, that I'd done enough of that. My obsession had blinded me. I regretted it, now. I could have left it all alone. Should have left it alone. Spirits, but I was a bitter, cruel old man. I'd objected to the love that she'd found with Dantry only partly from a sense of fatherly protectiveness. The other part was black, bitter envy.

'Stay alive,' I said. 'Do that for me.' She didn't reply.

The riders appeared first as a column of dust, dirt tossed into the sweltering Misery-air by their mounts' bloodied hooves. A vicious heat rose around us as the sun crested the horizon. Above, two of the moons had already started their slow crawl towards one another. Eala would follow last, her orbit the shortest. Three great spheres of crystal, focusing the power of our yellow sun down in a spear of magical intensity so powerful that even the Nameless craved it. Acradius was out in the Misery, exposed, but if we failed, Kanalina and North would be forced to pass our own weapon into his hands.

Fail now, and everything was over.

I began to make out the front ranks of riders as they came on. They did not travel at full-tilt, but their mounts continued relentlessly, pace by aching pace. The ridge had a sharp peak, keeping us from their eyes and in the racket of hooves scraping at the earth they were unlikely to hear us. I lay in the dirt, looking out. They drew closer, a mile away, half, and then below me, the first riders began to pass by. The drudge were the corpse-blue-skinned breed, intricate glyphs across their faces, the magic so deep that it furrowed their flesh. Prayer strips streamed from their arms and legs, and at their fore, a huge warrior encased in sweltering steel bore Acradius' own banner on a twenty-foot pole. The drudge clattered on past. Dust and grit clung to them, the hurks' muzzles thick with foam, but every eye stared resolutely onwards towards Adrogorsk. The column was huge, stretching back across the Misery. The sight of that vast horde was enough to put an icy chill through the bones of every soldier there, me included. But they were stretched out, a ragged, hell-bent charge. If they were massed together we'd have no chance, but spread – that was our opening.

More than three thousand had ridden past when the anchor came into view.

The cadaver faced west, one mummified arm outstretched, signalling the direction, binding them to the thought-rope stretched between Acradius and Adrogorsk. Its gilded throne was dragged on a sleigh by a dozen of the hurks, a mocking indignity for a long-dead sorcerer-king.

'That's the target,' I said to Dovroi and Vurtna, who lay beside me. Vurtna had woven a web of light over us to conceal us from any drudge that might look up at us, but none of them had. They were focused, intent on their destination. Not expecting an assault. Not caring about one, maybe. 'Do whatever you can.'

'We're doomed,' Dovroi said quietly. 'There's no escape once we attack.'

'No,' I said. 'Probably not. You have my thanks, for whatever that's worth.' The tall Spinner didn't look at me.

'I have family in the city-states. It's them that I'm doing this for,' she said. I nodded. It was the same for me. Why Vurtna had come, I couldn't have said.

The sled bearing the dried-out corpse ground by beneath us.

'It's time,' I said. I stood, the dawn light reflecting from my armour. 'Now.'

Dovroi channelled phos from her canisters and sent a flare of light out over the lip of the ridge. It sped down towards the drudge below and detonated in a flash. Bodies flew into the air, screeching as limbs disintegrated. It was the signal to attack.

The cavalry surged forwards over the lip, a black-armoured

tide of horse and steel, and their hooves churned red dust into the air as they galloped full-tilt down the slope. I saw Amaira amongst them, her cavalry sabre high above her head and my heart reeled. Charging onwards, the cavalry ploughed towards nightmare. Here and there a horse lost its footing, crashing down, bringing down other riders behind it, but the wedge held. The drudge began to wheel their mounts around in an effort to meet them.

The Marble Guardians erupted from the sand on the far side of the gulley. Buried, lying in wait, sunlight caught on the polished steel of their glaives as they burst forth. The drudge raised a keening wail as the huge, white-skinned warriors began to advance. Spears and axes found hands and the best that the drudge could send against us readied to meet a charge from legend.

Is this all you have to bring against me? Acradius hissed in my mind, his words floating out from the corpse. Leathery old skin split, ancient bones cracked as the cadaver's head turned in my direction. I had no reply worth giving.

The Marble Guardians charged. The drudge, organised swiftly by one omnipotent will, kicked at their mounts and charged right back into them.

A cavalry charge is a terrible thing to stand against. Without a solid wall of pikes in front of you, or a ditch, or a wall, there's little way for infantry to stand against heavily armoured lancers, and most men will break and run, or throw themselves down and cower, praying not to be trampled by the thundering hooves. Only disciplined soldiers, long drills overriding the natural urge to save themselves, could fight the urge to run, knowing that their best odds lay in bunching tight and hoping. It is discipline and numbers alone that can face such a stampede of beast and steel.

The Guardians had little discipline and were few in number. They still met the charging line like a battalion of battering rams. With a crash, they smashed beasts and riders out of the way, or took the impact head-on and went rolling through the sand, tangled with arms and stirrups, legs and fur. In moments the organised lines broke down into a swirling, thrashing melee. A single swipe of a glaive opened a drudge soldier from shoulder to hip, a drudge lance punched through a Guardian's chest, but didn't slow it. The press of drudge bodies became a wall through which the Guardians began to drive, smashing enemies from their path with the hafts of their weapons, hooking them down and sending sprays of blood into the air as they dealt death blows. One of the Guardians took a savage axe stroke to the neck but carried on fighting, grabbing one of the drudge that had struck it and ripping its arms off.

They were magnificent.

The soldiers met greater resistance. The enemy were the drudge's best, their biggest, toughest warriors, bred for war. The din of battle, the screams of men and beasts filled the air. A drudge-spear punched through a rider's side, but he rose up in the stirrups and delivered a colossal stroke with his sabre that carved the drudge's helm and head apart before he toppled from his saddle. I saw a man dragged from his horse, a knife flashing. I saw a woman blasting around her with pistols, then hurling them at the enemy that two lead balls hadn't stopped. A swirling, bloody mass of hacking, firing, spearing mayhem.

I looked for Amaira, but she was lost to me in the mass of swirling bodies and hacking blades.

Our gunners and archers lined the ridge and poured fire and arrows down into the packed drudge. There were no volleys, just tamp and spit and stoke and fire, nock and draw and loose, a continual cracking of guns and thrumming of strings. Smoke rolled down the ridge like plumes of swamp mist.

The drudge who had already passed had heard the sounds

of battle, and turned back. Those advancing from the east began to press in. Our nine hundred men looked pitiful in comparison.

'Get ready,' I said to Dovroi. 'Wait for your chance.'

The two Spinners siphoned power from their canisters. Their skin took on the faint, smoky glow of gathered phos energy. Lights on their canisters winked out as they absorbed the power slowly, calmly. Their magic was calm, controlled, but there was fear in their eyes.

The Guardians were warriors like I'd never seen. One reared up, a pair of spears lodged in its chest, tongue lolling as it brandished a broken glaive like a sword. The mushroom-white of their bald heads was slicked with red, but they were gaining ground towards the corpse-king, even as more and more drudge pressed in from fore and aft. The drudge were better, stronger than any I'd seen before. Their weapons were honed, their muscles bunched, but even the fine armour they wore buckled beneath the impact of the Guardians' blows. A drudge who must have weighed more than I did was tossed ten feet into the air. But still more came, and the Guardians' advance slowed as they smashed and tore at the wall of bodies before them. Drudge surrounded the Guardians. Spears punched into their backs, arrows whipped into them, and though the Guardians weren't going down easily, still their advance slowed.

A group of drudge had seen us up on the ridge. They drove their mounts up the slope, hooves clawing up sand behind them. Arrows lashed out to meet them, riders and beasts falling, but others reached us. The first came at me with an axe raised over its flat-faced head, but the long spear I held had the reach to meet his charge head-on and I struck him from the saddle. The second faltered as the body crashed into its path, and I went after him before his stumbling mount could right itself. I speared him in the face, forced him from the saddle, then went after each of them in turn with a flurry of thrusts. Some found armour, but others found exposed flesh, driving into muscle and organs. North worked alongside me, as fast as he'd claimed to be, gunning them down as he worked through his brace of pistols. All five were spent in short order, and our attention was back on the fight below.

The black tether of power that bound the sorcerer's corpse to Acradius swelled with energy, and then ribbons of twisting night blossomed around it. They lashed out, finding two Guardians that had managed to draw close. The warriors went rigid, their hacked and pierced bodies shaking as the energy bore into them, and then they began to tremble. A further surge of power, and they detonated, bloodless fragments scattering in all directions. Wasted corpse-lips, long since drawn back from yellow teeth, flexed in what might have been some kind of a smile.

They were not the only Guardians to have fallen. Those that had lost their heads fought on sluggishly, then slowed, their bodies gradually losing spirit until they collapsed. Sheer weight of numbers began to bring them down, one after another as they tried to batter their way through the drudge's elite. A second lance of dark energy tore another Guardian in two.

Our soldiers were nearly surrounded, and hadn't got as close to the corpse-anchor as the Guardians. They were doomed.

Amaira.

'Do it now!' I told the Spinners. 'We won't get a better shot.'

Dovroi straightened her jacket collar. She shared a look with Vurtna that said more than I should have seen, and they clasped hands as they stood.

'For the republic,' Vurtna said, and Dovroi nodded. The light coiled around them as their working began. The warmth of the day was replaced with a new kind of heat, hard and bright, unnatural and metallic. I fell back from them as tendrils of clutching phos snaked towards me. The Spinners' remaining canisters whined and a sudden rushing sound preceded their implosion, metal shells crumpling as the power was sucked from them.

The Spinners unleashed and the air around the sorcerer's corpse shimmered with sudden heat. Bands of pure white light appeared around it, overlapping, forming a sphere. The corpse's eyes glowered in our direction as the bands took form, and then, contracted. It was a deadly binding spell, more than enough to turn a husk into ash.

Something went wrong. Whether it was the magic that Acradius had bound within it, or the long-dead thing held power of its own, a series of wards rippled in the air around it, glimmering glyphs of fire and smoke. The Spinners' power caught on them, tangling, catching on insubstantial gleams of long-forgotten words, and then their casting came right back at them.

I had no time to scream a warning. No time to do anything at all.

The power redirected between heartbeats, the bands of energy rushing back up the slope. The sand beneath the Spinners' feet superheated, liquefied, and Vurtna and Dovroi plunged into the white-hot quagmire as though a platform had been ripped out beneath them. It was sudden enough that they didn't scream, hot enough that they were gone in an instant, nothing more than bubbles in the boiling pool of liquid glass.

Below, only a handful of Guardians battled on, their limbs hewn and splayed open, trying to wade towards the cadaver through a mounting wall of bodies. Five left. Four, as a pair of drudge hammered axes down into the skull of one of the Guardians. Another had gone blood-mad, its teeth locked into a drudge corpse, drinking greedily even as hammers and blades rained down blows.

The bubbling pool of liquid sand hissed and from within, a skull rose, wrapped in liquid glass, features forming into a drudge-like semblance of humanity. It rose on a sinuous, shimmering neck.

Is this all? Is this everything that the Nameless can throw against me?

It made no sound, but it was laughing at me.

The awful truth was, it was. It was everything I possessed to stop the drudge. Shallowgrave's elite warriors, the citadel's Spinners, and for all the Misery that I'd soaked up I was still just a man with a spear.

We had failed. Bodies littered the canyon floor below, the cries of the wounded ringing against the screams of the dying and the clashing of steel. The brave horsemen fought in a tightening circle, hemmed in on all sides as countless drudge swarmed around them. They were doomed. All of them. They had died for nothing.

The matchlock gunners and archers around me knew it. Squadrons of mounted drudge had wheeled from the main line and were coming at us from east and west. The officers desperately tried to form them into volley-lines to meet the enemy.

The liquid glass collapsed, the skull falling back to be swallowed once more. In the midst of the fighting, the last Guardian hurled back the drudge that were hacking at it. It was missing an arm, half of its head and half a dozen crossbow bolts protruded like spines from its back, but with a bellow it swung a drudge-warrior like a flail, gaining itself a clear space. Blood ran from its jaws, and its one remaining eye spun wildly as it looked for prey and saw an opening. It ran straight for the mummified sorcerer.

The wards met it, engulfing the Guardian in flame, but that didn't stop it. With a bellow it reached for the cadaver and when its fingers gripped the sorcerer's skull the flames leapt across to it. A deathless shriek rose up, above the battle, above the cacophony of swords and death throes, and the dried husk of the sorcerer went up in flame, even as the Guardian disintegrated, flesh burned away, bones charring to ash. The drudge bearing the throne collapsed, deadly magic spilling from the sorcerous corpse in waves, melting eyes and boiling blood in their skulls.

'Fall back,' I shouted. 'Fall back!'

The gunners did not heed me. They were settled into their lines, weapons primed and ready to meet the charge. I grabbed a sergeant's arm, yelled that we had to move, to get away now before the drudge swamped us. There was no fighting our way out of this, only running.

'We'll not leave our men behind, Captain,' the sergeant said. 'Not while they might still win free.' There was no hope in his voice.

'Everyone who stays here is dead,' I said.

'Aye, sir,' the sergeant said. 'Just have to hope we done enough, sir.'

I was about to turn away. About to abandon them to their deaths, when I saw her. Amaira, my little crow, struggling across the slope on a dying horse. Broken spears jutted from its side, and despite her heeling, it staggered sideways and then crashed to the earth. Amaira tried to roll clear, but I saw the horse come down on her foot. She screamed. I screamed. The fastest of the drudge were right behind her.

I tried to go to her but the sergeant and another man grabbed hold of me. My eyes were locked forwards, and I was stronger than they were. I began to drag them towards her.

'We need you, Captain!' the sergeant cried, 'We need you to get back. No!'

Another two men piled onto me, pulling, dragging. Their bodies swamped me. I stared helplessly as the drudge came towards the woman I'd helped to raise.

Amaira rose, sword in hand, unable to put her weight

on the foot that had been caught beneath the falling horse. She was already red from head to foot, and the first drudge to reach her took her sabre through the centre of its head. She let rip a banshee scream as another swung an axe at her, batting it aside and ramming the sabre's point into its mouth. Her ferocity checked them, but it would only be moments. Four quick-footed drudge circled around her as she tried to yank her sword free. Her teeth were locked, her eyes wild. I was going to watch my daughter die.

A huge horse ploughed back towards them from the retreating line. The drudge saw it coming, tried to ready themselves, but like a black thunderbolt the warhorse smashed two of them to the ground. The armoured man hacked down at them, his bladework artless, frenzied, killed another. A drudge-spear punched into the horse's neck, and as it reared he fell from its back, hitting the ground hard.

The Deep Kings, the Nameless, they all saw love as a weakness. But to need someone on your side doesn't make you weak; it makes you strong.

I was screaming Dantry's name. I was screaming Amaira's name. The sergeant and the soldiers pulled me back, farther and farther, my feet skittering against the sand as I tried to throw them off. I had no purchase, no way to bring my strength to bear.

Amaira cut through the last of the drudge, her skill far beyond anything that I'd ever mustered, then fell to her knees beside Dantry, alive but struggling to rise. Tears cut pale tracks through the blood spatters across her face. She got an arm under his shoulder, managed to drag him, stumbling, to unsteady feet. Concussed, or broken by the fall, but she forced him up.

Drudge-riders charged up behind them. They could never outrun them. I could never make it to them in time.

Dantry had been right. We'd given up everything. We'd become what we despised in order to see it done. And still, amidst all that, they wouldn't let each other go. I couldn't let them go either. I wouldn't let them go. Nothing was worth that.

I hurled the sergeant from me, let my weight take us all to the sand.

'I'm asking this thing of you,' I growled, though the Misery did not need my words to understand. 'I entered your shadow-gate. I gave you what you needed. You'll do this for me now.' I felt the broken earth beneath me shifting, the currents and flows of energy that passed beneath us in their ever-hungry quest for change turning to my will. I'd marked the Misery with drops of my own blood, and the Misery remembered them.

I looked back at Amaira and Dantry, limping towards us, knowing their doom closed in behind them.

'I love you both,' I whispered. 'Be good to each other.'

I surged down into the Misery, power I'd taken coursing back into the ground. My waypoints lit up in my mind like a beacon and I gripped them tight, ordered them into a line no more than ten feet long as I moved everything between them out of the way. I channelled distance and rock and stone, I reordered the world to my own making. The world shifted and changed, forced into a blood-road of my design. Dantry and Amaira felt it, felt the turning of the earth beneath their feet.

Amaira locked eyes with me, her mouth falling open as they took another step forwards—

And were gone.

One hundred miles to the west, the path I had forged finished. Three feet to run, a vast distance crossed, and Dantry and Amaira would blink and stagger and find themselves no more than a mile from the Range. They wouldn't understand. Would never know what I'd given up for them. But they would live.

Pain ripped through my head as so much of my

Misery-strength tore out of me. The sky blazed for me in fresh colours as reality convulsed against me. With a snap it bounced back to what it had been and the impact smashed me onto my back. Blood sprayed from my nose, my mouth. The world rotated around me, spinning, spinning.

Drudge closing in from the north. Drudge closing in from the east and west. Those still fighting would make their final stand here, as we all must in the end. Parts are played, and when the final lines are spoken, the cast retire back beyond the curtain, there to fade from memory until their performance no longer means a thing to the world. Maybe the gunners would have chosen to run if they'd thought they could get away, but they didn't. They couldn't.

I couldn't shift the world again. I hadn't enough strength left to do it again. The desperate soldiers dragged me to my feet, pulled me along.

I spared a glance for Acradius' sorcerer-king. It was a blackened thing now, charred and smoking. Teeth, exposed where the wrappings around its face had burned away, seemed to grin upwards at me. It wasn't done yet. Not entirely.

I stumbled towards my horse. It was not my time to die. Not yet. I still had a part to play.

32

A handful of gunners broke rank and followed me. Maybe thirty men in all. The sounds of matchlock volleys cracked behind us as we booted our horses on. I didn't have time to take a reading and my mind was scrambled, flaring bursts of light and colour threatening to throw me from the saddle; we simply rode, hard and fast, south and away from the numberless drudge. Four times the volley fire sounded, and then they too were done. I glanced back, and what I saw sat sour and heavy on my heart.

I'd known I was leading those men into death. They had known it too. That didn't make it any easier. General Kazna had led the charge and she'd been as good as they come, cut from the same stone as Marshal Venzer. There would be no state funeral for her; but then, there probably wouldn't be any states left soon.

I had saved those that I could. A paltry thing, in the face of so much slaughter.

The soldiers looked to me to lead them. Nenn was absent, and I missed her. I figured she'd be waiting for me back at Adrogorsk, but there were plenty of other old friends to keep me company. Some of those who'd died during the failed ambush were riding in circles around us as well, performing carnival tricks on their horses. I enjoyed that. It was good to try to keep things light in the Misery. The cowardly gunners who'd run with me gave me worried glances, but they should have tried to enjoy the show as much as I did.

I felt emptied, hollow. I'd hoarded the Misery-power for so long, only to expel it. On what? I couldn't remember. I found something to eat. It tried to turn into liquid as a defensive measure, but it was too slow and I got most of it down. My lips burned, my throat burned, and I laughed at the ridiculousness of it all. The pain did not last long. I wasn't sure why I was eating the things in the Misery. There had been a point to it, once upon a time. A purpose. But it was confused and lost beneath layer upon layer of the Misery's burying silt, fossilised beneath mounds of time, pressure, and rust.

The fields all around us were lush and golden with the summer's bounty. Wheat, crisp and golden bright, stretching out to the river. My father and mother were bathing down there. It was good to be out from beneath their gaze. It wasn't often that I got to ride as I wanted to, pushing my horse harder, faster. I loved the animal beneath me. I could have ridden him forever. Ridden him on and on, into the vineyards, through the olive groves, all along the sea coast. It was a beautiful day to be a boy without cares in the world.

I blinked and somehow the sun was starting to set. I crouched, apart from the soldiers, rocking on my heels, my arms wrapped around my knees. There weren't as many gunners as I'd thought there were. I saw bodies laid out in a row, six of them, and I didn't know what had happened. I didn't remember. The gunners wouldn't speak to me, other than to throw fearful glances in my direction.

I let myself soak into the Misery. The headache that had been plaguing me for days loosened, the flickering lights at the edge of my vision drifted away, the tightness in my chest dissipating. Like my parents taking their bath, I relaxed in it. Lay down against the sand, ran my blackened fingers through the grit. I could taste it in the air, in my gums, everywhere. I could feel it, working through my veins, spidering through the muscles in my arms and shoulders. Relaxed.

I was drunk. Vicious drunk, and looking to start fights. The tavern, if it could be called that, stank of all the piss soaked into the walls and the dogs that roamed beneath the tables. I looked across the men at the tables, looking for someone big enough to be worth fighting. I didn't care why we fought, I was just angry and hell-bent on doing some damage to something, someone, anything, anything to give me some pain to focus on so that I didn't have to be so damn alone in all the misery swirling around inside. Disgraced, rejected, fallen from a lofty commission down to nothing and nobody.

Ezabeth stood before me, golden and resplendent, but we were in another time and another place. She was not my Ezabeth. She was something else, something infinitely vaster and yet somehow emptier. Marble pillars lined a great hall, framing her soot-blackened throne. A queen, a goddess perhaps. I knelt in supplication. We all knelt. She was glorious.

When I finally remembered to take a reading, I found myself alone, crouched in a shallow cave. I don't know what happened to the gunners. My horse was gone. I didn't know where I was until I reached down and sent myself pulsing out into the world.

Deep Emperor Acradius saw me. He was closer now.

A small, hardened fragment of my mind shivered and squealed in terror. I had given too much of my strength to send Dantry and Amaira away. My mind was reeling, torn and billowing like a ragged, storm-sodden banner. My defences, stacked together over years, had collapsed around me. I knew what I was doing was wrong, that it was madness, that I was not myself any longer. But like a drunk, reaching for yet another bottle when he knows there is no coming back from it, I went on anyway.

The black palanquin was borne in the middle of the column. Horned and spurred, a weight of great iron that contained the essence of the one true god. Acradius saw me before him, though the sides of the palanquin were solid iron. We existed outside the spheres understood by mere mortals. The enormity of presence within the palanquin bore down on me. Not a carriage, but a sarcophagus, fronted with a vast metal face. He had become so great that whatever physical part of him lay within, it did not merely have to be borne aloft: it had to be contained.

Son of the Misery, Acradius said. His voice was the rushing of waterfalls, the splintering of ships upon the rocks. *Do you come to bow in supplication at last? Have you understood the true futility of resistance? Will you bend the will of the Misery to my purpose?*

'There is no purpose,' I said. 'We are the essence of instability. Change, and change again, she says. Never stop changing. Never end the flow of possibilities. There is no purpose. There is nothing. We are all nothing.'

'This is bullshit, Ryhalt,' Nenn said. She drifted alongside me. Acradius didn't see her, didn't sense her. She was a flicker of my old life, come to haunt me. I ignored her. I was something so much larger than I had ever been before.

There is but one true purpose, Acradius thundered, the weight of the aeons carrying through each word. *And it is mine.*

Even he did not understand the power of The Sleeper, the meaning that lurked behind his words. He thought himself mighty beyond compare, but he was as much a puppet as I was. A mouthpiece for an entity that should never have been awoken. Not that I cared. The Misery would endure. Change is inexorable.

'You had a purpose once,' Nenn said. An annoying fly. She was part of the Misery, wasn't she? She should have been with me. Should have understood. 'You've lost it. You need it back.'

'There is no fate,' I said. 'No purpose. No being. We are nothing but dust, blown on the wind.'

You are a fool to think so, Acradius said. *The Misery erred in creating you. By making you her own she has opened herself to frailty. Feeble human emotion. An attempt at understanding. An attempt for redemption. Is that what she wants, Son of the Misery? To make herself weak?*

I shook my head, rambling laughter spilling through whatever spirit form I had taken.

Bow before me, the Deep Emperor growled. *I will make you mine. I will make the Misery mine. Everything shall be mine.*

The mouth on the iron face of Acradius' sarcophagus seemed to yawn wider, and a thread of sickly pink light emerged. It drifted through the air towards me. The thread of magic approached me, and I reached out to touch it.

Our worlds collided.

The depth of hatred was so strong that despite whatever strength the Misery had given me, I felt my being ripple, strain against existence. Not just one hatred, but four, all opposing one another, all screaming like furious children in incoherent rage, came together.

I felt a presence stir in a lava-pathed tomb, felt something of a carrion bird's old grandeur screech utter fury back through me. Crowfoot and Acradius saw one another as they never had before. Acradius met him head-on like a snarling hound, teeth bared, all pretence at dignity and godhood undone in his all-consuming rage.

The third appeared like a rising headache, a sandstorm blowing across a desert floor. The Sleeper, bonded to Acradius but lying beneath the surface, the source of power that not even Acradius realised was biding its time, waiting to escape its confinement and return. The Nameless and the

Deep King were spitting dogs, but The Sleeper was the slow encroachment of a malevolent tide, implacable as it moved to wash everything away. And then there was a woman of gold, who somehow lived within me, even after all this time.

The loathing of immortals was a shallow thing. It served their feuding, the petty fucking feuding, that had cost so many innocents their lives. But mine was born from something much stronger. It hit me like a winter-flooded waterfall, a torrent of sudden awareness that spread my mind open wide.

But it wasn't magic. It wasn't power. It was only hatred. A pitiful, dismal thing, less threat to me than a sick kitten. They seethed at each other across the gulf of space, seeing each other for the first time in more than a century. The hate speared deep through the world. And it was nothing.

'No,' I said.

I rejected them. Change, and change again. The pink light that had wrapped around me shattered outward, Acradius' honour guard of Darlings went flying in their circle.

'I see you clearly now,' I said. 'What you come from. What you are. You are hunger. You are emptiness. You reach for everything, because nothing can ever sate your lust to consume. But hunger is not substance. It is the absence of substance. It is nothing. For all your bluster, all your rage – you can't hold me back.' I snarled, more fury than sound. 'Not you. Not the Nameless. None of you can stop me now.'

You cannot resist me, Acradius roared. As the thought rang outward, his army of drudge collapsed in waves, clattering to the Misery soil in their armour as they clutched at their heads. *Your resources are spent. I am not this voice alone. I am a million lives. I am armies. Even now they bear down on your last hope. You will serve me. All will serve me.* Threats washed over me as light as a summer breeze.

'I know what I serve,' I said. 'And it will never be you.'

You are nothing! Even your own master betrayed you! Acradius screamed, dignity shattered, the falling of towers, the sundering of a belief held so long that it had nearly become a physical law. All had been forced to obey. Even his brother Kings had been made to submit. But here I stood. Defiant.

'Crowfoot is an arsehole,' I said. 'But he's still worth more than you. Than all this.'

And what would Nall have said to that? What would your Bright Lady tell you of the loyalty of crows? Acradius sneered.

I shook him off like a dog emerging from a black and stormy ocean. The world beyond the cave mouth whirled around me, lights dancing before my eyes, the cracks in the sky rippling with barely controlled fire. The Misery was reaching through me. Grasping me, filling me, and soon I would be as much a part of her as the gillings, the Dulchers, and all the other nightmares that I'd struggled so long to contain. I'd done this to myself, made myself part of her madness. I didn't know whether I'd truly spoken to Acradius or whether it was just another hallucination, a random vision sent to blind me, bind me, bring me further to her side. What was real?

I buried my head against my knees but the Misery pushed through, grasping my mind. Red-and-black desert stretched out on all sides, rising and falling in broken waves. Some directions were north, others were also north, still more were north again. Possibility and difference lay all around me, a chaotic miasma of radiant nothing that could be everything if only it were believed. There were tears on my face. How they had got there or whose they had been, I didn't know. There was too much I didn't know. I had so much understanding, I knew how all things worked and why, but it didn't seem to matter anymore. Knowledge without purpose. Without goal or reason. It was the essence of the universe; chaos and entropy.

Clouds roiled across the sky. Dense and dark, purple and thicker and heavier than they had ever been before. I was safe within my cave. I could lie here and simply be, let my flesh waste away, my bones grow to be part of the rock. No need to fear, no need to venture out to where the world hurt, and burned, and torments of the past flocked to stab at me with barbed beaks like vultures tearing at a carcass.

'You have to know the truth,' Nenn said.

'The truth?' I almost choked on the word. 'There is no truth. There's nothing but chaos. Disorder. Nothing but endless living and dying and suffering. I don't want truth.'

'Maybe not,' she sighed. 'But you need it.' She took me by the hand and pulled me to my feet. Outside, the rain swept in, black and hissing as it struck the hot earth.

'What if I don't want to know the truth?' I asked.

'What we want doesn't matter all that much,' Nenn said. 'It's time you knew. You can't finish this unless you do.'

'The rain,' I said. 'It's Nall's memories. It's the story of the Crowfall.'

Nenn nodded. She was waiting for me.

'Are you ready?'

'I think so,' I said. It was time to face it. 'Yes. I'm ready.'

The rain burned against my skin as I stepped out, into the deluge.

33

The first drops struck, and I didn't even feel them. My skin had grown too crusted, too scaled, too hardened by the Misery-pollution. I spread my arms and leaned into it.

There was pain. Stinging at first, then burning. For a moment I thought that I had made a terrible mistake. I stood shirtless, letting the fire of the black rain wash over me, head tilted back, eyes closed. Let it come, let it burn. *Ask the sky*, Nall had said. Some part of me had known what had to come. What I had to see. Was I strong enough to bear it? I'd learn that now.

I was soaked in moments as the full strength of the downpour hit me. It was cold, but the pain that lanced through my skin and into the muscle beneath barely registered. Images began to flicker in my mind. An ordinary, everyday sort of face. The face of a man, one of many, one of thousands. Nall, Nameless but dead all the same. I breathed the moisture from the air, scorching the inside of my mouth, my tongue. *Endure*, I told myself. Latched onto the word. Clung to it, though every other word seemed lost to me. I could not remember how I had come to stand here, why I was standing here, only that I had to endure it. It was only pain. And this would not be the worst of it.

Minutes passed with nothing but uncontrolled, wild thought passing through my head. Thoughts so great and deep that I could never have contemplated them, visions of things so small that no man alive could have seen them, so vast that they defied description. The knowledge of a wizard, cast out into the sky to fall on the cowering mortals below.

And then I was there.

The place of power. Not shattered, as it had been when I had travelled through the Duskland Gate, but as I'd first seen it. An endlessly flat plain, the ice perfectly white, the sky above endlessly black in the night, a million stars bright as hope. The cold was intense, but while I was aware of it, it didn't touch me. I could feel the power all around, a cosmic fog in the air. The body I inhabited sat cross-legged as one point of a triangle.

Crowfoot sat close by, cheeks, nose, and lips black with frostbite. Shallowgrave made the third point, his indistinctness unchecked by the freezing cold. The Nameless were united, as they had not been in centuries. They were my brothers, alike in their uniqueness, and utterly unalike in every other way. I quested for the knowledge, to know what the Nameless truly were, in a moment of greedy thought. Nall's memories did not respond to my wish. I was an observer only.

They were engaged in battle, and it had lasted for months.

It is easy to hate the Nameless. They seem to care nothing for us, and their motivations are self-serving. But they were here, locked in a struggle of wills against the Deep Kings, and it was only their fight that kept The Sleeper bound beneath the waves. That kept us alive. Chains of thought and power spread from them in invisible lines, driving into the ice, flaring away into the sky. Glittering, invisible webs held together by concentration alone.

Nall drove along one of the chains, probing, searching. Through his thoughts I saw the Deep Kings, mustered together half a world away from the plain of ice. They sat beside a tranquil sea whose water was clearer than finest crystal, on an island of white sand, the sun bright above them. Five creatures, as unique as the Nameless. Iddin, a baleful cloud, eyeless and weeping. Nexor, old fire, burning and rolling back on itself. Philon, whose matted grey hair wrapped her like a funeral shroud, Balarus, a dirty smear of thought in the air, and Acradius, furnace iron and spite. Five points of a demonic star. For a mile around, the sand held intricate symbols that never shifted in the wind, each surrounding relics of the past, ancient artefacts imbued with great magic. Swords, crowns, jewelled cups. Mummified bodies, tattered shoes, a broken arrow. The Deep Kings had crafted their own place of power. Through the energy pouring out of them, I sensed The Sleeper. It was not awake, but it acknowledged them as they sent their collective energies towards it. Unified in purpose, just as the Nameless were joined against them.

'It stirs,' Nall said. Back to the ice plain. 'We are failing. Even here, we do not have the strength to hold it.'

'No,' Crowfoot snarled without sound. 'I will not allow it back into the world.'

'All the same, we are failing,' Nall said.

I felt the weakening within him. He was taxed, drawn to his utmost. The well of power that grew within his wizard's heart was depleting, day by day, hour by hour. Even speaking had cost him. The Nameless settled back into their working, unpicking the Deep Kings' spells as fast as they formed them, setting obstacles in their path through the void, through the aether, through any measure they could. Everything was calm, but their thoughts worked frantically, scrambling three at a time to match their enemies'. The Deep Kings threw up barriers, tangled the complications into knots, then bound the Nameless' channels to silence. Their spell continued.

The cracking of an eyelid resonated through Nall's mind. An eye, wider than a house, opened far beneath the ocean's distant depths for the first time in millennia. Entombed deep beneath the biting ocean cold, it saw.

'It awakens,' a new voice rang out. It seemed too small to be part of these titanic events and it crashed against my heart in a way that no ocean demon's rising could. Too small, too human. With an effort that seemed greater than all the magic that Nall was pouring into holding back The Sleeper, he managed to turn his head, shards of ice flaking away.

Ezabeth stood in gold and blue light, a phantasm of gleaming energy. She was an island of beauty in the blistering cold. The wind did not touch her curling hair, didn't stir the dress in which she appeared. The same dress she'd worn the day she burned herself into the light.

'You are not welcome here, Bright Lady,' Crowfoot growled. 'Do not interfere.'

'The Sleeper awakens,' Ezabeth snapped. 'I feel it, crushing me back against the light. It comes. You must destroy their working now.'

'You are not one of us,' Crowfoot intoned. 'You are not Nameless but an abnormality. Begone from here.'

He threw himself back into the webs of power, discarding her, but Nall looked on.

'We need you,' he said. 'Join us.'

'Tell me how,' Ezabeth said desperately. She flickered, and through her insubstantial, shimmering form I could see the distant horizon, flat and continuing on into the sky. 'You have never shown me how.'

'You must become Nameless,' Nall said. 'That is all. You have the power. You have become the light. Committed yourself so greatly to a concept that it has sought to become one with you. But you still hold to the world. And while you do, it will never let you ascend. Join us.'

'I can't,' Ezabeth said. That frustration, that desire to succeed that I'd missed so much struck a hammer into my heart. I ached for her, as I'd ached through all those years. 'I still don't understand. All these years and still you keep it from me. Tell me the truth!'

There was a shudder, felt through the plates of the earth. Almost unnoticeable, it was so far away, but the ice around Crowfoot's frozen eyes cracked as they widened by the barest of fractions. I saw something in them that I had never expected to see. Terror.

'I've told you all I can,' Nall said. 'It is for you to understand, or not.'

'They raise it,' Ezabeth said, her metallic voice breaking. 'They raise The Sleeper.'

I felt Crowfoot's ire burn hot, so deep, so strong that it came from him in waves. He poured it into the magic.

'We must act now,' Shallowgrave whispered, the rustling of corpse-shrouds. 'Act now, act now.'

There were no flashes, no fires, no colours, as the Nameless committed their conjoined will against the Deep Kings, slamming down against them as though against the opening of a tomb. Red lines broke across Nall's cheeks as blood vessels ruptured. Ice that had settled into the folds of his face cracked and fell away in jagged shards. The weight of magic crushed down.

Distantly, so distantly, that sinister eye continued to open. The Sleeper's long, binding slumber began to withdraw.

The Nameless began to babble things that made no sense. Instructions to one another, spells maybe, explanations for the manipulation of forces that should never have been unleashed. They were old arguments, old plans brought back to the fore in sudden desperation.

'We cannot hold them this way,' Nall said.

'Failure means annihilation,' Ezabeth said.

'There is only one recourse left,' Crowfoot said. 'We knew it might come to this. A direct assault. The Lady of Waves must act.'

379

'Too dangerous,' Shallowgrave whispered. 'Too dangerous, too dangerous. In making such an attack even we would be vulnerable.'

'There is no other choice,' Crowfall snapped.

'We can fall back,' Nall said. 'There is always flight. Save what power we can. Retreat across the western ocean and beg an alliance with the Earth Serpents.'

'I will not allow them to take this land from me,' Crowfoot snarled. 'Never. Retreat is nothing but a slow death, and I will not lose. Not ever.' He sent out a bolt of thought that raced across thousands of leagues as if they were nothing, crossing seas, lands that I'd never known existed, to Pyre where the Lady of Waves lay in the depths of her lagoon. 'Now,' Crowfoot told her, though all the Nameless felt it. 'Strike now. Destroy their relic field and, in the depths of their trance, we may succeed.'

The Lady of Waves did not speak, but her savage glee raced back along the thought-line. Like some terrible kraken, she had been unleashed, and she had craved this for so long.

The weight of The Sleeper's slow rise towards consciousness groaned back against the Nameless.

Out along the lines of power, so far away, ocean currents that had been manipulated for three long years subtly altered their course in perfect unison. Their directions barely had to change in order to create new swells, new channels of flow. Deep below the waves, in the night-dark cold, great pressures shifted. In the shallow waters around warm, distant shores, gentle tugs lessened. Choppy waters around headlands calmed, fishing boats on placid waves began to rock. Throughout the oceans of the world, the Lady's power was felt. But it was not just her power. She was not just commanding the ocean, she was the ocean. This, I suddenly understood, was what it meant to be Nameless.

A wave came into Nall's mind. Just a swell, no different from any other that rose and fell, out in a stretch of ocean my people had never known existed. But unlike those around it, this wave rose, and it did not fall. It grew, gaining momentum as fifty thousand currents merged and met; a sudden rush of energy brought it higher. The Lady drove it on, and on, gathering tides, picking up momentum. A wall of water that would have dwarfed the Grandspire rose across the ocean, carrying whales and shoals of fish as tumbling passengers, kicking salt and sweeping a ship from its path like a toy. It bore down on the Deep Kings' island, their relic field. Thousands of tonnes of roaring ocean. Enough to smite a kingdom. Enough to drown a mountain. I saw the Lady's image in the foaming spray, savage glee at finally being allowed to release her greatest working.

The tidal wave reached the island – and with a deafening crack, stopped, churning with white foam, cascading sheets of water. Iddin and Balarus had risen from their places, and pitted their will against hers. The wave was held back. I sensed the Lady's rage, her fury at being denied. She poured her energy into it, expending magic in a flurry, and the Deep Kings did the same, battling to keep the vast force at bay. They did not fear for themselves. Not even this great torrent could unmake them, not even if it broke the bodies that they currently dwelt in, but the relics that they needed, the power that they drew on to rouse The Sleeper would be destroyed or lost. And that, they could not allow.

'They hold us,' Shallowgrave whispered. 'It awakens.'

The Sleeper's eye, one of hundreds, opened. As though an engine had kicked into life, thought began to process behind it for the first time in thousands of years. Consciousness blossomed like fireworks in the night.

'Attack The Sleeper directly,' Ezabeth said. 'While it is still weak. You have no choice.'

'Silence, ghost,' Crowfoot snapped. Blood ran from his eyes as his body began to buckle under the strength of will required to maintain the battle. A bone in his arm snapped.

'We are too far to strike that way. Half the world away. Even had we the power we have no avatar to wield it.'

'Then use me,' Ezabeth said. 'I am nowhere, but I am everywhere that there is light. Channel your power through me.'

I felt the thrumming communion between the Nameless, thoughts so rapid that they had no words as new plans rose and fell between them.

'She would take our power,' Shallowgrave hissed.

'No,' Nall said. 'She will not.'

'How can you know?'

There was almost sadness in Nall's blood-filled eyes.

'Because she is not one of us. She still has a name.' Muscles that had been frozen solid for months flexed, turning Nall's head to look at the Bright Lady in their midst. 'Go, Ezabeth Tanza. We strike through you.'

The wall of water raged half a mile high, restrained by invisible forces, but it was diminishing. The currents that the Lady had manipulated rebelled, trying to reassert nature's rhythms and streams. Even against her will, the oceans of the world sought to reject their new, unnatural, pattern.

Ezabeth vanished from one place of power to reappear in another. She floated, a flickering, insubstantial mote of light high above a roiling ocean, a great whirlpool surging below as The Sleeper's many, curling limbs began to churn the water. The flames that ever sought to consume her played around her feet. Nall could feel the power that had grown within her, still a tiny thing compared to that of the leviathan below.

'You may not survive this,' Nall told her.

'All things come to an end,' Ezabeth said. 'And I died a long time ago. I am ready.'

I wanted to cry out, to scream at her to stop. But I wasn't there, and this was only a replaying of things that had happened years ago.

Somehow, she knew what to do. They all did. Ezabeth dove towards the ocean, summoning every shred of power she had managed to gather and retain since the day she saved me from Saravor's minions, and rushing flames surrounded her. She blazed, brighter than summer sun, hotter than the seventh hell as the Deep Kings below sensed the new attack, Nexor and Philon rising and turning their will against it. Their wave of power struck up at her, but in the heartbeat before they made contact, the Nameless poured their own magic into her, abandoning their efforts to keep The Sleeper restrained now that four of the Deep Kings were engaged against them.

Nall's essence was trickery, cunning, deceit, and illusion. I caught a glimpse in that outpouring of power of the man he'd once been, a man so down on his luck, so bereft of friendship that he had abandoned all pretence at the truth. The lies had swallowed him, had remade him, and he had become Nameless.

Shallowgrave was the veil of mortality. He was caught between two worlds, both living and dead, the uncertainty in the moment when one becomes the other. There was too much madness swirling around him for me to know his origins.

And I saw a young man, torn and twisted by fate to do things which he had never wanted nor intended, to abandon all pretence at humanity and to accept his place amongst the carrion birds.

Ezabeth's light magnified a thousandfold as the Nameless poured their energy into her. They emptied themselves, and the world groaned with that outpouring. The Deep Kings that opposed her were brushed aside, their barriers shattering like glass. She tore down through the water, the heat of her passage evaporating it in a tunnel around her as she streaked down, down towards the ocean bed where the light had never reached, down where the pressure would have broken every bone in a man's body, and crashed against The Sleeper.

And stopped. The beast was not just flesh and stone, but was something more primal, something that had lived long before there were mammals and birds and fish. Only the barest part of its mind was working, but even that part had the magic to resist the combined fury of the Nameless. The blazing energy drilled against The Sleeper. The physical was unimportant. Only power remained.

'I will not lose!' Crowfoot roared. 'I will never lose!'

The Nameless screamed in unison. Their power was at its limit, every last drop draining into this final, desperate assault. In their place of power, the sky howled and cracked, a shuddering wail emanating across the plain. The ice buckled, breaking apart in deafening crunches. Chunks of glacier spiralled up into the air as the depth of their anger howled around them.

'It's not enough,' Shallowgrave whispered.

'We need more power,' Crowfoot said, and the desperation in his voice revealed his own fear. He had bound himself to the malice of crows, because no matter who lives or dies, the crow never sees defeat, only another opportunity. And now he saw it slipping from him.

'Give everything,' Nall gasped, 'everything!' His avatars around the world began to drop, collapsing one by one as he siphoned every shred he could take.

'Not enough,' Shallowgrave whispered.

Crowfoot glowered, blood leaking from rents in his skin. One arm burned away in a rush of flame. The wrinkles on his face smoothed, and then the skin split apart, sharp black feathers jutting through the tears. His eyes fixed on Nall. His anger had diminished and there was only steel and determination within them.

'There is always more power,' he said.

Crowfoot, Nall realised in those last moments, had held

384

something back. He, the Lady of Waves, and Shallowgrave had committed their all, but not the raven. The corvid succeeds because it adapts, takes what it needs wherever it finds it. Nall would have done well to remember that.

The Nameless before him were utterly exposed.

'No,' Nall hissed. 'You need me. Without me the Engine will not fire and even you are defenceless.'

'Your Engine has already failed us,' Crowfoot said. 'But I will endure.'

Crowfoot's spell tore Nall's heart from his chest, ribs exploding outwards, and consumed the power. He sent it rushing through the void, into Ezabeth, their instrument. The force of a wizard's death is a terrible thing. I'd seen the aftermath at Cold's Crater, and again when Shavada's heart powered the Engine. It was not the first time the Nameless had betrayed one of their own.

The surge of magic ripped through the world and Ezabeth burned through The Sleeper's defences, a missile of blazing energy that punched a hole straight through it both in the corporeal world and through the infinite, impossible strands of magic that held it into being. It glowed from the inside as she raced through, lighting up the ocean, scattering the eyeless things that groped in the darkness. But Nall was barely paying attention. He met Crowfoot's eyes as his own essence wavered, dissipating, broken, fleeing to shelter in those few bodies that remained. There was no remorse in Crowfoot's expression, only a look of hollow, empty victory as the avatar disintegrated, charring and turning to ash on the wind.

I opened my eyes.

I knew whose tears lay on my face now.

I was the Misery.

I was Ryhalt Galharrow.

34

My mind had not felt so clear in months.

I knew who I was. I knew what had to be done. I felt the Misery-guilt like a weight in my chest, but in facing the truth I had driven it back into itself. I was not the body, polluted and corrupted by years of imbibing the toxins of the Misery: I had existed before, and would exist beyond, if we survived.

Everything was clearer now. I saw the flow of sunlight, the depth of stone. The Misery had clouded my mind for so long, I'd not seen the true paths. She was still within me, part of me, of me, but I was lighter now. I floated through the world. Much of the Misery's influence had burned out of me as I hurled Amaira and Dantry back across the desert, and the black rain had scoured away the crust of mould that had grown up around my thoughts. There was more to it than a simple equation. I'd needed the truth, and finally, I had it.

I couldn't afford to use the blood-trail again to get myself back to Adrogorsk. I'd squandered the Misery-essence I'd hoarded so long to send my friends back to safety. A moment of weakness and now I didn't know if I had enough power to see it through, or even to send Valiya to safety. I put a hand down into the sand, navigated the treacherous shifting land around Adrogorsk, and the Misery greeted me eagerly. I walked a day's distance in less than an hour.

The walls of Adrogorsk, jagged and broken, came into

view. I knew that I was returning to them one final time, and the news I brought weighed me down.

In the dawn, a solitary figure stood in a sorcery-carved breach in the wall, looking out across the sand, a spear in his hand.

'This doesn't bode well, neh?' North said. A film of Misery-dust coated his darkened lenses. 'Should I assume the worst?'

Even as my mind rode currents in the air, my body felt spent. My muscles, clenched tight as bow-strings, seemed to give way suddenly. I sat heavily on a chunk of cracked masonry, armour clanking. Slowly, I nodded.

'The Guardians are gone. Everyone else is dead, or lost. I think.'

'You failed us,' he said, but he didn't look at me. Instead he looked out instead towards the Misery. 'Failed us, and lost our only hopes of defending the loom. I should put you down for what you've done, but what would be the point?' He shook his head slowly, a grim turn to his lip. 'How long until they get here?'

'They've slowed,' I said. 'We may have done enough to delay them. The thing that's guiding them took a hit, and Acradius' link isn't as powerful as it once was. But they're still coming. They'll be here tomorrow.' I'd watched the progress of the moons as I stalked back from the failed ambush. Rioque was up and over the horizon, Eala tracked across the sky from the west. The eclipse was a day away. The few minutes in which three great lenses of crystal would be purifying and distilling, channelling the light of the world, over which we were all fighting. I thought of the wonders that could have been done with the power the heart could provide. Heat, light, motion for thousands of people, for years. And it would be wasted on prolonging a battle that had lasted for a millennium, and would last long after everyone I'd ever known was dead. Suffering and misery, waste upon waste, never ending.

'You look different,' North said. 'Sound different. Are you back with us, Galharrow?'

'I feel different,' I said. I couldn't explain it, not well enough for it to make any difference. Everything was cut from sharper matter now. I had it all in focus, finally. I had accepted the rain, and with it, truth.

'It's going to be close,' North said.

'We might make it by hours,' I said. 'Or we might be hours dead. Hard to tell.'

I was lying. The drudge would arrive before the eclipse.

'Nobody survived? Dovroi? Vurtna?' North's question surprised me. I'd not expected him to have taken note of their names. Maybe there was more human behind those eyeglasses than I'd given him credit for.

'No,' I said. 'Everyone else is gone.'

'But not you, neh?'

I shook my head. North's glare deepened.

'What do we have left, then?' North said.

'Prayers,' I said. 'And not many of those.'

North was silent. He leaned against a hunk of broken stone, staring out as though he would see the enemy on the horizon. He would, soon enough. I should have gone to the loom, to tell Kanalina and Valiya what had happened, but I would only be bringing them news of certain failure. I could leave them in hope for a time longer. It was all that I had to offer them now. Clarity was not always a gift.

'Was I right about you, Galharrow?' he asked. 'No, don't answer that. It's too blunt a question. It seems that in all this heat and chaos I've started to lose my subtle edge. This place will do that to you, I suppose. Tell me this instead: what were you trying to do out here?'

'Same as everyone else,' I said. 'Trying not to lose. Not to die.'

'Is that so?' North said, the snide, mocking tone settling

back across his tongue. 'Where are the rest of the Blackwing captains, Galharrow?'

'You know where.'

'I do. They're all in the dirt. Seems strange, doesn't it? With Captain Amaira gone, you're the last one standing.'

I stayed silent. He didn't need to know what I'd done to send Dantry and Amaira back to the Range.

'Tell me this, Galharrow. When it comes time to unleash the weapon, are you really the man to pull the trigger?'

'I'll be there,' I said. 'At the end.'

'I don't trust you,' he said.

'Should I trust you, North? You want to stand there, with the light blazing all around you and usher in another apocalypse?'

'I'll do whatever has to be done,' North said. 'Death holds many terrors, but to be changed, twisted, made to walk in eternal servitude to something that calls itself "emperor"? I'd rather die on my feet than live on my knees.'

'We live on our knees all the same,' I said. 'You and I more than anyone. We belong to the Nameless.'

'Perhaps that is the difference between us,' North said. 'You Blackwing captains serve because you're terrified of breaking your deal and being turned inside out by your own master. But the Lady of Waves – I love her more than I would ever have believed possible. I know what you'll say – that the Lady has compelled me in some way. But it's not true. I went to her. I loved her before I even laid eyes on her.'

'Why?'

'Why do we love what we love? I don't know. None of it makes any sense, does it?'

He was right, of course. We don't know why we love any more than we know why we can't control it. A jumble of a thousand different tiles that all combine together to make a mosaic that's both beautiful and utterly chaotic, imperfect and full of flaws. But we desire the flaws even as we desire the whole. Had any of us been able to choose where and whom to love, the world would have been a simpler, kinder place.

Sudden anger took him, and North slammed the butt of his spear against the ground.

'Is this it, Galharrow?' he snapped. 'Is this truly it? Nothing left in the canister, no more bolts in the quiver? It can't end here like this. There has to be something we can do.'

'It would take an army to stop the drudge,' I said. 'And there's nobody out here but you, me, and the ghosts.'

I sat with Valiya. She was taking stock of the provisions and munitions on the wagons. Stacks of powder charges, spare ramrods and rolls of bandages were laid out in neat, named piles, one for each soldier that had remained. She'd moved on to the food. There was far more than we needed, now that we were so reduced in number.

'You don't like the creamed beans, do you?' she asked.

'No,' I said.

'I like them,' she said. 'I'll allocate you more of the salt pork instead.' She popped open another crate and began to count packets.

'Valiya.'

'Or the pickled fish, if you'd rather.'

'Valiya.'

'What?' She rounded on me.

'Just rest. For a while, just rest.'

She ignored me and went back to her stock-take. She counted up the jars of disgusting pickled fish, which for some reason I'd pretended to enjoy whenever she handed me one. I hadn't needed the food from the wagons, not with the Misery-creatures that I'd hunted along the way. Every jar had been a waste. Every time she'd offered it to me, I'd still taken one.

'Here.' She passed me a phos canister. 'The Spinners took most of them when they deserted, but they left this. Give it to Maldon.'

'Valiya, just—'

Valiya slammed the lid of the crate down. Her shoulders shook.

'Give it,' she said quietly, 'to Maldon.'

I hung the canister from my belt. I had nothing else to say.

'There's no rest, Ryhalt,' she hissed. 'There's never been time to rest. Never time for anything.' She rounded on me. 'What did we do it all for? Why did we give up everything that we could have had? For this? For some dream?'

I didn't know what to say. I ran my fingers across the polished steel vambrace on my arm, caught sight of my reflection. I didn't recognise myself anymore. My eyes were full of amber light, my skin threaded with black cobweb lines, scaly, pebbled. My teeth had taken on feral, Shantar-fang shapes. Maybe it was easier for me to accept. I'd already given up everything that I had.

But my mind had cleared. The rain had washed through me, burned me back into myself. The Misery was part of me, was threaded through me, but I was not the Misery. I was a man.

'There was never anything for me,' I said.

'That's not true,' Valiya said. She had never shown me her bitterness before. It rose to the surface and boiled over, and eyes that had once been silver shone brighter with pain than they had with any magic. 'There was a future. And you chose the past. But there is no past. It doesn't exist, it's dead, it's done. So look forwards, damn you. Look forwards and find us a future that doesn't end with drudge spears and the world bound and cowering.'

'I'm just one man,' I said.

'No,' she said. She drew up her composure again, the

outburst retreating back beneath her skin. 'You're not a man. There's barely any humanity left in you. You've gone this far. So go further.' She gestured at the wagons, the boxes of provisions. 'I sealed up every sewer tunnel I could find, to keep the gillings below us. I searched the buildings for anything useful. And I'm going to ensure that every fighter we have has the very damn best in our inventory.'

'What for?'

'For *everything*,' Valiya shouted. 'It's all for everything. Not you, not me, not *Her*. It's for the millions of people back in the republic. It's for the land that they walk on, and the sky that's above them. But you can't see it. You *won't* see it.'

'Everyone dies,' I said. 'Everything falls. Look around. This city was once home to thousands. I brought men here to defend it and watched them die. They're still here, ghosts, reliving their last days in eternal silence. In a thousand years, nothing any of us have done will matter.'

Valiya couldn't bear to look at me any longer. She turned back to the wagons and began counting through the sad jars of pickled fish. Fish that had swum, died in nets, been stripped down, and bottled up, never to be eaten. Their deaths had served no purpose either.

'And that's why it matters all the more,' Valiya said. 'Because time is brief. Because life is brief, and if we don't make the most of it, then it really is for nothing.'

'I can send you back,' I said. 'Just as I did Amaira and Dantry. If you want to go, I can get you there.'

'No,' Valiya said. 'You can't expend any more of your strength on something so meaningless. And besides. I'm needed here. Get us past this next hurdle, Ryhalt, and I'll get us over the last. I know what I have to do, even if you don't.'

I watched a line of long-dead soldiers marching along the street. Two of them, young lads, were out of rhythm, struggling with their halberds. I caught myself before I called out to their officer to get them in line. Just ghosts, I reminded myself. I had to keep focused now. I couldn't afford to let the Misery get in my head again and send me sliding back towards oblivion.

'Here,' Valiya said. I'd not noticed what she was doing. She held out a wrapped bundle. 'You should have this.'

'What is it?'

'A reminder. And here's another.'

She reached up and put a hand on the back of my neck, drew my head down, and kissed me on the cheek. It was awkward. My skin was raw and still stung from the rain, and I felt a sudden surge of humiliation at the taste of the Misery that was ever present. But her lips were warm, and something that had long lain shivering inside me came to life. It did not last long. Just a kiss on the cheek. It left me more breathless than any fight had in thirty years.

She smiled at me, foxlike, and wiped her mouth on the back of her sleeve. I couldn't have tasted good.

'Remember who you are, Ryhalt,' she said. 'Blackwing captain. Leader of men. Shavada's bane. Saviour of Valengrad. Friend, father, and, most of all, human, acting for love. Be that again for me now. Do what you have to do, and I'll do what I have to do. I know that this isn't over. You should know it too. Find a way to buy us the time we need. This isn't over.'

'How do you know?'

'Because I won't let this be the end,' she said. 'Now go. Solve this. We're so close. And I need to get these kits distributed to the men we have left to us.'

As though she'd not just turned my whole world upside down, Valiya turned and went back to work.

Fate is a spinning coin, balanced on an edge so fine that the slightest breath of wind can set it spiralling away from you. But sometimes, in a moment of utter certainty, you have to slam your hand down upon it and make the call.

35

The black thread that brought the drudge screaming across the desert tightened. The Misery railed against such order and control. Dulchers ploughed into the column of drudge, goring and tearing. Great skweams appeared in their path, insect legs slashing. Sinkholes erupted before them, clouds of finger-long Misery flies descended on them as though the Misery herself tried to bring every terrible thing she'd ever made to bear against them. Still, the enemy ploughed forwards, ignoring the moans of their wounded as they left them to bleed out in the dust. We had hours before they arrived to destroy us.

Three moons tracked together, distorting the light as they caught it and cast it down on us below. The world took on rainbow hues, shimmering and changing, ghost-colours and flowers of sunlight mottled across broken walls and avenues of sand, the red-stained bones dancing in brilliant splendour. The eclipse edged closer.

We would all likely be dead before it happened. A coal-hot anger seethed within me at the injustice. After all we'd done, after every life given and drop of blood shed, the drudge would arrive an hour before the eclipse. North had said it would be close, and he was right. It couldn't have been closer. But close is not victory. Nearly alive is not alive.

The soldiers moved with purpose around the palace, raising barricades, digging pits, creating killing zones that would force the drudge to face our guns head-on. If they reached us before the heart was ready, it still wouldn't be enough. The palace gave us the best chance of holding the drudge, slim as it seemed.

We were pitifully few, atop the palace, waiting. First stood with his arms folded, impassive and blank as marble. He was alone in the world now, his ancient brethren torn apart out on the sand. If he felt anything at all at their passing, he gave no sign of it. Six of us looked out across the desert. Four captains, a citadel Spinner, and a blind child.

'We can make it,' Kanalina said, resolve forced into her voice. 'Just four hours more and the moons will reach their alignment.'

'Is the loom ready?' I asked. I glanced over to the huge contraption of iron and brass plates, glass lenses and copper wire.

'Everything is in place,' she said. 'The light's so pure. I could charge a canister in minutes. But during the eclipse it will be magnificent.'

The loom sat ready on the platform, tall, dark iron and polished lenses. One of a kind. Once the light began to flow through it, it wouldn't stop.

'I could start now,' Kanalina said. Eager. 'It wouldn't be much, not compared to the full eclipse, but ...'

'The heart will charge in less than a minute once the moons get in order,' I said. 'I don't want that thing out of its box for any longer than is absolutely necessary. You saw what it did to the longhorns.' Reluctantly, Kanalina nodded acquiescence. 'Have the heart ready,' I said. 'We'll begin as soon as we can.'

'When the heart is charged,' Kanalina said, running a hand across her brow. 'What then?'

'Then the Nameless do their part, whatever that is,' I said. 'Crowfoot says it's a weapon. He'll make use of it.'

'And us?' Kanalina asked. I just shook my head. The

drudge would get us. Or, if Crowfoot activated the heart, then I doubted that any of us were going home. 'I suppose I never expected to come back from it. A suicide mission all along. We came out here to die.'

'Not to die,' Valiya said. She took Kanalina's hand, causing her to flinch, but the Spinner didn't pull away. 'We came so that others will live. So that children get to grow up, to love and laugh and grow old.'

'To grow old,' Kanalina said. A wan smile found its way across dust-chapped lips. 'What a beautiful thing that would have been.'

'Four hours,' North said. There was bitterness in his voice. 'We don't have that long. Look.'

He pointed out into the Misery where dust and dark shapes swarmed on the horizon.

They were here.

Exhausted, mounts broken by their mad charge across the desert, torn and bloodied by the Misery's defiance, they would not last long. They were driven past the point of collapse by Acradius' roaring will, past the point where thought was necessary. A single, indomitable purpose drove them like a hurricane, forcing them onwards, tumbling over themselves, slipping and sliding on bloody feet. A ragged, ruined army. But still they came.

I'd hoped that it wouldn't come to this. I'd prayed to the Spirit of Mercy to grant us the time we needed. She hadn't listened. She never listened.

'How long?' Valiya asked.

'They'll be at the walls in under three hours,' I guessed. 'A little more before they reach us.'

'There must be something we can do,' Kanalina muttered. She didn't like me, but I'd come to admire her resolve.

'There's one last defence we can try,' I said. 'Get everyone together.'

We gathered in the sand-garden around the palace. They

all deserved to hear it. The soldiers who'd been left behind looked ashen. It wasn't just that they were the last. They'd lost a lot of friends. Hundreds. And they were probably next.

'It had better be a damn good plan,' Kanalina said. The blood had drained from her face, dark shadows around her eyes. 'We've fifty men, a few light artillery pieces, one Guardian and me. We have nowhere to run. If we can't prevail we need to keep it out of the enemy's hands. I'll not deliver them a weapon of this power. I'll destroy it before I allow that to happen.'

'If that's even possible,' I said. 'But no. Without the heart, Acradius wins anyway. We're here to the end.'

'Empowering the heart is the only hope,' North said. He gave me a knowing look. The Nameless had spent everything they had trying to keep The Sleeper beneath the waves, and he knew it as well as I did. North seemed to be backing me up more and more often and I didn't like it. I could never forgive what he'd done to Giralt and Tnota. Some men you just hate at a basic level.

'Your last plan ended in disaster, and now there are thousands of drudge bearing down on us,' Kanalina said. She forced her desperation back behind gritted teeth. 'We'll never survive this.'

'Our mission was never to ensure our survival,' I said. 'Just to give you enough time to spin the light into the heart and let the Nameless act. That will have to be enough.'

The soldiers shifted uneasily. They knew the situation was rough as sandpaper, but that didn't mean they favoured a plan with no way out.

'We've done what we can to make the palace defensible. But we're too few to hold the bridges,' the captain who'd been left in charge of them asked. He was an older man, one ear long since chewed away by something or other.

'We don't try to,' I agreed. 'We fall back into the palace, then blow the bridges.'

397

The moons sparkled overhead as they approached alignment. Rays of startling colour, wild and bright, fell like spotlights across the city. It would have been beautiful if we weren't all doomed.

I had no more to say.

'If we blow all the bridges … we're trapped,' the captain said. I nodded. He didn't understand. Didn't realise that it didn't matter if we were trapped or not once the light had been drawn into the ice fiend's heart.

'Yes,' I rasped. 'We can't hold even one bridge. But that sludge in the moat – that's death to the drudge as sure as it is us. It'll suck them down sure as quicksand, and that's not water it's mixed with. It's Misery-poison. We can cut them off from the palace, and if anything tries to get across the moat, we sink it. It's not much of a plan. But it's the best we have.'

'At least we get to go down fighting,' Kanalina said.

'Yes.'

I kept my face hard and empty. No coercion, no games. No words of hope, no suggestions that there might be some devious method of escape. I'd held this last back from them until the hour of fate was upon us. I couldn't risk them deserting, or refusing. Sometimes I thought that I'd changed, but no. Treating people like tools, just as I always had. I wasn't just asking them to believe me. I was asking them to decide how long their lives were going to be.

'I'm in,' North said. 'It has to be done.'

'It's the best chance we have,' Kanalina agreed, though she still looked angry about it.

'We'll talk it through,' the captain said. 'Way I see it you're not giving us a lot of choice. But I'll not order my men to their deaths. Those that would rather take their chances in the Misery get to.'

I nodded. It was our strongest plan. The drudge wouldn't have siege equipment to cross the sludge in the moat, but their leaders could be inventive and I wanted armed men ready to meet anything that made it across. Valiya came to stand beside me.

'Desperate times,' she said.

'The most desperate,' I agreed. 'You don't have to join us.'

'I do,' she said. 'Nall gave me a final command. I made my bargain with him, and I'll see it done.'

'Nall,' I said, shaking my head. 'Gone, but still pulling the strings. What did he ask of you, Valiya?'

'Not so very much,' she said. 'And everything.'

The soldiers' discussion didn't take long. The captain returned, his face dark.

'We'll start unloading the munitions from the wagons, sir,' he said. He didn't meet my eye, but he saluted me as though I were in command. I nodded to him. Maybe I was.

Bringing men across the Misery had been the hard part. The rain had prevented us marching in our thousands, but munitions in wax-sealed barrels hadn't been an issue. Marshal Davandein had outfitted us with blasting powder for a thousand men. Six wagons, each one holding a dozen barrels. Potent stuff. I'd set half the men to smash holes in the centre of each bridge. We'd load as many barrels into whatever they could dig before we detonated them. If we simply heaped the barrels on top of the bridge, I doubted that the explosions would bring them down. Most likely we'd just have some scorched and broken flagstones, and we couldn't afford to waste anything. But a detonation from inside would send the impact all the way through the structure, destroying the keystones and collapsing the whole span. Positioned between the legs that held the bridges out of the toxic quicksand, I hoped that it would be enough.

We'd find out soon.

The quartermaster – long gone, when the majority of our

Spinners had abandoned us – had not unloaded. He'd simply rolled the munition wagons into an open-faced temple to keep them from the rain. It had been smart thinking at the time, but now the powder wagons were backed in by two dozen wagons of weapons and food supplies. To hitch teams up and move them all would have taken too long. We moved them by hand.

I heaved barrels down from the cart. I could lift them easily enough, handing them over to teams of three or four men who struggled with the weight. This was no time to stand back and let other men do the work. Once we'd unloaded we'd split up, roll the barrels onto the bridges, and hope that five-hundred-year-old, Misery-blasted architecture wouldn't stand up against what we had. Each of the bridges was roughly the same width. Valiya had assessed how much powder it was going to take. Even Maldon had made himself useful for once, cutting fuses for grenadoes.

'This is a mad plan, neh?' North said.

'Mad as everything else out here,' I agreed.

'Once the spinning starts, you're expecting more instructions?'

I looked down at the tattoo on my arm. It had been silent for a long time. But when it came to it, Crowfoot would be there. He'd put every last resource he had into getting us this far. This was the final turn of the cards. A desperate play, but it was what he had. The Lady of Waves too.

'I doubt he'll miss the climax,' I said. 'Whatever it is. We might not want to be here when it happens, but he'll come.'

The captain gave directions and the barrels rolled away down the streets.

Davandein had provisioned us well, and the men who'd been digging holes had attacked the bridge's stone with frantic energy. They'd managed to dig a good five feet down. No need for the barrels themselves; we staved the wax-sealed lids and poured the grainy black blasting powder like wine. The soldiers were as good as I'd been promised, quick and efficient. When the fuse had been laid we packed earth back in over the top of the powder. The more contained the explosion, the better.

'Everyone back,' Valiya ordered when it was done.

'You'll want to cover your ears,' I said. 'This is going to be loud.'

The captain lit the fuse and we ran for the cover of a nearby ruin. For nearly a minute there was nothing, and I started to wonder if the fuse had gone out. And then, past the hands clapped over my ears, a terrific growl echoed through the city. The ground shook, dust sifted down from the melted ceiling above us. We ran to see the result of our work. I found a grin. A huge cloud of dust filled the air over what had once been a bridge, the midsection of which was now a gaping chasm. Pieces of stone were strewn across our side of the moat's bank, and pieces of rubble poked sharp edges up from the sludge.

'Well, it works then,' I said.

'You weren't sure, neh?' North asked.

'Nothing's certain,' I said. 'We don't have much time. Let's move on.'

The second bridge went down in a cloud of reddish dust, masonry splashing into the poisonous porridge below. I sent everyone who wasn't needed over the bridge to take up their positions in the palace and the soldiers began rolling the barrels towards the final bridge. We were in a rat-trap of our own devising, and once that bridge came down, our fate was sealed. We'd fulfil our desperate mission in relative quiet. I wondered, if we survived, whether that would be any consolation as we sat, surrounded, and slowly starved to death.

'I'm going to be stuck here forever, aren't I?' Maldon asked. He sat on top of an empty powder barrel, knees tucked up beneath his chin, a length of fuse dangling idly between his small hands. The soldiers were digging out the final pit for the last batch of explosives. Barrels stood stacked all around their frantic efforts. The third bridge was the biggest, widest, and we were going to try to blow three separate charges at once to bring down the central arch. We had a good lot of powder.

'I wouldn't count on that,' I said. 'Not if it goes down as we planned it.'

'You think that it will?'

I rubbed at the scars I'd carved into my arm in the Endless Devoid. I hadn't understood their meaning at the time. But I'd learned it. I'd given my all to it. I couldn't fail now.

'I've never been more certain.'

Maldon smiled. A true smile, one that I'd not seen since the day he'd vanished from Valengrad. My old friend, still there under all the pain and torture he'd endured. It had taken a long time for that light to shine through.

'What's that?' he asked, pointing at the heavy wrap of canvas I'd tied to my belt. I'd nearly forgotten it.

'A gift from Valiya. Just my ego getting the better of me, I suppose.'

Maldon smirked at me.

'Spirits, Ryhalt. We've come a long way, haven't we? And still it seems too soon for it to all be over. Seventh hell, but I could use a drink.'

'Why the fuck not.'

I reached inside my coat for the flask Nenn had given me, all the way back before we'd started out into the Range. Silver, the inscription *Always with you, boss* engraved across it.

'Thought you never drink anymore,' Maldon said as I handed it to him.

'Never's a long time.'

Maldon raised the flask to his lips and took a swig of the brandy within. As I reached for it, North walked towards our end of the bridge. He had that jade-tipped spear resting on his shoulder. I nodded to him, but he did not return it. He stopped at the bridge's edge, fifty feet away, and looked us both over. He was tense. We were all tense, brought to the frayed edge of our nerves, but I read his posture. I read the blank look on his face. He watched me, hard, but calm.

'We need to get over to the other side,' I said. 'This bridge needs to come down. The drudge will be on us in less than an hour.'

Rays of dappling moonlight shimmered across the ground, lighting the world in reds, blues, purples, sandstorm yellows, spring bloom greens. The cracks in the sky let out a sonorous wail, long and deep. I started towards the bridge.

'If only I could let you,' North said, no remorse in his voice. 'But your road ends here.'

I stopped. The bridge to the palace lay behind him.

'What are you doing, North?'

'You knew it would come to this,' he said. He twirled the spear through the air, the point whispering through the sand. 'What happened to Captain Amaira? Where is your criminal friend? Did you send them to their deaths, or did you kill them as you did the rest of the Blackwing captains?'

'Don't do this now, North,' I snarled. 'Whatever you think you know, you've got it wrong.'

'You think that you've played the whole damn world for a fool,' he said, without anger. He removed his glasses, tucked them into a pocket. Getting ready. He shouted, loud enough that the soldiers on the bridge could hear him. 'Captain Josaf, drowned in a ditch? It would have taken a big man to hold him down. Captain Klaunus, dead in a locked room, with only a window to escape from – but you'd survive that drop from the clock tower, neh? Captains Silpur and Vasilov, conveniently vanished on a mission with you. Captain Linette, garrotted and a Darling at the scene? But it wasn't a Darling, was it? It was this child-creature you've brought into the Misery with you.' The waves that lurked in his eyes rose and swirled. 'You betrayed your fellow captains. Then you took our men out there on a hopeless mission and destroyed them. You've betrayed the Range. You've betrayed your own Nameless master.'

I flexed my fingers. 'I'm no enemy to the Range,' I said. 'You know that, North. And he's just a child. He's no Darling.'

North's smile was a cold thing, the echo of sunken ships and the drowning cries of sailors.

'Only one way to be sure.'

Lightning fast he whipped out a pistol and shot Maldon in the chest. Maldon flew back from the barrel, blasted over by the force of the shot. He rolled across the dirt and lay still.

'You chose now, of all fucking times, to see this out?' I snarled.

'We should have been four,' North said. Smoke curled from the pistol barrel. 'Me for the Lady, you for Crowfoot. The Guardians for Shallowgrave, Winter for Nall. But we'll face the drudge as three. Your time here is over.'

'You want me to just walk away?'

'No,' North said. 'You're far too much of a risk. Not even human anymore. Do you want the heart for yourself, Galharrow? Is that why you turned yourself into a monster? You want to take the heart's power to become Nameless yourself, and cast the rest of us into the fire?'

My brows drew in. My lips curled back from my teeth, baring them like a dog. I reached for my sword.

'The mistake you're making right now,' I snarled, 'is to think you can stop me.'

I'd expected this betrayal. Crowfoot, for all his self-serving cruelty, was in this to win. But I'd known that the Lady of Waves never intended to see Crowfoot's plan through. There was too much power on offer, too much for her to gain. She was vanity and she was never going to allow something so precious as the ice fiend's heart to go to waste, even if it meant giving up the Range. She was not Crowfoot. Survival mattered more to her than the victory. I just hadn't expected him to act here and now.

North was as fast as he'd claimed. Pistols leapt into his hands and I lost him in the clouds of smoke and fire. One ball punched into my left shoulder, the other lodged in the muscle of my gut. I barely felt the impacts, ignored them, didn't care. I'd taken far worse and come out grinning and the Misery had long since made me immune to such minor wounds. I charged for North, but by the Spirit of Judgement, he was fast. He flicked the jade-headed spear up from the dirt with the toe of his boot, caught it, and whirled it around, blocking my sword stroke in a shower of sparks. I cut again but he scampered back out of distance, his spear dancing. Thrust after thrust, a rapid succession of darting jabs towards my face, my chest, so fast that had the Misery not empowered me, I'd have taken the first strike through the throat.

The soldiers on the bridge paused in pouring the powder into the holes that they'd created, watched.

There is a reason that every army since the dawn of history has given its men spears. The spear is the king of weapons. It turns out that against all our cleverness, our intricate forging and metal craft, there is little more effective than a spike on the end of a stick.

I parried once, twice, striking the shaft aside and trying to snatch at it, but North was too good, too sure, too fast. He wove the point in tight, deadly little circles, one way, the other, withdrawing, jabbing and eventually I could not keep up with him. He hammered the spearhead against my leg. The jade head scored across my left thigh, just above the knee, tearing the leather of my riding trousers and scraping the skin beneath.

North backed up. He'd expected that blow to punch right through the meat of my leg but my Misery-hardened flesh had ridden the impact and cast it aside.

I growled low in my throat.

'Not the effect you were expecting, was it?' I said. 'Don't you get it yet? I'm not just a man. I'm more than any of you. I—'

I stopped talking as a wave of icy numbness hit my knee, and I buckled into the sand. Something was wrong. North's blow had barely scratched me. Just a scrape. But the cold was emanating upwards through my thigh, and down through my knee. I pressed a hand against it, not taking my sword's point from North.

'Your arrogance is colossal,' North said. 'You're not the only one who plans ahead.'

'What have you done?' I growled.

'I told you, didn't I?' North said. He allowed himself his own small, cruel smile. 'The Lady of Waves forged this weapon. Strong enough to take down even the most terrible monster in the Misery. And it has. You see, Galharrow? We've been on to you from the start.'

'What are you talking about?' I growled. But the numbness was spreading. Through the tear in my trousers I saw my leg glittering like diamond. It grew heavier as flesh changed and grew stiffer, harder. I tore at the fabric and looked down at the gleaming, statue-smooth, translucent flesh beneath. I could see the muscle and bones through my own skin, but those too were hardening, locking up as they transformed into sparkling diamond. The black veins continued to pump blood through me, a dark network in a prison of glass. The Misery-taint within me shivered away from this magic. It was different; it was alien; it was raw with the crash of surf and tempest waves. The Lady of Waves' own power. The Misery-taint crashed against it and was driven back, screeching like claws of flint, but not strong enough to resist the Lady's curse.

'Do you recall throwing me a broken quarrel back in that nothing-town?' North said. He leaned against the spear now. 'You gave me your blood and the Lady forged it into this spear. She knew Crowfoot could not be trusted. She sees so much, Galharrow. The rivers and oceans of the world are all hers. She knows what your master did. I'm surprised you didn't realise that she'd see that. And there's power in blood, Galharrow.'

I tried to heave myself back up to my feet, but my knee had locked solid. The numbness was moving inexorably down my shin. I couldn't stand. Panic hit me. I saw my own death coming, too soon, and not death in battle as I'd always imagined, but slow transmogrification into silent crystal. With a bellow, I threw my sword at North with all the strength that I had. He swayed, neatly and without excitement and it sailed past.

'Your master betrayed the Nameless,' North said calmly. 'He even betrayed the Bright Lady, who should have ascended long ago. She should have joined the ranks of the Nameless, but Crowfoot crushed her. He would never have activated his weapon. He would have kept the power for himself. You know that.'

His words were dizzying, but I couldn't focus on them. My groin was gone now, my foot too. Feeling was leaving my body, as inch by inch the Lady's enchantment worked through me. I felt the Misery inside me still warring with it, fighting battles for glands and arteries, clutching to bones before the Lady of Waves' power drove it back. I drew breath with difficulty.

'The Lady of Waves will never claim that power,' I wheezed. 'You've lost.'

'Not yet,' North said. 'Perhaps it is time for the Lady of

Waves to strike a new alliance. The Deep Emperor cannot be stopped now. But my Lady will endure.'

My chest began to constrict. The muscle that let me breathe, whatever it was called, was locking into a plate of rigid diamond inside me. I thought of Valiya. Pictured her in my mind as she'd been in the good days, when we worked together side by side. See something beautiful when you go. Amaira had told me that, once.

To have come so far. To be so near the end, and then to suffer this indignity. What a way to die.

Up on the bridge, a soldier stood over the powder-filled pits. He took out a phos-powered sparker, held it over the bed of black powder. It was too soon. The fuse had not been laid. But then, with a rush of horror that swept through my crystallising body, I saw the twin tracks of blood running from his eyes. I caught the stench of rotten entrails, saw the mismatched colour of his eyes.

Impossible. No. No, no no. I thought I knew the game. I thought I knew who the players were. The weight of my own arrogance descended on me.

The soldier had been fixed. Saravor was dead. I'd *seen* him die. But somehow this man still obeyed his will. A soldier shrieked a warning, lunged for him as he struck sparks from his device.

The bridge went up in a thunderous roar. I stood immobile as soldiers went flying in all directions, stone showering outwards in a deadly rain. North was bowled over by the impact, tumbling across the ground. My ears pounded with the noise, but my body was still locking up, piece by piece. I strained against it, willed my crystallising limbs to move, willing the Misery-magic to free me, but the numbness was pushing up through me. I couldn't move my legs at all.

Maldon had been shot through the heart and playing dead, but he sprang up now and ran for North, a curved black spike as long as my forearm in his hands. Snarling, he raised it above his head in both hands, ready to plunge it down into North's back.

North heard the patter of feet and lashed out with the spear, grounded though he was. He swung a wide arc, the haft cracking against Maldon's legs and sending him crashing down. Maldon rolled, one leg flopping broken beneath the knee. He struggled to rise and crashed down again. Groping blindly, North struck out with the spear, the jade head piercing Maldon in the back. He screamed, but he'd taken worse and the magic of the spear had been tailored against me. It might not be killing him, but the spear pinned him. He raised the Shantar's stinger and with a grunt, threw it at me.

What did I have to lose?

Wordlessly I caught it. I felt the Misery thrum through it against my hand, ancient power from the purest days of the Misery's transformation. It was a weapon that would do for North, but my last breath was wheezing out of me as my chest and lungs became crystal. I had nothing to lose. No way back.

I thrust the Shantar's stinger into the base of my neck, seeking the major artery. I felt the bite of the point, the tingle of the venom, then squeezed the venom sack. Blackness flowed through my veins, sudden pain, vicious ants swarming inside my skin, biting and tearing. The venom crawled, then roared as dark energy swam down through me, challenging, screaming. My mind seemed to detonate, flooding outwards into the sky as raw, primal power overrode my control. This was no feeble scuttling beast. The Shantar was a relic of the Misery's beginning, when the power to change had been at its pinnacle. Piece by piece, the Misery's purity burned back through me.

It should have killed me, should have melted me as it had the Guardians, but I had long since become immune to even

409

the worst of the Misery's venoms. I was steeped in them. Part of them. We were one.

Exultation. A rush of power coursing through me. The Misery powered through me, railed against the Lady of Waves' magic, and drove it back. Feeling returned to my chest and gut as muscle flexed and softened once again. The lead shot that North had put into me was forced out, bouncing off the debris. My skin darkened to the gleaming obsidian of the Shantar's hide, wisps of smoke rising from it as its power consumed me. I felt the bones in my face changing, warping and welding back into new shapes. Spurs of pain ran through my jaw, through my fingers as my nails blackened and grew harder, sharper. My skin blackened to the gleaming obsidian of the Shantar's hide.

The Misery had taken my body, but I held on to me. Whatever me was. My fingers were black talons and the man with the spear would be torn apart. The world could be torn apart.

I screamed. A cloud of oily shadow erupted around me blotting everything out, fraying and re-forming, a swirling cloud of smoking Misery-essence. My eyes blazed with the Shantar's power, and when I cracked my lips to roar, my teeth were sharp as knives.

North ran for the bridge. I felt the fading of dying soldiers as their last breaths gave out. I felt the dark presence that awaited the traitor on the far side, a presence I thought I'd dealt with once before but was somehow, impossibly, here amongst us. But even as the Shantar's dizzying power coursed through me, stronger, more violently than any-thing I'd ever consumed before, those things seemed small concerns.

Out beyond the walls, I felt the drudge army tearing across the last miles towards us. Desperately holding on to thought as the Misery-energy tried to flood my mind, I saw, as the coiling smoke cleared around me, that the explosion had not destroyed the bridge. Bodies littered it, torn and smoking, but the traitor had detonated it too early, before the earth had been packed atop, and most of the blast had launched upwards into the air. Three shallow craters made hollows in the stone, but it was strong, and broad, and the drudge were going to swarm across it like a flood of rats.

36

Betrayed on all sides. Enemies before, after, and within, and a fire raging through me. Change and change again. Ripples of unmaking swam across my skin, smoke curled from me in waves, light bled from my eyes.

Maldon managed to force himself up onto one leg using a twisted matchlock as a crutch.

'Ryhalt,' he coughed through the smoke. 'It didn't work. The bridge is standing. Spirits, Ryhalt, you're – you're—'

I shuddered as the energy coursed through me. My toes wanted to bury themselves in the sand, lay down roots, become one with the ground. I shook my head, fighting back the Misery's desire to claim me. It needed me. Needed me as its outlet, needed me to channel all the dark hopelessness forced upon it. But I held it back.

I should have known that it would all come back here in the end, to Adrogorsk, where I'd first given that devastating, pride-crushing order. Where I'd done the thing that I'd always sworn that I'd never do in the face of the enemy. I had led the rearguard. It was my task, to hold the drudge back as what was left of our forces evacuated the city. But then I'd looked out at the drudge as they prepared for yet another bloody assault. *Fall back*, I'd signalled. Fall back and run. Run, and run, and keep on running back home where we could shelter beneath our mothers' skirts. And there had been no rearguard then, and the drudge had descended on our soldiers and the orderly withdrawal became a chaotic, bloody rout.

Fall back.

Not this time.

So much guilt. Guilt upon guilt. Guilt for failure, guilt for the things that I'd done, guilt for the things that I hadn't. The pain of seeing my own men die on my orders. The agony of reading that my wife had thrown herself and my children from the tower. Guilt for Ezabeth, whom I couldn't save, for Nenn, whom I couldn't save, for Venzer and Herono and all the others who had paid the price for my failings. Hadn't been strong enough, clever enough, brave enough. Adrogorsk had broken me, and I'd spent my life hiding and running, fleeing the fights that I couldn't win.

I loved Ezabeth because she made me see past that guilt. She gave me something to fight for. Something that I was willing to give my all to. I loved Tnota, and Amaira, and Valiya, even Maldon in some bizarre way. I looked at the blackening, oily smoke curling from my skin. What did I hold there but the guilt of a weapon? Crowfoot's guilt, maybe, so purely distilled that it lingered on in physical form. It wraps us, binds us inside ourselves and makes us into something less.

Black Misery-essence coiled within me, smoked from me, threading down into the earth. I could see them all around me now. Faces from the past, weapons shouldered, waiting. They'd been waiting for me all this time.

'You understand, don't you?' Nenn had said. But I hadn't. *'You're here for her. But we're here for you too. Not just me, and Betch and Venzer. All of us. We're here, when you need us.'*

It would take an army to stop the drudge reaching us. But I had one.

'I'm going to meet them,' I said, picking up a spear. 'Stay here. If anything gets past me, you'll have to stop it.'

'We need you here!' Maldon said. 'North has to be stopped.'

'I'll deal with North later,' I said. I felt calm. Everything was as it should be. 'But I'm needed out there.'

His questions faded as I walked back towards the city walls.

'You sure you like these odds?' Nenn asked, walking alongside me.

'I never like the odds,' I told her. 'But then, we never played fair, did we?'

'Awful lot of them out there. You think you can handle them all?'

'No. Of course not. But then, I won't have to.'

She grinned at me, a shit-eating grin that won my heart.

'By the fucking Spirit of Misery, I think he's finally getting it,' she said.

'About damn time,' Betch agreed. Marshal Venzer nodded enthusiastically.

I ran through the silent streets of Adrogorsk amidst the din of ghosts. They stamped and beat the butts of their weapons against the ground. I nodded to them as I passed by, returned their salutes. Faces I hadn't seen in thirty years, faces that I'd forgotten, faces that had never grown old. They were me, and they were the Misery, and they belonged to us both in equal measure. I passed through the great, empty eastern gate and stood outside the walls to look towards the army that descended upon us across the horizon. A blanket of churning shapes, thousands of them, with lance and axe and sword and hate enough to tear through cities. This mindless, senseless devotion, the willingness to disregard thought and choice and to kill and maim and enslave was what awaited all of us.

And so, it comes to this, I sent across the Misery. In the black iron palanquin, Acradius heard me. I felt the weight of his presence rise like the wave that had threatened to swamp the Deep Kings in their place of power, a rushing, roaring wall of destruction.

I see you before your broken walls, Acradius intoned, his voice the silence of a supernova, the quiet of falling oaks. *For all that you've worked towards, for everything you and your Nameless guardians have thrown in my path – this is all that stands against me now?*

He did not understand. He would never understand.

I stand against you, I told him. *And people like me will stand against you until their last breath. Until the battles are over, until the sky boils and breaks and tears the world apart. Someone will always stand against you. You will never have the dominion you crave. You will never be whole. You will always be nothing.*

I could make out individual riders as they drew closer. Their mounts were gasping, dead on their feet, ragged and pressed past the limits of their endurance, animated by will alone. Here and there, one of them crashed down, beyond exhaustion, spilling its rider. But while they may have been a ruined army, they were still an army.

'Hope you know what you're doing here, Captain,' Nenn said.

'You don't have to call me that, Major,' I said. 'Or should that be General?'

'I always liked it best when you were the captain,' she said.

The moons were so close now. Rioque, slowest in her orbit, began to cross the sun's path. The world shone in bloody red magnificence, blood in the sky, blood on the earth.

'Good times, weren't they?'

'No,' Nenn said. 'They were pissing awful, mostly. But they were ours. I'm going to miss you, Ryhalt.'

'I'm going to miss you too,' I said. 'Again. I'll always miss you.'

We clasped wrist to wrist. I met Betch's eye. Betch, whose life I'd taken with my knife when he couldn't run from the drudge. He'd understood, but the guilt had weighed heavily all these years.

'Look after her. Wherever you find yourselves when all this is over.'

'Always intended to,' Betch said. He put an arm around Nenn's shoulders.

The swarm came on. Faster and faster, urged by Acradius' dark will. It was an energy, behind them, a tornado of spite and longing. None of the Misery's poisoned ugliness could match the intensity of that inhuman hatred. Nothing but hate. That had always been the Deep Kings' weakness. They had nothing else to fall back upon but their own eternal darkness.

'Drink for the road?' Nenn asked.

'Hells,' I said. 'It's about time.'

I took out the flask that she'd given me. Had impossibly given me, when she was of no substance and, I'd thought, only in my mind. But our reality is shaped by our minds. There's more than sand and water, skin and bone, iron and starlight. Without that which exists in our minds, there's nothing at all, just an empty, desolate tangle of tiny particles that claim to be separate things, but in truth, are all one and the same. If the Misery had taught me anything, it was that our reality is not fixed.

I tipped the flask to my lips and let the brandy burn down my throat.

I smiled. Closed my eyes. Reached out all around me. Into the air, into the ground, I sent my Misery-senses out across Adrogorsk, across the Misery.

'I feel it,' I said. 'I understand now. It's time to make amends.'

What makes a place? The rock, the soil, the trees? Buildings, sky, rivers? It is all those things, and it is everything that lives within them, around them, understands them, exists alongside them. And they were still here. They were me, and they were them, and they were the Misery as sure as anything was. The Misery was not just twisted magic and polluted rock. It was spirits, and sky, and the endless pain of what it had been, what it had been made to do, and what it had become. And it responded to my call.

What's this? Acradius thundered in my mind. Loud as a feather's touch, booming like a summer smile. He had no subtlety. Too much arrogance, too much blinded pride. *You summon old, dead magic. The power of the Heart of the Void was spent long ago. Look around you and see how it was wasted.*

Not wasted, I told him. *Diffused. Scattered. But the core remains. It was terrible, and it destroyed countless lives, but it was put to a purpose, to save others while you are purposeless but to placate your own insanity. This soulless land is more capable of feeling remorse than you ever could.*

The riders had seen me. They beat their flagging mounts, and when those collapsed beneath them, crawled to their feet and began to run. On one side of the column, huge, screeching sandworms reared from the grit, dragging the drudge down into sand and jaws. From the other, sickly hands reached from clouds of drifting mist to pull riders from the saddles even as the mounts trampled the bodies of other things, unnamed things, that the Misery had thrown in their path as they crashed onwards. But there were still thousands. They would be upon me in minutes.

The Misery-essence welled inside me, rumbling in my chest as it found new form, spreading through the black veins of Misery-essence that wormed through skin and flesh and bone. It coupled with it, intensified. My head rushed, my vision shook. It was power beyond that which any man should have consumed. Acradius had been right: I was the Misery's voice. I was the one outlet through which it could feel, through which all the pent-up suffering and rage could be felt, could be exhaled in a titanic rush of raw fury. I was a conduit for both the living and the dead.

Guilt, is that what you seek to wield against me? I could feel the immortal's mockery in every word. It was beneath him to even say the word.

I thrust the butt of the spear into the brittle earth, screwing it down into the sand. I drew on a string, and the bundle that Valiya had wrapped for me unfurled from the shaft, caught and blown by an eager, rising wind. A single silver fist on a field of scarlet flowed out, Valiya's patient stitching bringing the torn pieces of my pride back into something whole.

'You see this, Acradius?' I roared. 'You remember this banner, raised over the walls of this city? This city is mine. I said I'd be waiting for you. Well, here I am. Bring everything you have.'

Acradius' laughter was the roaring of an avalanche, the chittering of fledgling birds. No longer in my mind, instead it crackled across the Misery, warring with the howls of the broken sky. I saw a face in the dust cloud left in his army's wake, narrowed eyes, a mouth contorted in rage.

Your defiance is the last feeble show of power from the Nameless, Son of the Misery. Where are your masters now? You are just a man. You are nothing without them. You stand alone.

I looked to my left. Nenn stood at ease, her sword resting on a shoulder. To my right, Betch gave me a nod.

'No,' I said. 'Never alone.'

I plunged my fist down into the Misery-sand and unleashed. Not just raw, primal magic. Not just the Misery-essence, but the guilt that had plagued this broken land for ninety long years. The guilt of an ancient being, forced to destroy; my own guilt at all the lives I'd failed and lost along the years; and they coiled together like tangling serpents, wrapping and binding together as they pulsed through the sand. Black shadows flowed out of me, billowing, roaring as they spread across the desert.

'Never alone,' I whispered, my voice like knives. Louder then, 'Rise up. Rise up, those that fought and died. Rise up, you that bled, and loved and were afraid. Rise up, you that were lost and broken before your years. Rise up with me now and stand against the darkness one last time.' I straightened and raised a fist into the air, black energy coursing out of me, into the ground, into the air, blazing through the sky. 'Rise up with me now, Children of the Misery.'

The sky roared, an echoing howl of grief and rage and the white-bronze cracks shuddered and sparked with lightning in the bloody red light. The ground shook beneath us, stones skittering, jets of black steam bursting forth as a vast wind swept in. The dust swirled, a blinding red cloud all around me as shapes began to form from the poisoned dirt. Still I poured the Heart of the Void's power back into the earth, still I threw back the agonised guilt it had borne all these decades, screaming, burning, unleashing it all.

I opened my eyes.

To my left and right they stood to order. Ghosts no longer, but carved from rock and sand, images of men and women from the past. Some I knew, others had died in this maniacal war long before I was born. They rode phantom horses of shifting sand, or stood in battalions with pikes shouldered. Shards of black Misery-stone made breast-plates, eyes glowed with the light of the cracks in the sky. The spirits imbued within those bodies glowed with star-light intensity, bleeding out from their new forms, overlaid across them as they held them together. An army. A whole damn army of the dead.

My army.

The drudge pulled up a couple of hundred yards short,

even Acradius' driving fury faltering in the face of this spectral army.

'We'll take it from here, Captain,' Nenn said. She glistened like she was formed of the white essence in the Endless Devoid. 'We'll buy you the time. And you need to be at the palace to see this through.'

I hugged her.

'This really is good-bye,' I said.

'I know,' she said. 'But I bet there's some fucking great adventures to be had wherever in the hells we end up. And besides. You gave me another chance to kill some drudge, and that's all I ever really asked for. You coming, beau?'

Betch helped her onto her horse. He took the reins of his own brilliant white mount.

'Love her well, Betch,' I said.

'Always,' he said. He smiled, and maybe in that smile, there was some forgiveness.

'Alright, you fucking lot,' Nenn called. 'We've been dead for far too bloody long and it's time for some payback. We're going to hold this fucking line.'

The drudge charged and the dead set their spears to meet them. Nenn bellowed her war cry, a perfect, ululating sound, taken up by thousands of roaring, ghostly warriors. With a crash, the two battle lines met.

I drew my sword, leaving the spear to carry my banner on the wind as I ran back into the city. I staggered as a lance of pain ripped up the bone of my left arm.

'Not fucking now,' I said, but the heat was rising through skin and flesh and I felt the beak within, driving upwards as it formed. My master was coming. 'Not fucking now,' I said. I was so close, so close that the last thing I needed was Crowfoot on hand as a witness. But he was here, writhing beneath my skin, and he wasn't going anywhere. I ran my sword blade across my Misery-hardened arm, sawing at it, barely feeling it. Black ichor and yellow fluid ran from me where blood should have been, as I sawed at myself. A small, black-feathered head emerged, sticky and slick with oil and mucus.

'Galharrow,' it whispered. A feeble sound, barely audible over the crash of spears on shields, of drudge screams and spectral battle cries. 'The Lady's captain will seek to present the power of the heart to her. You must be the last captain standing. I come now. When the heart is charged, I will be with you to consume its power. Do not let them take it first.'

He'd come pretty late with that particular warning. I stared at the bird in my hand. I felt no anger. I was not even surprised.

'There is no weapon,' I said. 'There was never a weapon. You don't intend to unleash the heart on the enemy. You're going to use it to replenish yourself. All of the Nameless have had the same plan all along.'

'Did I know that the Lady would betray me? Of course,' Crowfoot hissed. The baby bird's head lolled on its neck, broad, milk-blue eyes unseeing. 'Nall would have figured it out too, but he was gone before there was ever a need.'

'Because you killed him.'

'My hand was forced,' Crowfoot hissed at me. For a moment I thought that there might even have been pain in his fledgling voice. 'I need this victory at any cost, Galharrow. You of all people should understand that.'

He was right, and it wasn't like Crowfoot to try to reason with me. I understood then the utter depths of his powerlessness. He teetered on the edge of life, if what he had could be described as life at all.

'I understand,' I said.

'Good. The Lady's captain will attempt to take the heart. Stop him. Do not fuck this up.'

37

No time now. The eclipse was nearly upon us. I had to move fast.

First stood at the foot of the stairs that led to the palace roof. His robe had been torn and shredded away, the milk-white flesh beneath hacked and pierced by a dozen blows. Gunshot wounds raked his torso, but none of it seemed to bother the first amongst the Marble Guard. He carried no weapon. He needed none but his bloodstained fists, and a broken body lay at his feet.

North must have put up a staggering fight. The number of blows he'd dealt to the Guardian were testament to that. His ensorcelled spear lay across the square, broken into pieces, discarded like driftwood. But no matter how fast he'd been, how skilled, the Lady of Waves had put her faith into a man, and Shallowgrave had put his into the hands of a monster.

I was glad that I didn't have to go up against North. Somehow it seemed calm here, even as the din of battle cascaded over the shattered city walls.

First saw me as I crossed what had once been palace gardens. The moons were clustering over the sun, their alignment drawing closer, closer, and the world blazed in scintillating rainbow hues. North lay twisted in a way that told me his spine had been snapped in two like a twig. I could see the fight in my mind, North twisting and striking, spear leaping like a snake. And then First had got a hand on him, and in that mountain-weight grip, he'd been raised and broken in two. I remembered the impact of First's fists as they'd smashed me to the ground.

'Get out of my way,' I said. My voice was a shadow-thing, a nightmare growl.

I held Crowfoot's pathetic avatar in my left hand, the right around the hilt of my sword.

'He was a traitor,' the Guardian said, his words forming with difficulty through granite fangs, a corpse-dust whisper of breath.

'I know. Now get out of my way,' I said.

'The moons draw into alignment,' Crowfoot squealed. 'Brother, I am needed above. Do not delay me.'

'The moons draw into alignment,' First hissed. He raised a fist to his lips and a long red tongue snaked out to lick North's blood from his lips. 'Come.'

I hesitated. Intuition held me back a moment. North had bided his time. He'd waited, patiently, for his moment. As First turned away, I saw that his back was clean, unmarked by the myriad blows that had cut into his chest and abdomen. If North had decided to take First down, he'd have been better off pushing him from the platform or putting a pistol shot through the back of his skull. But the gunshots were all down First's torso.

He had not been the one to attack.

Maldon appeared from behind a stack of melted rocks on the far side of the garden. He looked meaningfully at First and shook his head at me.

'First,' I said slowly. 'You aren't one of the Marble Guard anymore, are you?'

The Guardian's crimson eyes turned back to me. Slowly, as though it were the first time the face had ever worn such an expression, as though such a face had never been intended to make it, the lips peeled back into a grin.

I knew that look.

'Oh, Galharrow. Always thinking you're one step ahead, when you're one step behind.'

I knew that voice, too.

'I don't know how you're here,' I said, my teeth locking together, the words spat through them. 'I don't know how you fucking survived. I'm just glad I get to kill you again, Saravor.'

The Guardian laughed.

'Kill me? I don't think so. You couldn't kill me when I was a man. Look at me now, Galharrow. Look how I have remade myself.'

'Your blood,' I said. I remembered the broken, charred body, missing a great chunk of flesh where one of the Guardians had taken a piece of him. First had swallowed part of Saravor and the sorcerer had used it to make the creature his own.

'Isn't it delicious?' Saravor said. 'What did you think? That I'd gone on some noble mission to save the world, throwing myself against the Nameless' creatures? I can barely believe that convinced anyone, least of all you.'

'For all the good it'll do you,' I said. I looked upwards towards the moons. The sky was awash with lights, glowing and rippling in waves as they spread outwards like the northern sky-flames. 'I've beaten you too many times to worry about it now.'

'There is no time for this,' Crowfoot's avatar squealed. I shoved him into a pouch on my belt.

'This body is incredible,' Saravor mused. 'It holds the essence of mountains. Strong enough to hold the power of the fiend's heart, which I shall make my own. Strong enough to ascend.' He flexed long, pale fingers, slick with North's blood. 'Strong enough to crush you again.'

Saravor stormed towards me, huge feet thumping against the flagstones. I held my sword up against the shoulder, only having seconds to plan my move. A sword wasn't worth much against that thing, but it was all I had to hand and maybe that brandy I'd chugged was giving me a recklessness I didn't deserve.

Saravor lunged for me, trying to get those huge fists on me, but I danced back and slashed out. The blade struck his stony arm and glanced away, opening a shallow little wound that neither bled nor slowed him. He swiped again, far faster than a thing that big had any right to be, and again I kept my distance and swayed back, cutting in to slice him across the shoulder. Anyone else would have gone reeling back, but the blow made little impact on marble flesh. He swung a fist then, not trying to grab me but a backswing that crashed into my breastplate and lifted me from my feet. I flew through the air, clanging and clattering as I rolled across the ground. No pain. Nothing hurt. Just off balance. He wasn't the only one who could take a beating.

Go again.

I rushed him this time, keeping low, and hammered the sword against the meat of his upper leg, but it wasn't meat and he didn't care. His fist slammed against my helmet and I rocked back. I thrust at his face but Saravor wasn't just big, he was fast and at eight feet tall, he had all the reach. He caught the sword blade with a downward swing of his hand and held it there. His grin opened wider, showing me his bloodstained teeth.

'I don't even need to fix them anymore,' Saravor hissed. 'The blood is all I need. North is inside me now, too. I know what he knew, have learned the things that he learned. I can be anyone. I can be *everyone*.'

He tore the sword from my grip and I staggered back. Swords were no use here, and that was something I never thought I'd say. Saravor surged after me and wrapped huge arms around me. He crushed down on me and I felt my battered breastplate flex under his vice-like grip, steel

425

screaming. I fumbled for the canister I'd hung from from my belt. Saravor pressed his face up against mine, and I stared into the whirling madness in his bloody eyes.

'You're so fucking hungry for the light,' I said. I ripped the arming fuse from the canister. 'Here it is.'

The phos canister detonated between us in a blaze of blue-gold intensity. I shot fifty feet back across the sand-garden, crashing against a pillar. The straps holding my armour together burned away and I tore free the buckled breastplate and helm as I spat dust. Crowfoot's little avatar had not fared well, a roasted carcass. I faced Saravor bare-chested. The light hadn't been able to hurt me for a long time and for a moment the glittering, ember-filled cloud of smoke gave me hope that it had been enough. But then the shadow rose within it. Slower now, Saravor stepped through, blackened and charred but still grinning.

'Nothing but tricks,' he said. 'Is this all that you have, Galharrow?'

I caught a glimpse of Maldon, climbing the stairs towards the roof. The moons were so close now, the world washed in sparkling shades. Saravor came after me, faster than I was, smoke curling from him like burned meat. The impact against the pillar had knocked the wind from me.

Saravor's blow crumpled me against a wall. Another massive fist rocked my head back into it, stone crunching, black blood spattering. He lifted me as though I were a child and hurled me through the air with a savage roar. I crashed through a section of crumbling wall in an explosion of stone shards. I spat blood, felt the hot wetness and sharp pain of a rib protruding from my side. I crawled back to my feet but Saravor was on me again. He smashed me down into the ground, my nose breaking against the stone. Vision blurred. A fist found my hair, dragged me upwards. The next blow sent me back through the wall again in a spray of mortar. I ragdolled across the sand, over and over, until a dry old fountain stopped me.

Every part of me thrummed with pain. Even through the Misery's protection, the Guardian's body was awesomely powerful. Shallowgrave had given his creatures the strength of the mountain from which they were born. Lights danced before my eyes, my broken rib screamed, my broken nose spat sparks of fire through my face.

I bunched my fists. Out of weapons. Out of allies. Out of options. Only I remained. I spat blood, spat shards of sharp teeth. Forced myself back to my feet as Saravor stalked out of the building as it collapsed behind him towards me.

'Strength,' I said. 'Maybe back in Valengrad I wasn't a match for First, but look where we are.' I cast a hand out around us. 'This is my domain, the seat of my power. I'm the Son of the fucking Misery, and what are you? A small-time sorcerer in a borrowed body.'

'You're just a man,' Saravor hissed. He raised one of those huge fists and swung it down on me.

I caught it midflight. The impact was like being kicked by a horse, my feet skidded back in the dust, but I didn't fall. Saravor's red eyes widened in consternation.

I roared and let fly with my own fist and Saravor was smashed from his feet. He crashed through half of a melted pillar. And then I charged him.

I'd fought a dozen barroom brawls and this was no different. My fist thundered into his chest, and then I dragged him upright and slammed it into him again. As he staggered to keep his feet I ducked low, drove my shoulder into his midriff, lifted him and heaved him off balance. Propelling forwards, the Misery's strength surging stronger and wilder inside me, I drove towards another pillar and we crashed into it together. Red stone crashed down around us in jagged shards. Saravor swung upwards, smashing me full in the face and I reeled back. He raised himself from the rubble.

427

Small shards of jagged stone jutted from his indestructible body as he came at me, and blow followed blow. I gave one back for each that he threw, uncaring whether his landed. I was stronger than him, just as resilient, and though we staggered and rocked as we hammered blows into each other, there was no ground to give.

The moons, the fucking moons were getting so close. I had no time for this.

I caught Saravor by the neck, drove my fist upwards at his eyes, one, two, three. My knuckles cracked under my own force and Saravor's marble brain must have rocked against his skull because he showed a moment of dizziness. I kicked out, sending him flying into a wall. I couldn't break him like this. Might as well try to punch out a house. So I did what I always do when I can't win a direct fight: I ran.

I heard him coming as I reached the stairs that led to the palace roof. Without pause I forced myself up them, legs burning and the old spear wound growling that I should remember that it was still there. I looked down, saw the streets below me, spread like a map, and suddenly I saw it. Saravor stormed up towards me, huge and trailing smoke and red masonry dust. He took the stairs five at a time, bounding up after me.

'Nothing can stop me,' Saravor shrieked. There was madness all around him. 'Nothing can kill me. Not even the Misery. Your master will never have the power. Everything you've worked towards has failed.'

I couldn't hold back my unnatural smile. There's something in every warrior that makes him want to gloat, to spill his most tightly held plans in his moment of victory. And I saw mine approaching now.

'He'll never have the power, that's true,' I said. 'But then, you're assuming that I ever intended for him to have it.'

Saravor's eyes widened just a fraction before I charged him again, and we sailed out from the stairway and into open air. Down, rushing down, hurtling down we plummeted towards the streets and the sewer entrance that Valiya had so diligently covered with a slab of stone. With a crash the stone cover shattered and I came down on top of Saravor, my knees driving into his chest. His arms and legs lashed wide, keeping him from going down into the hole but the impact had stunned him. From below, a seething babble of excited voices chorused in sudden, eager anticipation.

'Seventy-three, seventy-two!'

'Evening, master, care for a good time?'

'Death comes!'

I rolled from Saravor, took hold of one arm, and heaved it up. Saravor tried to force it down, and by the Spirit of Judgement he was as strong as the winter is relentless, but I had my whole body behind it and I kept a foot planted on his chest as I heaved that arm higher. I was filled with a blazing hatred that not even he could match. Hatred for what he'd done to Nenn, to Dantry, to me and all the other lives he'd taken. I stamped down, and his shoulders growled lower into the hole.

'Not this way,' Saravor hissed, panic in his voice. 'Not this way!'

'Don't worry,' I snarled back, 'you won't feel a fucking thing.'

I stamped down a final time and Saravor plummeted into the dense carpet of squirming, potbellied little bodies. He had no time to scream before the gillings sank their teeth into him, leg and arm, neck and scalp. Tiny, razored teeth latched on, injected their numbing, paralysing saliva from head to toe as they began to frantically chew at him. He tried to flail at them, shaking them off, but there were hundreds of them, swarming through the tunnel to reach him, to taste him. Teeth broke from gilling mouths as they gnawed. He crushed two of them together, swatted three flat, but as the venom took hold, his flailing dimmed. Paralysis spread through his limbs. He stared at me, face contorted in disbelief that after everything he had accomplished, all the power and knowledge he had accrued, he was going to be eaten alive by a swarm of Misery-spawned babies. Slowly. Really fucking slowly.

I ran for the stairs. No time, no time. The moons were aligning.

38

The sounds of distant battle continued as I reached the platform.

Just four of us left now.

Kanalina sat at the loom, heavy industrial goggles over a reddened, sweat-drenched face, taking readings from the dials. She plucked at control wires, testing their frequencies like a harpist, examining meters. There was no way to look directly at the sun, the shimmering colours were too bright, too chaotic to look on. Valiya stood a short distance away beside the iron box that contained the fiend's heart. Maldon crouched by the stairs. Kanalina was too intent on her work to have noticed him.

I must have looked monstrous, worse than ever before. Broken, bleeding, skin like charred wood. Valiya looked ashen when she saw me, but kept her face under control. I knew what she wanted to say. She knew I couldn't hear it, not now, so close to the end.

'North and the Guardian?' Valiya asked.

'Gone,' I said.

'Three minutes,' Kanalina said. There was excitement in her voice. Whatever danger was all around us, she was about to draw the purest power in existence, to harness it and bind it. She didn't know what was coming.

'Are you ready?' Valiya asked me. I took her hand in mine and kissed the back of her knuckles.

'I have to be,' I said. 'I'm so sorry.'

'I know,' she said. 'But you'll do what must be done.'

'Two minutes,' Kanalina said, fingers working. 'Get it in place.'

I looked into Valiya's eyes, but she turned her face away.

'Valiya, I—'

'Not now,' she said. 'Not now. Get the heart.'

I knelt and flipped the box lid back. Within lay a fossilised, blackened lump of what could have been stone. Without having to touch it, I sensed the chaos that writhed around it. It had waited, thousands of years, to live again. It sensed the forces converging on us, the focus brought to bear. I wrapped it in cloth, then lifted it free and carried it to the loom. Below the vast lenses, a four-clawed pedestal stood ready to grasp it. Carefully, reverently, avoiding the copper wires and refracting crystals, I laid it down. It settled with a hiss. Expectant. Waiting.

'Ninety seconds,' Kanalina said. She drew on gloves, thick and heavy.

'Move away from the loom, Kanalina,' I said. 'Now.'

Either she didn't hear me, or it didn't register at first. The click of a hammer being dragged back on a pistol brought her attention back to us, though, as Valiya levelled it at her. Mouth open, Kanalina pushed the goggles back from her face.

'What are you doing? The eclipse is coming. We can't stop now.'

'Step away, or I'll shoot you,' Valiya said. 'Move slowly.'

'You're mad!' she cried. 'This is our one chance. The only chance we have to stop Acradius and save the republic. It's our only weapon—'

'The Nameless never meant to turn the power of the heart against Acradius,' I said. I took her by the arm and drew her from the chair. The Misery-essence in my skin

432

squealed against the phos in hers like fingernails breaking on a chalkboard. 'And neither did I.'

'What – I – I don't understand – then what ... why?'

I drew her away and gestured to Maldon, who strode forwards from his place by the stairs, walking with more determination and pride than I'd seen in him in all his life. Spine straight, shoulders back, he took his seat at the loom. He locked his fingers together, flexed them.

The sun and the moons came together across the sun and the world pulsed in waves of gold, blue, and red light. One after another they sheeted out, rippling as they washed the world in beautiful, scintillating colour. Maldon began to work within the loom. He dragged threads at first, drawing strands of shimmering colour down, one after another, clawing them from the air. He laboured hard, tearing them into a different form, but as he worked the threads began to come to him more willingly, following the flow of the others, thickening and multiplying as the loom fed them down through its many lenses. Down, and into the heart.

A growl, the voice of a god long dead, rose from it as it sucked in the light. It drank the power eagerly, a dry sponge taking up water. Veins of blue-white energy rippled across its stony surface. Still Maldon worked, drawing light, feeding it into the fiend's heart, strand after strand, ropes of light coruscating down through the loom, twisting and twirling together in helixes as they answered the call.

Away to the west, a dark shadow appeared on the distant horizon, crossing the sky towards us. A vast murder of ravens, come to claim the prize. Crowfoot.

'You'd betray your own master?' Kanalina cried. 'You've been planning this betrayal all along?'

'Call it what you want,' I said. 'Dantry, Maldon, and I have been working towards this for a long time. You're lucky. You get to watch the resolution.' I glanced towards

433

Valiya. She gave me a slow nod. Whatever Nall's purpose, she was with me on this.

'If not for the Nameless, then what for?' Kanalina demanded.

I crossed the platform and stood beside Maldon.

'I need it,' I said. 'Ten years ago, something precious was taken from me. And I swore that no matter what it took, whether it took me a hundred years or more, I was going to get it back.'

Kanalina's eyes went wide.

'The ghost in the light,' she said. 'The Bright Lady.'

'Ezabeth Tanza was burned from this world and into the light. She died saving us all from the drudge. And she saved me. Not just from the enemy, but from what I'd become. I can never repay her in full. But this, I can do for her. I can draw her back.'

'But how?' Kanalina demanded. 'With what? The Bright Order thought she was coming back, but there isn't enough power ...' She looked to the fiend's heart. 'You can't be serious.'

'I'm serious.'

'Don't be a fool,' Kanalina snapped. 'You're no Nameless wizard. You can't shape these forces. If you attempt to use the power of the heart to break her from the light, the backlash will be impossibly strong. It will come down on you like a hammer.'

I showed Kanalina my bared arm. The words still stood there, scarred into the skin.

BECOME THE ANVIL.

'Six years,' I said. 'Six years soaking up the Misery. Six years becoming part of it. I'm not just Ryhalt Galharrow anymore. I *am* the Misery. I am the anvil on which that power breaks.'

She flung a hand out to point at the storm cloud of ravens as they came down towards us.

'Crowfoot will eviscerate you for this. You're Blackwing, you wear the raven's mark.'

'Maybe,' I said. 'But he'll be too late to stop me.'

Maldon's body smoked with the phos. He drew light in glimmering strands, faster and faster, fingers a blur as he dragged power from the sky. A rippling heat distortion surrounded him and the loom. One of the lenses cracked, wild strands of phos spearing across the platform. Kanalina and Valiya threw themselves flat as a stray flare shot over them. One of the strands washed over me, deflecting and blazing away across the city. The sky itself grew darker, the light of the sun focused down upon us in its entirety.

The iron contraption could no longer take the strain of the vast forces being worked within it. With a metallic tearing sound, the supports began to buckle. Wires zipped free, snapping and pinging, the glass components shattered, raining down over the heart. With a cry, Maldon ripped one final, tree-trunk-thick beam of light down into the heart. It blazed down upon it, writhing like an eel on a line, pure and dazzling. And then it was gone. Surrounded by the wreckage of the loom, the fiend's heart glowed with a purplish cast.

I looked from the onrushing birds to the prize that the Nameless all so desperately craved. Walked to it. Picked it up. It weighed little, for all the fury of the cosmos having been gathered inside it.

I saw into the fiend's heart then. I saw other times, ancient places where beings vaster than mountains had stepped across the world in its earliest days. I saw rivers of fire and forests that never ended, swirling storms that lasted for centuries. A primal world, long forgotten by all but these sleeping ancients that we now put to our own purposes. And within, I sensed the blazing power of the light. So much light, so much power. A world-ending force, resting on the palm of my hand.

435

'I suggest that you run,' I said. Valiya ushered Kanalina across to the stairs but remained on the platform, her pistol still trained on the Spinner. Maldon pried his burned hands from melted metal and staggered after them.

Galharrow, Crowfoot's birds whispered across the sky, *We had a deal!*

'We did,' I said. 'But you're no stranger to treachery.'

What are you doing? he demanded, his words born in the shapes of the wings as they flooded the sky.

'What do you think I'm doing?' I said. 'I'm going to fuck this up.'

I gripped the heart tight against my chest with one hand, and drew back the other. Punching things is not always a good solution to a problem, but on this occasion, it would have to do.

I drove my fist into the ice fiend's heart. I reached for the light. I reached for Ezabeth.

The world disappeared in a flaring cataclysm of blinding purity. All the power of the sun directed itself outward to release, but it met the Misery head-on. The sky bellowed, a roar of utmost pain and fury as the power in the heart released, backlashed, all that immense energy directed not just against me, but against the magic soaked through me, and against the magic that lay all around us. Every force requires a counter force to keep it in balance, and the Misery and the light could never be one. The phos energy drove against me like a lance, but I held it tight, redirected it back into the light. Two worlds, the spirit in the light and the man of the physical world, unable to touch, unable to cross the barrier. More power than the Engine, more power than a god, a backlash that had to be contained so that it would not rip the world in two.

The Misery speared back, and my body became the divide. The black veins of corruption bled from my skin, hissing and steaming in the air. I felt layers of me burning away, charring, driven out of me as the light strove to unmake the Misery itself, as the backlash sought to strike back against the light that had made it, and the Misery insisted on change, change and change again, on its ongoing existence.

As the colossal force of the heart met the Misery anvil that I had forged myself into, I saw the wall that lay between them all, the barrier between the worlds. And into that, I hurled myself after Ezabeth.

Into the fire.

Into the brightness.

Into the void.

39

I sat across a table from her.

Just us. Just a table. Around us, a storm of fire as far as the eye could see. No floor. No sky. No walls. Nothing but the rush of blinding flame and behind me, a shadowed gap in the flame that led back into the true world. The table wasn't a table. It was just the idea of a table.

We were the only things that really existed, but then for me, perhaps that had always been true.

Ezabeth sat demurely, her hands in her lap, back straight, a serious expression overlaying the sadness on her face. Half of it smooth, a woman in her prime. Half of it rippled, ridged, smooth, and scarred. She was as beautiful as she had ever been, if she even existed.

Perhaps this was oblivion. The afterworld, if such a thing could exist. It was enough for me.

Flame raced by on all sides, a swirling corridor of intensity. The essence of light.

'I saved this part of me,' she said when the silence had grown to a hammering crescendo. 'I had to hope it was enough.'

'Any of you is enough for me,' I said. Too quickly. Too eager. Like a child.

'No,' she said. 'That isn't true now, and it wasn't true before. I'm just here to keep you company, and ...' She faltered and lost her words. She glanced away. 'It isn't easy for me, either. Even this part of me remembers. Holds to it. It was so bright.'

'What?' I asked.

'Love,' she said. She smiled then, with the sadness the world must feel when the last of a great species falls to extinction. 'It was glorious, wasn't it?'

The finality of it. The weight of her words drove down on me. The detonation of Crowfoot's weapon couldn't have hit me with such force.

'It's not over,' I said. 'It still exists. As long as you do. As long as I do. It still exists.'

Ezabeth rose, stepped from river of fire to river of fire.

'Love blooms bright,' she said. 'But it's no more constant than the wind, Ryhalt. I had hoped you would have come to see that by now. It would have made this easier for you. But the wind changes. It lives only in moments, and when its roaring abates there is nothing left to show that it ever was. That doesn't mean that the wind was weak, or that it didn't matter. The world is changed for having known it. You see it in the movement of the seeds as they drift on, to make new life elsewhere. You see it bring down walls that have stood for centuries, wreck ships, or cool a child's brow. We are no different, you and I. Just a wind passing through the world. We have left our mark, and left it well. But the wind changes direction. Clouds come and go, and the sun rises and falls, and nothing is as it was. You can no more cling to the passage of love than you can the wind.'

She looked me dead in the eye, and in the power of her surety I felt the cracks tearing through my chest. My heart. Through everything.

'This can't be it,' I said. I rose to whatever my feet might have been in that place and leaned across the table. 'I won't let that be it.'

'You have done great things,' she said. 'Great, and bloody and terrible. But all things must end. Even you. Even me. I

439

was Ezabeth Tanza. But the wind has changed, and I must change with it.'

I slammed my fist down against the blackness of the table and it shattered into shards of thought, carried away in the torrent. The flames around us quivered and rocked, swirling, raging.

'Everything I did,' I shouted, 'everything I became. I did it for you. To bring you back.'

The floodgates had opened and everything poured out. Everything that I'd held back those last ten years, everything that had made me, driven me onwards, let me do unspeakable things, let me become an anvil that would defy the hammer of a god.

'This is not it!' I roared. 'I have broken reality for you. I have broken space, and light, and time, because spirits damn the world I *deserve* to have you back. You didn't deserve to die. If I have to tear down the walls of the afterworld and rip every damn soul free, I'll do it.' I looked around into the endless, raging torrent of fire. 'Do you hear me? Spirits or gods or whatever rules this world? Do you hear me? I'm taking her back.'

'It wasn't just for me,' Ezabeth said quietly. Calmly. Like she'd known that this tempest would come. 'It was for your friends. For Nenn, and Tnota. For your child, Amaira. For the children that were lost to you. And for Valiya, whom you love but cannot love, because you cling to my memory so tightly that to let it go feels like a betrayal. But there's no betrayal, Ryhalt. And you'll see that. Our story wasn't the one that we wanted, but it was still a good story.'

She moved closer to me. She was tiny and fragile, but there was so much power within her, so much more wisdom than I'd ever managed to accrue. She shivered in the inferno, eyes drifting to the dark portal behind me, smaller now than it had been.

'It's closing,' she said. 'The tear you've made between these worlds will not endure.'

'Then I stay here.' Ezabeth shook her head.

'I will miss this part of me,' she said. 'The woman, Ezabeth Tanza, loved you so much. Oh spirits, so much. When we were young together, for all you did then, and everything you did after. But I have to go. I should have done it when I died. But I can't go while my name still holds such power. You understand, don't you?'

'No,' I said. 'I refuse to understand.'

'I have to let it go,' she said. 'I was Ezabeth Tanza, and then I had a chance to become something else. And I couldn't … but I cannot be Ezabeth Tanza, not anymore. You know why. Don't you?'

Tears streamed down my face, hot and burning with the pain of ten long years, with the hopes and dreams that I'd stored deep inside where the light never reached.

'Tell me,' she said.

I screamed. I balled my fists and shook with the pain and the rage and the unfairness of it all.

'Tell me,' she said gently. She took my hand in hers and when I opened my eyes she met them dead-on. 'Tell me,' she whispered.

'Because you have to ascend,' I said. 'You have to leave yourself behind. That is what it means to become Nameless.'

I bowed my head in sorrow.

Ezabeth leaned in and put her arms around me. I clutched her hard against me, held her tight, as if somehow I could drive back the passage of fate. It had always been building to this. Of course it had. There was no other way it could have gone.

'I will be different,' she said. 'The wind moves on as it gathers strength. I will not understand love as I do now. But I have to let go. And I can't, while my name still lives on in you.'

The fire around us billowed and roared, rushing by in a hurricane of bright heat. It sought to dislodge me, to send me spiralling out into the fury. The portal shrank smaller, flame swirling around it in a torrent. It diminished further, nearly gone. I took a deep stance, breathed in fully as scorching flame flowed into me. The roar of the fire grew louder.

'I know,' I said. And it was all that I could say. 'You have to leave. You have to do what you were unnamed to do.' I looked around. There was nothing but the blaze, hazy through my tears. 'I don't know the way back. I'm not of that place either anymore.'

My feet began to drag along the missing ground, losing purchase. My grip on this existence was faltering and the light was drawing me into its grasp. Part of me wanted to remain. Let Ezabeth and me dwell here in the blazing brightness as spirits or ghosts or whatever we were now. It would be such a relief to let it all go. I looked around into the torrent, but there was nothing. It didn't matter.

'There's no way back,' I said.

A hand burst through the walls of fire, outstretched, the torrents of heat whirling around it. And upon the arm that followed it, words shone bright, and silver, and dazzling as they reflected the inferno.

BRING THEM BACK.

A second hand followed, clawing through the fire, splitting it apart, tearing the rift anew. Valiya stood framed there, head thrown back, a silent scream on her lips. She forced the tear open again. Holding the path. For me. For us.

Nobody had ever smiled with such sadness as Ezabeth did then. The last of her, what remained of the woman that I would have died a thousand deaths for, still felt the hurt of it.

'Humanity,' she said. 'It was what they never understood. The enemy, the Nameless; humanity. Humanity was always the key.'

'Ryhalt,' Valiya whispered. She couldn't see us. She stood alone in another place, holding back the fire with nothing but strength of will. Tears burned as they rolled down her face. 'Come back, Ryhalt. Please. I need you.'

'Take her hand,' Ezabeth said softly. 'As you should have done years ago.'

One final moment in her presence. That was all that I would have, and I felt it more powerfully than the raging maelstrom around us.

I looked back to Valiya, shrouded in dark flame, risking everything – everything – for one last chance at a future. A future I had dreamed of but had never let myself believe was within reach. The fire was not my place. It was not my world. Valiya had carried me, kept me together as I did all that had needed to be done.

I needed her too.

'You had my heart,' I said finally. 'But I understand. You have to go on.'

'We both must,' she said. And the smile that lit her face was bright, and the sorrow melted away into the beauty of the love we'd shared. 'Good-bye, Ryhalt.'

'Good-bye, Ezabeth.'

I took her hand, and through it I sensed the greater power beyond it, vast and filled with knowledge, and fury, and so much that would always be beyond me. Then I reached behind me, and took another hand, and it was warm and it snapped tight around mine, and with a strength greater than any magic, dragged us from the fire.

40

I blinked. I was sat up against something. I didn't know where I was.

Understanding returned slowly. There were arms around me, a weight. A chin, Valiya's chin, nestled against my shoulder. Her hair was loose, grey strands fallen across my chest. I could hear her voice in my ear, but I couldn't make out what she was saying. My vision began to clear, and I looked down at my hands. The black veins were gone, burned out of me. My skin was raw and smooth, but it was also fresh and clean, the Misery's colours no longer rooted through it. Burned out of me, burned away. I ran my tongue over my teeth, and found that they were just teeth. The same couple missing, but not sharp. Naked, clothing burned to nothing in the flame, I had absolutely no body hair left. It seemed a laughable thing to be concerned with.

The moons had moved on. The world was still aglow with colour but it seemed somehow softer now, gentler, and the sky had ceased its howling.

I eased myself up, and Valiya helped me right myself.

'Did it work?' I asked. My throat hurt, every muscle ached as though it had been hammered straight and reshaped, but my voice had lost its brutal rasp. Even that felt fresh and remade.

'Ryhalt,' Valiya said. 'She's here.'

'I know.'

'Ryhalt,' Valiya said again, her voice a breathy whisper. 'She's magnificent.'

I turned, weak and unsteady on my feet, to see the power that I had brought into the world.

The Nameless wizard was looking east. She was small, but taller than she had been. Golden from head to toe, long hair streamed behind her, its tips licked with gentle flames. She was pure and whole, the scars of her life scoured away. She wore a silver-blue gown, elegant, modest. The face had the rough shape of Ezabeth's, but everything that had made it hers was gone. The fire, the determination, the intelligence, and beyond all, her love for the world and her need to save it. She was no more Ezabeth than I was the Misery. We had uncoupled from our pasts, set them alight, and let them burn away in the conflagration.

When she turned her head to look in our direction, I saw that her eyes were utterly blank, filled with a light that I didn't want to look upon. She was silent, hands clasped before her.

A shadow loomed over us, the rushing flurry of wings as a storm of ravens came down to alight on the low wall surrounding the platform. The largest of them, its feathers old and scuffed, fluttered down to the platform's centre. It looked between us, one to the other.

'So,' Crowfoot said. The word held all the darkness of the night. Fury cannot begin to describe it. Human beings cannot feel the level of ire that he did, for what I had done.

'Greetings, brother,' the shimmering woman said. Her voice was deep, the resonance of a booming gong in pillared hallways. 'You have come to welcome me to this world.'

'You think so?' Crowfoot snarled.

'I am not asking you,' she said. 'I am telling you that you have come to welcome me. If you wish, you may watch as I lay waste to those enemies you have failed to destroy.'

'You address me with such disrespect? You, fresh-born and barely part of the world?'

'Respect must be earned,' she said. 'You are weak. Drained. In time, perhaps you will be useful as an ally. But you have nothing I need. Be grateful that I see future potential in you.'

'What?' Crowfoot snarled. His outrage was echoed through a billowing squawk. More and more of the carrion birds were trying to alight on the wall, but there was far too little space. The rest of them circled the platform, cawing and screeching.

'Eternity is a long time to live,' the golden figure said. 'It makes us forget that we are but parts of the greater whole. Even you, Crowfoot. There is so much power in me right now, so much potential. I would hate to have to waste any of it on unmaking you as well.'

The raven took a step back.

'Who do you think you are?' it squawked. 'You don't know what I'm capable of.'

'I am the Bright Lady,' she said. 'And I know exactly what you're capable of. Nothing.'

The furious bird rounded on me. Valiya's arms went tight around my chest. I placed my palm over her hand.

'But *you*,' Crowfoot snarled. 'My own captain. You bound yourself to me. You took my mark, and in return your children lived. Your torment will be legendary. Your name will come to mean *suffering*. Children will cut off their ears rather than hear the things that I'm going to do to you. I'll spin your life out over a hundred years. You are mine, and—'

'Yours no longer. And I will not permit harm to come to my captains, or those they care for,' the Bright Lady said. 'They wear my mark now.'

I didn't grasp what she meant at first, but then I looked down at my arm. The raven tattoo was gone. In its place,

446

a brilliant phoenix lay white and silver against my skin. I was suddenly aware of the gentle warmth of it against my arm. It was bright, and cool, and made of her fire. Valiya placed her arm against mine. An image that mirrored my own stood stark upon it where Nall's last message had been.

'Impossible,' Crowfoot snarled. But he looked from me to her and I saw how little there was left to his threats. It would take him years to amass his power again, decades if he wanted to challenge the Bright Lady before him. She glowed with newborn energy, brimmed with it.

'Retreat to your lair, Brother,' the Bright Lady said. 'I have work to do. Trouble me not until you are useful to me. And carry the message to the others too. We still have need of them.'

In a frustrated snarl of billowing feathers, the birds launched into the air, a black cloud rising around us. One of them took a swipe at my head with his claws as he went past but there was no heart in it. Only for show.

'Well done,' the Bright Lady said. She looked to Valiya and then to me. 'I am pleased with all outcomes.' I almost thought the slightest twitch of a smile reached her smooth, ageless face. 'Now I will bring the apocalypse against the Deep Emperor and drive him back. He is old and strained, and I am fresh-made. It will be no contest. I do not advise looking to the east. The light will be bright.'

And with that, she vanished.

Valiya and I stood alone on the platform in the new quiet. A piece of tangled iron fell from the remnants of the loom to clatter against the tiles.

'It's done,' she said.

'It's done,' I agreed.

'What of us now?' Valiya asked.

The phoenix on my arm seemed to warm a little more and gentle flames flickered along its length. I heard a whisper through my mind.

The Misery sleeps, for now. The war with the light has drained its potency and the way back to the west will be stable. I will call on your services if I have need of them.

'Indeed,' I said. 'What of us?'

'It's all changed,' Valiya said. 'The Nameless. The war. Everything is different.'

'We're still us,' I said.

'No,' Valiya said. 'We're different too.'

'Maybe different is better?'

'I think it is.'

A light began to rise in the distant east, far away across the Misery. The Bright Lady was as good as her word. She had wasted no time in committing herself to war with the Deep Kings. She had been waiting to engage them for a long time.

The streets were silent. The battle beyond the walls was over, and looking out I saw a field of the dead, but only the true dead. Nenn had done her work well. The ghosts were resting now, or maybe gone. Maybe I just didn't see them anymore. I would miss them, in my own way. But, as with Ezabeth, their time had come, and they had moved on to something else.

Maldon and Kanalina waited for us at the bottom of the stairs. There would be time for questions later on. The sounds of enormous detonations were breaking the peace and quiet.

'Fuck's sake, Ryhalt. Put some clothes on,' Maldon said. He grinned like the arsehole he was. 'We won then?'

'We won,' I said. 'Why are you itching at your sleeve?'

'I don't know,' he said. 'It's hot for some reason.'

'Please tell me he's not—' Valiya started, but I cut her off.

'Save it for now. I'll enjoy telling him when we're back in Valengrad.'

I found some spare clothes on one of the supply wagons. They didn't fit very well, but were better than nothing. We gathered up what we could, got some animals hitched up. I didn't do much of the work. I felt like I'd been trampled by a herd of bullocks. I looked out to what I figured was going to be west for a while.

'You know, back when I wore a uniform, my commanding officer told me that only three kinds of people enter the Misery. The greedy, the desperate, and the stupid.'

'Which do you think we are?' Valiya asked with a smile. She took my hand in hers, and it felt right there.

'None of them. We were determined. And that's what mattered, in the end.'

Our journey back to the Range began. The Bright Lady was right. The Misery was sleeping.

41

A blue sky. A silent sky. Nothing but calm, dandelion clouds drifting on a spring breeze. I breathed in the lushness of the meadow. Tasted the season on my tongue, as the year turned towards summer. The river at the foot of the pasture flowed happily, my cattle bowing their heads to drink. It was all very green, here. The sun kissed my face with warmth. I couldn't remember such enduring quiet.

A mile away, on the road that led to the estate, a carriage approached. Not hurried, just clattering forwards with steady purpose. I eased myself to my feet, feeling every year of my half century in my lower back. Getting old did not sit well with me, but most days, I bore it without complaint. I'd sat down for too long, let too much of the gentle country air lull me. It was like that out here. Green hills, farmers, quiet lives. A vineyard, a wine press, horses to be shod, and servants to chastise when they were sneaking off under the stairs together instead of polishing the silver.

The carriage bore no markings but I knew who was coming. They would reach the villa before I did. I started down the hill.

'G'afternoon, Master Galharrow,' one of my farmhands said, tipping his hat to me as I passed.

'Looks to me like we'll have a good harvest this year,' I said. I didn't know anything about farming, but it seemed like a good thing to say.

'Looking so, looking so,' he agreed through the blade of grass in his teeth. I nodded at him, smiled, and continued on to the villa. It was a beautiful old structure, white walls, red tiles on the roof, three sides forming a hook around a central courtyard. The carriage rested there, empty now, the driver reclining in the sun.

Valiya had heard me come in, met me in the corridor. She looked flush with health, warmth in her cheeks, light in her eyes. So beautiful.

'I was wondering where you'd got to,' she said fondly, reaching out and taking my hand. A soft smile on her lips. I wanted to kiss her. She dodged my attempt. 'Not now,' she said. 'We've company.' I caught her and kissed her anyway, and for a moment she relaxed into me. Electric, every time. 'Come on,' she said, pulling away and drawing me towards the kitchen.

A woman dressed all in black: high riding boots, a close-fitting tunic beneath a sword belt. She smiled at me, though her once-perfect smile was now split by a blade-fine scar that ran from ear to chin. She looked hale. Strong.

It had been months. I hadn't known what she would say or how this would go. Amaira and I looked at each other for several moments. How to start? What to say? I had never been skilled with words.

'I got your invitation,' she said.

'I'll just get us some tea,' Valiya said. She glanced from me to Amaira. 'Tea for everyone? Good.' She stepped outside and closed the door.

'Not that awful tea,' Amaira said. She tried another smile. 'Spirit of Mercy watch over us.'

'I never told you I was sorry,' I said.

Amaira walked up to me, put her arms around my neck, stood on her toes, and kissed me lightly on the cheek.

'You don't have to,' she said. 'I know what you did. For me, and for Dantry. Thank you.'

We sat. It was still awkward.

'How is he?'

'Living quietly, trying not to draw attention. Pardon or not, there are plenty of people still angry about the mills. He helps me, where he can. There's still a lot to do.'

'And you're doing it,' I said.

'There's much needs doing,' Amaira said. 'After the Bright Lady took the war to Acradius, he lost his hold over the Deep Kings. Even though she destroyed his army and turned him back, they weren't destroyed. They're out there somewhere, across the Misery. Plotting. Scheming. They'll come again, one day. It's only a matter of time.'

'I know,' I said. 'But hopefully not for a while.'

'And the Bright Lady,' Amaira said. 'Have you seen her again?'

'No. But she's out there too. Somewhere.'

Things were better, now. The black rains no longer came, and those that had suffered from their effects had begun to recover. Whether they had blown themselves out, or the Bright Lady had done something to fix the world, we didn't know. But for now, the world seemed to be exhaling, letting it all go.

'How is Valiya coping out here in the quiet?' Amaira asked.

'Bored, mostly, though she claims to be content,' I said. I smiled. 'Did you ever see such a well-run estate as this? She's planning to buy out the farms in the next valley, though she pretends that she's not.'

'And you?'

'I read. I tell the farmhands they're doing a good job, as though I know better than them what that would be. I listen to a lot of disputes about whose wall should go where. It's peaceful here. I like it.'

We talked of small things. Amaira seemed so much older than she ever had before, but then, she'd done and seen things beyond those that anyone her age should have. We were all of us changed, those that had borne the Misery, that had survived. I held off on asking about her work, but it was important to her. It had to come up eventually.

'Crowfoot is very, very angry with you,' she said. 'But he's sleeping, I think. There's a new den of Brides somewhere in Valengrad, or maybe just an old one we didn't find before. The world doesn't stop turning for a moment, it seems. I can't stay long. I just wanted to see if the stories I'd heard could be believed. Ryhalt Galharrow, gentleman farmer.'

'Hard to believe, isn't it?'

'Much too hard,' Valiya said as she came back into the kitchen. She gave us her horrible tea, which I drank. I always drank it now, but only because I knew she liked to make it. 'Now,' she said. 'Tell me what you know about these Brides.'

The simple life was never going to work for Valiya. I followed her back to the frontier.

I stood on Valengrad's walls one night, looked out into the Misery and listened to the new song it had begun to sing. It was different now. Changed. Nobody knew what it meant, but somehow, I liked to think that there was less grief in those notes now. It had gone back to its old shifting, and the things that lived there were no less dangerous than ever they had been, but perhaps, somehow, a part of it had been laid to rest. Or perhaps I was just getting wistful in my old age. Across the cracks in the sky, for a moment I thought I saw the flicker of gold, a figure of fire. But likely it was just my imagination.

'Was it worth it, in the end?'

I looked around. I was quite alone. I leaned back to rest against the wall, scratched at my arm.

'Yes,' I said. 'It was worth it.'

'It's not over.'

'No,' I said into the stillness. A whisper from the dark reached me on the wind.

'But we'll be ready.'

I laughed into the sky. We were never ready, but we didn't let that stop us. The enemy were still out there somewhere, their poisoned thoughts reaching back towards us, searching for an advantage.

Of course, they'd have to go up against me again. They were as close to gods as a man would ever meet in the flesh, but they would be up against the smartmouthed Amairas, the sharp-minded Dantrys, the Valiyas, and that annoying little bastard Maldon, who seemed likely to live forever.

They would be up against free people under a clear sky.

People who saw that there was a better world worth fighting for and were willing to hold on to it.

They were up against swords and walls and powder and magic, and above them all, hope.

Bad odds.